Queen of Light and Solace

Crescent Queens

Book Two

Tricia Meyers

For everyone who believes in love, in all its many forms.

Content Warnings

Please review these content warnings before reading:

-violence
-explicit sex
-blood
-on-page death
-the death of a parent
-torture
-strong language
-sexual threats/threats of SA
-PTSD/panic attacks

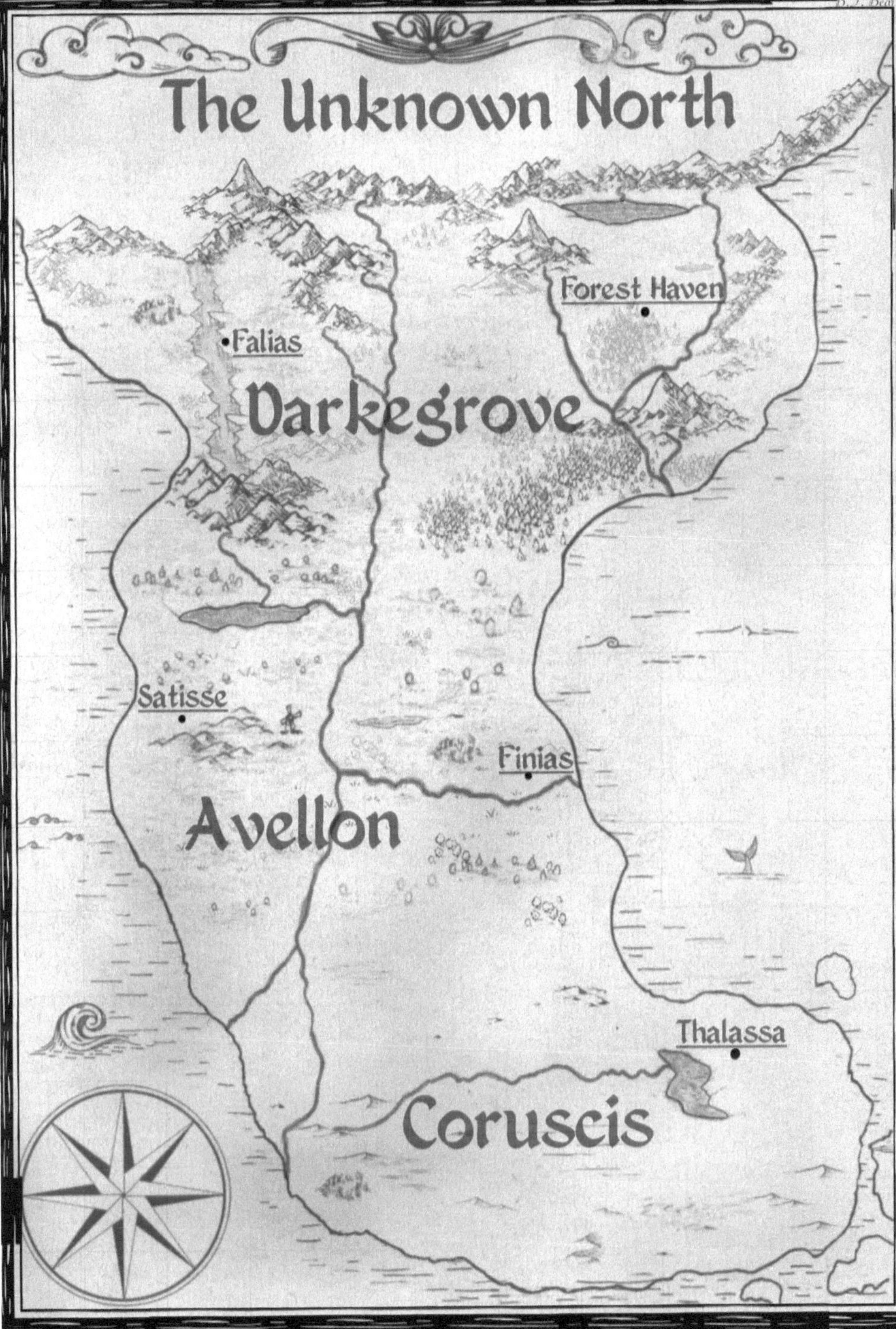

B.J. Bear
The Unknown North
Forest Haven
Falias
Darkegrove
Satisse
Finias
Avellon
Thalassa
Coruscis

PRONUNCIATION GUIDE

Evelyn- eve-lin
Riona- ree-oh-na
Callan- cal-en
Aldrich- awl-drich
Leysa- ley-za
Valerian- vuh-lair-ee-in
Cathal Vaderyn- cuh-hall vuh-dare-in
Aurelia- or-ell-ee-uh
Aelius- ay-lee-us
Vallyse- vuh-leese
Bastien- bass-tee-in
Sybella- sigh-bell-uh
Eyla- a-luh
Avoden- ah-vo-den
Alyere- ahl-yare
Brida- bree-duh
Maren- mare-in
Naia- n-eye-uh
Kore- cor-ee
Arawn- uh-raw-n

Lucia- loo-see-uh
Alyona- al-ee-oh-na
Zia- zee-uh
Amias- ay-mee-us
Jabez- jah-bez
Gorias- gore-ee-us
Avellon- ah-vell-on
Coruscis- cor-oo-sis
Finias- fin-ee-us

Relevant Members of the Pantheon

Macaria - Goddess of Death and Destiny - (muh-car-ee-uh)
Keithia- Goddess of Life and Earth - (ki-thee-uh)
Helie - Goddess of the Sun and Healing - (ey-lee)
Araceli - Goddess of the Night Sky and Prophecy - (air-uh-sell-ee)
Astraia - Goddess of Judgement and Justice - (uh-stray-uh)
Lir- God of the Sea and Storms - (leer)
Endri- Genderfluid God of Dreams and Inspiration - (in-dree)
Vidar- God of Silence and Restraint - (vee-dar)

PROLOGUE

The vision held her in place, its grasp on her mind as unyielding as always.

She could do nothing but watch as a golden crown, topped with sharp points reminiscent of rays of the sun and gleaming from light that seemed to come from the crown itself, fell to polished marble floors, landing soundlessly.

Dread washed over the dreamer as the brilliant points of the sunburst crown dimmed.

This vision would be a warning, then.

The sound of a woman speaking drew her attention next, and she turned in place, searching for the source. A prayer was being sent up to gods long-gone, spilled from female lips. The dreamer couldn't see the woman who offered the supplication, but she could hear the desperation, the outright desolation in every uttered word.

Sympathy weighed heavily on her heart; soon replaced by something utterly foreign to the one who had watched so many scenes of death play out before her mind's eye.

Fear.

She turned her attention to the dull golden crown in time to see a second crown, topped with shells and aquamarine, fall to the marble alongside the first. Lightning arced through the endless black of the vision as the crown landed, cleaving in two.

As if in response, a second woman screamed with such violent rage and despair as to rival the brutal storms that often crashed against the dreamer's coastal home.

Instinct warned the dreamer that this was no normal omen.

The dreamer pushed at the firm hand of prophecy that held her in place, making her bear witness. She didn't want to see this. Knowledge was power, in many cases, but in hers, this calling was a burden she did not want.

The vision held firm, refusing to allow her to flee, to block out what was to come.

When the third crown, woven of branches and precious stones, fell to the floor, the very earth shook violently, rumbling with such intensity she thought perhaps the outside world was collapsing around her as she dreamt.

A third female voice joined the plaintive chorus.

Unlike the first two, she was calling for someone. A single name, woven between prayers of desperation and screams of rage, cried out with urgency and anguish.

The dreamer sat up in bed, rubbing her chest as if that would ease the ache that had settled there.

Many visions had been given to her over the years, yet none had left her feeling so heavy in soul and heart. She didn't know what it meant, not yet, but that was hardly unusual. The meaning of the warning would reveal itself to her in time. All that could be done now was wait.

Fate had been laid at her feet, and there was no escaping it now.

Within moments, the dream was hidden behind the fog of memory. She could recall the imagery, the way it made her feel, but little else. Such was the way of visions. When the time arrived, she would recall what was necessary–whatever warning it was she needed to impart.

Only the name that had been screamed remained clear. Cried out so heartbreakingly by the woman who belonged to the third crown.

She had no idea who this Callan was, and she could only hope that she found him in time to save him.

CHAPTER 1

LIA

"Has Eve Darrow sent a reply yet?"

The click of Lia Vallyse's heels echoed through the sunlit atrium, adding punctuation to the question. The tempo of her steps echoed her quickened heartbeat. Worry had been her companion since her sudden departure from Darkegrove, for Eve, of course, but also for her own family.

Every one of the gilded halls of Sunholde were a sight to behold on sunny days, but none shone brighter than the great atrium. The floors, white marble veined with gold, were opulent, and polished to mirror shine at all times. The walls bore little decoration save for a small number of portraits of past rulers, each held by a gilded frame that perfectly complimented the white wallpaper, hand-painted with tiny sunbursts in the trademark gold of her house.

Her ancestors had certainly intended to impress their neighbors, human and fae alike.

"Not yet, Highness," came Alfie's muffled reply. He was still holding the thin book under his chin as he shuffled papers in his hands, struggling to keep up with her brisk strides.

Lia slowed her pace. The poor man would suffocate himself on the book her father had requested, an old scholar's notes about fae ruins in

Darkegrove, in his effort to be of help with her task. She had no idea why he'd suddenly taken an interest in ancient fae kingdoms north of Avellon, as his field of study had primarily remained within their own borders in the past.

Perhaps Eve and her decision to change her own kingdom's history had something to do with that, she mused.

Or, she thought, frowning, *it had something to do with the prophecy he's been so obsessed with that he sent me to warn Riona Darrow.*

That visit should have extended through Eve's coronation, but her return had been requested sooner by an urgent message arriving in the wee hours one morning. There hadn't even been time to say goodbye. King Aldrich Vallyse had taken ill and she had been recalled to be at her father's side, but also to be prepared should the worst occur and she needed to ascend to the throne.

So far he had held on, but the healers had little hope for his recovery.

"Please let me carry something for you, Alfie," she offered, not for the first time.

"I couldn't possibly, Your Highness," came the expected reply. He shuffled the papers once more, finally arranging them in an order he deemed correct, and tucked them neatly against the book now resting in his hand. "I've got it now."

Before coming to live at Sunholde and serving the ruling family of Avellon, Alfie Barre had been a scholar, studying the ancient fae. For years, Alfie had served faithfully as her father's secretary and personal librarian, his experience and interest in the long-lost fae no doubt having intrigued the young king with his own near obsession with the subject.

They arrived in her father's makeshift office moments later. One of the receiving rooms on the first floor had been converted to make his meetings and never-ending studies more comfortable as climbing to the third-floor office he'd occupied for all of her life was now an impossible task for the king. A large table was situated in the center of the room, with a heavily cushioned chair pushed behind it, where her father's too-thin frame now rested.

His normally tanned skin was pale, ashen. The long hair tied at the nape of his neck, once as golden as her own, appeared dull, grey as a winter sky before a storm. Her heart ached in her chest, a fresh wave of grief coursing through her as she paused in the doorway, looking him over. For all of her life, he had been so vibrant, so much larger than life. Softspoken and studious, but strong, and shining with an inner light that had always drawn people to him. Now, that light had dimmed.

It wouldn't be long now.

"Alfie has found the book you requested, Papa," Lia said gently, dismissing the guard at the door with a smile.

He was awake this time at least, leaning over the desk, quill in hand. Making notes in his journal or perhaps writing to the university to the east, where much of the research he'd commissioned took place.

"Thank you, Alfie," he uttered, his voice as frail as his body. The sound of it drew a wince from Lia.

"Leave us please," Aldrich added, finally looking up from his desk. Dark circles had formed under his honey-brown eyes. The eyes that had always sparkled with excitement over every new book he discovered, every artifact no matter how small, were so tired.

Alfie gently placed the book, along with the papers he'd brought on Lia's behalf, on the desk and departed with a brief bow.

"I've brought some things for you," Lia began, stepping forward and laying a finger on the small stack of papers. "The town of Braedor claims to have found new ruins we've never seen, but I'm not sure if they're as old as they claim and–"

"I need to speak to you about something of importance, Little Light."

Lia's gaze shot to his instantly at the use of her childhood nickname. Nobody had called her that in years. "Papa?"

Placing a shaky hand on the arm of his chair, her father inhaled deeply before responding. "It is time for you to take the throne."

"Absolutely not," she stated with conviction. "You are the king of Avellon, Papa. You will be the king until the moment you take your last breath, and then I will take your place. Not a moment sooner."

Accepting the crown meant accepting his death, and though she knew the truth, she simply wasn't ready for that yet.

Aldrich leveled a gentle gaze on his daughter. "We both know that time is coming faster than anticipated, Little Light." Turning to the paper resting on his desk, he frowned. "And, I am afraid certain events are forcing the issue."

"What events?" Lia asked, peering over the desk at what appeared to be a map of Darkegrove just beside whatever he'd been writing.

"Stoneweald has been taken."

"Taken? What do you mean taken?" Lia's hand drifted to her throat, toying with the gold sunburst charm hanging there. Had civil war broken out in Darkegrove? Eve's rule was opposed by many, but surely–

"An army of unknown origin, bearing a banner we don't recognize, attacked in the middle of the night four days ago. A merchant from Hythe happened to be in Forest Haven when the attack occurred, and managed to escape the city before it was too late."

"And?" She prompted breathlessly, head spinning.

"Stoneweald and Forest Haven have been seized, and we've been unable to get word from anyone inside."

"Eve?" Her voice was little more than a whisper as dread settled into the pit of her stomach like a stone.

"Missing. Two councilors, along with some castle staff, managed to escape and have taken refuge in a small village not far from Forest Haven. They have reported that Queen Evelyn and her personal guards also escaped, but did not accompany them."

"Where did she go? Was she taken?" Lia asked, drifting to the nearby settee and sinking down onto it slowly.

"The councilors either don't know or won't say." Her father lowered himself into the wingback chair behind the desk, groaning quietly. "Darkegrove has called for our aid, and Aelius is already rallying our forces. I am...hesitant to send our full strength."

"They need our help," Lia countered, frowning. "We are their allies."

"Yes, Little Light, but we do not know the full might of this army, or what their plans may be. They may stop at Darkegrove, or they may set their sights on us next. Remember, they managed to sack the city in a single night. If Darkegrove's forces were so easily overcome, this enemy must be greatly skilled, and high in number."

"Light above," Lia whispered. "How can you expect me to take the throne amidst all of this?"

Aldrich leaned back, offering Lia the cryptic smile that so often irritated her. He had his reasons, but he wouldn't be sharing them.

"It is done. You'll take the throne tomorrow."

"Tomorrow?!" Lia snapped to her feet, ignoring the sound of her gown ripping as it snagged on her heel. The soft blue color of the eastern sky, the dress had been her favorite, but she'd worry about that later when her father wasn't entirely losing his mind. "Are you insane?"

"Perhaps," he chuckled weakly. "Regardless, it's happening. If we are to go to war, it must be with a healthy leader sitting on the throne. Avellon cannot survive a war if her monarch dies in the midst of it."

Taking the throne would be the final acknowledgment of the inevitable. She was going to lose her father–but putting Avellon in greater risk would do nothing to stop that.

With a heavy heart, Lia nodded once, accepting her fate.

"Tomorrow."

CHAPTER 2

EVE

Eve stared out the window in silence, her eyes on the eastern sky. Frost lined the window pane, and more than a few small fluffy flakes had begun to fall sometime in the wee hours of the morning. Winter had arrived overnight it seemed. Her thoughts were on the people of the kingdom she had called home her entire life and had fought so hard to rule. Being Queen of Darkegrove, leading them into a new future had been her destiny, the one thing she desired above all else.

Now, she wasn't so sure.

"Eve?"

Her attention drifted back to the small group gathered by the fireplace. They'd arrived a little more than an hour ago for their meeting in the sitting room attached to the bedroom she now shared with Callan, and still, nothing had been decided.

In fact, nothing had been decided in the three weeks they'd been in Elesiya, the capital of Falias. The ancient fae kingdom was long forgotten about since its disappearance, along with its inhabitants, five hundred years ago.

"I'm sorry, what did you say?" Eve spent most of her days adrift, preoccupied, and impatient to return to Stoneweald to free what remained of her people, and to exact her revenge on those who had taken it from them.

Valerian offered her a smile, empathy softening his umber eyes the way it often did these days. "I asked if you needed anything before Leysa and I go, to prepare for the ball," he repeated patiently.

Seated beside him on the smaller of the two sofas, Leysa nudged his knee gently with her own. "This one needs to get prettied up for your celebration."

Offering them a smile, Eve inclined her head. "No, I think we're done," she began, glancing at the others for confirmation.

Mason Sinclair merely shrugged, having little to add to the conversation. He seemed nearly as distracted as herself, Eve noted. His gaze lingered so often on the lovely fae female across from him, it was a wonder he'd heard anything.

"Did you get the hair combs I asked Lydia to bring you?" Cora asked. At Eve's nod, she beamed. "They'll match your gown perfectly."

If she'd noted Mason's long looks, she gave no indication as she rose, followed soon after by the others. "We'll leave you two to do...whatever...." She said, earning a laugh, barely concealed by a feigned cough, from Valerian as the four of them retreated.

"What's troubling you, dove?" Callan asked, concern lacing his tone. From his position on the sofa, he let his gaze roam over her. Ocean eyes met her own after a moment, making her heart give a gentle tug in his direction.

His support of her had been unwavering. Despite his return to Falias meaning Cora would soon step aside so her brother could take his rightful place on the throne, he had delayed, instead focusing on helping Eve to settle into being fae and everything it entailed. Namely the inevitable loss of her own kingdom. Since she had been made fae by the once-forgotten gods, her claim to her own throne seemed to be tenuous at best.

Darkegrove was, and always would be, a human kingdom.

"Just thinking," she replied honestly as she moved to sit beside him on the larger of the two pale silver sofas.

"Darkegrove?"

"What else?" She sighed, dragging a hand through dark red curls gently. "Must we go tonight?"

"We could skip it if you like." Pausing, he trailed a fingertip along the side of her neck slowly. "But I happen to know of a particularly private terrace we could disappear to for a while if we go."

Eve laughed, desire coiling in her gut at the promise in his darkly whispered words. "I think that will more than make up for having to go."

"I thought so," he replied with a grin.

His touch, and the sinful promises he made, lightened her mood significantly. But there was more on her mind than just Darkegrove and her own throne.

Callan was the High King of all of Falias. He would need to claim his throne soon, despite his insistence on delaying for her sake. What that would mean for her, for their relationship, she didn't know, and she couldn't stop thinking about the possibilities.

"You're going to need to accept the crown soon," she said without preamble.

His slow trail over the side of her neck halted instantly. "Ah, that."

"Yes," she said, twisting so that she was facing him. "That."

"I wanted to give you time," he said slowly, pulling his hand away. "Because there is something I need to tell you about that." Huffing a laugh, he amended, "Something I need to tell you."

"What is it?" *There is always more I don't know.*

"When I declare you my mate publicly...the crown will no longer be mine alone."

"Callan, you can't mean..." she began, frowning. Her heart skittered in her chest, palms dampening. He couldn't possibly be going where she thought he was. Things were complicated enough, difficult enough without–

"You'll be High Queen of Falias, Eve."

Later, she found herself wandering into the bathing chamber they shared, her attention locked on the large porcelain tub on a raised dais that dominated the room. She hadn't been able to use an actual tub since the attack at the Black Pool. Hadn't been able to even consider sinking into the water again.

The very thought had her lungs seizing, unable to fill with enough precious air as she gasped and gasped, constantly seeking a steady breath that just wouldn't come.

Eve had made do with buckets of fresh hot water, and though washing her hair still sent fresh waves of panic through her every time her maid, Adriana, poured water over her head, it was nothing compared to the idea of actually being submerged. She missed being able to luxuriate in a warm bath, to soak her aching muscles after training with Callan, hours spent honing her gifts and learning to defend herself in a more physical way.

"What are you doing, dove?" Callan's voice had her nearly jumping out of her skin. She'd been so lost in her fear that she hadn't heard his approach.

Taking a breath to steady her racing heart, Eve turned to greet him with a wan smile. "I was just..." she began, but faltered, searching for the words.

What **am** *I doing?* She hadn't called for hot water, and yet here she was in her dressing gown staring at an empty bathtub as if it were a serpent ready to strike her at any moment.

"You still haven't used it." A statement, not a question, and filled with such sympathy that it had her heart aching.

Turning, he left the room without a word.

For several moments, she stood there, wondering what had just happened. Had her fear, her brokenness been too much for him to bear? Callan had never shied away from her darkest moments, even before they had made promises of love to one another, so why would he do so now?

She was about to follow, demanding an answer to just that, when he returned, a small army of servants in his wake, each of them carrying buckets with steam wafting from them.

Hot water. For the bath.

Panic rose like bile in the back of her throat. *No. No, no.* The words repeated in her mind, but she choked on them, unable to voice her terror. Shaking her head, Eve's panicked gaze met his, endless blue depths soft with patience and love.

"We'll do this together," he said, taking her shaking hands in his.

Together, she repeated silently, nodding her acceptance.

The moment the tub was filled and the servants had gone, Callan swiftly undressed himself before tugging the ties of her robe loose.

His fingertips were a gentle caress on her skin, from her shoulders down her arms as he slid the robe free, leaving her bared before him. His touch, her anchor in the storm of her fear. "Together, dove," he repeated softly.

The steaming water reached his chest as he sank into the tub and then reached for her, holding his hand out patiently. She knew without asking he would wait for her as long as she needed him to. The water would go cold, and he would simply call for more; and if she decided she couldn't do it, he would try again tomorrow.

With a steadying breath, she placed her hand in his, closed her eyes, and stepped into the water.

The water was cold—so cold.

Her soaked gown was heavy, pulling her down into the endless dark.

Devlan shoved her head under now. She fought, scratching and clawing at his hands uselessly. She was going to die. She had failed her kingdom, her mother, herself.

She had failed, and she was going to die.

Her lungs burned, and she couldn't get out—

I can't breathe,

-can't breathe,

—breathe.

Strong hands gripped her hips, and she pushed at them, but they only tightened. Not enough to hurt, but enough to keep her from moving. Her eyes flew open to find that rather than the dark water of the Black Pool, the polished and pristine marble of the bathing chamber surrounded her.

Falias. I'm in Falias.

Her legs trembled so violently she thought they might give out at any moment. "I can't...I can't..."

"I'm here," Callan's voice, always her lifeline in a storm, reached her ears above the dull roar that had taken hold. "I'm with you, and you are safe."

Her heartbeat slowly returned to normal as Eve took in her surroundings cautiously.

The water she stood in was hot enough for steam to rise steadily from its clear surface. Not cold, not black, she realized as she finally looked down, and certainly not dragging her downward.

She forced herself to breathe slowly, deeply. The water welcomed her like an embrace as she lowered herself into the tub, the worst of her panic eased with every deep breath.

Those were Callan's hands on her skin, comforting not hurting, his gaze never once leaving her face. His hands stayed on her, now beneath the water, roaming over her thighs and down her calves.

"Nobody will ever hurt you again," he said with a fierceness that would have frightened her if he had been anyone else.

"I know," Eve replied, tone hushed.

She did know, not only because he would do anything to keep her from harm, but also because she now knew that she had it within herself to fight back, to keep herself safe. With the help of her magic and the inner strength she was beginning to realize she'd had all along.

Never again would she be weak, and afraid to fight back.

With a slow exhale, she let herself relax fully, leaning back against the porcelain, cool against her skin above the waterline. For several moments, she sat in silence, relishing the feeling of warm water as it soothed her, body and soul.

Callan's hands had stilled, just on the inside of her knees, and suddenly her pulse was quickening again for reasons that had absolutely nothing to do with fear. Letting her knees fall apart, she slid lower until the water splashed against her chin. To her surprise, only a wisp of a memory of the last time water had gone over her head flashed in her mind, the flaring panic quickly extinguished as she willed herself to remain in the present.

His eyes, darkening with the same desire she felt, kept her in the moment.

With him.

Her mate.

Agonizingly slow, Callan's hand slid up her thigh, his thumb scraping against her inner thigh, leaving chills in its wake. "Do you want me to touch you?" He asked, his voice thick.

"Yes," she breathed.

"Ask me," he replied, hands stilling at the top of her thigh. He was so close now, leaning as far forward as the water would allow.

"Please touch me."

"Mm," he purred, hands caressing her thighs. Water sloshed over the edge as he tugged her closer until her legs were around his waist, the apex of her thighs pressed against his hardened length. "Say it again."

"Callan, please," she all but whimpered. Her core pounded, a steady beat sending desire thrumming through her. Her hands wound into his hair, thumbs resting against his jawline.

"I love the way you say my name," was his smoky reply.

Lowering his head, he flicked his tongue against the peak of her breast while his free hand slid between their bodies. His thumb pressed against the sensitive bundle of nerves just hard enough to draw a gasp from her parted lips, a delicious jolt of pleasure coursing through her veins.

He laughed then, low and husky, as he began moving his thumb in slow circles. Claiming her mouth with his, he kissed her deeply. It was enough to send her soaring toward that precipice, but just before she climaxed, he lifted her hips. Lowering her onto him gently, the water added friction, discomfort edging toward pain.

"I want to feel you crash against me. Say my name when you come, dove."

It was enough to make her come undone then and there. His name passed her lips on a sob, as she wrapped her arms around his neck, closing what little distance remained between them. He held her tight through each crashing wave, each breathless moment of utter bliss until his own release found him.

Weightless and spent, she lay her head against his shoulder. "Thank you," she whispered, pressing a kiss to his damp skin gently.

"Now when you think of water, think of this instead," he murmured against the top of her head.

"I think I can manage that," Eve laughed leaning back to look at him. "Thank you," she said again, more seriously this time. "For all of it."

Nodding, Callan pressed a swift kiss to her lips. "There is nothing I wouldn't do for you."

Chapter 3

Eve

Hours passed, and she was still reeling from what Callan had revealed. A part of her was angry that he'd waited so long to tell her, though, in truth, she understood his reasoning. If he had thrown that information at her right away, then she might've crumbled under the weight of it. She'd needed time to sit with everything that had happened and was still happening.

Losing one kingdom had been strain enough, she hardly needed the burden of another kingdom. Even now, the thought of it made her feel more than a little ill. Her priority would be Darkegrove, she'd told him. Always. Her people needed to be liberated, and then the matter of the crown would be settled....somehow. She could turn her attention to Falias, and what it would mean to be their queen afterward.

Falian scouts had been able to find precious little information about what was happening inside of Forest Haven and nothing at all about Stoneweald itself. Eldred and the others she'd left at Roskirk were safe, a blessing at least.

Standing at the window, dressed in a glittering silver gown with long, sheer sleeves, and a skirt that dusted the floor when she walked, her gaze once more turned to the east. Guilt weighed so heavily on her that for a long moment, she considered taking the dress off, calling for a horse, and riding back home alone if need be. She could use the powers gifted to her by the goddess of life, Keithia, to reclaim her fallen kingdom, and—

"That would be rather unwise."

The soft voice of the very same goddess shocked her out of her daydream, and she spun in place, turning to find Keithia standing just a few feet away. Dressed in a simple, gauzy emerald dress with a flowering vine trailing along the bodice, she perfectly embodied earth and life itself.

"The mind reading is rather unsettling," Eve remarked, her fingertips moving to rest on the tattoo left by the goddess on her opposite arm.

"I've been told," Keithia laughed, then sighed. "Though even without it, one could easily guess the direction of your thoughts."

Having no reply to that, Eve merely shrugged.

"My time is short, but I've come bearing news of great importance. The second, her time draws near."

"I don't understand. You must mean Naia?" she asked, referring to the prophecy that had claimed three queens sitting on three human thrones would each be keys to bring about the return of the fae. All of them.

Already, Eve's near drowning, gift of power, and subsequent coronation had turned the first lock, dropping the veil that separated the fae of Falias.

Keithia merely offered a slight smile. "I must go," she said gently. "Be well, my most favored child." Lifting a hand, she paused. "A bit of advice, dear girl? Allow yourself some happiness, wherever and whenever you can find it. Every moment of your life needn't be tragic."

Before Eve could formulate a response to that, Keithia vanished, leaving nothing behind to signify she'd ever actually been there. Of course, the goddess had failed to actually answer the question. Huffing irritably, Eve glared at the now empty spot where Keithia had stood moments before.

"Were you talking to someone?" Callan asked, emerging from their bedroom. Dressed in a black suit with his hair pulled back from his face, he was the picture of masculine perfection.

"Keithia deigned to drop in with more cryptic messages," Eve replied. Desire coiled low in her belly as his gaze swept over her, slowly, methodically, as if drinking in every inch of her.

"What did she have to warn us about now?" he asked, voice low.

Eve swallowed hard. "The second lock will be turned soon."

Dragging a hand over his face, Callan sighed. "Which one?"

Eve straightened her dress, more to have something to do with her shaky hands than for any practical reason. Irritation with Keithia and desire for her mate were certainly wreaking havoc on her nerves, she noted. "She wouldn't say."

A knock at the door interrupted his next question, and Leysa poked her head in, raven curls bobbing gently. "Oh good, you're dressed!" Pausing just inside the room, she clasped her hands in front of her, the fabric of her flowy maroon dress shifting with the movement. "You look amazing!"

Eve offered Leysa a smile in return. "So do you! Valerian is going to be drooling."

"Oh, I am." Valerian's voice sounded from behind Leysa, the warrior still hidden from Eve's view in the hallway.

"You should see him," Leysa said in a loud whisper. "I am going to climb him like a–"

"Are we ready to go down then?" Callan interrupted, humor lacing his tone. When nobody objected, he added, "Great, let's go before they start taking their clothes off."

Like humans, Eve discovered, the fae nobility spent inordinate amounts of money on food and wine for their celebrations. Long tables overflowing with food of more varieties than she could count lined the walls. Wine flowed freely, served by fae dressed in the livery of the Thorne family: navy blue with a trio of silver stars embroidered near the right shoulder.

Hours after it began, the ball was still in full force, showing no signs of slowing down. Callan had yet to take her to the terrace he'd mentioned before, but the gleam in his eye as their gazes met across the room seemed to promise her it wouldn't be much longer.

"Ah! Here they are!" Leysa exclaimed, having pulled Eve away in search of apricot pastries that the shifter claimed would change her entire life. Her joy, Eve noted, was perhaps a little enhanced by the several glasses of wine she'd had.

Eve, not far behind in that regard herself, giggled. "I prefer strawberry, but if it's as good as you–"

"Oh, shit."

Leysa's muttered curse had Eve tearing her gaze from the truly delectable-looking pile of desserts. She turned to look at her friend, puzzled by the scowl on her friend's lovely features. Following the direction of Leysa's gaze, she was surprised to see Callan was the source of Leysa's outburst.

"Let's just go–" Leysa began, placing her hand gently on Eve's arm.

A blonde fae female was speaking with Callan, standing so close that her breasts nearly grazed his chest with every breath she took. Backed against a wall, Callan began to step to the side, an attempt no doubt intended to put distance between them, but the ruby-clad female placed a hand on his arm, effectively stopping him in place.

Thanks to the music, conversation, and distance between them, Eve couldn't make out Callan's exact words, but his meaning was clear. He was telling her to back off, his expression offering not one ounce of welcome as he pulled his arm free of her grasp. Full, red lips pouted as she leaned forward, whispering something that had him shaking his head.

Jealousy, fierce and sharp, coursed through Eve. Without thinking, she let the magic flare to life within her. The familiar feeling of rightness, of strength and power, flooded her senses immediately, and she grinned as she turned her gaze to the potted plant just behind the female who'd dared touch what belonged to her. Roots slithered free from the top of the marble pot and snaked their way around her ankles before yanking.

Hard.

The blonde fell flat onto the marble floor, managing to break her fall at the last second, thanks to fae speed. Several dancers nearby stopped to help, confusion sweeping over them. None of them, including the female now picking herself up off the floor slowly, seemed to have any idea what had just happened.

Guilt warred with a sort of sick satisfaction as Eve's gaze moved from the blonde to Callan, who was staring directly at her, smirking.

Oops.

CHAPTER 4

LIA

Lia had been the queen of Avellon for all of a week and already her head was full of details about the strength and locations of her armies, and which noble houses were prepared to come to their aid if called upon. She had been raised to rule from birth, and though she felt educated and prepared to take her birthright, the circumstances of her coronation still haunted her. Her father's health had declined rapidly. Now he rarely left his bed, let alone his room. Her mother, Hemera, had not once left his side.

"The Devois forces continue to watch the northern border of his demesne, but so far there has been nothing of note. More refugees from outside Forest Haven arrived in Cirrane yesterday, but they had no new information for us." Aelius sighed, flopping unceremoniously onto the settee.

He tossed an apple into the air, catching it just before it struck him in the face that so closely resembled her own. Her younger brother by no more than three minutes, it was a wonder in her mind that he had never held any resentment toward her over the throne. Aelius claimed no interest in ruling, instead vowing his unending support for her reign.

"Has there been any sign of Eve?" She asked, eyeing the gauzy white curtains that danced on the afternoon breeze. The window had been left cracked open, despite the chill of winter that crept in. Lia hated the stuffiness of a completely closed-off room, even if it meant being a little cold from time to time.

"No, sorry," he replied, catching the apple for a final time. "I think it's time to face the possibility she–"

"Don't say it, I can't bear it."

"I'm just saying. Nobody has seen or heard from her since that night..."

"Enough, Aelius." She knew her friend was likely dead. Murdered the night of the attack, despite reports that she had been seen afterward, escaping to the west.

Nobody could understand why the Queen of Darkegrove, and the others she had taken with her, had gone west. There was nothing but unending forests and monstrous beasts in that part of Darkegrove.

Still, Lia would continue to hold onto the hope that Eve was perhaps in some small village or perhaps even heading south somehow, to seek aid and refuge.

"The seer is requesting an audience," he said idly, shifting the conversation away from the one that had her normally sunny expression clouded with worry.

"Papa's seer?" she asked, brow raised. "Why?"

Lia held no belief in such things. There were so-called fortune tellers and seers with nearly every traveling troupe of entertainers, and every single one of them were frauds. They preyed on naive people looking for guidance, in hopes that perhaps love would find them soon, or seeking proof of their spouse's infidelity. She was a hopeful person by nature, but some things were just too good to be true.

"I don't know," Aelius said around a mouthful of apple. "She didn't say. I guess just to offer her services." Wiggling his brows at Lia, he added. "She's very pretty."

Lia groaned, instantly looking for something to toss at her twin. Luckily for him, the sofa was free of anything but a small pillow, which he deftly smacked away with his free hand. Aelius had tried to find her love for years, being largely unsuccessful as his taste in women often turned toward the 'I'll stab you if you look at me the wrong way' type.

"I'm sure I'm not interested, Aelius," she said, rolling her eyes.

"Don't count her out just yet sister," he grinned. "I have a feeling about this."

~

Hours later, in the office that had once been her father's Lia awaited the arrival of this seer. The 'prophecy' her father had asked her to deliver to Darkegrove had apparently meant nothing to either Riona Darrow or Naia Colvari, according to Aelius when he'd returned from Coruscis. This seer was simply another opportunist looking for payment from the crown for her services.

At least this one was smart enough to come up with an interesting, albeit strange, little poem, she mused. *I'll hear her out, then politely dismiss her back to whichever troupe she came from with our thanks.*

"Miss Sybella Avoden, Majesty," the page announced as the door swung open. As he stepped aside at her nod, the girl Aelius had described as pretty stepped into view.

Pretty had been a lousy word to describe the raven-haired beauty that stood before her. Dressed in a simple black dress that hung loose from her slender frame, her night-dark hair, braided and hanging over one shoulder, was a stark contrast to her pale skin. Silvery-grey eyes set in an angular face scanned Lia openly, curiosity lighting them.

"Thank you for seeing me," she said tightly, before pressing her full lips together in a thin line.

Clearing her throat, Lia snapped her own gaping mouth shut. "Yes, um...My father seemed to be fond of you, and I thought it was the least I could do. What did you wish to speak to me about?"

"I had another vision," Sybella began, stepping farther into the room. Her back remained close to the wall opposite Lia, maintaining a healthy distance between the two of them. "I believe it to be a warning."

"Oh?" Lia maintained her polite smile, awaiting the request for payment or the dire warning that would ensure the seer's continued presence at court.

Stunning as she was, she was still a fraud.

"I think the three crowns of Aestera are in grave danger."

Thoughts turning to Darkegrove, Lia frowned. "This is in exceptionally poor taste," she began, shaking her head. "I assume you've heard what is happening to the north, and you're looking to secure your position here by issuing well-timed warnings."

"No, I swear I–" The seer stepped closer finally, raising a hand toward the queen.

Lia scoffed. "I apologize for being so harsh with my words, but let me speak plainly. My father may have believed in you, but I do not. I will ensure you are paid whatever it is you are owed and then seen safely to wherever it is your troupe is located so that you may rejoin them."

Sybella stiffened, dropping her hand to her side. "I have heard so many tales of your kindness and grace, but somehow none have mentioned how impossibly stupid you are."

Lia blinked, mouth falling open in shock. "Excuse me?"

"I am not being paid, by your father or anyone else. I have no troupe, and I am not trying to swindle you. I was taken from my home. **Taken**. By your father and his men, to be used as his own personal divination tool." Sybella's cheeks were flushed, chest heaving with anger. "If it is your plan to dismiss me, then I beg you to do so. But you must hear my warning first. As much as I despise your family, I love Avellon and her people. I will not stand by and do what little I can to help, even if that means helping my enemy."

Lia's thoughts scattered like chaff in the wind. Any preconceived notions of this woman's intentions vanished instantly.

That's impossible...isn't it?

She had never known her father to be one to take prisoners, especially women innocent of any crime. If what Sybella claimed was true, then everything she thought she knew about him was patently false.

"I don't know what to say..." she said lamely, as Sybella continued to stare at her. "There must be some mistake."

Snorting, the seer straightened her shoulders. "If you don't believe me, ask your father. Or any of his guards," she said practically sneering at the last word. "I want nothing from you but my freedom, and to help save my home. Will you listen to me?"

Allowing her to speak her mind was the least Lia could offer. Afterward, she'd have words with her father. A great many of them.

"Tell me everything."

CHAPTER 5

EVE

A month had passed since her home, her crown, and her people had been taken from her, and Eve was still in Falias, with no plan of attack on the horizon. Callan had finally agreed to step back into his role as king, something Cora had thanked him profusely for.

Ruling, she'd declared, was boring.

Curled up in her favorite chair, Eve was trying and failing to occupy her mind with a captivating novel about a fae princess and three very handsome guards when Callan returned from his latest meeting with the nobles of Falias.

The fae were prolific writers, she'd discovered, and though she had found many odious tomes regarding their impossibly long history, she had also found a rather extensive collection of very dirty romances. Reading them had become her source of entertainment when she wasn't training with Valerian, shopping with Leysa, or alone with Callan in their room.

She needed a break from thoughts of Darkegrove, and what this day was.

"It's all settled," he said by way of greeting. "The proclamation has been signed and sealed. I am once again High King."

Twirling the silver ring fashioned to resemble ivy around her finger, Eve waited until he took his seat across from her to reply, using the time to let the words she'd been holding onto take shape in her mind.

"What about the other matter?" she asked, closing the book gently. The time for distractions was over.

"I think that's up to you," he replied gently, leaning back against the couch. "Do you want to make the announcement?"

She sighed in response. Truthfully she had no idea what she wanted anymore, aside from the chance to reclaim what had been taken; and even that had begun to feel like a distant dream.

Rather than admit she didn't know, she asked, "What's that?"

Callan's brow rose at the change in subject, but he didn't remark on it as he glanced down at the small wooden box resting on his lap. "Did you think I forgot what today is?"

"I kind of hoped you did," she laughed halfheartedly.

"Here," he said, holding the box out for her. "Maybe you'll decide once you've opened this."

Reluctantly, she took the box, running her fingers over the smooth, unadorned lid slowly. Her thoughts turned to her last birthday, the last she'd had with her parents. Grief washed over her. Time and the chaos of her life had lessened it, but the pain was still there, dull and aching.

"You'll have to open it first," he teased, with a nervous laugh.

Why would he be nervous to give me a birthday gift? Offering him a bemused smile, Eve lifted the lid, revealing a deep blue velvet interior. Resting in the center was a silver ring with a large, square-cut sapphire in the center, three smaller diamonds set around it.

Her heart skipped a beat. "Callan," she breathed. "Are you proposing?"

It was stunning, and clearly an heirloom of his house. Movement across from her drew her attention, and she looked up to find Callan kneeling in front of her.

"The fae," he began, voice low, "as a rule, do not marry but..." Taking a shaky breath he dragged his hand through his hair. "I wanted to make a promise, to honor your human side. If marriage is what you want, then we will do that. But this ring," he paused, taking her right hand in his. "It was my mother's." Clearing his throat, he continued, voice thick with emotion. "I wanted you to have this symbol to promise my heart, my life, and my house to you."

Chapter 6

Lia

If she hadn't already been sitting, Lia may have ended up on the floor by the time Sybella finished her story. The seer had been taken from a small fishing village on the eastern coast of Avellon, a little more than three months ago. Lia's father had never allowed her to be harmed, but he had also refused to allow her to leave.

The doubt she had initially felt had been quickly dispelled, doused like a flame beneath water, as the seer recalled details she couldn't possibly have known without firsthand experience; descriptions of her father's favored guards and even the name of his horse.

"How did he find out about you?" Lia asked quietly. Nausea swept over her in waves. The man she had called Papa, the man she had looked up to, who had been known as kind and fair by all, had taken someone from their home and held her against her will. Who knew if Sybella was even the first?

Seated in the chair across the desk from Lia now, Sybella shrugged. "I have no idea," she replied. The worst of the anger in her eyes had dissipated, silver eyes no longer molten. "My visions often come as warnings, but they are usually small in scale, an incoming storm or a fishing boat capsizing. My gift it's..." She sighed, flipping her braid over her shoulder. "It's the kind of thing everyone knows but nobody really acknowledges."

"Do you think someone from your village–"

"No," Sybella cut her off. "Alyere is small. We look out for our neighbors there, and we certainly don't go spilling secrets to outsiders." Tensing her jaw, she admitted, "But I suppose it must be possible."

Lia nodded, only partially understanding. As well loved as her family was by their kingdom, even Sunholde, the castle she called home, was a hotbed of gossip. "I am sorry, for what it's worth."

Sybella lifted a shoulder lightly. "I don't need your apologies."

"Well, you're free–"

The door burst open unceremoniously, revealing an unusually pale Alfie. "Majesty, there is news from Darkegrove."

Lia rose as her heart leapt into her throat. "Tell me."

"The castle of Stoneweald, and Forest Haven, they've been relinquished."

"Relinquished?" Lia frowned. "You mean the invaders have gone?"

Alfie nodded slowly, eyes as wide as saucers. "Yes, Majesty, and we've received reports that a great host is marching south from Darkegrove." He swallowed hard. "They're marching on Avellon."

"The light of the sunburst crown went dim," Sybella murmured.

Lia turned an incredulous stare on the seer. "Will you stay?" she asked quietly.

Her disbelief was slowly fading. This was no normal army, to take Darkegrove unawares as they had, to move so swiftly and to have suddenly appeared as if from nowhere.

If they had sailed from across the sea, the port towns would have been the expected choice for the first attack, and yet none had been touched. They had sacked Stoneweald first, an illogical and supposedly impossible task, unless they had come from either the south or sprung forth from the Sgiath Mountains.

Sybella nodded. "For Avellon, I will."

Just after dusk, Lia found herself in the meeting room. Her brother, commander of her armies, and Lord Auclair, head of her council, joined her. Aelius braced his arms on the table across from her. White sleeves had been rolled up his tan arms, and his blonde hair fell forward, blocking his eyes from view. "At least we were prepared," he muttered.

"Hardly," Lord Auclair snorted. "But better than Darkegrove I suppose."

The mysterious invading army, she'd been told, had swept down from the north, then turned west, carefully avoiding the areas patrolled by Lord Devois' forces. His scouts had seen no sign of them, not until they were already within Avellon itself. Another supposedly impossible feat.

"Better than Darkegrove is what matters," Lia remarked, moving to look at the map laid out on the table. "What do we do now?"

Aelius drummed a finger on the table a moment before lifting his gaze to hers. "We fight, sister. They approach from the east, so I've ordered the bulk of our forces to take positions to meet them. The eastern lords have been kept abreast of the situation, and are rallying their own forces to join us, except for the ones in immediate danger of being overtaken."

"Can we send aid?"

"Not likely, Majesty," Lord Auclair said. "It would leave Satisse at too great a risk, and with the speed it seems they're moving...it's not likely they'd make it in time anyway."

"Light above," Lia whispered. Her first challenge as queen was proving to be a colossal one. She had no idea what to say, what command to issue now. Aelius would lead the armies well, as he always had. But beyond small skirmishes with bands of raiders from beyond the seas, the armies of Avellon had little experience. "Keep me informed," she ordered before leaving.

Gods be with us.

Upstairs, in her private sitting room, she found the seer waiting just where Lia had asked her to wait after their meeting in her office earlier.

"Do you believe me now?" Sybella asked, tilting her head to look Lia over. Silver-grey eyes swept over Lia's face, searching.

"I don't know," she replied truthfully. "Can you tell me more?"

"I've told you everything. I saw the three crowns falling, and then heard women weeping and screaming. I assume it to be the three queens of Aestera." Sybella paused as Lia plopped into a soft chair across from her. "But my visions are not necessarily set in stone. They are simply warnings so that the course can be corrected... usually."

"Usually?" Lia frowned. She didn't like the sound of that.

"Sometimes nothing can be done." Twisting the fabric of her skirt between her fingers, she added, "I have no way of knowing which visions can be changed and which cannot."

"Please excuse my bluntness here, but that seems utterly useless right now."

Sybella offered Lia a half smile. "I agree."

Lia dragged a shaky hand through her blonde hair. "This is a lot." Looking beyond Sybella to the closed window, she inhaled deeply. Desperate for a change in subject, she asked, "Where is your room?"

"Excuse me?"

Lia turned her attention back to Sybella, who was staring at her with a raised brow. "I've never seen you. I wondered where you've been living these last months."

Sybella's tense expression shifted to something more unreadable, something darker. "The south tower. I wasn't allowed out of my rooms when you were in residence."

Lia blinked. As the oldest part of the castle, the south tower was dreadfully cold in the winter and oppressively hot in the summer. It had been neglected by at least a few generations of her family, and for all she knew was home to little more than bats and spiders. Certainly the place to hide something, someone, you didn't want to be found.

"I'll have a room made ready for you in the guest wing," she said quietly. Anger and shame roiled within her. How had she not known her father's true nature? "Someone will fetch your things and take you to your room shortly."

"I have no need for your pity, Majesty," Sybella replied, lip curling.

"It's not pity," Lia sighed wearily. War was apparently on the horizon, and her friend was still missing, presumed dead. She was exhausted. "I'm simply offering you basic human respect. If you would prefer to make the journey home or return to the tower, you are welcome to do so."

Sybella paused, whether because she was, in fact, considering those options, or because of Lia's tone, Lia couldn't tell. "Thank you," the seer said finally, tone lacking the bite it had nearly every other time she'd spoken today. "I'll take the guest room...until Avellon is safe."

CHAPTER 7

EVE

"We found her," Valerian announced suddenly, plopping down beside Eve on the library sofa. There was no need to ask who he referred to; they'd been searching for her nearly from the moment they arrived in Elesiya.

"Where?" Eve asked instead, closing her book, another of the fae romances she was becoming increasingly fond of, with a snap. There was little else for her to do now but wait, wait until Callan could convince the nobles of Falias to come to her for the aid of her kingdom. *My former kingdom.*

As High King, he could technically order the armies to march, but with five hundred years of absence, many felt he had abandoned his people, no matter his reasons. War would be much more easily fought, and won, with their support. So negotiations had droned on, with Callan playing the penitent king, ready to rekindle friendships and alliances with each of the lords and ladies of Falias.

Eve would be included in those discussions as soon as they publicly declared their mating bond and she accepted the mantle of High Queen, but fear of becoming little more than a consort had her hesitating. Then there was the matter of Darkegrove and what awaited her when they finally liberated the human kingdom. They would never accept a fae queen, especially now, and she would never expect them to. But what did that mean for the future she had fought so hard for, had literally given her life trying to achieve?

"In the garden district, of all places. A mere five-minute walk from the palace," he laughed bitterly.

"Why did it take so long to find her?" Eve asked, brow furrowing.

Valerian lifted a shoulder. "Cal wanted it kept quiet, just in case she caught wind we were looking for her and fled, but it seems she was just at home, unaware anyone was looking for her."

"She's just been living a life here? Would she have run if she had known he was looking for her?"

"Cora says she kept tabs on Mara for a couple of hundred years after she arrived and was made fae. Mara apparently settled in well enough and just kind of started living a normal life. Cora made sure she was given a home, and money enough to live comfortably."

"That's...generous, considering."

"Yeah, that's what I said, but Cora is like that," Valerian laughed. "Anyway, you want to come and meet her? She's in the parlor down the hall with Cora and Leysa right now. Cal is in a meeting again."

"Sure," she sighed, shoving down the irritation that rose at yet another meeting she was not a part of. Her own indecision kept her from it, sure, but what sort of choice did she have anyway? She had given everything to be queen of her own kingdom only to have that ripped away, by fate or whatever the gods wanted to call it. Frustrated, she tossed the book on the sofa and headed out to meet the woman who had damned an entire kingdom.

～

"So you're the one." The soft feminine voice startled Eve as she entered the parlor. With her gaze landing first on Cora and Leysa, seated on the chairs to her right, deep in conversation, she hadn't immediately noticed the fae female standing by the piano to the left of the room.

Turning to meet the gaze of the petite, dark-haired fae, Eve's brow rose sharply. With jet-black hair that fell just past her shoulders in loose curls and dark brown eyes set in an oval-shaped face, Mara, the Queen of Despair, was stunning.

She was also eyeing Eve with an unexpected amount of cautious curiosity. What she had anticipated had been suspicion, fear, or even anger. She had expected a sultry temptress perhaps, or a cold and beautiful queen with little care for the mark she'd left on the mortal realm.

What she found instead was a woman who appeared nervous, of all things.

Indeed, Mara twisted the fabric of her violet gown between her fingers over and over, hovering just behind the piano, as if afraid to approach Eve.

Eve cast a glance at her friends, who had fallen into silence and were watching the exchange with interest now. Cora lifted a shoulder in response to Eve's look of confusion.

"Her?" Eve said finally, turning to look at Mara again.

"The Queen of Darkegrove, chosen one, Callan's mate." She paused, offering a small smile. "It's nice to meet you. I've heard a lot–"

"Can we not do this part?" Eve interrupted, frowning. "I know that's rude, but...you ruined my entire life, and the lives of countless other women in our, *my*, kingdom." Mara's expression fell, and to her surprise, Eve felt a small pang of guilt as she continued. "I just wanted to meet the person responsible. Well, the other person, as I've already had the extreme displeasure of meeting your lover."

Mara's expression sharpened at that, and she dropped the fabric, taking a small step toward Eve. "He's alive?" she asked breathlessly, turning her attention to Cora. "You didn't tell me."

Cora bit her lip gently. "I was asked not to. I'm sorry."

Eve's gaze darted between the two women. "Why are you apologizing to her?"

Leysa chimed in, "Eve there are things that Cora and the others were...made aware of...while locked away. There is a lot more to the story we didn't know."

More secrets. What a shock.

"Tell me your story," Eve sighed, casting a wary look at Mara. "Then I'll decide how much I hate you."

Mara ignored Eve's remark, moving to sit across from Leysa and Cora. "Then let us lay all of our secrets bare, including where Cathal is now, and how long we have until he comes looking for me."

CHAPTER 8

LIA

As it turned out, Sybella had precious few things to be moved. Little more than a small bag of dresses, a framed portrait of a young child, and a handful of books. It was all she had been allowed to bring with her when Lia's father, the man she had idolized her entire life, had kidnapped the innocent woman from her own home.

"You don't need to stay," Sybella called out looking up from the bag she was currently placing the last of her clothes in.

The room had been outfitted with a decent-sized bed, a scuffed wardrobe, and a small table with a single chair. Eyeing the table, Lia couldn't help but wonder what it had been like to be hidden away in this lonely room, anytime Lia had been home. As her eyes skirted around the room, pity and fury with her father warring within her, she noticed for the first time, what she'd missed.

"Where are you bathing chambers?" she asked, frowning. Even in the guest wing, each chamber had access to at least a semi-private chamber for bathing and seeing to needs. Some were shared between two rooms, usually designated for families. This one, however, seemed to be lacking that particular comfort.

Sybella's cheeks flushed a pretty shade of pink, her gaze raising to meet Lia's. "Down the hall."

Inhaling slowly, Lia stifled the urge to turn on her heel, stomp to her father's room, and demand to know what he was thinking. To ask when the father she had always known as kind and just had become someone so incredibly cruel. Instead, she began to take note of what the seer would require, in addition to new rooms.

She'd need some new dresses. The ones she had been able to bring were better suited for the warmer autumn months, not winter. Even in the better-maintained portions of the palace, it would get cold in the evenings, and if she wanted to leave at any time...Well, Lia would have to ensure she had proper attire.

"Can I get you anything?" Lia asked finally. "I've already ordered dinner to be brought to your new room. I thought you might like to get settled in tonight, but in the future, if you'd like to join me downstairs, you're–"

"No," Sybella cut her off sharply. "I have no desire to dine with your family." Plucking the small portrait from her bed, she strode across the room in long, elegant strides, coming to stop in front of Lia. "I appreciate that you feel bad for what your father did, truly. I can see that you are not the same, and I intend to keep my promise to remain here and help as much as I can. But I have not forgotten what he took from me, and I do not intend to behave as if I am a welcomed guest."

Lia tensed, ready to argue that it didn't have to be that way, that her father would be bedridden for whatever remaining days he had anyway, but the fire in Sybella's eyes stopped her. "I understand. If you need anything, I've assigned a maid to look after you. She will make sure you have anything you like, for as long as you stay." Turning to go, she paused. "I understand what he did, and if I could change it I would. I know you don't want it, but for as long as you choose to stay here, you will be treated as a guest, and with the utmost respect." Recalling the guards that waited for them outside, she added, "If anyone says or does anything out of line, I will ensure they are punished."

Men were men, after all, and if they believed the seer to be nothing more than a prisoner, who knew what the worst of them might do? Such things had never been tolerated in Avellon, and any soldier or guard who had been accused of doing harm to a woman had been swiftly and severely punished.

Yesterday, she might have simply held faith in the fact that her father would only allow decent men to remain employed here in Sunholde, but she wasn't so sure anymore.

"My daughter," Sybella blurted suddenly.

Lia turned to face her again, frowning. Confusion swept over her. "I'm sorry?"

"I have a daughter," Sybella explained, face flushing as she looked at the portrait in her hands.

It was difficult for Lia to make out any detail, but from where she stood she could just see the top of a young child's head, covered in raven curls. "Is she safe?" Lia asked, dread settling into the pit of her stomach like a lead ball. If her father had allowed harm to come to a child...

"Yes," Sybella answered quickly, gaze sweeping over Lia's face. "She is with a friend, safe in our village. They let me take her there before they forced me to go with them."

Lia sighed with relief. At least there was that bit of goodness left in him, little that it was. "You must miss her."

"Very much. I left a piece of my very soul behind when I had to leave her."

"Do you want to bring her–"

"Absolutely not." The fire ignited in Sybella's eyes once more. "She is safe from harm there, unaware of everything that is going on. If war comes to the east, then perhaps. But not before that."

Lia nodded. While she had no children of her own, the urge to protect a loved one was something she understood well. She felt it for her brother, for her mother. Had even felt that for her father, before everything she'd known had been turned on its head.

"I just wanted you to understand," Sybella continued, "why I cannot forgive him, and what I am giving up to help my kingdom."

It was tremendous. What had been taken from her, and what she was choosing to leave behind in order to remain close, to offer what help she could. It was more than Lia or her family deserved.

"Thank you," she said quietly. "You are a good person, Sybella."

The seer nodded once, gaze dropping to the portrait. She remained silent a beat, sliding her thumb over the young girl's portrait once. "Call me Bella," she said resolutely, before stepping into the room and closing the door in Lia's face.

Chapter 9

Eve

For several minutes, they sat in heavy silence. Eve had no words to describe the warring emotions within her. Anger, pity, and confusion were a tempest within her, each threatening to spill over at any moment.

Mara confirmed that Cathal had in fact tried to go to war with his brother over his refusal to allow the pair to be together; though she claimed the rift between the brothers was not the reason the fae had been sealed away behind their veil for nearly five hundred years.

According to her, it had been the threat that Gorias posed that led the gods to take that drastic step. It sounded like a lie, and Eve said so immediately. Only Cora's confirmation had changed her mind.

"You see, the goddess of judgment and justice, Astraia, brought Mara to us. Callan was still High King then, but he was away... seeing to Cathal." Cora frowned. She'd avoided any conversation regarding her brothers and their feud up to this point.

While Eve could understand the discomfort it might cause, there was too much at stake to be concerned over uncomfortable feelings. "And?"

"And she explained the whole truth," Cora began. "It's...a lot, Eve. And–"

"I should be the one to tell the story," Callan said from the doorway, all four sets of eyes turning to look at him at once. His gaze remained on Mara for several seconds, unreadable and cold, before softening as his gaze shifted to Eve, though his eyes remained darkened with emotion. "May we have the room, ladies?"

Cora offered Callan a murmured apology as she passed, followed quickly by Leysa and Mara.

"Will the secrets ever end, Callan?" She was tired, so tired of all of the secrets and revelations. As he moved to sit across from her, she looked him over. Her mate. The man she loved. There was trust between them, so why the need to hold onto so many more secrets? "Tell me the whole truth now, please."

Callan's gaze dropped to the ground as he nodded, clenching and unclenching his hands. "You're right, it's time you knew everything. Where do you want me to begin?"

"At the start. What happened with Mara and Cathal?"

Callan dragged a hand through his hair with a sigh. "Mara inherited the throne of Darkegrove, around five hundred years ago. Shortly after taking her throne, she married a prince from an eastern kingdom, across the sea. The idea was to bring peace between their nations. Power was supposed to be shared between them," he explained, leaning back in his seat. "But it didn't take long for him to shift the power in his favor. He was backed by many of the lords of Darkegrove. Not all, but enough of them."

Eve rolled her eyes. It was the same old story. Men taking power from women, and women forced to accept it. "How surprising," she remarked dryly.

Callan nodded his agreement vaguely but continued. "Once she was essentially powerless in her own kingdom, he began to enact his plan."

"She had no backing?"

"Not enough," he frowned. "Not enough to stop Vikenti. Here in Falias, we grew...concerned. He was making moves against their southern neighbors, and we worried he might set his sights west next, so we decided to send an emissary to keep an eye on things."

"Cathal," Eve breathed, anger flaring. For a moment she was back in the ballroom, a collar of flame around her neck.

Callan's thoughts seemingly took the same turn, and shadows gathered around his hands as he replied, "Yes."

"What happened then?"

"I don't know all of the details," Callan admitted, shaking his hands once, dismissing the shadows. "But apparently they fell in love."

"We did," Mara's voice sounded from the doorway. As they both turned toward her sharply, she frowned. "I wasn't eavesdropping. Not intentionally. I just wanted to make sure my side of the story was heard." Her gaze settled on Callan. "As you said, you don't know the whole story, and I think it's about time I got to tell it."

Chapter 10

Lia

The door to Aelius' room closed with a decisive click behind her. Lia couldn't bring herself to confront her dying father, not yet, but she could damn well confront her brother.

He had made a remark about the seer, Bella, before she had been brought before Lia. She was determined to find out exactly how much, and when, her brother knew of their father's actions.

"Did you know?" she demanded, coming to a stop at the foot of his bed, where he lay sprawled on his stomach. His clothes were rumpled, and his golden hair fell loose, hiding what little bit of his face the pillow didn't.

"About what?" he asked, voice muffled and bleary from lack of sleep, too much drink, or both.

"Our father kidnapping and imprisoning innocent women," she replied more sharply than intended.

Aelius flipped over then, pinning her with an incredulous look as he sat up. "Light's sake, Lia, what the fuck are you talking about?"

"Bella."

"Who?"

"The seer. Bella," she sighed, frustrated, and waved a hand. "Sybella. He kidnapped her and imprisoned her in the south tower."

"No he didn't," he scoffed. "That's ridiculous."

"Oh? Where are her quarters then?"

"How should I know? I'm barely here, and when I am I hardly have the time to keep track of all of our guests. Which, as you know, are often numerous."

Lia snorted. "You usually know where the pretty ones are," she replied, eyeing his rumpled clothing pointedly. "Which nobleman's wife did you bed this time?"

Aelius bristled. "None."

His unexpected reaction was noted but was far from a pressing concern at the moment. "So you didn't know?"

"Have I ever lied to you?"

As children, Aelius and Aurelia were thick as thieves. Little Light and Whirlwind they'd been called, inseparable, even when they squabbled. He had never once lied to her, even if it meant telling her a truth that would hurt her feelings.

"Okay," she sighed. "I had her moved to one of the guest rooms, and she's free to leave anytime she likes."

Silence settled over them, thickening the air for a few moments before he spoke again. "He really did that?" His normally sunny face had clouded, and the guilt and shame she felt were mirrored on her twin's face.

"Yes, he did," she said quietly.

"Why?" He dragged a hand through his hair, shifting in the bed so that his legs hung over the sides now, bare feet resting on the wooden floors.

"I don't know," she answered truthfully. "I guess he wanted to use her for her visions. But kidnapping? That's so unlike him."

"I guess, unless there's more we don't know."

"That's what I'm afraid of, and the reason I haven't gone to see him yet."

Aelius nodded his understanding. Their father had been seen as a paragon for as long as they could remember, and for good reason. Aldrich Vallyse was known to be wise and fair, strong but kind. Everything they thought they knew about their father was being turned on its head. "I'll go with you."

"Aelius— I don't–"

"I know, Lia, but we have to know the truth before he's gone. We have to know who our father is."

48

CHAPTER 11

EVE

"He came to Darkegrove just before the summer solstice," Mara explained, taking a seat in a free chair near Eve. "The first time I recall seeing him was at the celebration."

"That sounds right," Callan added, eyeing Mara warily. "I asked him to go about a week before the solstice."

"Celebration?" Eve frowned. The summer solstice was an excuse to spend time in the little bit of extra sunlight, and perhaps go swimming in one of Darkegrove's many lakes or rivers, but beyond that, there was little in the way of celebration. Such things had been abandoned long ago, alongside the worship of the gods they'd lost.

"Things were different in Darkegrove in those days," Mara explained. "We had great parties, with huge bonfires burning all night. The doors to the ballroom would be thrown wide, and we would dance and dance. Inhibitions were all but nonexistent on that night. The summer solstice was the one night of the year where we were free to do what we wanted, wear what we wanted, and fuck who we wanted."

Eve's brow rose at the change in demeanor from the nervous-looking female to the now seemingly confident and brazen one.

Noting Eve's surprise, Mara met Eve's gaze levelly. "After our discussion earlier, and thanks to the fact you haven't attempted to do...whatever it is you do with your goddess-given gift, I've decided to stop being afraid of you and speak freely."

Rather than remind Mara that she could still, in fact, use that gift if pushed, Eve instead asked, "So you and Cathal?"

"Did I fuck him that night?" Mara asked, laughing lightly. "No, not that night. But we danced, and he flirted. We didn't actually touch one another until later."

"We don't need the details of your relationship," Callan remarked flatly.

Eve shot a glance at him but remained silent. She was a little curious, she had to admit, but he was right. The details wouldn't help them decide if he was going to continue to be an enemy they needed to be worried about. Or, as she hoped, could be convinced to at least stay out of their way while they dealt with what appeared to be the larger and more pressing threat; or perhaps, with Mara's help, even be swayed to help them.

Mara raised a brow but inclined her head in acceptance. "Alright. We fell for one another quickly. I couldn't be with him, not really, but... we were drawn to one another in an undeniable way. He saw how my husband treated me, and how he tried to war with our neighbors." Mara's brown eyes darkened. "He wrote to you for aid," she said, tone lowering as she turned to stare at Callan. "And you refused."

A muscle in Callan's jaw feathered. "I did."

"Why?" Mara's tone was full of something akin to accusation. "Why didn't you help us get rid of him?"

"You took care of it yourselves well enough." A non-answer that had Eve frowning in response. She would have liked more of an explanation for that herself, but now was not the time to demand it.

A low and bitter laugh sounded from the Queen of Despair. "That we did." Turning her cool gaze to Eve, she continued. "I took care of the problem my husband presented. We asked for his help again," she said, flicking a gaze at Callan. "This time, permission to marry. As an emissary and member of the royal family, the king's permission had to be granted for him to wed another royal." Lifting her chin, silver eyes brimming with tears, she finished. "He refused again. Cathal sought to… change his mind."

Now it was Callan's turn to laugh bitterly. "If by change my mind, you mean overthrow me, then sure."

"So is that why the fae were sealed away? To prevent war?" Eve asked, confused. She'd expected more somehow.

"No," Mara sighed. "That was just the excuse. Presented to the humans to keep you from panicking. Only those of us who were sealed away were informed of the truth."

"What truth?" Eve asked, growing impatient.

"Gorias is coming for us, for all of us, because of the Stone of Rule," Callan supplied.

"The what?" she blurted, shaking her head. None of this was making sense.

"Stone of Rule. Created by the gods, it amplifies the bearer's magic. For example, if one had the gift of water, they could go from conjuring a few small droplets to a torrent of rain," Callan explained.

"Basically, whoever has it can conquer a kingdom a hell of a lot easier," Mara cut in.

Eve's head was spinning. This certainly fell under the category of a lot, as Leysa and Cora had warned. "And what does that have to do with you?" she asked Mara.

"In truth? Nothing. But Cathal had hoped to frighten Falias into backing down and granting what we asked for. He'd heard rumors that the Stone was hidden in Darkegrove somewhere, and could only be wielded by fae hands." Again, she cut a glance at Callan. "So he claimed to have it. But he never did."

Warning bells started sounding in Eve's head.

"Gorias must have heard, and they began to make moves on Darkegrove," Callan said then. "The goddess Astraia took pity on Mara, hiding her here and making her fae. In order to protect the humans, the gods let them, as well as Gorias, believe that the reason for their intervention was to prevent war. Then Gorias quieted, I assume believing that the artifact was lost when Cathal vanished."

"Cathal's punishment," Mara explained, "was to be locked away from everyone and everything he loved for as long as the veil between humans and fae remained."

Callan's ocean eyes darkened. "And I remained behind to guard my brother, and to atone for my mistake."

"Which one?" Mara countered.

"All of them," Callan sighed.

CHAPTER 12

LIA

The cloying sweetness of lilies danced in the air of Aldrich Vallyse's bedroom. Someone had selected the very best blooms from the greenhouse, as even in Avellon, the cool kiss of winter meant no more bright blooms until spring returned. Likely a maid or even Archie, as her mother, Hemera, hadn't left her father's side for more than a few moments at a time since he had taken to his bed.

It smells like death in here, Lia thought to herself as she and Aelius hovered just inside the doorway. She hadn't expected him to look so frail today. When she'd last visited, yesterday, she realized with some degree of regret, he'd looked stronger than this. His tan skin had turned pallid, and the light in his eyes was nearly gone.

"Are my children going to come and say hello, or simply stare?" he murmured, barely loud enough to be heard across the room. Lia hazarded a glance at Aelius, who was staring out the windows at the starlit sky, refusing to look in their father's direction. Night had fallen some time ago, while they debated how they would approach the difficult discussion ahead.

"We have a question, Father," Lia began slowly, carefully.

"Did you kidnap and imprison the seer?" Aelius demanded suddenly, jerking his head to stare at the former king.

Hemera was on her feet in an instant. "Aelius, what has gotten into you?!" Tears welled in their mother's lovely sky-blue eyes. The eyes that Aelius and Lia themselves had both inherited. "To come in here and make such wild accusations that can't possibly be tr–"

Aelius shook his head, "Mother, you don't–"

"Please can we just–" Lia began, in an attempt to calm the fight that was already starting between mother and son.

"I did." Aldrich's quietly croaked response silenced the room.

Hemera gasped, sinking back into her chair, her eyes on Aelius who inhaled sharply, turning his gaze back to the window.

Lia however, spoke up. "Why?"

"I did what I had to do to protect and prepare you, Little Light." Aldrich coughed. "To learn what fate has decreed."

"That makes no sense," Lia replied, shaking her head. Her heart pounded, head reeling. She'd believed Bella instantly, without explanation, instinct screaming that the seer spoke true. That same instinct was now telling her that despite the wrongness of what he had done, he was telling the truth. Or at the least, what he thought was the truth.

"Aldrich, what did you do?" Hemera whispered softly, reaching for her husband's hand.

"What I had to," was his gravelly reply. "Ask her yourself, what she saw coming for you. If you still judge me for what I did, then so be it."

Aelius snorted, turning his back to the window as he surveyed his father. "Papa, when did you become this person? You are a man of wisdom, of education. Yet you kidnapped someone and held her hostage because she had some weird dream?"

"I had to find the truth," Aldrich sighed, eyelids fluttering closed.

"That's enough," Hemera said quietly. "You've gotten your answer, let your father rest now."

Lia had been taught by her parents from birth that the truth was more important than anything. Truth, wisdom, and light had been the Vallyse family motto for centuries. Now, on her father's deathbed, she was finding out that he had lied, based on something decidedly unwise– and she was struggling to find any semblance of light in the entire situation.

Still, he was her father, and if there was light to be found in this darkness they found themselves in, she would find it. She could not offer forgiveness, as it was not hers to give, but she could offer him peace in death, at least, with the love she still felt in her heart for him.

"I love you, Papa," she said quietly, before leaving the room for the last time.

Chapter 13

Eve

"Will he come for her?" Eve stared up at the dark ceiling of their bedroom, barely illuminated by the light from the bright winter moon that slipped through the space between the drawn curtains.

The pretty pattern of stars in the night sky, barely visible in the scant light, even with her fae vision, had been chosen by Callan's mother centuries ago. Most of the decor and furnishings in their rooms had been chosen by her. Out of love and respect, none of it had been touched. While Eve had added some things, more live plants and a few pieces of artwork that reminded her of Darkegrove, she was somewhat surprised to find she actually really enjoyed the same things Ferelith, the late Queen of Falias, had. The woman whom she would have loved to have met, if only to thank her for the incredible gift that was her son.

"I'm only surprised he hasn't already," Callan replied softly.

She knew he could hear it, the way fear made her heart thunder in her chest, as she could hear the steady beat of his own heart beside her.

"I can hear your heartbeat," she murmured.

"Yes," he laughed, barely more than a breath in the darkness. "I can hear yours as well. There's nothing to fear, dove. He will not touch you, not ever again."

Warmth spread through her chest at that. "That's not why I asked. I was wondering if every fae can do that."

Callan laughed again. "Oh, that. No, that's unique to mates."

Eve rolled to her side, facing him. Still lying on his back, he turned toward her. They were so close now that their noses nearly touched. "Really?"

"Mhm." Rolling to his side, he traced the line of her jaw slowly with one finger. "I can hear yours, as you can hear mine. Even across great distances, we'll be in tune with one another. We'll know if the other is in danger or injured. Or.....has died." His tone lowered at the end, hand stilling.

"I'm not going to die, Callan," she promised. "We're going to have an annoyingly long life together." Willing her heart to steady its staccato beat, she leaned into his touch. "We'll figure it out together, all of it."

A weighty silence fell over them, too many unspoken words hanging in the ether. There was too much left to say, too many secrets–and the decision she still had yet to make. The single word she wanted to say, if she could steel her spine and ask her own question.

The final blockade to her future with him.

Callan opened his mouth to speak, to say what she didn't know, but fear had her tongue loosening, and the words spilled from her lips in a rush.

"Would I be Consort or Queen in my own right?" she blurted suddenly, wincing. She hadn't meant for it to come out so abruptly, and not while they lay awake in their bed at the end of the day.

Callan's hand fell away from her face, and the sudden absence of his touch chilled her.

"Is that what you think of me, dove?" Moving so swiftly she had no time to react, he pushed her against the bed firmly, hovering above her so closely that their lips nearly touched as she took a sharp intake of breath. "Do you think I would do any less than make you queen of everything you see? That I would offer you anything less than the world?" he asked quietly, his voice thick with emotion.

Electricity danced along her spine as heat curled low in her belly. "And where does that leave you, my king," she whispered.

Callan's growl of approval had her toes curling. "With you, My

Most Resplendent, Magnificent Queen. For that honor alone, I would give anything. My lands, my heart, my crown, my very life. Whatever you ask for, it's yours."

Eve's breath hitched. Not only at his words, his devotion to her, but at the callused hand that was now sliding her nightgown up ever so slowly. Rough skin skimming against soft, the heat of his touch followed closely by the cool kiss of the evening air along the parts of her he left bare. "As I am yours," she replied softly. "In whatever way you ask of me."

He said nothing more as his mouth claimed hers in a crushing kiss that left her breathless. In one motion, he had the nightgown up and over her head, tossed to the side and forgotten. Leaning back, with her legs trapped between his knees, Callan's eyes roamed over her. Her skin prickled at his attention, breasts growing heavy and peaked as his gaze landed on them.

"Beautiful," he breathed, awe filling his tone just as he had the last time they'd been together like this, in her room at Stoneweald.

"Yours," she whispered, lifting a hand to his chest, palm flat against where his heart lay.

"Mine, as I am yours," he murmured in agreement. Sliding down the length of her body slowly, he peppered her chilled skin with kisses until he came to the small bit of lace that covered her most intimate place, hiding the last bit of her from his view. Hooking two fingers in the waistband, he slid them down her legs, discarding them alongside the nightgown.

Her core tightened at the sight of his head hovering between her thighs, breath coming in quick bursts. She felt heavy and somehow light all at once, gripping the sheets in anticipation, earning a roguish grin from him in response.

"I think, perhaps, my queen has need of me?" He breathed against the sensitive skin of her inner thigh.

"That she does," Eve replied shakily, trying and failing to use the haughty tone expected of royalty. "You know your task, Lord Thorne," she teased, a subtle reminder of their beginning. "See that your queen is not disappointed."

A husky laugh was the only reply before he languidly slid his tongue over the sensitive bundle of nerves at her apex. Soon, his fingers joined his mouth, and he took her soaring higher and faster than she'd thought possible. She was little more than dandelion fluff in a whirlwind by the time he had wrung every last ounce of pleasure from her.

"Is the High Queen of Falias pleased?" he asked, leaning his head against her bent knee.

"The High Queen of Falias is delighted," she replied, heart singing.

Callan's response was cut short by the sound of urgent knocking at the door to their bedchamber. "Go away," Callan called out, offering Eve a mischievous grin.

"Put your clothes on, Cal," Valerian shouted through the closed door, his tone devoid of any of his usual humor.

With a frown, Eve dragged the blanket around her as they both rose from the bed. Callan didn't bother to fasten his pants as he opened the door just wide enough for the pair to see Valerian's grim face.

"What's wrong?" Eve asked, tightening the blanket around her anxiously. Something had clearly happened, judging from the shadows she saw dancing in her friend's eyes.

"It's Stoneweald," he began, shifting his gaze to hers. "Gorias has gone. They're free."

Chapter 14

Lia

Aldrich Vallyse died two short days after the confrontation with his children.

Lia had spent the entirety of that time regretting their last minutes together; as much as she hated what he'd done, despite his claim it had somehow been done to protect her. She hadn't gone to see Bella but had been informed by her staff that the seer was being well looked after.

Now, three days after her father's death, she was ready to see the woman for herself, and to ask about the claim he'd made from his deathbed.

If she couldn't beg his forgiveness for the way their last conversation had gone, she could at least find the truth of the matter that had divided them before his body was placed atop the pyre upon the sacred Vespera Hill, yards from the Black Pool nearest their castle. His ashes would then be sprinkled over the depthless waters, sending his soul to the gods.

Such was the way of Avellon, the custom that must be upheld, whether she herself believed in it or not.

Before she could talk herself out of doing the very thing she'd been avoiding for days, Lia knocked.

"Yes?" Bella's voice sounded surprised, cautious even, as she called out from within the guest room she'd been given.

Steadying her strangely shaky breath, Lia inhaled. Why were her palms suddenly so sweaty? She pushed the thought away just as she pushed the door to Bella's room open, stepping inside.

The seer had been given one of their best guest suites. Bedecked in the soft hues of an Avellonian sunrise, white, pink, and pale orange, it boasted a large and comfortable bed, wardrobe, small sitting area with comfortable chairs and sofa, and a desk for writing. Attached was a bathing chamber nearly as opulent as Lia's own.

It was luxurious and soft, in the style most Avellonians thought of as beautiful.

Bella, seated on one of the overstuffed white chairs, looked entirely out of place. Still lovely, but in a more feline way. With her dark hair hanging freely, well past her shoulders, those strange silvery eyes fixed on her, and the sharp angles of her face tightened ever so slightly as she realized who had stepped into her room.

"Majesty," she said cautiously, rising to her feet and lowering herself into a curtsy. More deference than she'd shown before.

"Please, don't do that," Lia sighed. "I would like for us to speak as equals," she began, offering a smile that felt only a little forced. "If that's okay."

A dark brow quirked upward, and she paused for a beat. "I have a choice?"

Something in Lia's chest tightened at Bella's careful tone. "Always."

Bella considered it for a moment, the corner of her full mouth twitching downward. "Alright then, please join me, Ma–"

"Please call me Lia." Lia interrupted as she lowered herself slowly into a chair, the twin to Bella's.

"I can't do that."

"Why?" Now it was Lia's brow that rose.

"You're the queen. It doesn't seem right."

"What if I command you to?" Lia teased half-heartedly. "Really though, I would like...I would like to speak to someone as simply myself. Not as Queen of Avellon."

"It weighs on you, the crown," Bella observed, finally taking her seat again.

Lia frowned. She'd barely taken on any of her duties. Far less than she should have, if she were being honest with herself. The latest reports on the forces heading toward them had been murky at best, so she'd soon have to send more scouts, and reach out to the lords in the path of this strange army, requesting they do the same. That would likely be her next task, after this conversation. "It's beginning to," she admitted.

"Do you not have friends?" Bella asked, then winced. "I'm sorry, that was rude."

Lia shrugged the blunt question off. "I have a few. None who I can really....be myself with nowadays. My closest friend–" She hesitated. She had wanted this conversation, but how much truth should she be revealing to this woman, this stranger? "Well, I can't see her right now."

"That must be difficult."

She was delaying the inevitable, and necessary, conversation she'd actually come to have. But was a moment of normalcy too much to ask?

Bella watched her closely, seeming to judge the silent thoughts that no doubt danced across Lia's features. She never had been a very good liar.

The truth is always in your eyes, Little Light, her father often teased. Tears pricked at her eyes, thanks to the painful memory, and she quickly wiped them away with her palm.

"What did you come to speak to me about, Lia?" The sudden use of her name caught Lia by surprise. Bella's tone was soft, but not weak; bearing a steely strength that she had no doubt could be sharpened into a weapon if need be.

"My father claims– claimed," she corrected, wincing. "That he...did what he did, to protect me somehow. Because of some prophecy of yours."

Silver eyes flashed brightly. Lia could almost see flames, bright and unending, within them as Bella's temper flared. "Is that so?"

"It doesn't make it okay," Lia added, shaking her head gently. "Regardless of what he believed, he had no right to do that to you."

The worst of the cold blaze in Bella's eyes dampened slightly. "You want to know what the prophecy was." None of the cold rage Lia had glimpsed in Bella's eyes found its way into her tone, as she issued the simple statement.

"Please."

"Very well," she said, turning her gaze to the fire that roared in the hearth. "I saw you die. You died on a field of blood and muck, battling against an enemy I couldn't see. The Light of Avellon went out, and darkness spread across the lands. You died, and the last hope of Aestera went with you."

CHAPTER 15

EVE

Three days after the conversation with Mara, Eve, Callan, and their friends had gathered to discuss what would come next, regarding Gorias. Darkegrove was free, they'd been told, and under the control of what remained of her council. To her relief, Eldred had assumed his position of leadership once more and was spearheading the effort to repair what had been damaged and reassure the people of Darkegrove of their safety.

"He bids you to stay here," Mason said with a sigh. "His letter states that everything is under control, but warns that–"

The doors to the sitting room opened suddenly, and a pair of guards entered without so much as knocking. "Lord Cathal has been spotted approaching the gates," a stoic and stern-faced guard said, his hard gaze meeting Callan's.

Callan was on his feet in an instant. "How long ago?"

"Minutes, Majesty," the guard replied.

Holding a hand out for Eve, Callan looked to Cora. "We'll pace there. Cora...He's always listened to you."

Cora nodded, dark hair swaying. "I'll try to keep the two of you from killing each other," she sighed. The long-suffering sigh of a sister constantly caught between her brothers. But the smile she offered

Callan was too tight to be casual, and that was fear hardening her blue eyes.

Callan didn't reply, instead looking to Leysa and Valerian next. "Get Mara. We should let him see her, but don't let him close enough to take her. Perhaps if Cora fails, Mara can keep him calm." Ocean eyes turned hard as sapphires. "But be prepared in case her presence...upsets him."

Mason glanced at Cora, his gaze shuttered. "I guess I'll stay here," he said, expression tight. Cora nodded, only briefly meeting his gaze before turning back to the others.

Taking her hand in his own, Callan paced them. Her stomach lurched as they stepped between the shadows of the world, cold nothingness surrounded them, and in the span of a breath, they were standing just outside the gates to Elesiya.

Eve's heart sputtered in her chest, palms going clammy. Perhaps a hundred yards away, stood Cathal; dressed nearly identically to the last time she'd seen him, impeccable in black, hands in his pockets, and pinning Callan with a lethal grin.

"I thought you two would show up if I waited long enough." Callan stiffened as Cathal's attention shifted to Eve, gaze sweeping from head to toe and back. "It seems I've missed some very interesting developments," he mused.

Callan bared his teeth in warning, shadows gathering around him slowly. "We have no desire to fight you, brother." *But we will if you force our hand*, was left unspoken, hanging between them in the cold winter air.

Cathal snorted, attention shifting back to Callan. "I've no interest in you or your–" He sniffed the air slightly, the corner of his lips twitching. "Newly made mate? Interesting indeed. I've come to claim what is mine–unless you were lying."

"I'm wounded, brother. I thought you would've missed us," Cora called out sweetly as she came to stand on Eve's other side.

Something in Cathal's expression shifted as he turned to his sister. "How could I not miss you, sweet sister?" he said after a beat, tone as mockingly disinterested as always. Narrowing his eyes he added, "It must be painful to be treated so poorly by your own brother."

Callan snorted, drawing Cathal's attention once more.

"Do you recall my warning brother?" Cathal began, flames sparking to life around his hands, writhing around and through his splayed fingers like serpents. "The return of what is mine...or her life is forfeit."

"She is here," Eve said, hazarding a single step forward. "Do you intend to take her?"

"Take her?" Cathal laughed bitterly. "If I did, do you think you could stop me?" He challenged, lips curling into a cruel grin. The flames around his hands burned brighter, as he continued, "I have come to see for myself that my love, my wife, lives. After five hundred years."

Eve's own power surged in response, the ground beginning to tremble. A small quake, just enough to show him that she was no longer the girl from the temple, weeping and afraid.

She was strong and in control of her gift.

When the change had occurred, if it had been the night of her death or if it had happened sometime since her arrival in Falias, she wasn't sure. Perhaps the time with little to do but think, to plan, to grieve, had also given her soul time to heal and to accept the magic in her veins as a real and true part of her.

"That is unnecessary," Mara said quietly, from just behind Eve. Whether Mara's words were for her or for her lover, she didn't know.

All at once, Cathal's flames guttered, vanishing entirely as his entire body sagged, the sardonic facade vanishing entirely. Mara stepped past Eve, close enough to Cora that she reached a hand for the shifter princess, giving her hand a gentle squeeze.

As Mara approached, steadily, slowly, Cathal sank to his knees before her. A choked cry escaped his lips as she reached him, placing her hands gently on either side of his face before he buried his face against her abdomen. Mara's own sobs of grief, and love, and heartbreak reached them soon after, as she sank to the ground as well.

It felt wrong, intrusive, to bear witness to the reunion, but Eve didn't dare so much as move. Right or wrong, Callan had been responsible for the many centuries Cathal had spent believing the woman he loved was dead.

Before she could think further about what to do, Mara spoke again. "My love," she began, moving her hands to his shoulders. "There is so much you need to know, but first, you must try to forgive the many years that we were apart. We have eternity ahead of us, because of what he did, and...we need your help."

Cathal's gaze met Mara's intensely, never once leaving her face. "Help him?" he demanded with a lethal intensity that had Eve's power straining beneath her skin. "Why in the name of all of the fucking gods would I help him?

Casting a glance at Callan, she saw fear mirrored in the hard set of his jaw, the way his eyes remained locked on his brother. Beside her, Cora edged closer.

"No, help me," Mara replied firmly, hands sliding down his arms to clasp his hands. "Help save us all."

Weighted silence fell over them as Cathal simply stared at Mara. Each second that ticked by was a war drum in Eve's ears.

If he said no, if he attacked, how many innocent lives would be caught in the middle? Would Mara side with Cora, who she had apparently befriended in the last centuries spent in Falias, or would she side with her love? What powers did she even have, if any? Each question sped through her mind, growing louder and more urgent with every heartbeat.

"Fine," Cathal said suddenly, stopping her anxious thoughts short. "For you, my love," he said softly, almost too quietly to hear, lifting a palm to Mara's cheek. "Anything for you."

CHAPTER 16

LIA

The memory of Bella's words played through Lia's mind on a loop. *The Light of Avellon went out, and darkness spread across the lands.*

The Light of Avellon, in her father's opinion, had been Lia herself. An idea that she dismissed entirely. How could she, one person, be considered the light of an entire kingdom? Perhaps it was more metaphorical.

Could the light be the life of her people, or even hope itself?

Huffing, she rolled onto her side, bunching the pale blue comforter under her chin and staring out the window across from her bed at the starlit sky.

Snow likely wouldn't reach Avellon for weeks, maybe even months, yet. The skies would remain clear, in brilliant blues during the day and stunning starry skies at night. The moon, hanging high above, was nearly full now, and with the drapes thrown wide, the room was fairly well illuminated.

Her thoughts drifted from the prophecy to the woman who had issued it. Bright, silvery grey eyes flashed in her mind. They'd look like starlight if Bella ever laughed, she thought, lips curving at the thought of the seer happy and smiling. Not that she had many reasons to now, thanks to her father's actions.

Lia tossed the blankets to the side and rose from the bed. Grief was hard. It was cruel, and cold and lonely. Only one other person in the world would know how she felt.

This late in the evening, she thought, glancing at the ornate gilded clock atop the white marble mantle, *he is either asleep or deep in his cups.*

Hovering between her bathing chamber and bed, Lia hesitated.

Risk waking him or go back to bed and try to sleep?

Aelius had been a ghost of himself since the confrontation with their father.

Can he handle my grief on top of his own?

That thought alone had her turning and heading back to her bed. She couldn't bear bringing her twin more pain than he already had, even if it would possibly relieve some of her own. Lia had no more than covered her head when a knock at the outer chamber door had her dragging the blankets back down. At this hour, there could be no reason for a visitor; no good ones anyway.

There's a guard outside. Everything is fine.

The thought, designed to bring her some sense of security did little to quell the fear that sprang forth within her, flooding her senses and making her arms feel leaden. There was a dagger, just inside the bedside table. All she had to do was open the drawer and it would be in her hand.

"Yes?" She forced herself to call out, trying and failing to sound unafraid. Her voice trembled as she fumbled with the drawer pull. The door was opening now, with only the sounds of footsteps from whoever was now inside her sitting room in response.

"Theo?" she called out hopefully.

It had to be Theo, her nighttime guard who was always outside her door, ready to protect her. Not that there had ever been a real reason to, not in Avellon where the Vallyse family was so beloved amongst their people; but then the attack on Stoneweald had occurred in the middle of the night.

The Light of Avellon went out.

A thud and scrape sounded from just beyond the bedchamber.

Whoever was in her sitting room was moving furniture around, or stumbling, she couldn't be sure which.

"Hello, who's there?" she called out again, sounding like little more than a frightened child.

The drawer finally slid open with a whine. Wincing, and silently cursing the creaky drawer, Lia kept her attention on the door as she reached inside. The cool metal of the dagger's hilt was in her hand in an instant.

Do I even know what to do with this thing?

The footsteps were just outside her closed bedroom door now, followed by the sound of slurred cursing and a loud scraping sound.

"Fuckin' chair...Where'd you come from?"

Every once of fear within her vanished in an instant, replaced by irritation and a healthy dose of worry.

Aelius.

He was drunk again, and standing outside her bedroom, as he had a handful of times before. Usually with some grand story of his night out that would've ended up with him dead or in jail, had he been anyone else. The bedroom door handle jiggled violently, followed by another string of rather colorful curses from her brother.

Sighing, Lia tossed the blade back into the drawer. If she kept it, she might just be inclined to use it on the idiot once he finally remembered how doors worked.

"It's not locked, Aelius," she called out, not bothering to hide the disapproval in her tone.

"Unlock the–Oh." The door flew open finally, revealing her very intoxicated brother, who leaned against the doorframe. His clothes were rumpled, and most of his blonde hair had slipped free of the loose ponytail he'd tied it in at some point. "I knew that."

"What did you do?" Dragging a hand through her hair, she frowned at him. She'd been so worried about burdening him with her grief when she should've been concerned about how he was handling his own.

"Nothin'...just..checkin' on my favorite sister," he slurred, letting his head fall to the side. It bounced off the doorframe hard enough to draw a wince from Lia.

"You should sleep it off," she remarked, already rising to her feet.

She knew how this would go. He was too proud, even in his inebriated state to admit to what he really needed, the truth that lay beneath the drunken swagger and stories.

He was lonely, and just needed to be near the one person he trusted. So, she'd started keeping blankets and pillows in a chest in her sitting room, prepared to turn her spacious couch into a bed for him for the night; just so he wouldn't have to be alone.

He didn't respond as she brushed past him to the sitting room, but the shuffle behind her told Lia that he'd at least turned around. Without waiting to see if he was following, she set to work making up the makeshift bed.

"I would've stopped him," he mumbled, wandering over and plopping onto the couch with a huff. Before she could protest, Aelius kicked off his muck-covered boots...right onto the rug. The color of the sunrise, it was her favorite. Had been anyway. The stench of his boots had her wrinkling her nose in distaste. Turning her back to him, she picked up each boot between her fore and middle fingers.

"What in the name of the light have you been doing tonight?" Lia gagged. *I probably don't want to know the answer to that.*

"I promise, Li-Li."

The use of his childhood nickname stopped her short. Spinning to look at him, she frowned. "Aelius, don't..."

"I would've stopped—" Whatever else Aelius was going to say faded away as he either passed out or fell asleep, she couldn't tell which.

So it was more than just the grief then. She sagged a bit, nearly dropping the boots. Despite his reputation as a bit of a whore, Aelius was a good man. If he had known the truth about Bella and her presence at Sunholde, he would've done something.

"I know, Aelie, I know," she sighed, dropping the boots back to the already ruined carpet and patted her twin's head gently. "We'll try to make it right, together."

CHAPTER 17

EVE

In stark contrast to the respectful welcome that Callan and Eve received when they arrived in Eleysia, Cathal was greeted with many wary, and some outright hostile, stares. Despite the fact that the truth of their plight had been shared by Mara, and many among the fae citizens had come to call her friend, none had forgotten that his actions had nearly caused a war.

It seemed, Eve thought as they walked through the gallery to meet with Callan's advisors, that for Cathal, forgiveness would still need to be earned.

Within the assembly room, Callan's advisors waited patiently, Leysa and Valerian alongside them. There were only four to Darkegrove's nine and comprised equally of male and female members. Tension radiated off of each of them, nearly palpable as Eve and Callan stepped inside, followed by his siblings and Mara.

Here was the real moment of truth. They would soon discover if their tenuous truce, struck out of Cathal's love for Mara, would stand. The room was lined with the same style of artwork that lined the halls and receiving areas, and as expansive as most in this castle were. Lovely sunsets, depictions of various historical events, she'd been told, and a few still lifes.

"Lord Thorne," a white-haired female with bronze skin said in greeting. The trade advisor, if she recalled correctly.

"Vaderyn," Cathal corrected flatly.

A delicately arched brow rose slightly over warm hazel eyes. "Apologies, I was unaware you'd chosen to use your mother's name instead, Lord Vaderyn."

Beside her, Callan tensed, so slightly that she doubted anyone else would have noticed. Slipping her hand into his, she gave a gentle squeeze.

"Lord Vaderyn has agreed to aid us," Eve began. "Mara, Lady Hanen, has–"

A snort from the male standing to the left of the trade advisor drew Eve's attention. Callan's grip on her hand tightened. The finance advisor was as lovely as Eve was discovering all fae seemed to be, with pale skin and dusky brown hair that hung freely to his shoulders.

Sharp, moss-green eyes pinned Eve with an assessing stare. "I do apologize, High King," he began, not bothering to shift his attention away from Eve. "But as your mating has not been publicly declared, I must point out that Lady Darrow has no official place in these decisions."

Despite the afternoon sun streaming merrily through the windows, the room began to darken. She could hear Callan's heartbeat rising to a steady hammer, quickening alongside his anger.

Behind her, Cathal sighed, murmuring, "Temper, temper."

Eve opened her mouth, prepared to tell the male exactly what she thought of his opinion, but it was Cora who spoke up first. "Lord Alefin, I remind you that in this kingdom, we do not hold to such archaic beliefs as our human neighbors," stepping forward, she offered Eve an apologetic smile. "I must apologize to my sister-to-be, Queen Evelyn," she continued, adding emphasis to Eve's title. "And to our own Lady Hanen, as she also hails from the kingdom of Darkegrove. Perhaps we might remember our manners with our most esteemed friends, and soon-to-be High Queen." Baring her teeth in what was an anything-but-friendly smile, she stared Lord Alefin down until his cheeks turned bright pink and he nodded.

"My apologies, Queen Evelyn," he muttered.

Slowly, and with some effort it seemed, the darkness receded, the room once again taking on its cheerful and sunny appearance.

"Let this be a lesson," Callan said with deadly calm. "Disrespect of her will not be tolerated. By any of us."

Her steady gaze remained on the advisors, the three others turning amused smirks in Lord Alefin's direction, who remained silent, looking less than pleased at the veiled threat. She would not back down, not look away. Out of the corner of her eye, Eve spotted Valerian and Leysa at her side, nodding their agreement. Her heart sang with a sense of home, of belonging.

"Well if this little drama is finished, might we continue with the matter at hand?" Cathal asked, as if inquiring about the evening dinner plans, and not the fate of their newfound alliance.

"Yes, let us turn our attention to what really matters," the military advisor, Lady Greum, Eve recalled, said. "I do understand your desire to go to war with Gorias, but with their Samach at play, we are....hesitant. We are happy to send aid to Darkegrove, however, of course."

Eve stiffened at the imminent refusal. While Callan commanded the army, and could force them to go to war without the support of his advisors, he risked losing the support of his people. With five hundred years of absence to atone for, it was a risk he was not eager to take, which she wholly understood.

"Please, do not take this as refusal," Lady Greum added swiftly, tawny eyes softening. The corners of her angular, upturned eyes crinkled as a sympathetic smile graced her aged face. Soft lines etched into her tan skin, the first fae Eve had encountered who looked to be much more than middle-aged, by human standards. "I would very much like to help you, but we must choose our actions carefully. We cannot go into war, in the winter, with unprepared soldiers. Especially when we very well may be outnumbered. Perhaps if we had allies–"

"We will," Callan interjected, casting a glance at Eve. "Another of our cities will soon be restored."

"How can you know that?" Lady Eddara demanded, eyes narrowing.

Most of Falias had heard the story by now. The human queen resurrected by the gods and blessed with a new fae body and powers. Callan's advisors had been made aware of the true threat of Gorias, and what part it had played in the decision to lock the fae away from the rest of the mortal realm of course, but they knew nothing of Eve's true part in it all.

Ocean eyes met her own in silent question. Did she want to tell the story herself, or allow him to do so?

"The goddess Keithia told me," Eve said, dragging her attention away from Callan and back to the advisors.

Gasps sounded from all but Cathal, who snorted.

"She told you?" Shorter than Eve by an inch, with jet black hair and gentle amber eyes, Lord Kuran was left in charge of most things civil, outside of finance, overseeing things such as the city guard, building permits, and virtually anything else the citizens of Elesiya might require.

"She did."

"Tell us, please," Lady Eddara asked, gently.

So Eve shared the story, leaving each of them in stunned silence, each advisor looking to their brethren for a few moments that stretched on for a small eternity. Laying it all bare, every twist and turn of her story, every heartbreak, every moment of terror, left her feeling raw and exposed, but also lighter. Even as the weight of knowing that soon, one of the other human queens would share her fate continued to bear down on her.

"We will consider—" Lady Greum began, speaking for the military she commanded, only to be interrupted by a breathless page entering the room unannounced. At once, every fae in the room turned to stare at the red-faced teen.

"My Lady," he wheezed, fixing a wide-eyed stare on the military advisor. "An army has been spotted leaving Darkegrove. Marching south."

"Gorias?" Valerian asked, speaking for the first time since they'd arrived in the meeting room.

"The scouts thought so," the page replied, nodding. "They've already reached the human lands in the Vale."

Valerian folded his arms across his chest, frowning thoughtfully. "The Samach at work again. They hid their movements well, and for a reason."

"Agreed," Callan replied with a nod. "Thank you, leave us," he added, dismissing the page.

With a swift bow, the boy spun on his heel and departed. Waiting for the click of the door to ensure they were once again alone, Eve leveled her gaze at Lady Greum.

"Gorias marches on Avellon. Will we help them or leave them to their fate?"

Chapter 18

Lia

The sound of songbirds woke Lia not long after sunrise. The peachy pink and gold light of morning beamed merrily through the windows, drawing a sleepy smile from the Queen of Avellon. It didn't matter that her twin brother was asleep on the couch just beyond her door, sleeping off his drunkenness, after having done gods only knew what in what could only have been a literal pigsty judging from the state of his boots.

It didn't matter, because despite all of the bad and awful in her world she was going to face it with a smile and with bravery in her heart. She was going to set the world to rights today and–

A knock at the outer chamber door stopped her internal pep talk short, and drew a grumble from Aelius.

"Majesty," Alfie's familiar voice called out,. "something has happened. You are needed by the councilors at once."

Her heart sank. It could only be bad news if they were waking her at this hour, and requesting her presence in the meeting room. Still, she could face the day with grace and a determination to make the best of it she decided, pushing herself to a sitting position. Dragging both hands over her face to wipe away the last dregs of sleepiness, she sighed.

Today would be good, in some small way, she would make it so.

"Majesty?" Alfie called out again. "Are you awake?"

"Light's sake, Lia, answer the man," Aelius grumbled.

Shaking her head, Lia sighed. "Thank you, Alfie. I'll be there as quickly as possible. Will you ask for coffee to be brought to the meeting room, please? I think Prince Aelius will need it."

"Of course, Majesty," came Alfie's reply, followed by quick footsteps and the sound of the outer door closing.

Rising from her bed, Lia headed for the bathing chamber to see to her needs before dressing. "You should go get cleaned up, you'll be needed for this meeting, I'm sure."

"Yeah, yeah," he called out, soon followed by the sounds of his departure.

By the time she arrived in the meeting room a short time later, her good mood had begun to waver, if only slightly. Grief, guilt, and worry refused to be ignored for very long. But she could make them wait a little longer.

Today, I will be happy, if only for a little while.

The sound of boots against the marble floor behind her drew her attention as she reached the meeting room. Stopping to turn, she found her brother, dressed in blessedly clean clothing, approaching quickly.

"Feeling better?" she asked, offering a small grin.

Aelius gave her a flat look in return. "Let's not discuss last night, not just yet," he sighed, dragging a hand through his flaxen hair. "Do you know what's going on yet?"

Lia shook her head slightly as she continued toward the door. "I suppose we're about to find out."

The pair of guardsmen, dressed in the white and gold of their house, swung the double doors wide as they approached, revealing the controlled chaos within.

Lord Bastien Devois, the second-highest ranking commander of Avellon's armies, who answered only to Aelius, and now Lia stood behind the table, gesturing angrily at a map of Aestera. Around him stood several high-ranking Lords and Ladies, each listening with grave expressions, as he argued with Lord Marshall Charron, lord of one of their westernmost demesnes.

"They are coming *now*," Bastien said forcefully. "We must act accordingly."

"But are they our enemy? Just because there was some dispute with Darkegrove does not mean—"

A bitter laugh from Bastien had Lord Charron bristling. "Dispute? They sacked the capital, and have likely either murdered or captured their fucking Queen by this point."

Noticing Lia's arrival finally, the argument fell away as the gathered councilors dropped into low bows and curtsies.

"What has happened?" she asked glancing between Bastien and Lord Charron.

The former cast a cutting glare at the latter, answering swiftly, "As I was just informing, Lord Charron, this army, which we have yet to identify, has begun their march toward us. At the speed they're moving, they'll be here in a matter of days."

Straightening, he folded his muscled arms across his chest. The rolled sleeves of his grey tunic revealed scars along his olive-brown arms, earned from years of serving in Avellon's armies, most of which earned fighting raiding parties from the west. Approaching the table, Lia frowned at the map. There was little doubt of this mysterious army's destination. Even if Satisse was somehow not the ultimate goal, too many cities and towns in the eastern parts of Avellon were now at risk. "What do we know of them? Their numbers?"

Bastien shook his head. "Very little. Our scouts haven't managed to get close enough to get an accurate read on their numbers, but it's fair to say it's more than a raiding party."

Aelius took over then, running through all of the possibilities and strategies with input from Bastien and several of the others gathered. Following as best she could, Lia felt every moment as if a new brick were being laid upon her shoulders.

How many lives now depended on her making the right decision? Her fingers curled against the smooth fabric of her skirts, the tips beginning to prickle and tingle.

What would Father do?

The room was beginning to spin, but callused fingers soon squeezed hers gently in a familiar beat. One quick, two long, three quick. Inhaling slowly, Lia began to calm, the room settling back to its normal stillness as Aelius raised a brow at her in silent question.

Are you okay?

The small and hidden message in his grasp, one she'd nearly forgotten, from the secret language they'd developed as children.

Nodding once, she turned her attention back to the councilors.

"We must save our people. We march at once."

CHAPTER 19

EVE

For the first time in more than five hundred years, a fae army was on the move; headed by the High King of Falias, with the fae queen of a human kingdom at his side.

The decision had been reached only the night before. Eve would save her people, and those of Avellon, as Queen of Darkegrove. When the war was won, she would aid the Council of Nine, or what remained of them at least, in choosing her successor, and only then would she take up the mantle of High Queen of Falias.

If she was to give up the crown she had sacrificed so much to claim, she would ensure her kingdom would follow the path she had fought so hard to set them on.

"Will the snow be a problem?" she asked Callan as they marched southeast, toward the border. They had been riding for two days now, the border with Avellon still a couple of days away. Snow had fallen steadily throughout the morning, but slowly, accumulating no more than a few inches so far. Skirting the mountain ranges had been a necessity, given the season, but also made the journey longer than she would have liked.

Pacing had been discussed, but with the number of soldiers and sheer amount of equipment and supplies, it would have proven too taxing on the fae who were capable of doing so.

"It shouldn't be. Our horses are accustomed to the northern winters, and our soldiers are more than capable of handling this little bit of snow. As long as it doesn't get much heavier, we should be fine for just a couple of days."

"Do you think–" Her next question was cut short by the sound of a familiar hawk crying out overhead. The wolf that loped at her side yipped in response.

Valerian called the halt from Callan's other side, ordering the commanders riding behind them to give their soldiers a brief rest for lunch.

Leysa landed a few feet away, shifting into her fae form with a flash, dressed in the thick fur-lined leathers and boots she'd dressed in before they'd departed their camp that morning. Leysa had attempted to explain the magic behind it, but the complexity of it had boggled Eve's mind.

It worked because...well it just did. That was good enough for her.

"There's a host marching directly for us. They're perhaps an hour away now."

"Gorias?" Eve asked, casting a glance at Callan as they both dismounted.

"No," Leysa replied, shaking her head, raven curls bobbing lightly. "They're carrying one banner with a white stag on a field of green, and one of a gold mountain cat wreathed in flames on a field of burgundy."

"Impossible," Eve breathed, laying a hand against her heart.

The Fallwens and the Lyons.

Her mother's family. If they were coming, then that meant more of them had survived than she'd thought. Her heart soared.

The north could rally and put up a real fight, and it seemed they intended to do just that.

Her lips curved into a grin. Her people would rally. Of course they would.

"What's happening?" Valerian asked.

"The Lyons and Fallwen are coming," Eve said without preamble.

"Who?"

Still grinning, she replied, "I assume it'll be my uncles."

"Your uncles?" Callan asked.

"Yes, the Fallwens are my mother's family, headed by her brother, my uncle Ross, and the Lyons by my aunt Ailia's husband, Graeme. They were at Stoneweald, but they must've gotten out."

"They survived," Valerian said in understanding, giving her shoulder a gentle squeeze.

"It seems so. Though why they're heading west instead of the more direct southern route, or east to Stoneweald, I don't know."

"Well," Leysa began, looking eastward. "We'll certainly find out soon enough."

Leysa's estimate turned out to be nearly spot on. Just over an hour after her report, the first of the combined forces of the Lyon and Fallwen houses rode into the clearing where the fae host had stopped. Four riders, three men, and one woman stopped several yards from where Callan and Eve stood awaiting their arrival.

Dismounting, two of the men and the woman passed the reins to their companion and began to approach slowly. They were dressed in the typical style of northern warriors, warm leathers and furs, including, to Eve's shock, the woman now offering her an apprehensive smile.

Recognition nagged at the back of her mind. With chestnut hair and eyes nearly identical to her mother's, something about this woman, this girl, Eve realized as the trio reached them, was incredibly familiar.

"Cousin," the girl, who couldn't be more than twenty, said in greeting, stopping a few feet away. The two men with her stopped just behind, making it clear who among them was in charge. Eve blinked, shaking her head once.

"Brida?" Eve gaped. Her gaze darted from the girl in the front to the man at her right. "Leith?"

"Hello again," Leith said in greeting, dipping his head. Russet brown hair fell over his freckle-covered face, shielding it from her view.

Brida straightened, briefly surveying the group of fae that accompanied Eve. "We've come to help you," she announced.

"We appreciate it," Callan said, casting a sideways glance to Eve, who was still staring, still stunned by both their arrival and the fact that Brida led them.

"There's something I should tell you, I'm–" Eve began nervously. She couldn't have them joining her without knowing the truth of who and what she was now.

"Fae?" Brida supplied, brow arched. No sign of shock showed on her features at the statement, much to Eve's surprise.

"How do you know?"

"The scouts we met along the way directed us here and also shared much of your story. We were made aware of your recent...change."

There was little more to say on the matter, at least little more that Eve was willing to say. So she turned instead to the question screaming in her mind.

"Are you in command?" Eve asked carefully, eyes shifting to the silent man on Brida's left. He had a decade on Brida at least, judging from the white that peppered his short-cropped charcoal hair. *It must be you, they would never allow a girl to lead.* "Is your father with you? Or perhaps Graeme?"

Brida tensed, and the men at her back exchanged a glance. "They're gone. My parents were taken the night of your coronation, Leith's father during a failed attempt to oust the invaders."

Eve's heart nearly stopped. She hadn't known there had even been an attempt to retake Stoneweald. Of course she hadn't, because she had been hiding in Falias and attending parties while her people suffered and died.

Guilt, slimy and thick, settled in her gut. She was responsible for these deaths and countless others.

"We've received word that the army that took Stoneweald is moving southwest, I assume that's why you march toward Satisse as well?"

Brida's assessing gaze landed fully on Callan as he spoke up, attempting to steer the conversation to the most pressing matters.

"They abandoned Stoneweald and seem to have turned their attention on Avellon fully," she replied. "Some of us intend to spare our neighbors the suffering we endured." Turning to Eve again, she added, "Anyone left inside the castle when these monsters abandoned it was murdered. Few others made it out before that. Eldred Gray and Silas Morris set to work organizing the surviving lords. Leith and I lead our respective houses now."

"We sent Mason Sinclair with a group from Falias to offer aid. They should arrive in Forest Haven soon," Eve said. It wasn't enough, not nearly. "They allow you to lead?" she added, gaze darting to the older man at Brida's left once again. " Forgive me, but I find that difficult to believe."

"We follow her because she's proven herself a warrior," the man said finally, his rough voice filled with pride. "Lady Lyon saved several of our people from Forest Haven." Dragging a hand across his bearded chin, he added as an afterthought, "The aid will be appreciated I'm sure."

Brida smiled warmly at the man, returning her attention to Eve after a moment. "We have much to discuss, Majesty," she began, smirking. "Including the fact that you now lead the fae. Our scouts were quite confused when they were met by riders from the west, coming to share the news of Falias' return, and their promise of aid. Many people were quite happy to hear it."

She hadn't been sure, hadn't dared to hope, that the messages they'd dispatched before leaving had reached the human kingdom, and that they'd been well received. To hear both had been true had relief coursing through her like a cool stream, soothing the worst of the guilt, if only a little.

"How many do you command?" Valerian asked, ever the strategist.

Brida's smile widened into a grin. "Not many, but we march with the full force of our combined households, with some smaller numbers from a few others. Most are too afraid to leave their lands and homes defenseless."

"Understandable," Valerian replied, nodding.

"We know they're fae, the ones who are waging this war on us." Turning an arch look to Callan, Brida added, "Not friends of yours, I assume."

Callan laughed, a bitter sound with little humor. "No. Gorias is no friend of ours."

"Do you know what they're after?" It was the older man's turn to speak now, addressing Callan rather than Eve.

Callan merely gazed at the man for several long, tense moments. The cold winter wind whipping between them was not the only thing sending a chill down Eve's spine. Careful, they had to be so careful here. "We do," he said finally.

"Such things can be discussed later," Brida cut in, "when we've proven ourselves allies to one another; and there are far fewer eyes and ears."

"Agreed," Eve smiled, stepping forward to clasp hands with her cousin. "Let's catch up while the soldiers take their rest, and then discuss how we're going to win this war."

CHAPTER 20

LIA

"Take me with you." Bella's silver-grey eyes had turned steely with resolve.

Lia hesitated on the threshold of the seer's room. A page could have delivered the message, but she'd wanted to do it herself and to say goodbye. The need to see Bella face to face for what could very well be the last time was so strong, she couldn't ignore it.

What that meant, she didn't know, but the eve of war wasn't the time to look too closely at things like that.

"It won't be safe," Lia began, gripping the side of her gown tightly. *Who am I to deny someone the right to fight for their home?* Still, fear clogged her throat at the idea of the seer anywhere near a battlefield. "I would like for you to stay here..."

"I saw you die."

Lia blinked. "What?"

"I had a vision," Bella replied slowly. "Your death, on the field of battle. I want to come with you, to try to prevent it."

Bella stared at Lia, folding her arms across her chest. She'd dressed for travel in an indigo tunic and leather leggings. Somehow she must have known about the departing army before Lia had arrived to tell her, and her mind had already been made up. The set of Bella's jaw and the packed bag on the bed told Lia plainly enough that if she attempted to leave her behind, Bella would simply follow anyway.

"You said I was free to leave," Bella countered. "At any time."

Lia sighed. "Yes, I did," she conceded finally. "Can you fight?"

Bella nodded sharply. "When you live near the coast, you learn to fight or you die. The raiders don't care if you're a woman or child, or whether or not you pick up a sword. Satisse has left us to our own defenses for quite some time, Highness."

Lia's heart ached at the thought, guilt settling over her like a dark cloud. Bella's daughter had been left there, in that village by the coast. Far from the war, but also far from the protections of the city and its guards.

She considered it, refusing Bella and ordering her to remain here, despite the dire warning she'd just been given. But what sort of person would that make her?

"I'll have supplies prepared for you. We leave in an hour."

FROM THE MOMENT SHE'D LEFT BELLA, LIA'S THOUGHTS HAD been on the seer and the danger that threatened them all. While she'd retreated to her own rooms, changing into her own crisp white tunic and dark brown leggings, she'd thought about the battle to come.

Horseshoes clicked against the pale cobblestones of the courtyard as horses shifted nervously, sensing the foreboding and anticipation of their riders. The bulk of the army had been gathered outside of the city, but the men and women who would be accompanying Lia, Aelius, and her advisors gathered in the sunny courtyard of Sunholde.

From beyond the gates that would take them to the city of Satisse, sounds of everyday life in the capital drifted toward them. People chatting as they passed, wheels on stone rumbling, and laughter of children playing nearby, thanks to one of the many good things her father had built for the people of Avellon. A tree-lined park with plenty of space for children to run and play; freely available to everyone who called Satisse home, regardless of social rank or standing.

Lia pushed her father from her mind. Grief, love, anger, and betrayal warred within her. She had no room for that, not when the burden of each and every soul residing in her kingdom rested on her shoulders. But every time she allowed her mind to dwell on that weight, it was a certain seer's face she saw flashing in her mind. With the winter afternoon sun warming her face, she waited atop Zephyr for Bella to join them, patting the mare's neck gently as she turned her gaze skyward and shoved the fear down.

I am Aurelia Elaine Vallyse, Queen of Avellon. I will not let fear control me.

Quiet muttering from the men gathered nearby pulled her attention from the bright blue sky. They were all looking toward the castle doors, at a woman now descending the stairs toward them. She was the last to join them, though she'd been ready before Lia even had been. Chin held high and her dark hair braided back, Bella approached the group. Not an ounce of fear showed on her face.

"You said you'd have supplies for me," Bella said.

"Yes," Lia replied, ignoring the heart that had leapt into her throat and gesturing toward the mare she'd chosen for Bella. "Everything you need is already packed and ready."

Bella nodded, moving away to mount her own horse a few feet away.

"Will you ride beside me?" Lia asked before she could stop herself.

Lia ignored the glances being shot in her direction, gaze locked only on the seer, already astride the borrowed mare. The one she'd personally chosen for Bella because of the mare's even-tempered nature.

"Sure," Bella replied warily.

"If you're done flirting, sister, I think it's time we go," Aelius teased. She hadn't even noticed his approach. Giving him her very best death glare, she nodded.

Snickering in response to Lia's wordless threat, Aelius gave the signal for the company to depart, and they set off to meet with the rest of the army.

~

AELIUS RODE SEVERAL YARDS AHEAD, CHATTING WITH Bastien and some of the other commanders and advisors. Bella rode alongside Lia as requested, the pair falling into silence as they rode through the streets of Satisse. People stopped what they were doing as they passed, each of them offering a bowed head in solidarity with their defenders.

"Do they know?" Bella asked, voice low.

"They know," Lia confirmed. "Not all of the details, but they know that an enemy approaches and we're riding to face them."

Bella nodded, hesitating a moment before asking, "You've spread word to the outlying villages?"

Did you warn my people? That's what she really wanted to know. "Yes, riders were dispatched as soon as we were made aware of what was coming."

"Thank you."

The ride through Satisse was silent and heavy in a way Lia had never experienced before. So many lives were at stake, relying on Lia to make the right decisions at the right time.

Though she certainly accepted the council of Aelius, Bastien, and the other advisors, ultimately the orders were given by her; the educated, but inexperienced girl who had only been queen for less than a month.

Yet another thing she didn't know if she could forgive her father for.

He'd known that war was coming and had all but forced the crown onto her brow before she was ready. Had he given any thought to what she wanted? To what she could handle? Of course not.

Because he was sick. The oily feeling of guilt settled over her once more.

"Light above," Bella gasped, drawing Lia from her thoughts.

They'd crested the hill, coming to stop beside Aelius and Bastien who waited at the peak for Lia to reach them, each of them atop sleek black steeds. The valley below was covered with tents, with more people moving between them than she could count.

Lia's mouth fell open, and all she could do was stare. She hadn't known what to expect, couldn't begin to picture it when she'd been informed of how many soldiers would be defending Avellon.

"You'll need to pull yourself together before we go down," Aelius teased, adding more seriously, "You can do this."

Bastien's warm brown eyes darted between Lia and Bella. "I would suggest you ride alone at the front. They need to see you as strong and unafraid." His glance behind her announced the arrival of another rider. "Before we go, we've brought you a little gift," he added.

The soldier who approached pulled his own chestnut steed to a stop beside Bastien, a bundle wrapped in soft brown leather lying across his lap. The man passed it over to Bastien with a nod. "Just as you asked, my Lord," he said.

"What's this?" Lia asked, brow raising. Her gaze flicked from the stranger to Bastien, who had set to work untying the bundle.

"You want to make an impression," he replied with a grin. He tugged something white from within the parcel. A cape, she realized as he gave it a little shake, unfurling the fabric. As white as a swan's wing and so fine it was nearly sheer, the cape billowed on the wind. The edges had been embroidered with gold thread, matching the army's uniform closely.

"Beautiful," she replied with a smile. "But not very practical for a battlefield."

"Oh, I'm not finished just yet, Majesty," Bastien said, tugging something else from the package with his free hand. Gleaming in the afternoon sun, bright gold epaulets emerged from the parcel, chainmail, with small suns hanging from the sides. "You'll have chainmail to match," he explained. "But we wanted you to have something special for this occasion. They need to look to you as more than a woman, more than their queen. You need to be a symbol."

Tears welled in her eyes and her throat tightened. Pride squeezed her heart and the fear that had been her constant companion the last couple of days vanished. "Thank you," she said, looking from Bastien to Aelius. "Both of you."

Aelius beamed at her. "Well, put them on, sister, we don't have all day."

Rolling her eyes, Lia did just that, with help from her twin.

"One more thing," Aelius said as he straightened her epaulets. He pulled a familiar white velvet bag from his saddlebag, earning a gasp from Lia and a groan from Bastien.

"You had that in your saddlebag?" she all but shouted.

Shrugging, Aelius pulled the bag open and tugged the bright gold crown free from the bag. "You have more, if something happens to this one."

It was true, but this particular crown was the one most favored by her family. Gilded points soared skyward from the frame, reaching for the very sun it emulated. Small amber stones at the base of each point shone brightly in the sunlight.

As she placed it on her head, a small, choked sound from Bella drew her attention. Silver- grey eyes had gone wide, her face pale.

"Three crowns will fall," she whispered. Shaking her head, she added. "Wear another, any other. Just don't wear that one. Please." The knuckles of her fingers had turned white on the leather reigns, making her mare shift uneasily beneath her.

Aelius frowned. "I didn't bring another one. The rest are with the carriages," he explained.

Unease had Lia pausing, hands falling away from the crown that now rested on her head. She had asked Bella for her help, to share her visions with Lia to protect their kingdom. But riding into the camp wearing the crown was an important symbolic moment that she couldn't pass up.

"Did your recent vision have me dying in the camp?" she asked, gaze flitting to the men who watched in silence. She hadn't told her brother about this vision of Bella's, and judging from the way he stiffened, he was going to be angry with her for that.

Bella considered it, turning her attention to the valley below. "No," she admitted. "It was raining, there were soldiers fighting."

"Then I think it's okay, for now," Lia said gently.

Though Bella nodded her acceptance, her lips remained pressed together in a thin line. Discussion over.

"Let's go," Lia said, steering Zephyr toward the path that would take her down the hill and into the heart of the army camp. "We have a kingdom to save."

CHAPTER 21

EVE

"They didn't expect you to go out of your way for them," Brida remarked as they rode together. Soon she'd have to return to her own people, but for a short while they could ride together at the head of the joined armies to talk, and plan. "My grandmother and the Queen, your mother, hadn't spoken much for a long time."

Brida's grandparents and parents had been at the coronation, though Eve hadn't made time to see them, and the guilt over that weighed on Eve more heavily than she'd expected.

Eve nodded absently. Riona hadn't been particularly close to any of her relatives during Eve's childhood, but family was family. She would carry the guilt of her role in their deaths, alongside all of the others in Darkegrove, for the rest of her very long life. She couldn't bear to meet Brida's gaze, so she kept her attention on the road ahead.

Snow that had fallen so lightly earlier was strengthening now, so much so that Valerian had warned they'd need to pick up their pace or risk being snowed in when they stopped for the night. The border with Avellon was still two days away, and if they didn't make it farther south, where they had at least a little hope of the snow letting up, two days could easily turn into four or more.

Any delay could prove perilous for Avellon, and the thought of leaving another kingdom to suffer what Darkegrove had was more than she could stand.

"I need to get back," Brida remarked, drawing Eve from her thoughts. Her cousin's gaze was turned skyward toward the grey clouds that hung above, dropping fat wet flakes on them. "I'll see you when we stop for the night?"

"Yes," Eve replied, offering a weak smile. Brida broke away without another word, leaving Eve alone. She watched in silence as Leith and Baird, as she'd learned he was called, fell into pace behind Brida. The trio disappeared into the ranks soon after.

The familiar yip of a wolf announced Cora's arrival, soon followed by a second. *Leysa*. Casting a brief glance behind her, she saw Callan riding toward her, atop Tenebris, his night-black steed who terrified many of the stablehands and even most soldiers; despite being little more than a sweetheart with a serious apple addiction once you got to know him. They had fallen back to give her a few more moments of relative privacy with Brida, while she could.

"Pushing back against archaic traditions is a family trait," he remarked, bringing Tenebris alongside Eve's mare, Ventia.

Eve tossed him a grin. "It seems so. I wish I had gotten to know them more, before all of this."

"When we've stopped Gorias, you'll have plenty of time to get to know them," he assured her.

"If we all survive," she sighed.

"We will," Callan stated with a certainty she wasn't sure was genuine.

"What did you think of her? Of them?"

Taking the change of subject in stride, Callan laughed lightly. "I think she's every bit as fierce and stubborn as you are, and Leith, I'm not sure what to make of him yet."

Eve nodded, keeping her gaze on the path ahead, the few riders who rode a short distance ahead ensuring the way was safe for the High King of Falias and fae Queen of Darkegrove. The wolves, her friends, bounded ahead keeping pace between the front line of riders and Callan and Eve.

"I want to fight," she said suddenly, turning to look at him.

A muscle in Callan's jaw feathered, but for a moment he didn't speak. Stiffening, she prepared herself for the argument, for the denial. Her grip on the reigns tightened, but just as she inhaled deeply, prepared to argue against his refusal, he turned to her with a smile. "Okay."

"Okay?" she repeated, blinking.

"Okay," he confirmed. "I want to ask you to stay back, to watch from a safe distance. But I won't do that. You are the queen of two kingdoms. You are powerful, and you are the bravest person I've ever known. If you want to fight, you'll fight. I have no right to deny you, despite the utter terror I feel at the thought of you being anywhere near danger."

Eve's heart swelled in response, every bit of anxiety simply melting away. "Thank you," she said after a beat, mentally cursing the fact that she couldn't simply grab him and kiss him right now, thanks to the horses beneath them.

"You did this yourself," he replied with a light shrug. "It's all you, dove."

To that, she simply smiled. It wasn't true, not in her mind, not when so many people had helped her along the way and had quite literally saved her life. She wouldn't be here without each and every one of them. Her mother's face flashed in her mind. Grief surged so powerfully within her she had to blink back the tears that threatened to fall.

Not now, she thought. *Cry when you're alone.*

"How long until we stop?" she asked, using the mundane distraction to calm herself.

If he sensed the reason behind the shift in conversation, he didn't let on, only glancing skyward before replying. "A few hours, I would think. There's still plenty of light left, and we need to try to beat the snow."

"Tell me again what we're facing."

His gaze sliding toward her once more, Callan's ocean eyes lingered on hers a moment. "Monsters. Soulless monsters, dove."

CHAPTER 22

LIA

As Lia rode through the war camp, every soldier she passed paused in their task, offering a bow to the Queen who would be leading them into battle. She would gladly carry this burden, but the enormity of it was already taking its toll on her, and she was already exhausted.

Do not let them see how it weighs on you, she reminded herself silently. *They need you.*

"They've stopped," Aelius began without preamble as she stepped inside the tent that would operate as their center of command. "It will take us a couple of days to reach the valley. They've already positioned themselves on one side, taking high ground. Our scouts couldn't get any closer."

"Will we be at a disadvantage?" Lia asked, frowning.

"It's possible but we think we've found a way around it," Bastien replied, dragging his finger along the map. "If we take up a position here, we should be able to at least even the field."

The conversation dragged on for hours, with each of her advisors giving their opinions and arguing with one another over every tactic and possibility. By the end of the evening, a decision had been made, one that each of them agreed offered the best chance at their victory. But without more information about their enemy, they couldn't be certain of their success.

Trailed by a pair of guards, she was heading back to her tent when she found Bella. The seer's tent had been erected near Lia's at the Queen's request. In case she had another vision, Lia had reasoned, though the more truthful answer would have been that she simply wanted to keep her close. Out of fear, or for some other reason, she didn't know.

Sitting on an upturned bucket just outside the tent, Bella stared up at the starry sky.

Following her gaze, Lia lifted her own head. The winter sky was dazzling, with more stars than she could ever dream of counting lighting the dark like diamonds in a sea of indigo. A silver-white streak danced across the sky, drawing a gasp from the Queen.

"Shooting stars," Bella said, voice filled with what Lia could only describe as longing. "I've counted five so far."

"They're stunning," Lia replied, grabbing a nearby bucket of her own.

"You'll get dirty," Bella remarked, eyeing the white cape that Lia still wore.

A wave of her hand had one of her guards stepping closer as Lia unfastened the epaulets and cape, passing them over to the tan-skinned woman. "Please see these safely to my tent, thank you." Turning her attention back to the seer, she offered a smile. "Now I don't have to worry."

The wonder she saw in Bella's strange eyes had her heart skipping a beat. They were stunning, those mercurial eyes of hers. Lia took a seat beside Bella, who watched in silence, just far enough away that they wouldn't be touching.

If a glance at her eyes had sent Lia's heart skittering, then she wouldn't dare touch her for fear of melting right at the seer's feet. When had sympathy and respect begun to shift into this strange fluttering in her stomach, making her stutter and blush like a teenager?

"How did it go?" Bella's attention had returned to the sky, that faraway look of longing returning; as if she had once descended from the stars themselves and they now called her home.

The thought had Lia smiling, despite the serious turn the conversation had taken. "As well as I expected. We have a plan, at least. But we need more information."

Bella nodded, though her gaze remained skyward. "I'm wishing for a vision of our victory," she replied quietly. "But the vision of the crowns...it has me worried. For you." Closing her eyes for a moment, she added, "For all of us."

There was no way to respond to that, so Lia instead looked to the stars. Another silver streak darted across the sky. "I've heard they're considered good omens in some places," she offered. Perhaps the gods are sending a sign."

"The gods are gone, or dead," Bella replied in a sharp tone, rising suddenly from her makeshift seat. "I'm tired, please excuse me."

Stunned by the sudden shift in mood, Lia barely managed a nod in response. Without another word, Bella left Lia to watch the night sky alone and contemplate the silver-eyed seer who dreamed of the future and wished upon stars.

CHAPTER 23

EVE

With half a day's ride left to go before they reached Satisse, the combined forces of Falias and the houses of Lyon and Fallwen set up camp for the night. The snow had stopped falling some hours before, and as they reached the border of the kingdom of Avellon, temperatures had warmed finally. Still cold, but not as frigid as the northern kingdom had been.

In the shelter of her tent, she kicked off her boots before peeling off the outermost fur coat, tossing it onto the bed inside the lavish tent she'd be sharing with Callan, and sighed with relief. It had been a hard journey, and every muscle screamed and ached.

Size enough to accommodate a large bed, a small tub for bathing, and a table for sharing their meals, the tent was quite comfortable and surprisingly warm thanks to the small domed brazier in the center.

A shock of cold air breezed through the tent as Callan stepped inside. "The scouts brought news," he said, expression grave, ocean eyes dark. "Avellon's forces have already begun their march to the southeast to meet Gorias." He paused, tugging his own fur-lined leather coat off and tossing it onto the bed as Eve had earlier. "Led by their queen."

Eve frowned. To her knowledge, Hemera Vallyse rarely left the city of Satisse. The idea that she would be leading the army in place of her husband was strange at best, given what Eve knew to be a rather shy nature and little interest in military matters.

Callan must have read the confusion in her expression, and added, "Queen Aurelia Vallyse."

Sinking into the nearest chair, Eve gaped. "Aurelia has taken her father's throne?"

"Apparently illness claimed him, but before he passed he had Aurelia crowned."

The words of a goddess replayed in her mind. "Keithia said the second lock's time grew near. I assumed she meant Naia, but...."

Callan nodded. "I had the same thought. What if it's Aurelia? If it is...and she returns Finias, it could greatly improve our odds of winning."

"Finias?"

"The middle fae kingdom. Ruled by a High Queen, Lucia. She was a dear friend of my mother's. If I sent Cora to request aid, I think they would come. They know the danger that Gorias presents even better than I do."

"But we don't know if that will happen, or how. I had to nearly die to receive my powers from Keithia. Do we just wait for someone to try to kill Lia?" The very idea of it made her feel ill. "Unless the gods have something else in mind?"

Callan shrugged. "There's no way to know." Glancing around the room, he added loudly, "Unless someone would like to share their plan with us." Snorting he shook his head. "No, Macaria and the others will keep it to themselves. We can do little more than wait and see. I'll have Cora ready to run if it happens."

"How will we even know?"

Shaking his head lightly, Callan sat on the edge of the bed. "I suppose we'll have to wait and see about that too. It took some time, but when yours emerged there was an earthquake. Perhaps there will be a similar sign when hers takes hold. We can try to reach her before it happens and explain what is coming."

Her head was aching. There were so many hidden plans, lives in danger, dependent on those secrets being kept from them. Rubbing her temples in slow circles, she frowned. "There are far too many uncertainties."

"Then take a moment to think about the things we can be certain of, dove." His tone was low, and when she lifted her eyes to his, emotion swam in depths of endless blue.

Rising from her chair, she crossed the tent, taking his face in her hands. "Of this I am certain, I love you. I will love you until my last breath, into the Otherworld and whatever lies beyond. Forever. I am yours, as you are mine."

He said nothing in response, simply reaching for her, and with his hand behind her head, Callan pulled her closer, claiming her mouth with his. Deep and with every ounce of love they felt behind it. He pulled her onto the bed, twisting so that she lay beneath him. He slid her tunic upward, revealing the pale skin beneath, every movement slow, reverence lighting his eyes.

Lifting her arms he pulled it free, followed swiftly by the binding she'd used to keep her breasts in place while riding, tossing them to the side before pressing his lips to the column of her neck. The tips of her breasts peaked in response, both to the cool kiss of the chilly air and Callan's attention.

"Of this, I am certain," he whispered against her throat. Sliding downward, he trailed kisses to her belly button. His warm breath against her skin sent goose pimples scattering. With deft hands, he tugged the laces of her leggings sliding them downward with agonizing care.

With her leggings discarded, he set to work removing her undergarments with no less care and attention than he had her other clothes. Once she was bared before him, Callan brushed his lips against hers, featherlight. "My heart has been yours for an eternity. Before I knew your name, before I saw your face, it was yours."

Lowering so that his head was between her thighs, he pressed a kiss to her clit gently. Eve barely stifled a moan as her core tightened and pulsed, dampness pooling between her legs. "Before either of us was born, when we were little more than ether floating on the winds of time, I loved you."

With the first gentle swipe of his tongue, she sighed, arching her back. He worshipped her with his mouth, bringing her to a glorious climax that had his name spilling from her mouth; as quietly as she could manage thanks to the guards and soldiers who no doubt stood mere feet away from their tent.

Rising, he positioned himself between her legs, lifting each of them so they rested on his hips. "Of this I am certain," he said, voice husky, his eyes darker and more endless than she'd ever seen them. "I will love you until our very world is little more than a whisper of a memory, even to the gods."

Slowly, carefully, he entered her then, and she took every glorious inch of him. Pulling back until only the very tip of his length remained within, he drove home again, sheathing himself inside of her. Over and over he moved. She met his every thrust, arms wrapped tightly around his shoulders. He claimed her mouth with his once more, with a ferociousness and intensity that took her very breath away.

"Forever," she whispered against his lips. "Forever." A word of hope and a promise.

"Forever," he agreed. The sound of it had her coming undone again, and this time, they broke together. Breathless and spent, they fell onto the bed, side by side.

Laying her head on his shoulder, hand on his heart, Eve let the tears fall. Forever, they'd promised; both knowing that forever may be no more than days.

Whatever forever might mean, however long it was, she would savor every moment of it, and try her best not to worry that the next day may be their last.

Chapter 24

Lia

The breaking dawn found the Queen of Avellon alone, standing atop a small rise and gazing at the gently rolling hills ahead. Rippling in the chill morning breeze, the golden grasses were a sea of gold and yellow, all but glowing in the first rays of morning light. It was little wonder why Avellon had been called the Halcyon Vale for as long as anyone could recall.

The armies would meet in the Paix Valley, two days ride from where they currently camped, if all went according to plan. She had been to the valley only once in her life, visiting the Lady Blanchet, whose family had laid claim to the region for nearly five hundred years, since the fae of the Avellon had vanished alongside the others.

Her thoughts turned to those long-forgotten people as she bent, letting her fingers drift through the tops of the grass. It was tall, even now in the winter months, nearing her knees. In spring, it would grow near to her waist and bright blooms of red would cover nearly every open space.

Had it been the same when the fae had ruled the area? When humans had laid claim only to a small region surrounding what was now Satisse. A frivolous thought, but one that at least pulled her attention from the danger they faced.

"Lia?" Aelius' voice sounded from behind her, and she turned to face him.

Behind him, the tents were each being taken down and packed away, and soldiers finished the last of their breakfasts.

No time for dallying when war was at hand, she thought with a sigh. War.

How would the fae of the Vale have met such an invasion? If they had remained, would her kingdom have flourished as it had or would they have simply remained little more than a city-state, overshadowed by the sprawling fae empires that surrounded them? Would her ancestors have called upon their fae neighbors in times like this?

It mattered little, she supposed, as they were all gone now and beyond their help.

"Is it time?" she asked, meeting her brother's flat stare with one of her own.

"Yes," he confirmed. "And the seer is asking for you."

Surprised, she blinked at him. "She is?"

Aelius hesitated, gaze flitting over his shoulder briefly.

"Just say it, brother."

"Are you two...?"

"Are we what?" Eyes widening slightly, she looked beyond him, to where she knew Bella must be, though Lia couldn't see her from where she stood.

The corner of his lips tugged upward. "You seem to be getting close," he remarked. "The ride together, and I've heard whispers about visits to her room back home."

Lia's heart pounded a staccato in her chest. "People are talking?"

Aelius' grin faltered slightly at that. "I can try to stop them if it's distressing you Li-Li."

"No, you know that would never work," she sighed, dragging her attention back to him. "We aren't...nothing is happening."

"Okay," he held up his hands, stopping her protest before it began, "Not saying it is, but if it were, I think it could be good for you."

"Why do you say that?" she asked, ignoring the way her heart sang its agreement.

"Just a feeling," he replied with a shrug.

The sight of a familiar dark head peeking around a wagon, just beyond Aelius, had the reply dying on her tongue. As Bella stepped around the wagon, every thought scattered from her mind as if on a phantom wind. "Go, Aelius."

"Go where?" he asked, mock hurt flashing across his features as he placed a hand on his armor-clad chest. "Are you so tired of talking to your brother already?"

"Please," she whispered loudly.

Following her gaze, Aelius smirked. "A twin's intuition should never be discounted," he laughed, sauntering away.

Ignoring him entirely, Lia steadied herself as Bella approached. She barely resisted the urge to wipe her suddenly sweaty palms against her leggings and tried not to stare too hard at the way Bella's own leggings hugged her thighs. Instead, she focused on the small smile the seer offered, the way her lips curved, and the almost imperceptible scar on her right cheek, noticeable only now that they were a mere foot from one another.

"Majesty," Bella began, voice tentative, nervous.

"Please call me Lia," she replied instantly.

"I wanted to apologize," Bella began. "About last night."

Tilting her head, Lia offered a warm smile. "You've done nothing to apologize for."

As Bella's gaze shifted down toward their feet, Lia took a breath to calm her nerves. The heady scent of a bloom she could picture, but couldn't quite recall the name of, hung between them, drifting toward Lia as Bella moved.

"I was rude," Bella continued. "I was having a bad night, and the gods...they're a difficult topic for me. I just–"

"Moonflower," she breathed quietly. "You smell like moonflowers."

Bella's head jerked upward and silver-grey eyes pinned her with a wide-eyed stare. "You've seen moonflowers?"

The question came as no surprise. Moonflowers were exceptionally rare, only found in the oldest and wildest of places, such as the deepest forests of Darkegrove or the many ruins scattered across Aestera. As large as her hand, the pale white flowers opened only under the bright light of the moon. Their scent was utterly unique and so lovely it was impossible to forget them.

"Once," Lia nodded. "A long time ago."

The surprise in Bella's eyes had given way to something else now. "Where?" she asked, her tone several degrees cooler than it had been just a moment before.

Lia offered a confused smile. "There are some ruins near the border with Coruscis, on the eastern shore. An old temple, my father believed, though little remained. He liked to explore and research the old sites, and sometimes he would take me along with him as a child."

Bella stared at Lia, silver eyes hardened to ice. Mentioning her father had been a mistake, but Bella had asked. "We camped nearby and one night, he took me to see the flowers," Lia continued, smile fading. "I'm sorry, I shouldn't have–"

"It's fine," Bella sighed, casting a glance over her shoulder to where horses were being brought around for the royal party. "Anyway, I'm sorry for being rude. We should go."

"Ride with me again," Lia blurted before she could stop herself.

"What?" Bella's attention turned back to Lia.

"I...I enjoy your company, and I would very much like to have a conversation with you that doesn't involve my father," she replied, cheeks heating. "Or the gods. Though I'm not sure what to discuss."

The last of the ice in Bella's eyes melted away as she smiled at Lia. "I'm sure we'll think of something. I would like that very much, Lia."

CHAPTER 25

EVE

The sun shone brightly overhead by the time the northern forces reached the armies of Avellon. Gone were the warm furs that had been a necessity in the colder northern climes, exchanged instead for only a thick sweater and riding leathers.

Only a handful, led by Eve and Callan, would ride into the camp to meet with Lia, as ordered by Eve. The arrival of an entire army of supposedly extinct magical beings would no doubt cause at least a small degree of panic, and she'd wanted a moment to speak to her old friend before things got too complicated.

Word had apparently reached the new Queen of Avellon. As Callan and Eve, followed closely by Leysa and Cora, arrived, they found her waiting for them at the center of the camp. Valerian had remained behind, in charge of their own forces in Eve and Callan's absence.

"You're alive," Lia all but sobbed, rushing forward and embracing Eve in a near bone-crushing hug.

"I'm so sorry I didn't let you know," Eve murmured, returning the hug with equal enthusiasm, while being careful not to exert too much force, so she didn't actually crush her friend with her fae strength.

Yet another thing to feel guilty over. She could have sent word, and though she'd never admit it, the primary reason she hadn't was a strange sense of shame.

Shame over the secret she was hiding even now, with her hair carefully braided to cover the tips of her ears. Cora had been working with her, teaching her to glamour, but for reasons she didn't understand, this particular form of magic eluded her.

"I am rather upset about that," Lia replied, pulling back. Eyes the color of a summer sky scanned Eve as if to make sure she was real. "But I am so very glad to see you."

"Me too," Eve replied with a tight smile. "You remember Callan?" she said, stepping back to draw attention to the male at her side.

"Of course, hello again, Lord Thorne," Lia smiled, inclining her head toward him politely.

Callan met Lia's smile with one of his own, not bothering to correct the incorrect title just yet.

Turning to the women who now stood at her other side, Eve gestured to each of them in turn. "This is Lady Leysa Ashford, my dear friend and protector, and Lady Cora Thorne, Callan's sister, also a dear friend."

Lia offered each of them the same polite smile and greeting before turning her attention back to Eve. "I am so happy to see you, but...how are you here? Why are you here?"

Eve tensed, nodding once. "Yes, that..."

"I think this is a conversation best had in private," Callan interjected smoothly. "May we step inside your tent, your Majesty?"

"Of course, ah..." Lia smiled turning to lead them inside. A dark-haired woman stepped out as they approached. Lia, cheeks blushing slightly turned back to them. "Oh, um, this is Sybella Avoden, one of my advisors, and a friend."

The woman, whoever she was, offered Lia a half smile. "I'll come back later," she said quietly, offering only a brief inclination of her head to the group before disappearing into the bustle of the busy army camp.

Once they were safely ensconced in the relative privacy of Lia's temporary home, Eve asked finally, "Who was that, really?"

Lia laughed nervously, sinking into one of four chairs around a low table near the tent's center. "Please have another chair brought in," she said to the guard positioned at the entrance. "And then my guests and I would like some privacy, please. Ensure that nobody interrupts."

Eve settled into one of the chairs, followed by Cora and Leysa, and Callan took up a position just behind her, resting his hands on the back of the gilded wood. His fingertips grazed the nape of her neck, left exposed by her braided hair. Even after months together, entire nights spent wrapped in his arms, his touch still sent a shiver of anticipation and desire through her.

"She," Lia began, unaware of Eve's quickening pulse or the slow, small circle Callan was currently tracing against Eve's goose-pimpled skin. He was most certainly aware of the reaction she was having to his touch, Eve knew. "Sybella– Bella, she's...complicated. Perhaps we should discuss where you've been and why you're here first?"

Lia's nervous tone was so unlike her that it drew Eve's attention from Callan's touch. Either her tone or the change in topic seemed to have captured his attention as well, as his fingers stilled instantly. "I suppose I should just say it," Eve began carefully. "I...have been with the fae."

CHAPTER 26

LIA

Utter silence settled over the tent. Lia's heartbeat sounded in her own ears, a drumbeat warning against something she didn't understand. "The fae?" she repeated lamely.

"Yes," Eve nodded. The claim she was making was so outrageous, so impossible, there was no way that it could be true...and yet. "I know it sounds impossible," Eve continued, as Lia stared blankly. "I thought it impossible myself until I saw proof of it." Pausing, Eve glanced behind her to Callan.

Callan, the mysterious warrior whom the late Queen Riona had called upon to keep her daughter safe as she took her throne. The way they looked at each other, there was little doubt as to what was between them; what Lia had so clearly witnessed beginning to bloom in the short time she'd spent with them in Darkegrove. What did he have to do with this?

A shock of cool air drew all of their attention as the guard finally returned, delivering Callan's chair. As soon as they were alone once again, the warrior took his seat. "Tell me," Lia said finally, eager to hear the rest of the unbelievable tale.

As Eve laid out the story, a pit opened in Lia's stomach. The truth of the gods' return, of the fae not only still existing but returning to their realm, and the fact that her friend was now one of them. That the enemy at their doorstep was of a fae kingdom. That even Callan, High King of this Falias, she thought with a wince, thought them gone.

It was too much to take in. She was dizzy, like when she'd been a girl, and Bastien and Aelius would twist and twist the old tree swing as much as they could and then release her. She would spin and spin, like one of the wicked storms that would sometimes spring up on the plains, whirling masses of air and debris that would wreck anything in their path.

It was impossible to accept, to believe.

They were staring at her patiently. Four sets of immortal, or near enough, eyes waiting for her to process, to respond. "I don't know what to say," Lia admitted finally.

Eve offered a gentle smile. "I know, I felt the same when I found out. It's...a lot. But the important thing is that we've come to help. I've asked Mason Sinclair to go to Darkegrove, to help them regroup and rebuild what they can. My cousin Brida is here with a small, but fierce, contingent of her own house and that of my cousin Leith's."

"I appreciate it. You know that I am your friend and that I– that I will accept this as soon as I've had time to wrap my head around it. But my people, Eve, they're going to have a hard time with this."

It was Leysa, the beautiful fae warrior to Eve's side, who spoke up this time. "People are generally okay with whatever they need to be to survive," she remarked, dark brow lofting slightly.

"That's true," Lia conceded, pausing a moment to consider the next steps. She would have to tell Aelius and Bastien first. The thought of their reactions had her sighing. They would either be thrilled or horrified, and it was impossible to tell which.

In either case, Aelius would likely be looking for the prettiest fae woman to try to lure to his bed. "I'll speak to my generals immediately."

It was a dismissal, one they immediately understood. Each of her unexpected guests rose from their seats. Callan and Eve shared a glance, one that conveyed some message only they understood. "We are making our camp on the northern side of yours," Eve said. "Callan and Leysa's husband, Valerian, will meet with your generals as soon as you are ready. And then perhaps you and I can speak?"

There was a lot to discuss, beyond the coming battle, beyond the unbelievable truths that had been dropped in her lap. So much had changed about both of their situations in the last few months. Beneath the mantle of a queen, she was still just Lia, a young woman who wanted to confide in her friend about the woman she was beginning to have feelings for; Lia, who was terrified of those feelings and what the future might hold.

Nodding, she offered a smile. "Of course, I'll send someone for you when I've spoken to Aelius and the others."

With nothing more left to say, they departed, with a brief hug between the queens. Lia had been alone for little more than a few minutes when Aelius and Bastien strode in and plopped into the recently abandoned chairs.

"Ready to tell me what that was about?" Aelius asked, in his standard casual tone. As if he hadn't also believed Eve Darrow to be dead little more than an hour ago.

Bastien, at least, donned a somewhat more serious expression, likely considering the strategic implications of the northern army's arrival.

When their scouts had announced the arrival of an army from the north, flying an unknown banner alongside that of Darkegrove, each of them assumed that the Council of Nine had sent what aid they could muster and that the other banner had to belong to some lesser known lord or another, expecting there to be little impact from the arrival. How very wrong they had been.

She shook her head gently. "You won't believe it."

Aelius did little more than stare, at times with mouth agape, as she relayed the story she'd been told. When she finished, he laughed. "Well, was the fae princess attractive?"

Bastien, as expected, kept his mouth pressed together in a thin line.

"Gods, you are impossible," Lia rolled her eyes. Gods. Right. They did exist, and they were watching, listening. Bella's remark, and the anger behind it, flashed in her memory. How would she react to all of this, Lia wondered.

"On a serious note," Bastien interjected. "We know what we're up against now. I don't think we would have won without their warning, or their help. I'm grateful that they came. Assuming–" he lowered his voice, "we can trust them."

"We can," Lia stated with certainty. Despite her new status as fae, Eve was her friend, and instinct told her at least that had not changed.

Bastien and Aelius exchanged glances before nodding.

"Alright then. I'll call for the other lords and we'll fill them in. I assume you know how difficult this is going to be, getting them to accept all of this," Aelius said.

"I'm sure we can handle it," she replied, rising from her seat. She could only hope she was right, that all of them would accept this new reality of theirs with grace and not fear, but human nature was unpredictable at times, especially in the face of the new and unknown.

"Also," Aelius added as he headed for the tent flaps, "the seer is out here. I think she's waiting for you. Want me to send her in?"

Lia's heart gave a thump. "Please."

"You only have a few minutes, sister," he teased. "Don't get distracted."

"It only takes a few minutes if you know what you're doing," Bastien declared.

Without thought, Lia grabbed the nearest object and hurled it, sending a fluffy golden pillow from her bed sailing toward them. "Get out."

Chuckling as they deftly dodged the harmless projectile, her brother, and the man whom she considered brother in all but blood, stepped out.

She was alone for only a moment before Bella arrived. Her cheeks were flushed, from what Lia couldn't tell. Perhaps it was simply the afternoon sun on her pale skin, or, to her dread Lia realized, she'd heard what they had been saying on their way out.

Light above, please no.

"Is everything alright?" Lia asked, hazarding a step toward Bella.

"I was worried," Bella admitted, gaze flitting over Lia briefly before their eyes met. "I saw those people and I had a feeling."

"A feeling?"

"Just...something felt strange," Bella replied, moving farther into the tent, but staying well beyond arms reach, a feat inside the tent, spacious as it was. "But everything is alright?"

"Actually," Lia sighed, sinking onto the edge of the bed in favor of the chairs. "You're right about something being strange. There is something...well, a lot of things, that I need to tell you."

Bella, her back to Lia, trailed her fingers along the oak dressing table that had been set up opposite her bed, against the far side of the tent. "What is it?"

"My friend, the Queen of Darkegrove, Eve. She's traveling with a fae army– and she's become one herself." Lia tensed, prepared for the confusion, the distress, that she expected.

"How?" Bella asked quietly, turning sharply toward Lia.

Lia blinked. No declarations of the impossibility of such a thing, no disbelief as she'd expected. Just one simple question.

"She says...she says the goddess of life is responsible. That she nearly died, and the goddess of life, and others, came to her. The goddess granted her powers, and then later, she actually did die, and Eve was given a choice...die or return as fae."

Bella's expression was shuttered, unreadable. For several heart-pounding moments, she didn't reply, barely moved. Simply staring and breathing. "How are they back?"

"What?" Lia asked, dumbfounded at the lack of reaction.

"How are the gods back?" Bella repeated, as patiently as with a small child struggling to understand a basic question.

"I don't know," she replied truthfully. That part of the story had not been explained, and when they departed, Lia had been left with the distinct feeling several pieces of the puzzle were left out deliberately; perhaps until the fae were certain the humans were indeed their allies. As much as it stung, she couldn't exactly blame them.

"This army we're facing, they're fae aren't they?" Bella asked quietly, moving to take a seat beside Lia on the bed.

"Yes," Lia replied, ignoring the way her stomach tightened at Bella's closeness.

"They've returned," Bella whispered, lowering her head, dark hair falling forward to hide her face. "It's actually happening."

"What is?" Lia asked, reaching for Bella instinctively, tucking her long hair behind her ear to see her face. She'd expected tears, for Bella to be upset, though she didn't know exactly why. Instead, she found only steely resolve on the seer's face.

Bella lifted her gaze to Lia's. "I want you to know that whatever comes next, I will be here to help you."

Chapter 27

Eve

"She took that better than I expected," Callan remarked.

They were alone again, Leysa having gone in search of Valerian and Cora, claiming a headache that required rest. Lia had reacted better than most would have, Eve agreed, but she had expected her friend to have a level-headed response.

"How will her advisors and commanders react though?" she sighed. "Her soldiers?"

Shaking her head, she leaned back, letting her gaze fall on the peaked canopy of the tent. The opening at its top, designed so that the smoke from their brazier could escape, had been covered, leaving only the sides open.

Rain had begun to fall, a gentle patter against the canvas above. It would muddy the fields and hills, making the battle to come that much more dangerous, Callan had said when it began an hour before. There was little to be done but adapt.

"I think," Callan said, rising from his chair and moving to stand in front of her, "that they will accept whatever help they can get, as shocking and frightening as it may be for them."

His fingertips trailed along the side of her face, moving slowly to the column of her neck.

"I'm scared," she admitted, straightening to look at him. His hand stilled at her collarbone, exposed now thanks to the loose top buttons of her tunic. She knew without looking that his fingers had come to rest on the top of her tattoo.

"I know," he replied, sinking to crouch in front of her. She followed the movement with her eyes. "I won't tell you not to be. Fear is normal; it keeps you from making stupid mistakes on a battlefield. As long as you don't let it consume you. Remember who you are, and what you are capable of, dove. You–"

A sudden burst of chilly air cut him short as the tent flap opened, revealing Valerian. "We have a serious problem," he said without preamble, expression somber. "They brought the Samach."

Within minutes they were out of the tent, heading for the center of camp. Their water conjurers had tried to replenish their supplies, but soon discovered they couldn't.

"We expected this," Callan said as they walked through the rain and muck. The sun was beginning to sink low in the sky. Night would soon be upon them, and from the bustle of activity around the camp, the watch was being set, preparations being made in case Gorias decided to use the cover of darkness to their advantage once again. "They used them at Stoneweald, so there's no reason to believe they wouldn't use them here."

"True," Valerian agreed. "But what worries me is how close they must be to be blocking us."

"None of us can use our magic?" Eve asked, tugging the hood lower as the rain began to pick up. It was going to be a miserable night for those on watch, and if the weather didn't clear up, a messy day tomorrow.

"Maybe the shifters, their magic comes from the goddess of wild things and the hunt. Certain gifts, like hers, are less easily suppressed. Chaos would be another example, but her gifts are rare," Valerian explained.

Callan snorted. "Thankfully. We don't need any of that tomorrow."

Valerian nodded grimly. "Let's hope Gorias doesn't have any."

Eve's heart sank, fear seizing it and dragging it down as she once had been. "Is it that bad?"

"It's pure destruction," Callan answered this time, as they rounded a corner around a small cluster of tents. The soldiers standing just outside gave grim smiles and bowed low as they passed. "Utterly unpredictable and sometimes uncontrollable even by the person using it. It would make things...very difficult."

"What's happening?" Eve's attention jerked to her right as Brida approached. She hadn't bothered with a hood. Despite being braided back, a few loose tendrils had come free and now clung to her face. She looked, Eve thought to herself, as if someone had tried to drown her.

The thought had her wincing.

"Trouble," was Valerian's only reply as her cousin fell into step with them.

"Of the fae variety or something more mundane?" Brida asked, her hand coming to rest on the pommel of the sword strapped to her hip.

"Magic," Callan said, not bothering to look at Brida as they neared their destination.

Peering through the open flaps, she could see perhaps a dozen fae gathered. "Water conjurers?" Eve asked, glancing toward Callan, who shook his head.

"Shifters."

"They say they have an idea of how to help," Valerian said as they stepped inside.

Cora and Leysa were standing in the center of the crowd, speaking in low tones to two older fae. Every set of eyes in the tent turned to them as they entered, but only a small, grey-haired fae with dark umber skin and sharp brown eyes spoke. "This is not a discussion for human ears," she said in a rich voice that reminded Eve of a bonfire with its warmth.

"She is an ally, and should be aware of what's happening," Valerian said before Callan or Eve could reply. "Grandmama," he added, lips curving into a slight smile.

Eve blinked in surprise, her gaze flitting between the two. The resemblance was there, and undeniable. Valerian had without a doubt inherited his grandmother's eyes, and as she looked at her grandson, Eve saw the same broad smile gracing the woman's aged features as she'd seen on Valerian's so many times.

"As you say," she replied, turning, at last, to look at Eve, followed by

Brida. "I meant no disrespect. It has been a long time since I last had the chance to speak with one of your kind, and I know that this must be difficult."

"No more so than our homes being threatened," Brida replied smoothly. "I cannot speak for all of my kind, but I think you'll find most humans to be remarkably adaptable." Despite the sharp grin and affable tone, Eve could see the tension simmering behind Brida's eyes.

"Of course," the elder replied. "Please do not take offense. Many of us lived alongside and loved your kind. We mourned when we were separated," she explained, casting a glance to the other elder at her side. "Some of us still do."

Her words earned a sharp look from the man, a silent rebuke that spoke of deeply carried grief. "Ursa," the man interjected calmly, only the faintest hint of color staining his sandy cheeks. Downturned brown eyes gave no hint as to what he was thinking as he gave a shake of his head, jet-colored hair peppered with grey shifting loose from the binds that held it back from his face. "Not now."

Nodding, Ursa offered Eve a grim smile. "We are here to help if we can."

"Many of our number," Leysa said, "have no gifts, and many of those who do can still fight with blade and bow, but we will need magic to win."

Eve looked at Valerian, the commander of their armies. "We are down several of our fighters now, and the battle hasn't even started."

He offered her an unexpected grin in response. "We have a plan."

Chapter 28

Lia

"Well that could have gone worse," Bastien remarked, watching as the last of Lia's advisors stepped out into the rain and darkness.

"It also could have gone better," Aelius countered, attention on the map spread on the table that dominated the space.

Straw crunched beneath her boots as she moved to look out at the night sky beyond the tent opening. Not a single star was visible, hidden by the clouds that now dumped rain by the bucket on the armies that waited restlessly for the day to come.

"They're frightened," she replied. "We all are. But they've accepted the truth, as difficult as it was, and our newfound allies." Turning to look at her brothers, she nodded once. "It'll have to be good enough."

Despite his doubtful expression, Aelius nodded. "It'll have to be," he repeated. Tapping idly on the oak table, he shrugged. "We should get some rest. It's going to be a long and very muddy day tomorrow."

"There is the other thing," Bastien began, and from the tightness around his eyes, she knew this was going to be something she didn't want to hear.

Aelius' eyes closed briefly. She was definitely not going to like this.

"Yes, that." Sighing he opened his eyes, looking at Lia with what she could only describe as apprehension. "We want you to remain a safe distance from the field tomorrow. Our scouts have found a suitable spot that should keep you far from the battle, but close enough to give orders as needed."

"Absolutely not."

Her firm denial was met with a frown from both men.

"Lia," Aelius began, taking a small step toward her. Whatever argument he was about to make was cut short by Bella's voice.

"You can't be on the field tomorrow." All three of them turned to look at the seer. The hood that had sheltered her head from the rain fell back, revealing her near panic-stricken face. "I had another vision."

It was as if all of the air had been sucked out of the tent. Lia held her breath, heart pounding so hard she could feel it in her throat as Bella, whose attention remained solely on Lia, continued.

"I fell asleep, and I had another vision. I saw the armies fighting in the mud. I saw...I saw all of you," she said, voice shaking. "And I saw an arrow pierce your chest." A small, choked sob escaped her. "I saw you die again." Crossing the distance between them, Bella cupped Lia's face between her hands. "More clearly than last time."

They had never touched like this, Lia had never dared. Electric shocks raced through her at the contact, her breath returning to her in a sharp gasp.

Something in her chest screamed with joy, at the rightness of it, only to be dampened by Bella's words. "Stay behind. Please."

"Okay," Lia whispered. She would have agreed to anything Bella had asked for in that moment, if only to see the fear and pain in those silver eyes eased. "I'll stay behind, and I'll stay safe."

Without another word, Bella pulled away, glancing at the men with a surprised blink as if noticing them for the first time. "I'm sorry," she whispered, disappearing into the night again.

Bastien scoffed. "Well if I had known that was all it would take I would have begged too."

"Unless you're a certain pretty, dark-haired seer, I don't think it would have made a difference," Aelius laughed.

"Shut up," Lia scolded, only half-heartedly. Her thoughts were still on Bella, and for a moment, Lia could swear she could still feel Bella's fingers on her skin. "I have to go," she said, not bothering to wait for their response.

Within moments of stepping outside, she was well and truly soaked, thanks to the cold rain. Protests sounded behind her, objections from her guards to her being out in the chill without at least a cloak, but she ignored them.

Where did she go?

Her gaze scanned the encampment, dimly lit with roaring braziers spaced relatively evenly throughout the camp and torches that managed to still burn, even with the heavy rain.

Bella had gotten a head start, and a combination of nightfall and the sheets of falling rain made it near impossible to see very far ahead. Lia's boots sank into the muck with a squish that had her wrinkling her nose but didn't deter her.

The walk back toward both of their personal tents was a blessedly short one, and she caught up with Bella in time to find the seer hesitating outside of Lia's tent. The small group of personal guards that had followed their sodden queen fell back as she stopped short.

"I won't die," Lia said suddenly. Bella spun in place, silver-grey eyes meeting Lia's suddenly. The queen couldn't read the emotions she found there in the seer's eyes, but there was something there, something that hadn't been there before.

"I saw it," Bella said, placing a hand against her chest. "I saw the arrow; it pierced your heart," she whispered, just loud enough to be heard, as she closed her eyes. "I saw you—"

"No," Lia replied, her own voice thick with emotion. Without thought, she closed the distance between them, taking Bella's face in her hands just as Bella had her own. "I can't die," she whispered.

Bella's eyes flew open, widening, and for the first time, Lia could so clearly read what was written there: the same need that had heat pooling low in her belly.

"Bella," Lia whispered, leaning so close that their lips nearly touched.

"You can't die," Bella breathed, before her lips crashed into Lia's. Her hand plunged into Lia's soaked tresses, pulling her closer and kissing her fiercely.

Lia couldn't say how long they stood in the rain, holding one another close as each heartbeat ticked away a small eternity. When they finally pulled apart, they were in Lia's tent, though she didn't know when they'd moved, or how.

Lia's heart ached with need and fear in equal parts. The battle to come could claim either of them. If all they had was this one night, then she would take every moment, every touch, every kiss, and savor them.

"I want this, with you," Bella said, brushing Lia's hair back from where it stuck to her rain-soaked face. "I need to forget, to feel something that makes me forget what might happen tomorrow."

Taking Bella's face in her hands, Lia pressed her lips to Bella's. They were every bit as soft as she'd imagined. Bella's lips parted as Lia flicked her tongue against them, allowing her entry. The kiss was full of hunger, of the desire that Lia had been stifling all of this time, and Bella met her with equal intensity.

Pulling back, Lia let her hands fall from Bella's face to her shoulders. Bella reached down, hiking the hem of her dress upward and over her head, tossing it to the side, where it landed with a wet plop on the carpet covering the straw floor. The sound had a nervous giggle bubbling from Lia's lips, and Bella grinned.

"I love that sound," Bella said quietly, brushing her thumb across Lia's lips gently.

Lia simply smiled, ignoring the way her heart thumped at Bella's words as she gently urged Bella backward toward the bed. She'd worn only lacy undergarments beneath her dress, Lia discovered with delight. Her small, perfect breasts were peaked and firm beneath Lia's palm. Bella fell onto the bed with a gasp, biting her lower lip so invitingly as her head fell back slightly. Lia's hand drifted lower, sliding down Bella's smooth abdomen with pure adoration.

Bella was stunning, in every sense, and she was going to savor every moment they had between them. "Lay back on the bed," Lia said, falling to her knees between Bella's spread thighs.

Bella obeyed instantly, inhaling sharply as Lia pressed her lips to the side of Bella's knee. A quiet groan escaped the seer's lips as Lia's hand slid lower and lower, grazing against the damp lace of her undergarment, proof of Bella's own desire.

"I love that sound," Lia laughed huskily against Bella's skin.

Straightening, she hooked a finger on either side of the lace separating her from Bella, the last barrier between them. Once they were discarded alongside the dress, Lia slid a finger down the apex of Bella's thighs, slipping between her folds gently. With two fingers, she gingerly began to work her fingers against Bella's clit, in slow, precise circles.

Bella groaned again, back arching against the bed. Lia grinned, loving Bella's vocal response to her touch, how wet she was for her. Moving her fingers lower, she gently parted the folds and pushed one finger inside Bella, crooking it upward to hit that sensitive spot inside of her as her thumb met her clit again. Moving her thumb in slow circles, she added a second finger and worked them in and out in time with the movement of her thumb.

"Oh, fuck," Bella sighed throatily.

Lia simply laughed, her own core tightening. When Lia leaned forward, replacing her thumb with her tongue, Bella arched again, thighs clamping around Lia tightly as her inner muscles squeezed Lia's fingers tightly, over and over as she fell over the edge of pleasure.

Bella's response to her touch was nearly enough to drive Lia over the edge herself. Rocking back on her heels, Lia pressed a kiss to Bella's inner thigh. She would never tire of hearing the sounds Bella made, of feeling her soft skin beneath her hands.

After a moment, Bella sat up, propping herself on her elbows. "My turn," she said, crooking her finger to beckon Lia closer. "Dress off."

Lia obeyed, tossing her dress to the side unceremoniously. Like Bella, she'd only worn scraps of lace beneath the dress. Impractical for their journey, but she was a woman who liked fine things. Bella, she was discovering, was the finest of all.

"Those too," Bella said, silver eyes darkened with lust.

When Lia was entirely bare, breasts peaked and goose bumps dancing across her skin, Bella reached forward, grasping her hips gently and tugging her closer. Without warning, she twisted, pushing Lia backward onto the bed so that she lay flat.

Rising to her knees, she placed her hands on either side of Lia's face, hovering just inches above her. She lowered her head just enough for their lips to brush against one another, their hips the only other parts of their bodies touching.

"I've been dying to taste you," Bella whispered, before lowering herself more. Lia couldn't help the gasp that escaped her lips as Bella set her skin on fire with a trail of kisses down her chest, between her breasts, to the planes of her abdomen, stopping only when her head was between Lia's thighs.

Looking up at Lia with a wicked grin that had her heart thundering, Bella slowly slipped her fingers inside of her. Lia shuddered in response, arching her back as need coursed through her. With only a few strokes of her hand, Bella had her soaked and going mad, nearly on the precipice.

When Bella licked the most sensitive part of her, setting her nerves on fire, Lia cried out, flying right over the edge. Her hand gripped Bella's raven hair, as she continued, not stopping until Lia said, in a pleading tone, "Please, I can't take anymore."

With a laugh, Bella lifted her head, licking her lips. "I knew you'd be delicious. Like fruit on a summer day," she said with a grin.

Sometime later, sated and wrapped in each other's arms, Lia realized she may never recover from falling into the stunning woman who slept soundly beside her.

Chapter 29

Eve

"That is the most ridiculous thing I've ever heard," Callan stated.

Eve had to agree, it was absurd and likely wouldn't work, putting many lives in danger. She wanted to refuse to allow it, but frankly, they had nothing else. "Do we even know if this will work?" she asked instead, certain that her doubt was clearly etched in her expression.

It was Ursa who spoke then, silencing her grandson with a look as he began to answer. "The risk is worth it. Unless the Samach are dealt with, and quickly, I doubt we'll have any chance of success."

"Which is why," Valerian interjected, "I believe this is the only way."

"Won't they be at risk?" Eve asked, shaking her head.

"We will," Leysa said. "But, as Ursa said, doing nothing is an even greater risk."

How many are going to die in the coming battle?

She had no skill in battle strategy, as she had never been expected to need it, but she was smart enough to consider the risks and listen to those who knew more about the subject than her. "You're all in agreement?"

"Yes." The response from each of the shifters, plus Valerian, was unanimous with only Callan disagreeing.

"No." He shook his head firmly. "We'll find another way, we'll–"

"I know that you would not have us take this risk, but there's no other way," Leysa said calmly. Casting a glance to Valerian, something unspoken passed between the couple. "It's our decision, Callan."

Callan sighed, outnumbered and with little alternative. "Alright."

Her heart ached at the idea of her friend, and the others, being put in anymore danger, but the decision had been made. "It seems likely they won't expect it," she added, hoping to smooth not only her own fear at the situation but Callan's as well. "If they assume they've successfully silenced all of our gifts."

"That's true, dove," Callan agreed. "But all of this hinges on the Samach being unaware that they can't stop them from shifting."

"As far as we can recall, they've never been used in battle against us," the elder male stated.

Callan turned to him, offering a grim smile. "I wish we had something more certain."

"Are you up for it, Corbin?" Ursa teased, though Eve caught the glimmer of concern that flashed in her eyes.

"I'm always up for a good fight," Corbin replied, looking rather ruffled by the suggestion he might not be.

Despite their conviction in their choice, Callan looked unconvinced. "I assume you've tried reaching out to–"

"Making plans without us, dear brother? How abysmally rude," Cathal droned, interrupting whatever Callan was about to suggest, and announcing his arrival.

She hadn't seen Cathal or Mara since their departure from Falias, both out of a desire to allow the long-separated couple some privacy, but also to avoid the oily disdain she felt as she turned to face him. She hadn't forgiven him for what had happened at Stoneweald, for taking Callan and nearly murdering her.

Still, his alliance was a necessary evil, and Mara, standing at his side, was supposedly keeping him in line. She had, according to Cora, found a life amongst the fae, and had somehow moved on past any old hurts during the five hundred years that had passed, despite the loss of the man she loved.

It must have taken an astounding amount of strength to do so, which earned at least some degree of respect from Eve; begrudging as it was. Mara too, had not quite earned forgiveness for her part in Darkegrove's history.

"An oversight," Callan replied, tension radiating from him.

"We understand," Mara offered, smiling patiently, before Cathal could say something that would likely end up in a fight between the brothers.

Gods, how I wish Cora was here to act as a buffer between them.

"Of course, my love," Cathal replied, looking anything but understanding. "Fill us in?"

As Callan did just that, Eve sent a silent prayer to the gods for their success, the safety of the shifters, and just enough peace between the brothers to see them through the next few days at least.

CHAPTER 30

LIA

The war drums began before dawn. A steady beat rolled over the hills, into the valley that separated the two armies. Lia sat up straight in her bed, reaching instinctively to the right where Bella had fallen asleep the night before, only to find cool sheets.

When did she leave?

The brazier that had kept the tent warm and comfortable overnight had dwindled to little more than coals, and the chill morning air that drifted in from the opening at the top of the tent had Lia dragging the nearest warm furs over her shoulders.

The drums continued as she dressed and made her way out of the tent in search of Aelius and Bastien. There was far less commotion in the camp than she'd expected, and no real sense of urgency. A short walk had her back at the command tent where she found them both, in a hushed and intense conversation.

Where is Bella?

She wanted to speak to her, to discuss what the night before had meant to her, to find out if it truly had been a simple romp to take their minds off the battle ahead. But for now, she needed to focus.

"What's happening?" Lia asked, casting a glance outside toward the nearest group of soldiers. Men and women were donning armor, sharpening blades, and even a few still finishing the last of their breakfasts. It certainly didn't appear that they were in any sort of hurry.

"It's an intimidation tactic," Bastien explained. "The drums are meant to fray our nerves, and make us shaky when we finally engage them."

That made sense, she supposed. It had certainly frightened her enough. "What are you discussing?"

"Our new allies were up to something last night," Aelius replied, tapping a finger on the spot on the map indicating the fae army's position. "We're not sure what, but we saw an awful lot of movement."

"You're spying on them?" Indignation rose within her. "Shouldn't we be more concerned with what our actual enemy is up to?"

"Of course," Aelius replied, straightening. "But it would be foolish to ignore the fae. They may claim to be our allies, but frankly, we know nothing about them." At Lia's scoff of protest, he added, "I know she's your friend, but we cannot risk our people."

Eve was her friend, despite the new and unexpected company she kept– *the Kingdom she now rules*, she corrected herself, but the fact remained that she had a duty to her own people first and foremost.

"Of course," she conceded, lifting a hand to her temple. He was right, as much as she hated it. "Tell me what they saw."

Bastien hesitated only a moment before speaking. "We saw...animals leaving the camp, less than an hour ago."

"Animals?"

Aelius rolled his eyes slightly, shaking his head. "That makes it sound ridiculous. Animals, yes, but also more guards on the eastern patrol than before, which was the direction the animals headed in."

"You're telling me you think the animals have something to do with the fae?" Lia asked slowly, not bothering to hide the doubt that had crept into her voice. "What sort of animals?"

Bastien's cheeks darkened ever so slightly. "Birds, mostly."

"A flock of birds flew away from their camp, and they added some extra guards on the watch that faces the enemy, so you think they're up to something?"

She couldn't believe the ridiculousness of what she was hearing.

That these men, trained warriors and strategists would be so disturbed by something so simple.

*And yet...*she thought, recalling the fact that these were fae, known to be blessed with magical gifts no human had ever possessed, she couldn't discount the possibility of things they simply didn't understand.

"Alright," she said after a moment. "We'll keep an eye out for strange birds, then?"

Before either of them could respond the drum beats in the distance stopped abruptly, leaving them in an eerie silence. Goose pimples that had nothing to do with the cold spread across her arms like wildfire. Somehow the absence of the constant drumming was more frightening than its sudden appearance had been.

Shouts erupted from outside, and the three of them ran to see what was happening. Her heart was in her throat. Was Gorias on the move? Had their soldiers finished preparing?

Running for the nearest small hill, one with a clear view of the expanse between the two armies, what she saw had her stunned. Rather than an approaching army, ready to conquer and destroy, she saw chaos.

Flames had broken out behind their lines, and even from this distance, she could see that men and women were scrambling to put out the fires and handle whatever had the sounds of screaming erupting from a place near their left flank.

"What do you think happened?" she asked her twin, as he came to stand beside her.

To her surprise, his face was split wide into a grin, as he pointed toward the mass of birds flying west. "Animals," he said.

"Fae," Bastien corrected from her other side, erasing any doubt that had remained in her friend.

CHAPTER 31

EVE

Just as Callan had predicted, the drums began early in the morning and continued on for nearly an hour before abruptly stopping.

It was a tactic well loved by Gorias and used during the last war, the war in which they had barely succeeded in forcing them beyond the mountains. They had remained away for so long, leaving no trace of their whereabouts that the other fae of Nidus, the continent they all called home, had long since decided they had either died out or moved to another continent, possibly to the east, to Anguis. Where, Eve had learned, dragons still roamed, alongside humans and fae.

"It looks like they were successful," Valerian beamed, as he returned to the tent. Armor donned and swords sheathed, they had all been prepared since before dawn to march. "The fires were lit, and they found where the Samach were gathered and have at least taken them out of the fight."

"Has Leysa returned?" Eve asked, concern for her friend at the forefront of her mind as well as Valerian's, she was certain.

"She's getting cleaned up right now," he replied, relief clear in his eyes.

"The humans?" Callan asked, rising from where he sat on the edge of the bed. Heat flushed her cheeks as she recalled what they'd done there the night before, where and how he'd used those shadows of his.

Callan's gaze shifted to Eve sharply. *Shit.* She'd forgotten he could hear her heartbeat and how it pounded when images of him, naked and– *Shit.*

His responding grin told her clearly enough that he knew exactly what direction her thoughts had taken, and the dark desire she saw in those ocean eyes of his also told her that he had every intention of acting on those thoughts, the moment they had the opportunity.

"If you two are done ogling each other," Valerian began drily. "The human queen has sent word, she's ready. Lady Brida has also arrived, and her forces are already joining ours on the line. It's time to see if the shifters were successful."

"I should do it," Eve suggested, earning another sharp look from Callan, but this time it was fear that deepened his blue eyes rather than lust.

"If they were successful, then it won't matter anyway, right? If the Samach are down, they'll be scrambling to figure out what happened, and nobody will be looking anyway. If they aren't down, it won't work."

"She's right," Valerian added.

"I know," Callan conceded, rising from his seat. "Just try not to cause an earthquake."

Rolling her eyes, she stepped out of the tent, where she would have a clear view of the mud and stone beneath their feet.

Feel and focus.

Reaching out with the intangible limb that was her magic, she felt for a small stone, hidden beneath trampled grass and earth, summoning it upward. As light as a feather, with little strain, the stone obeyed, erupting from the earth in less than a heartbeat.

"I think we've been successful," she said with a grin, lifting her gaze to Callan, only to find him staring at the path ahead, dumbfounded.

"I'd say so," he whispered.

Following his gaze she turned to see dozens of small stones in varying sizes, some as large as her fist, hovering in the air. Each of them had felt her power and obeyed.

"Gods," Valerian whispered.

"I didn't mean to do all that," she said, blinking. When had her powers grown so exponentially? Before they'd departed Falias, she had a good amount of control and could call upon plants or stones from a fair distance, but only ever individually. Never in this number and never unintentionally.

"When it begins, be very careful with your aim, dove," Callan laughed. "And very specific with your magic." Turning to face her, the humor in his gaze faded. "Only use it when you're certain it's the best course and only when you must. You are powerful, more so than I think any of us realized, but you will have a limit. I would like to find out what that is, but in a controlled way and not on a battlefield where it may cost you your life. If we had been given more time to practice. Before we go, I–"

Eve silenced him with a finger to his lips. She could hear the fear and worry creeping into his voice, see it in his eyes. There would be no tearful goodbyes, no heartfelt words. Not now, not again.

Everything they'd need to say had been said already, and when they saw the end of this war, they would say them all again. To say them now would be a curse, an invitation to disaster.

"We will have all of the time we need," she whispered, moving her hands to his armored chest. "You will teach me my magic, we will rule our people together, and we will have a life. Do not think this is the end, because it is not. Our story is only just beginning, and I intend for it to be a damn long one."

"Such language from a queen," he teased, voice thick with emotion. Her mind flashed to the first time he'd said such words, in a darkened garden, just before her entire world was upended. He was the one constant during the worst time of her life, and for that, she would be forever grateful to have found him. She had said goodbye to one family, one home, and thanks to him, found another.

"Let's go kill them all so that we can have our happily ever after," she whispered fiercely.

"I will follow wherever you lead, my Queen," he replied, pressing his forehead to hers.

CHAPTER 32

LIA

"Keep your promise," Bella begged, as the first wave of Gorias' soldiers began to sweep into the valley.

Their own forces surged forward, ready to meet them, and already the sounds of steel and men dying reached the small hilltop clearing where the Queen of Avellon would wait and watch, as Aestera's defenders fought and died.

"I will," Lia agreed, dragging her gaze from the battle below to Bella. "I wish you would stay with me. Your daughter–"

"Will know that her mother did everything she could to fight for her, for all of us," Bella interjected, voice firm with the steeliness in her eyes that Lia was beginning to love. "Make sure she knows."

"You'll tell her all about it yourself," Lia assured her.

Bella's only reply was a tight smile and a quick press of her lips to Lia's. "We have things to discuss when I get back," she said, before turning on her heel and heading down the hill into the fray.

For what felt like an eternity, Lia waited and watched. Occasionally reports from the front would arrive, keeping her abreast on the status of their soldiers. However, as the morning went on, they became less frequent, more sporadic and vague.

We're losing.

Her heart raced with fear. The last she'd heard of Eve's forces had been good news: the fae that fought alongside them had managed to hobble Gorias' left flank, charging into the main body of their forces and doing quite a lot of damage, but their progress had slowed significantly; even with the bears and wolves they apparently had aiding them.

The fighting raged on, far ahead from where Lia stood, but even from her vantage point atop the hill, she could smell the battlefield. The tinny scent of blood and gore, mixed with mud and the heaviness of desperation and fear. She should be down there, fighting with her soldiers, men and women fighting and dying to protect their homes and families.

But she had made a promise.

Bella, who was somewhere down there, sword in hand, doing exactly what Lia couldn't, had foreseen what would happen if she joined the fray. She scanned the battlefield, searching for a sign of Bella or Bastien, as unlikely as it was that she'd be able to pick them out in the chaos.

Aelius then, maybe she could find him. He'd been atop his horse, sword held high as he led the charge the last time she saw him.

It was no use. She could hardly separate her own forces from those of their enemies. Blood and filth coated the armor of fae and humans alike, leaving them almost indistinguishable from this distance. Lia strode anxiously from one side of the makeshift command table to the other.

I should be helping them.

Bella's vision had been clear about one thing: Lia would die; an arrow through the heart would take her down. So she had begged Lia to remain back, out of the range of the enemy archers.

"Please," Bella's silver eyes had been glistening with tears as she'd pleaded with Lia to agree, to remain behind where it would be safe. "You will die."

The where had been unclear; all that she could see was the arrow striking her heart, and Lia falling to the ground. Lia had announced that if she died in the name of saving her people, the risk was well worth it. Lia would die a thousand times if it meant saving them all, but Bella had only argued that her people would benefit far more from her in life than in martyred death.

Loosing a frustrated sigh, Lia turned away from the battlefield, letting her gaze drift to the nearby copse of trees. Someone was coming out of the dim treeline. A man, carrying a bow loosely in one hand.

One of the scouts perhaps?

Turning to the guards who had remained at her side, she opened her mouth to ask if they recognized the man striding confidently toward them, but the words never came.

Pain, bright and blessedly brief, sent a jolt through her chest, and she turned her gaze to the source. An arrow protruded through her chest, just below her breast.

"Oh," she breathed, lifting her gaze to the archer who now nocked his bow for a second time. The guards are her side were moving, some rushing toward her, others toward the would-be assassin. Too late.

The second arrow found its home in her heart, and Lia Vallyse fell.

LIA HAD BEEN TAUGHT FROM AN EARLY AGE THAT DEATH WAS peaceful. As easy as coming up for air from beneath the surface of the lake she swam in every summer. She was taught that she would simply awaken in the Otherworld, a land of beauty and endless light and joy.

If what she'd been taught was true, she would see her Papa again, to have the chance to ask why. Instead, she found herself in a room of stark white.

Not a room, a tunnel.

Staring ahead, as far as she could see, nothing but white, made from some material she couldn't describe, let alone name. A hazy sort of light enshrouded what she presumed to be the end, and she took a small step forward. Perhaps that was the way to the Otherworld, to the land of light and solace that she had been promised.

Bella.

The thought had her pausing. Bella was not in the Otherworld, nor Aelius, nor her mother. Bastien. Eve. So many people she loved or cared for remained, and she was leaving them behind. But what was the alternative? Steeling herself, she took another step forward.

I will wait for them, and love them until I–

"No, child, your time has not yet come."

The smooth, warm feminine voice had her spinning. Had her heart still beat, it would have been leaping from her chest.

Standing mere feet in front of her now was the most stunning woman she had ever laid eyes on; with dark brown skin that seemed to nearly glow against the gold fabric that draped over her slender form and bright gold tattoos along either clavicle, depicting the sun shining with golden rays.

There was little doubt in Lia's mind about whom she was seeing– a goddess stood before her.

"You're a goddess." Lia couldn't help her incredulous tone, nor the way her mouth fell open as she stared.

Bright gold eyes brightened in response. "Yes, dear. I am Helie, whom your people once revered as the bringer of sun and healing." Her full lips tilted downward in what could only be disappointment, though it was fleeting. "Before we were forgotten."

"I...why is the goddess of the sun here to take me to the Otherworld?"

Helie's answering laugh was warm and airy, and suddenly Lia had the sensation of running through a meadow in summer, carefree and warmed by sunlight. "A fair but rather incorrect assumption, I am afraid." She paused, tilting her head as if listening, though no sound met Lia's ears. In fact, the space seemed utterly devoid of any sound save their voices.

"Time is short," Helie continued. "I know dear Evelyn has apprised you of the situation, that you are the second key in an ancient lock that must be turned."

Of course, Lia sighed.

"You brought her back, or Keithia did?"

"Mm, that was the work of my beloved, as I am here to offer the same to you. But it must be your choice. Do you understand?"

"I think so," Lia admitted. "But I am frightened. What will happen?"

Helie's smile was warm and comforting. "You will be blessed by me, darling, gifted a small drop of my own power to heal, to light the way when the circumstances are most dire."

"Oh."

"Do you agree then? To be returned to the living world, to be granted this gift?"

Lia nodded instantly. Of course she did. How could she refuse, to pass on to the Otherworld when her help was needed? To choose to say goodbye to those she loved and to abandon the world to its fate when she was being given a second chance to help; the very idea was unfathomable.

"There is a small cost," Helie said, lifting a single finger.

"I will pay whatever it is, gladly," Lia answered with certainty. "To save my people."

Helie's expression turned grim. "You will no longer be of your people," she explained. "You will become fae, as Evelyn did. It is the only way for you to wield the gift I will impart."

Lia could only blink. Doubt coursed through her. She would be forced to give up her kingdom, her people, and her very mortal life. But if it meant saving those she loved, those she'd sworn to protect...

She had said she would be willing to pay any price, and had meant it.

"So be it," she said finally.

Helie stepped forward, placing a hand on Lia's forearm gently. "This may burn," the goddess warned.

Before Lia could reply, searing pain shot up her arm, like wildfire in her veins. A bright gold sun, nearly the twin to Helie's, graced the place where the goddess had touched, a permanent symbol of the goddess's gift.

Without warning, her chest began to ache and burn where the arrow had struck, and she closed her eyes, steeling herself and biting back the scream that threatened to erupt from her.

When her eyes opened once more, it was clear blue that greeted her rather than white. Clouds danced along the winter sky, and she blinked away the tears that swam in her eyes.

I've returned.

She inhaled deeply, filling her lungs with precious air and exhaling slowly as she stood. Shouts of surprise echoed from somewhere behind her, but her attention had settled on the battle still raging below.

There was no doubt now that they were losing. Gorias had nearly overrun them, and the fighting had nearly reached the base of the hill. She couldn't find them, Bella nor Aelius or Bastien. There was no hope of finding Eve, not with the fae line trapped in the middle of what could only be Gorian forces now.

Panic seized her, and she did the only thing she could, she screamed. Every ounce of fury, fear, and heartache spilled from her as she wept and raged.

Why bring me back for this? Why bother?

Perhaps it was some sort of divine punishment for some sin she'd committed, to watch those she loved, her kingdom, her very world, be taken and destroyed. To bear witness to the loss of all hope.

Eyes closed, she wept until strong hands gripped her arms, two men on either side, urging her backward. No. If they were going to die, she would die alongside them; her people would know that she remained, and did not abandon them, even when all was lost.

She screamed once more, this time with desperation and despair.

The mark on her arm, left by the goddess who had supposedly given her a chance to save them all, burned once more, drawing a bitter laugh from Lia.

So much for that. I have to do something.

No sooner had the thought crossed her mind when light erupted from her. Bright and unending as the sun, it expanded and spread until it cascaded down the hill, spreading over the men and women fighting below. Taking shape and form as it moved, liquid and serpentine, it moved with purpose.

Battle was hardly a silent thing. Wails of people dying, war cries, and the metallic clang of sword against sword, the thunk of shield after shield taking blows. Each of these sounds had been carried on the wind alongside the screams of men and women who still fought; the screams that had now shifted from those of rage, of ferocity, into something far more primal.

Sheer, unadulterated terror echoed throughout the valley.

Lia hazarded a step closer, breath stilling as she gazed below at her handiwork. The light that had poured from her, surging forward as an asp in search of prey, had finally begun to dissipate. At the edges of their line, frayed and broken, soldiers began to rise from the ground, earning shocked stares and outright cries of surprise from their compatriots.

Healed, she realized, as they began to feel at their arms, or chests, or heads.

But the screams hadn't come from them.

She let her gaze move farther then, toward the horde Gorias had brought against them. There, amongst the fae that had come to destroy them all, soldiers fell. Most covered their eyes with their hands, shrieking in what she could only assume was pain or fear.

Lia's heartbeat was steadily drumming in her ears, her pulse roaring as the words rang through her mind, *What have I done?*

As far as their line extended, soldiers lay dead or dying. Save for a small pocket, surrounded on all sides. Eve's people, she realized with a shuddering breath. In her wrath and grief, somehow she had managed to preserve her own people and those of her allies, while slaying the ones who would have conquered them. The pounding in her ears became a dull roar as her vision began to cloud, like rain on a windowpane.

"Majesty?" The alarmed voice of her guard barely reached her, and as darkness overtook her she wondered if this time, she might just ask to stay dead.

CHAPTER 33

EVE

"I love you," she whispered into the wind as the battle raged. She had no idea if Callan could hear her, even with his fae ears, over the sound of battle.

As planned, Eve had remained on the edges, as far from the heaviest fighting as she could but close enough to help, surrounded by the wounded who had managed to find themselves here, or had been carried here by brothers and sisters in arms. Kneeling on the ground, with mud up to her wrists, she poured her magic into the earth.

Healers moved among them, doing what little they could with the herbs Eve was able to call forth from the ground where they waited. Ahead of her, vines rose from beneath the feet of the Gorias, yanking them down before choking the life from them as she wrapped their bodies. She'd discovered she could take many of them that way, while also raising stones to hurl at their heads when able. Aim was difficult, even for her, amongst the chaos, and she was utterly unwilling to risk harming any of their own people.

It was an effort to keep an eye on all the ones she cared for, but she tried. Callan was racing ahead, Valerian at his side, as they led the charge that fractured the enemy's flank. Leysa, in the form of a wolf, was among the fae shifters; a mixture of bears, wolves, and mountain cats.

The russet fur Leysa preferred was easy enough to spot with her fae vision at first, but after a while, even the white wolves had been stained red with blood, making it much more difficult to track her friend. Cathal had been amongst the fae that followed Callan, and Eve couldn't help but fear the knife at his back, almost as much as the swords he charged toward.

Mara had remained behind with Eve and, it turned out, had also been given a gift. A small one, she'd claimed just as the battle began, given to her by Astraia, the goddess of justice and judgment. When Eve had asked what that meant, Mara only smiled.

"You'll see," she said. The former queen had remained by Eve's side, waiting, silent as a ghost, her pale face never once turning from the battle. Worry for their beloved was another common thread between them.

A shout tore Eve's attention from the battle, as a lone soldier, Gorian by his armor, charged at Mara, sword raised. Before Eve could so much as summon stone to shield her, Mara's attention jerked sharply to the man who, to Eve's shock, stopped dead in his tracks.

"Tell me your sins," Mara said softly, as coaxing as a mother with a reluctant child.

Eve watched in horror as the man fell to his knees before Mara, sword dropping into the muck with a thump. "I...I took her, against her will," he stammered, the front of his trousers going dark. "She didn't want me, and I didn't–"

Stepping closer, Mara placed a single finger on the man's brow. "There, now," she cooed. "Doesn't it feel better to say the words aloud? Do you wish to atone?"

The man was shaking now, and rather than answer, he whimpered.

"A nod will do," Mara said, gentle as can be, utterly at odds with the chaos that still reigned around them. The fighting had grown more intense, perhaps in small part because of Eve's inattention, but she couldn't tear her gaze away from the scene playing out before her.

The man nodded once, and that was all it took. Smoke the color of a stormy sky ebbed from the finger that still rested on the man's brow, pouring into the man's nostrils. He shook violently, just once, before falling away from Mara and onto the mud with a squelch that had Eve wincing.

"What did you do to him?" Eve asked. By the time her attention returned to the former queen, Mara had taken her place by Eve's side once more, seemingly unfazed by what had just been confessed to her, what she'd just done.

"He has been given a fitting punishment for his greatest sin," she replied darkly, casting a glance at her would-be attacker. "I suspect right now, in his mind, his victim is getting her revenge. He will fracture and then he will die; after he suffers sufficiently."

Eve shuddered. It was horrific, as deserved as it was. "And who decides that? Do you?"

Mara turned a grim smile on Eve. "Astraia passes the final judgment. I am simply her...well let's just call me her catalyst."

Eve could only gape. The gift Astraia had bestowed was beautiful in its irony, and anything but small. Before she could reply, a messenger, bloody and breathing raggedly, arrived, ducking and weaving his way through the fighting to find her.

"The High King begs you to retreat to safety. They've been surrounded now, there is nothing more–"

Warning cries from the healers nearby cut his warning short. Something was happening ahead. She could no longer see Callan, or the shifters, as what little view she had of them had been cut off by a fresh wave of Gorian soldiers.

"Shit," Eve shouted, Mara echoing the sentiment with a curse of her own. "We need to move." She began summoning a shield of stone to block the soldiers who now charged toward them. They were beginning to lose, badly.

Mara's response was undecipherable, drowned by a fresh wave of screams that erupted from somewhere to the south. Screams unlike any of the others they'd been hearing all morning. Light, beautiful, and terrible, spread from the direction of the Avellonian lines and racing over the battlefield, like liquid gold brought to life.

Eve watched in sheer horror as it speared itself through the eyes of each Gorian soldier, burning their eyes in the sockets, even as it gently caressed each of their own, mending every wound, even those that would have proven fatal in little more than a few minutes.

"Lia," she breathed, heart sinking even as relief crashed through her. "What has happened to you?"

CHAPTER 34

LIA

"What was *that*?" Lia demanded, her voice shaking as she advanced on the goddess Helie. She stopped short, casting around the space. Rather than the white tunnel, she found herself in a field that stretched for what had to be miles. Blooms in varying shades dotted the landscape, interspersed with high grasses. "Am I dead again?"

Seated on an utterly out-of-place, stark white chaise, Helie smiled patiently. "No, darling," she said soothingly. "Not dead, just sleeping. I thought you might appreciate an explanation after that display of power."

Lia turned her attention to Helie once more, as recognition sparked. She'd been here before, as a girl. The field, known as Solamen Steppe, was not far from the ruins where she'd seen the moonflowers that Bella so reminded her of. "I've been here before."

Helie shrugged lightly. "I pulled a location from your memory," she replied, glancing around. "It is quite a lovely place."

"What happened?" Lia asked again, more calmly this time.

"You were losing, so I offered a bit more aid than I should have." Helie leaned forward, the movement utterly feline in its gracefulness, and offered Lia a conspiratorial grin. "My mate will be quite cross with me, I'm afraid. Her own chosen did not display such power when she was granted her gift, but then dear Evelyn did not have such need of it," she explained, lifting a hand lightly.

"Will I–will that happen again?" Lia whispered, shuddering. The power she'd displayed had been terrible and frightening. Yes, she had healed, but what she'd done to the Gorian soldiers had disturbed her. It had saved her people, but at what cost to her soul?

"No," Helie stated. "Your gift can be manifested similarly if you wish it to, but on a significantly smaller scale, my dear."

Relief washed over her like cool rain, and she looked skyward to the pale blue expanse that had been pulled from her memory like a loose thread. "Is that what you wanted to tell me or is there more?"

Helie smiled as if she knew just how much her answer had been a balm to Lia's heart. "I bear a message as well. Look to the east at dawn. Be sure to tell our dear Queen Evelyn as well; she will be most interested in what is coming."

"And what is coming?" Lia asked, lowering her gaze, only to find nothing but grass and flowers where Helie had been seated.

She blinked, and when her eyes opened once more, it was not bright blue that greeted her, but the canopy of her tent and the dark night sky beyond, visible through the opening at its peak.

"You've come back to me." Bella's fingertips grazed Lia's cheek gently, her voice little more than a whisper. Dirt and gods only knew what else caked her lovely face, save for the twin trails left clear beneath both of her impossibly silver eyes.

"You've been crying," Lia said, shocked at the hoarseness of her own voice, the way her throat burned. Lifting a hand slowly, she cupped Bella's face.

"We thought you were going to die," Bella replied quietly, casting a glance toward the tent flaps and the guards waiting beyond, Lia assumed. "According to the soldiers who were with you on the hill, you *did* die."

Lia squeezed her eyes shut as the memory of her death and subsequent meeting with the sun goddess flashed in her mind. "I did," she croaked. "I need to see Eve, and Aelius, and Bastien. I have to tell you all–" She swallowed hard, attempting to ease the burning in her throat.

She'd been screaming, she remembered, screaming as she blinded them—

"Here," Bella said, bringing a cup to her lips. "Drink this. It's an herbal tea, it'll soothe your throat."

Lia drank deeply, rising to a sitting position as she took the cup from Bella. The tea was delicious, floral and earthy, soothing her throat almost immediately. "Thank you," she whispered, marveling at the lack of pain speaking caused her. "I know you will all have questions, but I have a message to share. Can you ask someone to send for them?"

"They're already here," Bella replied, taking the cup and setting it to the side. Rising to her feet, she glanced toward the tent flaps once more. "Queen Evelyn and the fae High King are waiting in the command tent, alongside Prince Aelius and Lord Bastien."

"Good," she replied. "But...Bella, there are things you and I should talk about—"

"Later," Bella interrupted, smiling faintly. "There are more important things that must be seen to first."

Lia nodded. "Yes," she agreed, albeit reluctantly. Waiting felt wrong, for some reason. Perhaps it was her near death that made her impatient to say the words, or maybe it was the threat that Gorias still posed, but time felt short.

As Bella started to leave, Lia called out, "Wait. Is Gorias—did I kill them all?"

Bella frowned, shaking her head. "No, not all. They took a hit, but the threat remains. I'm sure your brother will fill you in, once he sees that you're well."

As Bella departed, Lia rose from the bed, moving to a nearby chair. She wouldn't be seen as weak, not when so many depended on her strength, even to her friends. Gorias remained, as depleted as their numbers had to be after Helie's intervention, and they had certainly taken their own significant losses. How would they meet the threat that remained?

The tent flaps burst open suddenly as Aelius, followed closely by Bastien, ran inside. "Thank the gods," her twin said, all but yanking her from the chair and embracing her soundly. "You scared the shit out of me, Li-Li."

Hugging him tightly, Lia huffed. "I'll try not to die again."

"See that you don't," Bastien threatened half-heartedly as Aelius released her.

Minutes later, with Eve, Callan, Bastien, and Aelius gathered, Lia shared her story. From the first encounter with Helie, to how she had used her gift without intending to, and ending with the short interaction they'd had as she slept.

"She said to look to the east at dawn, and that you will be very interested," Lia said, looking at Eve. "I have no idea what that means though."

Eve and Callan shared a long look that told Lia she suspected the pair knew exactly what Helie's words would mean for them.

"Finias?" Eve asked, earning a nod from Callan.

"What's Finias?" Bastien demanded, brow raising.

"The fae kingdom," Callan replied. "I sent my sister Cora to request their aid if their veil fell."

"Which it should have," Eve added. "When you came back, as fae."

Aelius' startled stare bored a hole into the side of Lia's face. "When you what?" He demanded, voice rising nearly to the level of a shout.

Bastien merely gaped, confusion, betrayal, and grief swimming in his eyes.

Lia winced, shame and guilt flooding her cheeks. "I was going to tell you," she began lamely, searching for the words to explain why she hadn't. How could she possibly explain the necessity of the price she'd paid? They wouldn't understand, not at first. "A price was required to be given the gift–"

"But what was the cost for her?" Aelius interrupted, pointing directly at Eve, accusation flaring to life in his eyes. "According to their story, she didn't become fae until later. Why should you pay a higher price?"

"Watch your tone, princeling," Callan warned in a low growl, as the shadows in the corners of the tent grew deeper.

"My situation was different, yes," Eve intervened, placing a hand on her mate's arm gently. "We don't know why–"

"I believe I can explain that." The sound of Bella's quiet voice had each of them turning.

"You're a–" Callan said suddenly, tone somehow full of surprise and what could have been awe.

"Seer," Bella interjected, offering a tight smile. "Yes, and I think I can explain some of the missing pieces, if you'll allow me." When nobody argued, Bella nodded. "Macaria, the goddess of death, is who returned you to life, I'm told, though your blessing was given by her sister, Keithia, goddess of life," she began, looking to Eve for confirmation.

Eve frowned slightly but nodded, saying nothing.

"Macaria's domain stretches beyond that of death, into that of destiny. She would have been aware your true death was imminent, and therefore it was unnecessary to wait to offer the change until then," Callan explained.

Lia's heart stuttered in her chest. Eve had been forced to face death twice, and with no warning given by the goddess who supposedly considered Eve her chosen. What little care did these long-forgotten gods have for their own?

"But," Callan continued, tilting his head as he took a small step between Eve and Bella. "What really concerns me, *seer*, is how you know this to begin with. What are you?"

Lia's breath came in a whoosh as she too realized the strangeness of Bella's knowledge. No human should have had nearly this much knowledge regarding the gods, shouldn't have known their names, much less their domains of power.

"Lia, I–" Bella began, starting for her, only to be blocked by Aelius, who stepped in front of his sister protectively.

"I believe he asked you a question," Aelius said in a low tone. "I suggest you answer and do not take a single step in my sister's direction until we are satisfied."

She felt, rather than saw, Bastien take up a place just behind her, and Lia shook her head. No, this couldn't be happening; Bella was just a seer. She would make them see that, make them understand. But if that was true, why did she feel so betrayed, so lost?

Tension hung in the air, and for several heartbeats, nothing happened. With silver eyes locked solely on Lia, Bella spoke, tone etched with a brokenness that made Lia's heart ache. "I am the daughter of Araceli. I–"

A commotion outside the tent drew everyone's attention, save for her own, Bella's, and to Lia's surprise, Callan's.

Dark lashes fluttered downward as Bella inhaled deeply. "High King," Bella said softly, as a guard burst into the tent, "tell your Mother that Kore walks in the light. Tell her..." Bella shook her head, pausing only a moment. "Tell her all will be lost if the prophecy is not fulfilled. Do not delay."

Callan's stony-faced expression softened slightly as he nodded once. "I will tell her," he said quietly, bowing his head almost reverently. "Thank you for the warning."

Lia couldn't make sense of his change in demeanor toward Bella, or who this Araceli was. Bella had told her nothing of her family, aside from what little she'd shared about her daughter.

"Majesty, you must come at once," a guard interrupted, stepping inside and offering a sealed parchment. Aelius stepped forward to take the message he bore, tearing it open with more force than was necessary. His jaw tensed as he read the words silently, turning a grim face to Lia.

"A large force is marching directly for us, under a banner we don't know. They will be here within the hour," Aelius explained. "We have little left to fight them with." Whipping to face Bella, he demanded, "Is this how we end, *seer*?"

CHAPTER 35

EVE

The large force, marching under a banner bearing a white poppy on a field of silver, arrived as swiftly as expected but halted just south of where Gorias' now abandoned camp had been. A small group, led by a white wolf, had broken away from the main body, coming to greet the gathered royalty and their advisors.

"Cora," Callan said in greeting as their party joined the human commanders. "I see you were successful."

With a flash, the wolf was replaced by the form of the fae princess, offering her brother a bright smile. "Indeed," she replied, turning a dazzling grin to Eve.

"Apparently the gods have been busy sharing your story," she explained. "Queen Lucia of Finias was prepared for my arrival and rode out to greet me the moment their veil fell. They've come to help." She paused, scanning the group behind Eve until her gaze stopped, grin faltering. "So it's true then," she sighed.

"What is?" Eve asked, puzzled, casting a glance behind her. Among the human commanders, Bella and Brida stood behind her, the latter still bearing a stunned expression, likely thanks to Cora's sudden shift.

Most of the humans bore similar expressions, Eve noted. She could only hope their shock would wear off before the next battle.

Bella, however, looked resigned, lips pressed tightly together as she stared into the distance.

"Your mother is demanding your return," Cora said gently. "She appeared in person to Queen Lucia and charged her with finding you. She'll be along shortly," she warned. "I don't know how long you have, but she intends to send you home."

"I know," Bella whispered, gaze shifting to where Lia stood, watching silently. Her normally sunshiney face was shadowed, some unreadable expression darkening her eyes.

Callan broke the silence. "Where is Lucia?" He cast a glance behind Cora to the gathered fae soldiers, each dressed in stunning silver armor and bearing stoic expressions.

"She wanted me to smooth the introduction," Cora explained. "She is only awaiting word that you are prepared to receive her."

"Well, let's get on with it then," Aelius stated flatly, eyeing Cora up and down suspiciously. He was still hovering near Lia, pointedly remaining between his sister and Bella.

Whatever trust they'd gained with him may have been lost, Eve realized, now that he believed Bella to be another fae in disguise, lying to gain access to his sister.

The truth was so much more, and when they found out.... She shook her head at the thought. There were too many other things to worry about now. The truth of Bella's parentage would have to wait.

A messenger was soon dispatched to the waiting fae queen, giving Eve a moment to greet her friend, embracing her tightly.

"I'm so glad you're all safe," Cora said, moving to embrace Leysa next.

"We almost weren't," Leysa said softly. "But Queen Aurelia's change...it saved us all."

Eve nodded her agreement, shuddering at the reminder of what Lia's gift had done to the Gorian soldiers. "It was...."

"Disturbing? Terrifying? Amazing?" Leysa supplied with a grim smile.

"All of those," Eve agreed.

Cora exhaled slowly. "At least you survived," she replied linking hands with them both and giving a gentle squeeze. "We're here together for now, and that's what matters."

"She's here," Callan interrupted, pointing to the east.

Atop a stunning white mare, Queen Lucia rode at the head of another small group. Dressed in a sky blue gown beneath a silver breastplate fashioned to resemble a cloudy sky, her white curls arranged artfully atop her head surrounded by a gleaming silver crown, she more closely resembled a goddess than a fae queen.

"I am glad to see that you all survived until we arrived," she said by way of greeting. "I would very much like to meet with the changelings." Her gaze slowly roamed over the group, pausing when it landed first on Eve, then on Lia. "I would know you anywhere," she said. "Even in these new forms."

Eve blinked. "Excuse me?" Confusion swept over her, and she looked to Callan. Perhaps he had some indication of who Lucia meant. But she saw only her own confusion mirrored in his frown.

"A matter we should discuss privately," Lucia replied cryptically.

"We can retire to the command tent, where Lord Bastien Devois, the commander of–" Aelius began.

"I will speak only to the queens on this matter, and the high king," Lucia interjected, shaking her head once. "Long has it been since I laid eyes on you," she said more gently, looking Callan over. "You are the picture of your father. And where is your brother?"

"Awaiting us within our camp," Callan replied, not bothering to smile in return, "with his mate."

Lucia offered a knowing smile. "It would please your mother to see the two of you reunited."

Callan gave no reply to that, only stiffening slightly at her words.

"We can meet in my personal tent," Lia offered, coming to stand at Eve's side. They would be a united front, these fae royals who stood to defend Aestera. "We will have the privacy we require."

Satisfied, Lucia nodded and motioned for Lia to lead the way. "I would like the child of Araceli to join us as well. I believe she has a story to tell, and as I am tasked with her safe return, she will remain at my side."

Eve frowned, glancing at Lia, whose eyes had once more darkened, seemingly ready to argue, but Bella nodded her acceptance of the situation, settling a long look on Lia that kept the queen silent.

As they made their way to the tent, Eve slowed her pace to allow some degree of privacy with Callan. "Can we trust her?" She was fully aware her words could be heard by each of the fae that made up their party, but she didn't care.

"She was my mother's dearest friend," Callan replied. "And the oldest of us all." A non-answer, that told Eve clearly the real answer would have to wait until they were certain to not be overheard.

"We're going back to camp," Leysa announced suddenly from behind them. "Valerian, Cora, and I. We want to check in and keep an eye on Cathal and Mara."

Valerian, who had been unusually silent, met Callan's gaze with a hard stare, something unspoken passing between the friends. At Eve's curious look, Callan shook his head.

"Later," he said gently. With that, their friends departed, leaving them to follow the other fae queens to Lia's tent.

Once inside, a warm smile replaced the more regal expression Lucia had borne, and she embraced Callan tightly. "I am truly happy to see you, my dear," she said, cupping his cheek with her palm. "It is a balm to my soul to see you and Cora well." Adding, "And mated," as she looked to Eve.

Up close, the signs of her age were more easily read, as subtle as they were. Laugh lines marked her brown cheeks, along with faint crow's feet along the corners of her eyes—one a stunning golden brown and the other the blue of a winter sky.

She appeared to be no more than her mid-sixties by human standards, but Callan had named Lucia as the oldest among them, older even than Ursa, who appeared much older. A glamour, Eve supposed, to keep herself looking more youthful than she truly was.

"You have questions," Lucia stated before Callan could reply, stepping back with a swish of her gown. "As I myself do." The ancient queen's attention turned to Bella. "Why did you remain when you must have known you'd be discovered? Surely you've had a vision of what's to come, or has your mother severed that bond as well, child?"

Standing beside Bella, Lia's face tightened. Bella simply stared back, shaking her head once. "My reasons are my own," she replied flatly.

Lucia smiled. "Very well then," she replied darting a glance to Lia. "Who am I to question the whims of a goddess?"

CHAPTER 36

LIA

oddess. The word rippled through her like a stone in a pond. Lia would have understood fae, or perhaps even a witch.

But this, this was unfathomable.

A strange, rhythmic thumping sounded in her ears as dread settled over her. "You're a goddess?" she whispered, lifting a shaking hand to cover her mouth.

Her father had imprisoned a goddess. Perhaps all of this was divine punishment then. Her heart thumped; with a shake of her head, she dismissed the thought almost as quickly as it appeared.

The goddess Helie had intervened to save them, hadn't she? Why would she, or the goddess of life, who had aided Eve, have gotten involved if that was the case?

Bella reached for Lia, taking the hand that had covered her face and giving it a squeeze. "What I am changes nothing about us. To you, I am just Bella, I will always be just Bella."

Turning to face Lucia, Bella continued, still holding Lia's hand tightly. "To you, I am Sybella, demigoddess and daughter of Araceli, the goddess of the night sky and prophecy. I am the brightest star, and I am the harbinger of cataclysm. My mother may have tasked you with my return, but you will show me the respect I am due. You have no right to issue commands here."

Lia was too stunned to take note of Lucia's response, her gaze locked solely on Bella's profile. Fear and awe battled within her, a storm of emotion only made more chaotic by three little words that rang through her mind.

"Are we going to lose?"

Eve's voice startled Lia, drawing her attention back to the present once more.

"I don't know," Bella replied gently, lips curving downward. "I doubt if my mother even knows that," she added, looking at Callan. "Or yours."

Callan nodded. "Even fate is blind to some things," he agreed.

"Will she help us?" Lia asked.

"I think she already has," Bella answered, attention returning to Lia. "By waiting until now to send someone for me. She allowed me to stay long enough to meet you, to warn you about what is to come." Turning to Lucia, Bella lifted her chin higher. "I will be going nowhere with you, and I will speak to my mother myself."

Lucia inclined her head in deference. "Of course, Callan, my dear, would you be so kind as to accompany me to our camp? There are matters I would like to discuss. I will send my commanders to confer with yours, Queen Aurelia. I assume that is acceptable?"

"Yes," Lia replied, casting a glance at Eve. "We'll speak later?"

Eve nodded, offering a warm smile before the fae rulers departed, leaving Lia and Bella alone.

"You're a goddess," Lia repeated, releasing Bella's hand before wrapping her arms around her own chest tightly.

What other surprises were going to be thrown at her?

"Demi-goddess," Bella corrected, observing Lia's reaction carefully. "But it changes nothing."

"It changes nothing?" Lia scoffed with a laugh. How could that possibly be true? She wondered. It changed everything. "You aren't who you said you were, you aren't even human, you–"

"Neither are you," Bella interjected. "And it changes nothing. What I feel for you, what I think you feel for me," she said, voice lowering as she tugged Lia's hands from where they clasped her arms tightly. When their fingers were linked once more, she continued, "There are so many things I need to tell you, so many things," she whispered, resting her forehead against Lia's. "When the time is right, I will tell you the entire story."

"And when is that?" Lia demanded, pulling her hands free and cupping Bella's face so that their eyes met. "When will I know the whole truth, Bella?" The thumping in her ears grew in intensity, but she ignored it.

Bella's expression shuttered. "When I can, I promise."

Before Lia could argue, Bella stepped away and began to douse the lanterns that kept the tent illuminated. "I am going to call on my mother. It will need to be dark," she explained as she moved the brazier that dominated the center of the space. "I want you to watch and listen, but do not speak; she is not known for her patience."

Lia could only watch in stunned silence as Bella settled onto the floor where the brazier had been, tilting her head back so that she gazed upward at the starlit sky. For several moments, nothing happened. Bella breathed in and out steadily, deeply, gaze locked on some unseen point far away in the endless night.

"Bella, I–"

Without warning, Bella's back arched, and a low groan escaped her lips. As Lia's hand extended toward her, Bella's own hand shot up, signaling her to stop.

"Do not interfere," Bella's whisper was hoarse, forced as if it came from deep within her.

From the hole above fell a single droplet of silver, like a star in liquid form. As it landed on Bella's brow, time seemed to halt. Darkness fell over the tent, for a mere heartbeat, before a faint glow began to emanate from where Bella sat–no, had been sitting. In the center stood an ethereally beautiful woman, pale with luminous silver eyes and long, flowing jet-colored hair.

"Bella?" Lia whispered, terror seizing her heart.

The strangely lovely woman turned to Lia sharply, the corner of her full lips twitching downward once. "Human," she purred in a voice as melodic as birdsong. "Ah, but human no more. Once beloved, now chosen, and forever damned."

Lia's heart seized as the woman took a step closer, forcing her to take a shuffling step back.

Where is Bella?

The thought raced through her mind as the heel of her boot snagged on something, and she began to fall backward. A pair of hands gripped her upper arm, helping to straighten her to standing.

"Stop." Bella's voice was every bit as firm as her grip on Lia's arm. "Remember yourself, Mother," she added.

"Wayward child," the woman cooed, halting her progress to look Bella over. "Sybella, brightest of stars, harbinger of cataclysm, diviner of all things. Most beloved daughter."

Dark hair slid over her bare shoulder, flowing freely across the front of her silver gown as she shifted her head, still peering at Bella as if confused. "Why have you hidden yourself from one who loves you so? Have I not yet seen the cause?"

"Mother," Bella said more gently, releasing Lia's arm now as she took a step toward her mother. "Return to the present, look no further than now."

"Present," the goddess sighed, as if releasing great unseen weight from her shoulder. "I am here, I am now." Some of the light from the silver eyes of the goddess dimmed, and she settled her gaze on Bella firmly. "Your time is up, my beloved."

"I have until the task is done," Bella countered. "The end has not yet come."

"She's not going anywhere," Lia said suddenly, surprising everyone, including herself. Where had she gotten the nerve to speak to a goddess that way? Taking Bella's hand in hers, she stood her ground. "With all due respect, it should be her decision." Meeting Bella's widened eyes, she continued. "She has a life here, people who care for her."

For several tense moments, the goddess simply stared. Her gaze somehow slipped beyond Lia and Bella, as if she were looking through them, rather than at them. Lia blinked, surprised by the lack of response to her outburst.

"She's divining the future," Bella sighed. "Trying to see what will happen."

"You have days, maybe weeks," the goddess whispered finally. "It is unclear... but the darkness, she comes–" Araceli's voice cracked, suddenly thick with emotion. "Take no longer, I beg you, daughter. She draws near."

Without warning, the soft light that had emanated from the goddess vanished, leaving nothing but dark emptiness where she stood. Only the watery light from the moon above offered any illumination.

"What does that mean? Who is coming?" Lia demanded, breathing raggedly as fear rattled through her.

Bella's expression had turned dark, shuttered. "The Void. She is the end of all things, and she's coming to kill us all."

CHAPTER 37

EVE

"I would like to see your brother. I have questions." Though Lucia's words were a statement bordering on command, she smiled softly as if making a request.

Callan hesitated a moment before nodding once. "I suppose you're owed an explanation, and he deserves to tell his story."

Eve frowned, casting a worried glance at Callan. His non-answer regarding Lucia's trustworthiness left her wary, and where Cathal was concerned there was essentially no trust. He'd declared himself their ally, where Gorias was concerned at least, but that didn't mean she'd allow him the chance to conspire against them.

"What can you tell us about Gorias?" she asked, hoping to pause the discussion surrounding Cathal for at least a little while longer.

"Oh, now that tale is old and complicated," Lucia replied, donning a knowing smile as she sank into a chair, and gestured for Callan and Eve to do the same. "I assume you know a little of the story, Callan dear?"

"Only what my tutors taught of the history, which was not much," he admitted.

Lucia nodded. "That isn't surprising; only the oldest of us truly remember what Gorias was at its peak, and why they were forced to remain solitary."

Eve and Callan took their seats and waited for Lucia to continue. Glancing skyward, the fae queen paused, pressing her lips together. "Let me see if I can recall how it began," she sighed, and tapped her fingers along the arm of the chair. "Gorias was once as glorious and lovely as any of the Crescent Kingdoms-"

"The what?" Eve asked, confused. She'd never heard the term before, outside of the prophecy that had set her on this path to begin with.

When the gods touch the crescent once more, the lost children will return and herald a new age.

"That's what we were called, long before humans arrived on our shores and each of us handed over lands for them to establish their kingdoms. If you were to lay a map out before you and label each of the four fae kingdoms, you would find that we make the shape of a crescent moon and a star. Gorias was once the star of Aestera."

Lucia paused, whether to call upon memory once more or for dramatic effect, Eve couldn't be sure. Once the fae queen continued, a sort of light entered her eyes, a faint smile gracing her lips.

"And a star she was, lovely and full of life. Gorias was a beacon of art, music, and culture. For a time, they were the pinnacle of what it meant to be fae. Many of us were envious." A shadow passed over her features as she added, "Until *he* took the throne."

"Arawn, the Ruiner," Callan stated, frowning. As if a chill wind had blown through the tent, goose pimples danced along her skin. She had never heard the name before, but something deep within her recoiled anyway.

"Who was he?" she asked, voice barely above a whisper.

"The exact opposite of what his ancestors had been," Lucia replied, shaking her head. "Despite the fact that each of us had lived in peace for longer than even the oldest fae could recall, he chose to go to war. He looked at what Gorias was, how prosperous, and decided it was not enough. He decided he wanted to conquer the other three kingdoms, to build an empire with himself as emperor."

"That was a long time before the gods departed. Did they not intervene?" Eve asked, glancing at Callan.

Callan inclined his head. "They did, but they–" he began, only to be interrupted by Lucia once more.

"Oh, they most certainly did." Her expression shifted to a sly grin. "And this, my dear, is where you come in. But there is one more thing that even you do not know, Callan."

"I know about the artifacts," he replied, brow raised.

"I'll get to that in a moment, but here is the most interesting part of the story," Lucia said, waving a hand. "Arawn didn't act alone. He had the help of someone very powerful, which was what forced the gods to intervene. Had it just been a war amongst their children, they would have waited, allowed us to come to a conclusion on our own."

"Someone powerful? Another fae?" Eve asked, frowning. The other possibility, the idea that a god would have helped him, was too outrageous to consider. But then, wasn't she living proof that the idea wasn't quite so far-fetched?

Lucia laughed. "No, dear, someone much older and much more frightening. Her name is Kore," she said, lowering her voice to a whisper. The elder fae shuddered, just as Eve felt that same unease slithering over her, making the thing inside her shrink back once more. Bella had declared that Kore once more walked in the light, and now they were going to find out just who this Kore was, what she was.

Callan shook his head. "I don't know that goddess," he frowned.

"You wouldn't, because she isn't a goddess," Lucia explained. "She is something much older, and some might say more powerful. She is the Void itself. One of the oldest primal powers, existing before even the gods."

"The primals yielded themselves to give life to their children, the gods," Callan countered. "All of them are gone."

Lucia shook her head. "Most, not all. Some still walk the worlds, coming and going as they please and never interacting. Nobody knows how or why, but for some reason, she took notice of Arawn and decided to make herself known to him. Some say she fell in love with him, if such a thing is possible for primals. She is deadly, as cunning as she is powerful, and I imagine she is rather angry after what was done to him."

Eve's heart was a steady drumming now. If primals were more

powerful than even the gods, how did they stand a chance at winning? Fear loosening her tongue, she said as much aloud.

"The artifacts," Callan supplied. "Forged by the gods for fae hands to use. Like the stone," he added, glancing at Eve. "They were made to stop Gorias."

"Yes," Lucia replied. "The Stone of Rule, the Sword of Light, the Cauldron of the Sea, and the Spear of Conquest. But you're wrong about when they were made. These weapons were forged long before the war, for reasons lost to time. What I do know is that they are the only weapons capable of slaying gods and even primals, and now she seeks them. The spear was hidden in Gorias, so it's safe to assume she has that already."

"That's why she came for Darkegrove. She wanted the stone." Eve said, recalling what Callan had already told her about it.

"Yes, but now that she knows you are fae, as well as our dear Queen Aurelia, I think she will turn her attention to the last remaining bearer."

"Naia Colvari," Eve supplied, "Queen of Coruscis. But why would she turn away from us? Why not kill us and take the artifacts? Not that we even know where they are."

"Oh that," Lucia laughed. "You've had them all along, my dear. Each of them was placed with the humans for safekeeping, as human hands could not wield them. The ancient kings of Darkegrove hid the stone amongst those in your oldest crown. The Prince of Avellon carries the sword, I'm told, and the cauldron calls the shining palace of Evertide home, though I confess I do not know where. What little land Gorias allotted to humans was soon enveloped by the fae kingdom. The spear resides in the care of their king, and as such is under the control of Kore."

"She'd need the fae to wield it for her," Callan stated.

"I do not know if she's found the reborn bearer yet," Lucia shrugged.

"The what?" Eve blinked.

"That was the next part, and the most vital," Lucia's sly grin returned. "The part of the story you'll be most interested to hear, though it may come as a bit of a shock, I'm afraid." She paused, this time for dramatic effect Eve was certain. Anticipation and anxiety coursed through her veins, and the ground began to tremble slightly beneath their feet.

"Careful, dove," Callan whispered, trailing a finger along her arm gently.

Lucia, unbothered by Eve's display of impatience, continued finally. "The bearers are said to be reborn each time the artifacts come into play." Leaning closer she added, "The very same soul must bear the artifact, do you understand? Your birth, your death, they were all written on the pages of destiny long ago, when this world was more than a speck of dust. The three of you will save, or damn, us all."

Chapter 38

Lia

"Where are we going?"

Just as she had the last three times Bella had asked, Lia simply replied, "You'll see."

The revelation Bella had dropped on her had shaken Lia to her core. Fear was a living thing within her, tense and coiling, ready to strike once again the moment she looked too long in its direction.

And yet, she wasn't about to let it take her down. Not after everything they'd already been through. They would have to face the Void, this mysterious she that Araceli and Bella both feared so much, but for now she wanted a moment or two of peace with Bella.

Much like the night they'd shared before the battle.

"Just a little further," Lia reassured Bella, casting a glance to her side in time to catch the wary expression the apparent demigoddess wore. "It'll be worth it."

True to her word, they arrived at her chosen spot within moments, followed closely by a handful of guards and a few servants armed with long swaths of fabric and tent poles.

"What are we doing here, Lia?" Bella frowned, glancing at the moonlit pond before them.

"We need an hour, to just be Bella and Lia," she replied, gesturing for the servants and guards to begin their task.

They erected the poles, hanging the fabric between them to form a sort of privacy screen between the still nearby army camp and the pond. "The guards will remain close, and we're too near the camp to be in any real danger from Gorias. It's perfectly safe for a short time–"

Tugging her hand free from Lia's grasp, Bella shook her head slowly. "I know that, but what are we *doing* here?"

Lia's smile faltered. "I thought we could use some time to–"

Bella closed her eyes and exhaled slowly. "I don't want you to put yourself in more danger by–"

"That isn't your choice to make," Lia countered, brushing a strand of dark hair back from Bella's cheek. "It's mine, and I am perfectly capable of weighing the risks."

Dark lashes fluttered upward and ethereal silver eyes met Lia's once more, making her heart skip a beat. "I could never live with being the reason you got hurt," she replied, though the resolve in her voice wavered.

"Not being with you when I have the chance, that's what would hurt me, Bella. I couldn't bear not giving whatever it is we have between us a chance." Lia leaned forward then, pressing a gentle kiss to Bella's full lips. "Give us a chance. Even if it's only for a little while."

Bella's quiet reply was cut off by the sudden crack of thunder that sounded from over- head, the night sky rending in two as a massive bolt of lightning raced from cloud to cloud. Within seconds, buckets of rain were falling, soaking them both instantly.

"Majesty, we must get you back to the tent!" one of the guards shouted, as the servants hastily undid the work they'd only just completed.

Where had that storm come from so suddenly? she wondered, looking briefly at the sky before returning her attention to Bella. It had been a normal, sunny day when they left.

"You'll die," Bella said, just loud enough to be heard over the unex-pected storm. "Even with your long fae life, you'll die long before I do. We'll have such little time. My mother...."

"Then let us take what we can have," Lia whispered, leaning so close their lips nearly touched.

The words hung between them, as electric as the lightning above. For a heartbeat, Lia feared Bella would say no, would run away and leave her there, heart laid bare, in the rain alone.

"Okay. Whatever comes, we'll have this, then. As short as it may be," Bella breathed before her lips crashed into Lia's. Her hand plunged into Lia's soaked tresses, pulling the queen closer, and claimed her mouth with a fierce and hungry kiss.

She couldn't say how long they stood in the rain, holding one another close. Each heartbeat ticked away a small eternity. When they finally pulled apart, they were in Lia's tent, though she didn't know when they'd moved, or how.

Lia's heart ached with love and fear in equal parts. The battle to come could claim either or both of them. If all they had was one more night, then she would take every moment, every touch, every kiss, and savor them.

"I want this, with you," Bella said, brushing Lia's hair back from where it stuck to her wet face. Their lips came together in a rush of need, of love and desire. The tug that pulled her closer to Bella tightened to the point of pain as their bodies collided. Clothes were discarded in a rush, a desperate need to feel Bella's skin, to taste her, to hear every sigh, every quiet cry in response to her touch, drove her.

Bella flicked her tongue over Lia's lower lip gently before dragging her backward to the bed. They were bared before one another now, and like last time, Lia took a moment to drink in the sight of her. Her chest ached at Bella's quiet beauty. She was as gentle, as ethereal as moonlight in the way she moved, the way she spoke. So much of her was a mystery, even now, even to Lia, but that only added to the wonder that was her.

On their knees, they faced one another. Lia's hand slid from Bella's face to her chest, hovering over the place where her heart hammered against her chest so intensely that Lia could feel it beneath her palm. Bella was mirroring Lia's own movements slowly, gently, and her soft hand soon found its way to Lia's chest, to feel her own heart thundering in response.

Lower now she moved, sliding her palm over the gentle curve of

Bella's breast, and then down her sides to the flare of her hips. Bella's caress against her own breast had Lia's breath hitching, earning a delighted grin from the seer.

Pressing her lips to Bella's, Lia moved her hand inward. The dampness she found between Bella's thighs was mirrored by her own, soon discovered by Bella as she followed Lia's lead. A small groan passed her lips as the kiss deepened. With slow, gentle movement, she circled the sensitive bundle of nerves at the apex of Bella's thighs with two fingers.

Her own thighs quaked, as Bella did the same. Electric jolts of pleasure rocketed through her as they both increased their pace until release found them at the same moment. The kiss deepened, intense, as they fell onto the bed, wrapped in one another's arms.

Moments later, still in the afterglow of her orgasm, Lia rose to her knees once more. "I want all of you," she said quietly. "I want to taste you, as well as feel you."

"I am yours, in any way you'll have me," Bella breathed, pale face flushed, as she spread her knees for Lia.

Pressing a trail of kisses along Bella's inner thigh, Lia ran her tongue gently against the seam of Bella's folds before slipping her tongue inside of her. Her tongue worked in and out, drawing the gasps and sighs from Bella that she loved so much.

Slowly, she moved upward, her tongue circling over Bella's clit. Bella's legs clamped tight around Lia's head, her fingers winding their way into her hair as the orgasm rushed over her. When it was over, Bella's legs fell back to the bed and Lia climbed over her, pressing a gentle kiss to Bella's forehead.

"You are my own personal moonlight," she sighed reverently. "I could bask in your glow forever."

"And you are my sunlight," Bella whispered in return. "If this is all we get, I will remember. Even when we pass to the next life, I will remember this, with you."

"Always," Lia promised.

CHAPTER 39

EVE

Thunder cracked overhead, drawing a low curse from Valerian. Eve arched a brow at her friend's reaction.

"He hates storms," Leysa supplied. "Ever since he was a boy and–"

"Do we really need to tell that story, my love?" Valerian interjected, tilting his head slightly.

"We're all friends here," Leysa shrugged.

Valerian sighed. "I got lost in the woods once as a boy, while hunting with my brother. It was scary, to a nine-year-old." Rolling his eyes good-naturedly at Leysa, he added, "That's basically it."

"Oh there's definitely more, but it doesn't matter right now," Leysa teased, tapping the end of his nose gently.

"Don't tease him, Leysa," Callan chimed in from his position at the tent opening. "We all have our fears. Want me to rehash the tale of your run-in with that dragon?"

Leysa shuddered, waving a hand animatedly. "Absolutely not."

"Did you say dragon?' Eve asked, eyes widening. She'd heard rumors, of course, of their existence but had never met anyone who had actually laid eyes on the near-mythical creatures.

"Would you like me to introduce you to one, dove? Do you like the idea of a ride atop the back of a dragon?" Callan asked, turning to face her. Something wicked danced across his features, making heat pool low in her belly. "Perhaps we'll even—"

Valerian's gagging sound stopped him short. "Were we this obnoxious when we were first mated?" he asked Leysa.

"Worse," she replied with a delighted grin.

Eve couldn't help but laugh, even as her thoughts turned to the reason they'd gathered. Lucia had left them with the huge revelation that each of the three human queens, Eve, Lia, and Naia, were more than just destined to die, become fae, and wield some magical artifacts in order to stop the end of the world—they were also reincarnated.

Because any one of those things wasn't ridiculous enough, she thought, scowling.

"What are you thinking about that's got you making that face?" Valerian asked, as Callan moved to take a seat beside her.

"The idea that my soul isn't my own. Not really."

"It is," Callan countered. "You just happen to have a small piece of the ancient warrior within you, it doesn't define you."

Lucia had said as much, before leaving to meet with Cathal in his own tent. The fae queen declared that she had questions and she would be back at the first morning light to plan and regroup. Gorias would not be quiet for long, she'd assured them.

"It's still strange," she replied, shaking her head. "It makes me wonder how much of me is really me, and how much is her. I don't know if that even makes sense."

"It makes sense to me," Leysa replied. "Some shifters have a sort of similar concern. We sometimes wonder how much of us is animal and how much fae. Mostly we find a good balance, but some struggle with it."

Eve supposed she could understand that, the balancing act of having two natures. "Is that why I dreamt of Falias, you think?"

Callan nodded thoughtfully. "Maybe, or it could have been some part of our mating bond."

Eve smiled. Her heart sang at the mention of their bond. Hers. Forever hers, as she was his. "I hope it's that, rather than this other woman's soul. I hate the idea of her being inside me, separate enough to have memories like that."

Callan lifted her chin gently with his fingertips. "Do not let it worry you, dove. Whoever you once were, it's who you are now that matters."

Eve nodded, the warmth of his fingers against her skin bolstering her. "Of course." Turning back to the others, she looked at her friends. Valerian's easy smile and gentle reassurance and Leysa's warm eyes and fierce heart offered her as much strength as Callan. How lucky she was, to have found them all.

"Lucia says Gorias will turn to Coruscis next. Naia will be an easier target, she believes, assuming she hasn't yet been gifted her powers."

"I'd agree with that," Valerian replied, straightening. "It makes less sense to fight our combined forces head-on when they can sack Thalassa while we're stuck chasing after them." Looking to Callan, he added, "Think they'll be able to pace a large enough force that far?"

"Not the entire way," Callan replied. "They'll have a huge head start, though. Assuming they've recovered from Lia's attack."

A chill ran up Eve's spine at the reminder of what she'd witnessed on the battlefield. "That reminds me," she said suddenly. "Are you aware of what Mara can do?"

All three of them shook their heads.

"Apparently a long fae life wasn't all that Astraia gifted her. She can force people to confess their greatest sin and then kill them with whatever punishment fits, although I don't know exactly how. A soldier tried to attack us, and she took him down with almost no effort."

Leysa's eyes widened as she said, "Damn."

Callan remained quiet and thoughtful, simply shaking his head in disbelief.

"Wonder what she'd see if she used it on Cathal," Valerian mused, earning a sharp look from Callan. "I'm just saying," he said, lifting his hands in defense. "We know he has secrets, and I'm doubting what he did to you is the worst thing he's ever done."

"Fair enough," Callan sighed, dragging a hand through his hair.

Eve frowned at the memory of Callan on his knees, of them trapped inside the crumbling temple. "I just thought you should know," she said finally. "She seems to be on our side, but..."

"It's smart to be aware of it," Valerian said. "We'd be stupid to pretend there isn't a risk of either of them turning on us."

For a moment, uncomfortable silence fell over the tent before Leysa spoke up again. "So we'll need to go south then, right?" she asked, looking at Valerian.

He nodded. "Yeah, I think it makes the most sense. If Lucia is right, Coruscis is in danger."

"Brida should be part of this conversation," Eve interrupted. "I don't know if she'll want to go that far. She may want to return to the north, just in case."

"I've already sent an invitation," Callan replied. "She'll be joining Valerian, Aelius, and whoever is representing Lucia, to discuss battle plans."

Eve relaxed then, nodding. "Good." Pausing a moment, she examined the tattoo, peeking out from the sleeve of her gown. "I know I'm not one of them anymore, but the humans are still my people. I want to make sure they're given the same chance to defend their homes and lives."

"Of course, dove." Her skin warmed as his thumb ran over her cheek gently. "Anything you ask will be done."

Valerian cleared his throat pointedly. "Speaking of battle plans, we should go. We're due to meet soon," he explained, rising from his seat, followed by Leysa.

"I'm meeting with some of the soldiers," she said. "Some of them have asked to leave, to go to Finias. They have family there, or friends, who they haven't seen in five hundred years."

"Of course they should," Eve replied instantly. "But is it wise to do so now?"

Valerian shared a glance with Leysa. "We won't force anyone to stay, but we're hoping most can be persuaded to wait," he explained. "We can't risk losing numbers."

Eve frowned. He was right, and as much as she hated the idea of keeping loved ones apart after they'd already waited so long, they couldn't risk losing the war now.

"Don't worry," Leysa said, offering a smile. "We'll work it out."

Eve hoped her friend was right, and as Callan pressed a kiss to her lips, whispering words of love before leaving, Eve couldn't help but feel the cold hand of dread tickle her spine.

~

LEFT ALONE, EVE FOUND HERSELF SEATED AT THE DESK, drafting three letters.

The first, to a man she thought she'd never speak to again. Memories danced through her mind as she wrote her warning, her plea for Brodie to take his family and flee south or east before war made its way to his doorstep. His wife had been expecting if Emilia was to be believed. She may have even given birth by now. If she could spare them any pain or loss, she would do so. She could only hope the letter arrived in time.

The second was, in a way, easier to write. From one queen to another, speaking of the threat that loomed over both of their kingdoms. She was sure that Naia Colvari had already been made aware of what had transpired in Darkegrove, as Lia had. This letter was less a warning and more a plea. *Find the cauldron, and call out to the gods.*

Explanations had been made, but it was difficult to convey so much nearly unbelievable truth on paper, so she had included a line asking the Queen of Coruscis to allow a visit. She would ask Callan to pace her there, as soon as she received Naia's reply.

The third, a simple note to Mason. *I need the crown; I'm coming to get it. Meet me where we parted.*

She didn't dare return directly to Stoneweald. Not with the possibility that Gorias watched and waited for her to do so. The moment the letters were dispatched, to be taken to their various recipients by bird shifters, Eve sank onto the bed. They would be departing for Coruscis soon, she knew, and yet another battle would follow.

Another woman's life would end so that she could be forever changed, as she and Lia had.

Her thoughts turned to Lia, and guilt settled in her gut. She hadn't been to see Lia since the truth about the seer had come out. It had to have been a blow, especially given the way the two women looked at one another. She wondered if Lia knew that Bella's gaze tracked her at all times, especially when she thought Lia wasn't looking. The thought of them together made her smile. Lia deserved to be happy, she truly did. Hopefully, the matter of Bella's true nature didn't stop them from finding it somehow.

"Stupid, fucking arrogant," Callan's tirade announced his presence as soundly as the sudden gust of cool breeze did. "...son of a–."

"What did Cathal do now?" she asked, brow arching.

"Oh, it's not Cathal, not this time," he replied, angrily dragging his hand through his hair. He strode across the tent, from one side to the other and back, aimless and angry.

"What happened?"

"The human commander, the older one that rides with your cousin Brida?"

"Baird?" Eve asked, puzzled. "What did he do?"

"Their scouts caught sight of a group of Gorian soldiers, moving south. Just a small number of them. So he decided to take his party and go after them."

"Brida's soldiers?" Eve jumped from the bed, alarmed. "How many? Are they?"

"That's the thing," he replied, laughing bitterly. "He had no more than thirty with him."

Eve's heart sank. What had Baird been thinking? "They died," she stated, searching his eyes for confirmation.

"All but five of them. Baird still lives."

Rage quickly roiled within her. These were her people he had sacrificed, and for what? His own hubris? She may not be Queen of Darkegrove for much longer, but for now, she was, and she would see this crime punished accordingly.

She could feel Callan's eyes on her as she dressed, hands shaking as she fastened the buttons down the front of her steel grey gown.

"What are you going to do, dove?" he asked quietly.

"I am going to remind the men of Darkegrove that they still answer to me, whether they like it or not."

CHAPTER 40

LIA

They had laid together, limbs tangled, for a small eternity. Bella was tracing small circles along Lia's arm when she finally spoke, breaking the silence that had fallen over them. "I need you to send someone for my daughter," she whispered, casting a glance skyward at the stars visible through the opening at the peak of the tent, as if afraid they might be listening—and perhaps they were. "Her name is Eyla."

"Of course," Lia replied, pressing her forehead to Bella's. "Right away."

"I wanted her far away from this war, but now...."

"You're afraid someone will go after her," Lia whispered. "I understand."

Bella nodded silently in response, pressing her lips to Lia's collarbone gently before rolling away. The sudden absence of Bella's warmth had Lia groaning quietly.

"I don't know if my mother knows about her yet," Bella said, lying flat on her back now. "I thought about sending her to the Otherworld, to my family, for her safety. But...I don't know if they'd accept her."

Lia frowned. "Why wouldn't they?"

"She's more human than goddess," Bella explained. "Her father was human. He was a good man, kind, and he loved her very much. Right now, Eyla is with his sister."

"You loved him?" Lia asked, feeling sympathy more than jealousy for what had to have been a difficult loss. She watched as Bella's chest rose and fell in the darkness, her steady breathing hitching only a moment before she nodded.

"Yes, I did. Very much."

She'd had lovers, but she'd never experienced that sort of loss before, had never really loved any of them enough to feel much more than fleeting regret when it ended.

"I'm sorry," was all Lia could think to say.

"It's the past," Bella replied, rolling to her side to face Lia. "And I am always looking toward the future," she whispered, cupping Lia's cheek gently. "Always."

The words were a comfort, easing most of the worry she felt. But the truth remained that the ghost of Bella's former love would be there always. Was it enough to discourage her from continuing down the path she was currently hurtling with the seer who had so thoroughly captured her heart? No, but it was certainly something to be mindful of as they forged this future together, whatever came next.

Chapter 41

Eve

Thunder crashed over the heads of the five remaining survivors of Baird's failed attack as they stood, two of them held up by others, ready to be judged by the Queen of Darkegrove. Lord Baird Stewart knelt on the sodden ground a few feet in front of the others, just in front of Eve.

"You are charged with putting the lives of each and every soldier here in danger," Eve said, her tone as cold as the rain that fell on them. At her side, Brida looked down at the men with an icy rage so intense it was nearly palpable. "You failed to obey the orders of not only your commander, Lady Brida Lyon, but of your *Queen*."

Baird stared back, eyes simmering. "I did what I thought was best, *Majesty*," he spat at her. "You abandoned your people to play the whore for these...voidspawn. As far as I'm concerned you have no rights over my men anymore," he continued, struggling to rise to his feet thanks to his bound hands. "I will accept my punishment, but only because *she* has earned it." His gaze turned to a stunned Brida.

Shadows wreathed around Baird's throat, tightening until his face turned a deep purple. "She is your queen," Callan said, voice lethal and calm. "You will still your disrespectful tongue or you will lose it."

"He is my subject, for a little longer at least," Eve said to Callan, lifting a hand. Thick vines rose from the ground, wrapping around Baird's body like twin serpents, constricting as they grew. Callan recalled his shadows, and as Eve's vines found their way to Baird's face, she stepped closer, whispering for his ears only. "If you had been but a little more patient, you would have lived to see her crowned."

BAIRD'S BODY WAS BURNED SHORTLY AFTER. CRIMINALS AND traitors were not granted the peace of becoming one with the earth, by Northern customs. The others who had followed him were allowed to keep their lives and handed over to Brida's officers, who had rather creative ways of enforcing their rules, she'd been told. The thought had her shuddering, but she hadn't dared to question it.

Shortly after, inside Brida's command tent, the two cousins stared at one another over a low table, situated between their two chairs. "You want me to be queen?" Brida asked, stunned.

"I can think of none better," Eve replied.

"I don't understand," Brida said slowly.

Above, thunder crashed once more, giving Eve a moment to pause while she collected her thoughts. In the dim light offered by a scattering of iron lanterns hung on poles around the interior, Brida's face was a portrait of confusion.

"A fae queen cannot rule over a human kingdom. I cannot allow Falias to be seen as trying to conquer Darkegrove. I have to pass the throne to someone, and I would like it to be someone as committed to changing things, to protecting all who call Darkegrove home, as I am."

Brida exhaled slowly, looking to the side a moment as she considered Eve's words. "But the council–"

"May make things difficult," Eve interjected. "But how can they stand in opposition to one of the heroes who saved Aestera?" she smiled.

"Well," Brida laughed, "we haven't quite accomplished that yet."

"No, but we will." Eve paused. "Will you accept?"

Brida grinned, pride lighting her face. "How could I not? Someone has to finish what you started."

CHAPTER 42

LIA

"We're going south, toward Thalassa," Aelius said, pointing at the map.

Dawn had barely broken when the meeting had been called. Aelius and Bastien, alongside a handful of other Avellonian officers, gathered inside the command tent.

Somewhere on the other side of the massive combined forces camp, she knew, the leaders of Falias, Darkegrove, and Finias were each holding a similar meeting.

"Everyone was in agreement?" Lia asked, examining the path that Bastien had marked along the map.

"Yes," Aelius said. "Aside from the small group that idiot from Darkegrove attacked, there have been no signs of Gorias in the area. It's like they vanished after..."

"After she burned their eyes from their skulls?" Bastien finished helpfully, looking almost giddy at the idea.

Lia's cheeks heated. She'd saved her people but the violence of it still made her feel guilty, and frankly a little ill. "I didn't know that would happen," she mumbled, frowning.

"You saved us all," Bastien replied. "Don't feel guilty about that."

"Right," she sighed, nodding. "So, preparations have begun?" She already knew the answer but was desperate for a change in topic.

"Yes," Aelius replied, meeting her gaze. A small nod of reassurance was the only indication that he understood. "We need to resupply and regroup, but we should be leaving in two days."

"I need a couple of people we can trust to go and get someone for me," she began, casting a glance at Bella, who stood beside her. "A few men who can be discreet, but who are absolutely loyal, and a maid who is good with children."

Aelius and Bastien shared a puzzled look, but the latter nodded. "Sure, I can think of a few like that. Who are they fetching?"

"My daughter," Bella explained. "Her name is Eyla Avoden, and she's in the village of Alyere. I need her brought here."

Aelius stared at Bella for a long moment, not bothering to hide the disdain in his glare or his voice as he spoke. "And why would we do anything for you?"

"Because I am ordering you to," Lia replied instantly, temper flaring. "If she makes a request, it is to be treated as a command from me," she added, looking at each and every person gathered in the tent. "I want that to be made clear. Bella is to be treated with respect, and her requests are to be honored. If anyone has an issue with that they can come see me. Do you understand?"

Bastien grinned and Aelius frowned, but both nodded, followed by each of the other officers and advisors.

"Understood," Bastien replied for all of them.

"Now, have the men sent to Alyere immediately. I want the girl brought here safely. Bella will send a letter along with them for her caretaker, to ensure that she'll allow them to take her. I need her here before we leave."

Bastien eyed the map, noting the distance between Alyere and where they currently stood. "I think it can be done."

"Make it happen," she replied as she left. "Let me know when they leave."

∼

They were nearly back at the tent when Bella finally spoke. "Thank you for standing up for me." Her tone was enough to make it clear to Lia that such a thing was a rarity for Bella.

"You don't have to thank me for that," Lia said, stopping and taking Bella's hand in hers. "Not ever."

Bella's smile was nearly as warm as the bright sun overhead, and Lia's heart sang in response. This thing between them, as short-lived as it might be, was real, and for the first time in a long time, Lia felt truly alive and whole. She'd been happy before, of course. Her life had been blessed, and she had known lovers who had made her content, while it lasted. But the moment Bella had walked into her life it felt like suddenly she'd found a missing piece of her she hadn't even known existed. It was more than she could've ever expected to have.

"There's something I need to tell you. I've decided that I'm not–"

A shout from nearby drew their attention, stopping Bella short.

"Are you one of them now?" a soldier demanded, slurring his words as he stumbled closer. "Those void damned monsters that you've commanded us to fight?"

Bella pulled Lia's arm gently, urging her away from the intoxicated man as he approached. Lia gave no response but held her ground as other soldiers approached slowly, seemingly curious to hear the queen's response.

"I am no monster if that's what you think. I am the same as I have ever been, and I ask you to fight to save us all."

The man snorted at that, gesturing wilding in her direction with both hands. "Look upon the beast," he snarled. "The one who still calls herself our queen." He stumbled forward a step and still, none of the guards intervened. "My brother was there you know, on that hilltop. He saw what happened. He saw you die."

Lia's heartbeat was thunder in her ears. She had been covering her ears and had refused to speak of what had happened on the hill. But there had been soldiers with her, and they had witnessed her death and resurrection–had seen the light flowing from her and spilling over the battlefield. There had also been soldiers present for several of the meetings between herself and the other fae. It wasn't necessarily a secret, just something she hadn't addressed; admittedly out of fear. Her foolish mistake was now catching up with her it seemed.

It was time to speak the truth, even if this wasn't the ideal situation.

"Yes," she said, straightening and meeting his gaze levelly. "Your brother speaks true. I did, in fact, die." She paused, glancing around at the crowd that was beginning to gather. At Aelius and Bastien now shoving their way through to her. "And the goddess Helie, of sun and healing, intervened. I have been given a task to complete, one that required my death, and rebirth in a new form."

"Lies," the drunk man spat. "You're a monster like the rest, and you're going to get us all killed!"

Lia's gaze shot back to the man. "No, I, and the fae of Falias and Finias, are pledged to fight this evil that threatens us to save–"

"Lies!" he shouted once more, whipping his hand toward her so quickly that she didn't have time to block the blow to her face.

Her eyes closed as her head jerked to the side, pain lancing its way across her face. Thankfully, being so deep in the drink left him clumsy and his blow uncoordinated. As she opened her eyes once more, she found the man lying on the ground, staring at her, eyes wide with terror as blood dripped from his nose.

Bella was between Lia and her attacker, blood marring her knuckles, hands hanging loosely at her side. Lia's stunned gaze drifted to the side, where Aelius and Bastien shoved their way through the crowd of soldiers, none of whom made a move to help her to her shock. Instead, each of them fell to their knees, one by one, staring at her with a mixture of awe and terror painting their features.

The drunk man sputtered as Bastien hauled him to his feet. "Soleil," he murmured. "Soleil, soleil."

Lia frowned, not understanding the word or the reactions of those gathered. "What?" She asked, turning to Aelius with confusion, only to find her twin staring at her with wide eyes, awestruck. "Why is everyone looking at me like that?"

"You're...glowing, Li-Li."

Lia's gaze shot down to her hands. Tan skin now glowed, as Aelius had said, with light that seemed to come from within her. Bella spun to face her, expression still tight with anger from the man's attack.

Without thought, Lia took Bella's hand in her own, laying her palm flat over the bruised knuckles. Warmth seeped from her hand to Bella's, though she had no idea how.

Bella's sharp intake of breath had Lia releasing her, letting her hands fall to the side. The skin that had been bruised in her defense of Lia was now perfectly unmarred as if the act of violence had never occurred. Lifting her hand, Bella turned to the crowd.

"Does this look like the work of a monster to you?" she demanded of the soldiers gathered. "Do monsters heal? Do monsters save your lives when all seems lost?" Her gaze bored into the now silent drunken soldier who had struck Lia. "You owe her your life, every single one of you. Yet you attack your queen; or worse, do nothing to come to her aid when she is attacked. Pitiful, fearful, weak bastards. All of you."

With that, she grabbed Lia by the hand and led her the rest of the way into the tent without once looking back. By the time they were alone again, with the awfulness of what had occurred outside left beyond the tent flaps, Lia was no longer glowing.

"You've healed yourself too," Bella said, gingerly pressing her fingers to the place where the man's fist had connected. She had felt the blow, had fully expected to have a nasty bruise and probably an even nastier headache for a few days, but somehow felt none of that. She sent a silent prayer of thanks to Helie for that. Bella paused, her fingers stilling on Lia's cheek. "You didn't deserve any of what just happened."

Lia's skin tingled where Bella touched her, sending a wave of elation through her. "They're frightened," she replied, gaze roaming over Bella's face. From her starlight eyes, framed by thick dark lashes, to her lush mouth, with the faintest freckle just above her top lip. She could spend eternity mapping Bella's face and still find something new she hadn't noticed. "You'll have to forgive them, they don't mean it."

"For mistreating you?" Bella countered. "Impossible."

To Lia's disappointment, Bella stepped away, taking a few strides before turning her back to Lia as she idly toyed with something on top of the dresser. "But, I suppose I had better pretend, at least," she continued, tilting her head slightly to cast a glance over her shoulder. "If I am to remain at their queen's side, for as long as she'll allow it."

Lia's heart thundered. "What?" she blurted, in disbelief. "You're staying? I thought your mother wouldn't allow–"

"My mother may think she commands me, but she does not," Bella replied firmly, turning to face Lia. "She can demand my return, but she has no right to enforce it." Crossing back to Lia, she linked their hands. "The idea of not having a life with you, it's impossible. I have no idea how long we'll have, until time parts us or until you're tired of me, but I will stay by your side, in your arms, for as long as you like."

"Forever," Lia breathed before pressing her lips to Bella's. "Forever."

Chapter 43

Eve

It was finally time to return to the North, to retrieve the crown bearing the artifact that she was somehow destined to wield in order to save the world.

"I want to go back with you," Cora said, as Eve and Callan clasped hands, prepared to pace to meet with Mason.

"Why?" Callan asked, brow raised.

Cora straightened, somehow managing to look down her nose at her much taller brother. "I have my reasons."

Whatever Cora's reasons were, they had her cheeks flushing slightly. "We won't be there long enough for much conversation," Eve said gently. "And we need you here so that our absence isn't discovered."

Cora's gaze turned to the side, considering. "Will you deliver a note to Mason then? I– there is something I need to apologize for."

"What did–"

"Of course," Eve said, silencing Callan with a look. "There's parchment and a quill on the desk."

It took Cora only moments to write whatever apology she had to write to Mason and return the sealed note to Eve, who took it with a smile. "I'm sure you'll get a chance to apologize in person soon," she said.

Cora simply smiled, and stepped back as Callan wrapped both arms around Eve, prepared to pace.

"Remember," Callan said as the familiar wind and darkness began to gather around them. "We're here, in our tent and not to be disturbed."

Cora nodded, understanding. "I'll make sure of it," she said, and then they were gone.

Though she'd begun to become accustomed to pacing, the sudden feeling of freefall, then the encompassing darkness and sheer nothingness that surrounded them still made her stomach lurch at first.

Within the span of a few heartbeats, they were on the road just outside of Eleysia, where they had last seen Mason before his departure for Stoneweald, and theirs for Avellon. He approached from several feet away with a handful of human guards and a small case in his hands.

"We weren't sure how long it would take you," he said by way of greeting, offering Eve a tight smile as he reached them and ignoring Callan entirely. "We've been camping nearby since we arrived yesterday."

Callan released his hold on Eve, and she stepped free of his arms, catching just enough of a glimpse of his face to see the frown he offered Mason. There was still no love lost between them, she noted, though she hadn't really expected there to be.

"We tried to give you some time to find it and then make your way here," she replied. His response to the letter had been returned instantly, with assurances that he would find the crown and return to the meeting place as soon as possible.

"Well, here we are," he replied, offering the box containing the crown with outstretched hands.

Callan took the box, much to Mason's apparent annoyance. The human still failed to acknowledge her mate, earning a sigh from Eve. She'd have to try to smooth things over later, but more important matters needed to be addressed right now and she simply didn't have the time.

"I have a letter for you," she said, tugging the note free from her pocket. "From Cora."

Mason's surprise was sudden, and though quickly hidden beneath a facade as he took the note, genuine. "Oh?"

"She said she had to apologize for something. I don't know what happened, but I hope that you two get to speak and fix whatever it is soon."

Mason's expression darkened, his eyes swimming with some emotion she couldn't identify. "Thank you," he said quietly.

Callan extended his free hand to Eve. "If that's all finished, we need to return, dove. Cora won't be able to keep them at bay for long."

Eve wordlessly placed her hand in his and took one last long look at her home. Hope burned within her chest. Hope that she would live to see this place again, hope that they would win this war and wipe the threat of Gorias, and Kore, from the mortal world for good.

"Oh!" she blurted, remembering the question she'd meant to ask. "Lord Gray, is he well? Has he been to Eleysia yet?"

Mason shook his head. "Not yet. He says he's waiting to see it alongside his Queen."

Eve's heart gave a squeeze. "Then tell him I will do my very best to end this war quickly so that I may personally escort him."

Mason nodded, offering an approving smile. "I wish you well, Majesty."

As the darkness enveloped her once more, returning her to the reality of battle and death that awaited her, Eve inhaled the sweet fragrance of the northern forests that she so dearly loved and made a silent vow to do exactly as she'd promised.

CHAPTER 44

LIA

"I'm so sorry we didn't share this with you sooner," Eve was saying. Lia could barely hear her over her the warning bells sounding in her ears. There had been so much more to the story, and Eve was keeping secrets.

Her gaze shifted to the fae queen Lucia standing beside Callan, then to the sword and crown that rested on the table between them. "Why didn't you?" she demanded quietly.

"Truthfully?" Eve began, frowning. "I wanted to be sure I could retrieve the crown before I brought this to you. I was afraid it was already lost; that Gorias found it when they sacked the castle," Eve paused. "I was afraid of giving you false hope."

"That isn't your decision to make! You are not my queen, I am your equal," Lia snapped, surprising even herself. Eve's responding flinch sent a wave of guilt washing over her but she pressed on, this time in a more even tone. "I can understand and appreciate your desire to protect me, but you must treat me as your fellow queen, not just your friend. Not where this is concerned."

Callan's expression had darkened, she noted, and shadows were beginning to swirl around his shoulders, but she ignored it. Eve inclined her head. "Of course. I am sorry," her friend said sincerely.

"If you two are quite finished," Lucia said, her gentle tone at odds with her sharp words. "We need to discuss the third queen and the other artifacts."

"I sent word to her," Eve said, slowly, casting a wary glance at Lia. Yet another secret. Another action taken without bothering to tell Lia first. "I've asked to visit."

"How can you do that?" Lia asked. "It's at least a few days' ride to Thalassa and there's likely an entire army out there somewhere waiting to kill you."

"Pacing," Callan replied, as if she should know what that meant.

"You know I don't know what that is," Lia replied tightly.

Callan, finally looking somewhat regretful, cast a glance at Eve. "It's a way of travel that some fae can use. It's sort of like walking through the space between worlds. We can easily reach places across great distances, though it is difficult if we've never been there."

"You're going to pace to Thalassa?" Lia asked, the word feeling foreign on her tongue. "Have you been there before?"

Callan frowned. "Once," he admitted, "a very long time ago."

Lia's gaze shifted to Eve as she tensed beside him, presumably waiting for whatever Lia would say next. "Can you do it?"

"As long as they haven't changed the architecture of the palace too much," he replied drily.

Eve frowned. "We haven't heard from Naia Colvari yet, and we won't go until she's agreed. I don't think we'd receive a warm welcome if we simply appeared in her home. When she replies, we'll send another letter, explaining what to expect."

Lia sighed, resigned. There was nothing she could do about choices made in the past but choose to accept them and move on. "Well, I suppose this is what we have to work with. Let's make the best of it." Turning to Lucia, she gestured toward the crown and the sword Aelius had begrudgingly handed over. "What do we do with these?"

Lucia laughed, "Well, I suppose you'll have to ask the gods that. I have no idea."

"Okay," Lia replied, dragging the word out. "Do we know if Gorias has the spear?"

"Not for certain, but it's a safe bet," Callan replied. "It hasn't been seen outside their kingdom in centuries, longer even."

"How do we keep these safe until we get to Thalassa?"

Lucia gestured to Eve and Lia in turn. "I suggest you keep them close. If what the gods claim is true, then only you will be able to wield them, and if Gorias comes for them, you'll need them."

Lia met Eve's forest green eyes and nodded. "That is what we'll do then," Eve replied for both of them.

"Aelius is going to be so pissed," Lia mused, smiling despite herself.

CHAPTER 45

EVE

Another day passed without word from Naia, and it was time to move south. Eve had sent yet another letter to Naia, explaining what was happening, this time all but begging for an audience. Perhaps the arrival of their army, or that of Gorias, would spur the southern queen into action.

The silence coming from Coruscis had her worried. While Naia was known for her stubbornness and sometimes standoffishness, this was too much, even for her. Continuing to wait was foolish, and they were running out of time.

"If we don't hear back soon," Eve said, giving Ventia a gentle pat on her neck as she settled into her saddle. "We should send a messenger to request a meeting in person. Perhaps one of the shifters?"

Her previous letters to Naia had been sent the conventional way, through crows this time. They hadn't wanted to risk a shifter flying over the Gorian forces, on the off chance they were found out. But if something was wrong, maybe the risk would be worth it. Especially if the shifter they sent could gain a personal audience with the queen.

"Is it like her to ignore our letters?" Callan asked.

The horns sounded, announcing the start of their march south, and off they went. Thousands of men and women from four kingdoms, united in their resolve to defend Aestera. It would be slow, so slow, moving this many people and their supplies, but with so many to move and so few able to pace, there was little to be done about it.

"To delay her response until it suits her? Yes. She can be a little... difficult at times. But to ignore them entirely? No." Eve tossed her braid over her shoulder, giving a shake of her head. "She may be hot-headed and mercurial, but she is an ally. Her family have always been firm allies of Avellon and Darkegrove."

Her thoughts turned to a great fire that had ravaged the North a decade ago. A freak lightning strike had ignited a tree, and the flames soon spread. An entire forest had been decimated along with homes, farms, and nearly entire towns before the rainy season began and doused the last of the flames.

As a heavily forested kingdom, they were accustomed to the blazes that sometimes broke out, especially in the heat of summer, but this one had been monumental and had tested the kingdom's ability to recover.

Famine had swiftly followed, owing to the loss of farmland and orchards, and lack of habitat for the game animals they depended on. Their sister kingdoms had been called upon for aid, and both had responded swiftly.

Lia's family had sent grain and fruit stores from Avellon, with the Colvaris sending preserved fish, and other meats and vegetables from Coruscis in great numbers, saving many lives.

Even as a teenager Eve had understood the magnitude of the undertaking and what it symbolized for the kingdoms of Aestera. The treaty that bound them still held firm, and Darkegrove was not alone.

"They won't abandon us," she added. "If she doesn't reply by the time we reach the border, something is very wrong."

Callan nodded his understanding, saying only, "Then we'll send someone."

 from the border. She sat quietly on the floor of the tent, atop a pile of furs and rugs brought from home. The farther south they'd traveled, the warmer it became, and she'd found it unnecessary to have them on the bed any longer. Across from her, Leysa and Valerian were engaged in a quiet conversation that had Leysa giggling every so often. She could have easily listened in if she desired thanks to her heightened hearing, but she'd learned over the last few months how to tune out certain things.

The quiet moments with these people who had become like family to her were a balm to her troubled soul. It was the peace amongst the chaos of their lives. She sighed, leaning back against her mate comfortably. Callan's heartbeat was a steady drumming against her back, his fingers tracing idle paths along her arms left bare by the short-sleeved tunic she wore. The warmer weather certainly had its benefits.

To her shock, Cathal and Mara had decided to join them for dinner in their tent and had remained after, as had their friends. The pair sat to her left, with Cora acting as a buffer, physical and metaphorical, between her brothers.

"I'm going to ask a question, and I want you two," Eve said, leveling a flat stare at Cathal, and flicking Callan's thigh gently, "to behave. Understood?"

Cathal snorted, earning a sharp look from Mara who sat on his other side. "You agreed," she reminded him.

He immediately inclined his head, pressing a kiss to her forehead. "Alright."

"As long as the only flames in this tent are in this brazier, I agree," Callan replied in a wry tone.

"Good," Eve replied, not at all convinced. From the looks on Leysa and Valerian's faces, they weren't either.

Brida, seated to Eve's right, watched, eyes widening slightly. "Flames?" she mouthed, earning an apologetic smile from Eve in affirmation.

"So," Eve went on, returning her attention to Cathal, "I know that Callan thought he had..." She paused, searching for the right words, the ones that would get her point across without starting a fight.

"Imprisoned me forever?" Cathal supplied, not at all helpfully.

Mara rolled her eyes.

Eve winced. "Yes?"

"You want to know how I got free," Cathal said, his pale grey eyes flicking to Callan behind her. "I'm shocked he hasn't asked himself."

"I was waiting until more important matters were dealt with," Callan shrugged.

Cathal raised a brow, looking thoroughly unconvinced. "There was a fire," he explained finally. "Not mine," he added at the sharp inhales taken by several of them. "Nature herself caused this one, I suppose. But it destroyed what remained of the temple. I assume the wards were tied to the trees around it, or perhaps the very stones." He waved a hand dismissively. "I do not know, but whatever the case, there was a massive fire, and then suddenly my wards were gone."

Eve's heart skittered in her chest. "That was ten years ago?" she asked.

Cathal nodded. "The great fire that nearly burned your entire kingdom to ash."

"Lightning," she corrected, frowning.

"Lightning?"

"Yes, they think lightning struck one of the trees and started the fire."

Cathal's face split into a predatory grin. "How ironic."

"How so?"

His gaze shifted to his brother once more, something gleaming in his eyes that put Eve's nerves on edge. "Because Lir is one of the gods that created the artifacts, one of the gods destined to bless the three chosen queens."

"Who is Lir?" Brida and Eve asked in unison.

Cathal rolled his eyes as Leysa spoke up. "Lir is the god of storms and seas," she explained. "Lightning would be part of his domain."

"But," Valerian tacked on, "that doesn't necessarily mean that he was involved."

"After all of this, you really don't think they would push a little to ensure certain events unfold the way they wanted them to?" Cathal asked with a laugh. "You already know they do. Your mate, brother, is the perfect example of that. She wouldn't be here without the intervention of the gods, on more than one occasion. Tell me, was your dear mother, may her soul rest in the

Otherworld, aware of the intervention of the goddesses in her life?"

Callan tensed behind her. They hadn't known Cathal was aware of Keithia's intervention, that her help had been what allowed her parents to conceive her after years of struggling to bear a child. Five pairs of eyes shot to Eve.

"What does that mean?" Brida demanded, straightening.

Eve shot daggers at Cathal with her gaze before turning to Brida to answer. "My parents had difficulty conceiving. The goddess Keithia intervened."

Brida's eyes widened as she sat back again. "Wow."

"But that still doesn't mean that this god, Lir, nearly burned my entire kingdom to the ground to free you," Eve stated, turning back to Cathal with a frown. "Why not just let you out?"

"Because truth needed to be hidden as something mundane, I would assume," he replied with a shrug, looking utterly unconcerned. "But what do I know of the whims of gods?"

"It could as easily have been Aden then," Cora said quietly. "You bear his gift."

Cathal's expression darkened. "No, he wouldn't help me."

"People died in that fire. A lot of people. Those that did survive lost homes, farmland..." Brida's voice quaked with quiet rage. "Why do all of this just to free you?"

"You'd have to ask the gods that, human," Cathal shrugged again, lifting a hand to brush Mara's dark hair over her shoulder. "But whatever their reasons, I am grateful they did."

Silence, thick and filled with varying emotions ranging from contemplative to angry, filled the tent. While she certainly didn't know the inner workings of the minds of gods, Eve knew they had reason for everything they did. That much she had learned. If they'd gone through so much trouble to not only free Cathal but to hide their actions, then he was going to play a part in this unfolding drama of theirs, but what would it be? One thing was clear enough– If the gods wanted him free, they must have considered him beneficial to their cause.

Valerian and Leysa shared a look before the latter spoke up. "We're going back to our tent. We'll be leaving early, and this one needs his beauty sleep." Valerian made a show of rolling his eyes, despite the grin he offered his wife.

Soon after, Mara and Cathal departed, bidding them vague and half-hearted goodnights, followed by Cora and Brida.

Once alone again, Callan and Eve began to ready themselves for bed.

"Do you think that Lir caused the fire?" she asked quietly, a million thoughts and emotions raging through her.

Callan sighed, shaking his head. "Honestly? I think it's possible. If the gods needed him to be in our path, they would certainly intervene. Macaria would call it fate finding a way."

"A lot of people died," she snapped, yanking the sheets back harder than necessary. The ground beneath their feet gave a slight tremble at her tone as she dropped onto the bed.

"Careful, dove," he whispered, easing into bed beside her. "We don't know for sure, and even if Cathal is right, there is nothing to be done now."

"I know," she muttered, lying back against the pillows. "But it was a cruel way to do it. Surely they could have found a way to release him that didn't hurt so many innocents."

Callan murmured his agreement, pulling her into his arms, and she nestled her face in the space between his shoulder and the column of his neck. "Not all of them care for mortal life as much as Keithia and Helie. Their domains make their bond to the mortal realms more firm, but some are more...disconnected."

"When this is done, I hope I never see them again."

"Until we cross into the Otherworld," he agreed, caressing her hair.

"Until then," she agreed, before drifting off into a fitful sleep.

CHAPTER 46

LIA

"You want my sword?" Aelius stared at her, dumbfounded. "Why?"

"Apparently it's a gods blessed artifact that I need to wield," Lia replied, feeling ridiculous, despite speaking only the truth.

Aelius blinked a few times, no doubt processing the most recent unexpected news dropped into their laps by the fae. At least this latest revelation hadn't been delivered by yet another god, showing up out of the blue. Lia wasn't sure she could take another divine appearance just yet.

"Well, if that's all," he muttered sarcastically, loosening the sheath from his back and handing the sword over. "Take care of it."

"Thought I'd throw it in a lake and see what happens," she replied drily, taking the sword with no small degree of reverence. "Is it supposed to do something special when I hold it, you think?"

"Who knows? But maybe just...take it outside before you test that out. I'd rather not be blinded, or burned, or something, if your magic goes crazy," he replied, waving a hand.

Lia winced. He had only been teasing her, of course, but the fact was, it was entirely likely she could accidentally do just that. She had no control over when her powers manifested, or how. Perhaps Bella knew

199

some way for her to learn, and if not, there were plenty of fae around to ask. She'd have to ask Eve for some assistance. Perhaps there was someone skilled with magic similar to hers within their camp who would be willing to help.

"I'll be careful," she promised, unable to keep her voice as light as intended.

Aelius sighed, shoulders slumping slightly. "I didn't mean it, Li-li, not really."

"I know." She offered him a reassuring smile before leaving.

The walk back to her tent was short, especially now that he had insisted on moving his own closer after the incident with the drunk soldier. An unnecessary precaution, seeing as how most people now bowed a little deeper, some even sinking fully to their knees when she passed.

The blessing offered by the goddess Helie, and her new status as a fae, created by the gods, afforded her even more esteem than she'd been given as simply their queen, now that they'd seen more than just the destructive side of her magic. Many who had not seen it for themselves doubted that the magic they'd seen wipe out so many of Gorias' soldiers and heal their own, had come from her, but after the incident with the drunken soldier, too many had seen her literally glow with their own eyes to doubt it now.

Inside the privacy of her tent, Lia gingerly placed the sword on the table and turned to Bella, who eyed the artifact as if it were a serpent ready to strike.

"Be very careful with that thing, sunshine," Bella warned.

"How can I know what it even does? I'm afraid to touch anything but the sheath."

"We'll have to find a place to test it, where nobody is around. Just in case," Bella replied, dragging her gaze from the sword. "It should, in theory, only react when you command it to. But it's been waiting a long, long, time for you. It may be impatient and unpredictable."

Lia laughed nervously, as a chill ran down her spine. "You speak as if it's alive."

Bella shrugged, wary attention returning to the sword. "In a way, it almost is. Not intelligent, but alive enough to recognize its true bearer, and respond to your call."

A shudder ran through Lia at the thought. "That's...a little disturbing."

"Your magic isn't really any different," Bella replied. "You'll learn to control it, and soon enough it'll be little more than an extension of yourself– of your wants and needs."

"I was going to talk to you about that," Lia replied, all but falling into the nearest chair. "How do I control it?"

Bella grinned. "I can show you," she replied softly. "Give me your hand."

Lia obeyed instantly because she was desperate to learn, but also because she found that without Bella's touch, it felt as though a small piece of her was missing. The sensation of Bella's hand cradling her own had her racing heart calming, as a strange sort of peace washed over her.

Like stepping out into an early spring night and inhaling the cool air for the first time.

Lia watched carefully as Bella pulled a small dagger from her boot with her free hand, silver eyes meeting her own. "Do you trust me?" Bella asked, holding the dagger just inches from Lia's palm.

"With my life," Lia replied breathlessly, truthfully.

This woman had managed to lay claim to her heart. Every smile, every laugh, and every time she so bravely chose to remain and fight for the lives of mortals, made Lia love her just a little bit more. So much strength lay behind those silver eyes of hers.

They'd promised to accept whatever time they had together, but Lia wondered if there was any way one life would be enough. "What are you–"

Bella smiled, then sliced Lia's palm wide open.

Lia inhaled sharply as crimson bloomed in her palm. "Why did you do that?" she cried, attempting to pull her hand from Bella's grip, but finding that even with her newfound strength, she couldn't free herself.

"Heal yourself," Bella replied patiently.

"I can't!" Lia all but shouted, silently cursing the tears that welled in her eyes. Hurt, both physical and emotional, coursed through her. Nobody had ever intentionally wounded her before.

Nobody who mattered, anyway, she silently corrected herself.

Bella held the knife, brow raising as Lia jerked her hand once more, and released her grip finally. "You can do anything, but if you won't do it for yourself, then do it for me," Bella replied before plunging the knife into her own abdomen. "Now save me, my love," she whispered as the knife clattered to the floor.

Panic blossomed in Lia's chest like a sunflower greeting the sun. Her heart raced, pain in her palm completely forgotten as she quickly placed both hands against Bella's wound. "What do I do?" she demanded, voice rising an octave. "Someone call a healer!" She shouted for the guards outside. "Why did you do that?" She sobbed, anger and fear waging a war within her.

"Heal me," Bella replied shakily. "Just focus, feel what you want your magic to do for you. It's a part of you, make it bend to your will."

Lia's hands were quivering, so much so that blood seeped freely through her fingers as she continued to press as hard as she could. Closing her eyes, she took a steadying breath. This magic may not have been something she had been born with, but it was hers. It was a part of her, as Bella said, and she would make it obey.

Heal her, save her, heal her, save her.

The words echoed through her mind as warmth flowed through her veins. She pictured the sun above, a sweet summer day, a warm breeze lifting Bella's hair as they walked hand in hand. Bella laughing, tilting her lovely face to the sky. Unharmed and whole.

"Open your eyes, my love," Bella whispered. "Open your eyes."

Lia did no such thing.

Squeezing her eyes tighter, she shook her head. Tears rained down her face, she could feel it. She should listen and look into Bella's eyes one more time, just in case the healers didn't make it in time. *Why had I been so stupid?*

Her magic was so new, she had no idea–

"Open. Your. Eyes." Bella's commanding tone had Lia obeying finally, and what she saw had her jaw dropping.

Not only was Bella smiling, but a warm glow surrounded them both. Dropping her hands, Lia saw that not only did the blood no longer flow, but Bella's wound was now closed, leaving only a pink scar that was already beginning to fade.

Bella leaned forward, cupping Lia's cheeks gently with her palms. "You did it," she whispered.

Relief washed over her. Bella was going to be okay, her wound was healed and she was going to be okay. She could breathe again, and her heart seemed to beat for the first time since Bella had plunged the knife into herself.

The light guttered as the tent flap opened.

"Majesty, you called for a healer? Are you injured?" the soft tones of an older woman drew Lia's attention briefly.

"We're fine, it was a misunderstanding. Leave us please," Lia said as calmly as she could, dismissing the frowning woman with a forced smile.

The moment they were alone once more, she pulled away from Bella's touch, pressing the back of her bloodied hand to her mouth. "How could you?" she whispered hoarsely.

"I needed you to see that you could do it," Bella retorted, giving Lia a surprised look.

"I thought you were going to die!" Lia shouted. She was shaking now, her entire body trembling with anger or fear– likely both. "You had no right to–"

"If you weren't afraid, truly afraid," Bella countered, rising from her chair, "you would have let your self-doubt keep you from seeing how truly incredible you are." Bella dragged a hand through her midnight hair and scoffed. "You have no idea, do you? How amazing and powerful you are, even without your new gifts. Aurelia, you could do anything, anything in this world, and yet you hide behind fear and doubt."

"I don't hide," Lia shot back, anger rising. "I am not a coward."

"No, you aren't." Bella crossed the space between them, taking Lia's face in her hands. "You are brave and selfless, but only when it comes to saving others. Allow yourself to be powerful, to be right," Bella whispered.

"I'm not– I don't," Lia began, unable to deny the fact that self-doubt was a struggle she faced. The uncertainty of her ability to rule had caused her to argue with her father about taking the throne, despite having been raised to one day rule. It was why she so often allowed others to make the decisions, or at least heavily influence them. Aelius in particular had been a crutch for her for a very long time.

"Show your people how capable and strong you are," Bella breathed, pressing a kiss to Lia's lips softly. "Show the world you are truly the Queen of Light. Bring solace to this damaged world. It needs it."

CHAPTER 47

EVE

It was time to continue their march south, and still no word had come from the Colvaris. Worry nagged, and Eve shifted uneasily in her saddle. "I think we should send someone."

"We'll be at the border by nightfall," Callan replied. "We can send someone when we make camp."

Eve nodded. "I was thinking of asking Brida to go," she began, casting a look over her shoulder at where her cousin rode alongside Leysa, the pair engrossed in conversation. "She has met Naia's sister, Maren, a few times and they get along well enough, I believe."

Callan nodded as Eve's attention returned to him. "That sounds like a good–"

Shouts of warning erupted from ahead as horns blasted. Three in quick succession, the pattern to signal an incoming force.

"Fuck," Callan muttered as the entire host came to a sudden stop.

She could see nothing from where they were, the armies of Avellon ahead of them. Lia at the head of their column, with the army from Finias to the east. The massive plains of southern Avellon had allowed them to spread out some, something that may just save their lives, she thought.

A rider wearing the colors of Avellon raced toward them, eyes wide and breathing heavily.

"Are we under attack?" Callan demanded the moment the rider came to a halt. Shadows clung to his body, weaving and dancing. His power prepared to seek out their enemy if he willed it.

"We're not sure, Majesty," the young man replied. "Our scouts report something strange ahead."

"What does that mean?" Eve demanded.

"Everything is dead," the messenger replied. The color had leeched from his face, and sweat beaded on his forehead.

"What do you mean, everything is dead?" she asked again.

"All of the grass, the trees...they're all brown and...well, dead."

Callan muttered another curse and looked at Eve. "It's an attempt to stop or slow us," he explained. "No vegetation for the horses to graze on, and I'm willing to bet they think it'll stall your powers."

Anger flooded her veins. "Then we'll show them how wrong they are," she replied darkly. If they sought to starve their horses, their soldiers, she would use her gifts to grow what they needed, assuming it was possible after whatever Gorias had done to the earth. "Tell Queen Aurelia to continue, and that I will ensure we are fed. Make sure the others are notified as well."

The messenger looked skeptical but nodded anyway, departing to report to his queen.

"We may have to alter our path. I'm not sure I can–" Eve began, only to be interrupted by Leysa and Brida.

"What's going on?" her cousin demanded.

"Gorias destroyed the grasses and trees ahead, in an attempt to slow us," Callan explained. Meeting Eve's gaze levelly, he added, "Eve is going to grow what we need for the horses and soldiers."

Brida glanced between them. "Well damn," she replied, earning a laugh from Leysa.

"Do you need me in the air?" the shifter asked.

"Only if you'd rather be there," Eve replied, knowing that was likely the case if she was asking. Eyes in the air were useful, but they already had other shifters on it, taking turns as they got tired, or simply wanted a change.

Tight dark curls bobbed as Leysa nodded once. "Yeah, I think I will. I'll let you know if I see anything interesting." With a light wave, she fell back and passed the reins to a nearby soldier before dismounting to shift. In the blink of an eye and a bright flash, Leysa was a hawk, soaring skyward.

"I don't think I'll ever get used to seeing that," Brida muttered. "I'm going to find Leith and fill him in." As Brida fell back, a horn blared, signaling the host to march once again.

Eve allowed her gaze to roam as Ventia settled into a steady walk. There was little to see in this part of Avellon aside from gently rolling hills and expansive plains. Small copses of trees dotted the landscape here and there, with wildflowers adding splashes of color in an endless sea of high amber grasses that danced lightly on the breeze. The air had little chill now despite being winter, and with every passing hour, it grew warmer still.

It was lovely, she could admit, but the lack of trees and mountains left Eve feeling a little lost. She was so very far from home in so many different ways, adrift and exposed.

"What are you thinking?" Callan's voice drew her from her thoughts with a start.

Here's my anchor, she thought, gaze roaming his features. She had every plane and line memorized now. His face was there when she slept—when thoughts of the future offered her bright dreams, he was the shining light that made them alluring and hopeful, and when thoughts of the past haunted her nightmares, his face reminded her that she was safe and loved.

"Just thinking how empty it is here, compared to home," she replied with a smile. "I miss the trees."

Callan nodded his agreement, his gaze sweeping over the landscape briefly. "I never liked coming this far south," he replied, rolling his shoulders. "It feels too big...too open. Though the night sky is pretty spectacular."

"But they don't have Lucerna," she replied wistfully. The colorful lights that danced across the spring sky were only visible in the northernmost parts of Aestera, and only during a short weeklong window in spring. Nobody knew why or how, but it was a spectacular sight that some people traveled from great distances to see.

Callan laughed, and the sound made her heart sing. "That's true," he replied, offering the crooked grin that seemed especially reserved for her. He turned his gaze forward, then. "We'll be making camp in a couple of hours, and then you can show them how incredible you are."

~

If the lovely plains made her feel adrift, the dead, barren one left for them by Gorias made her feel utterly desolate. True to what the scouts had reported, not a single blade of grass was left green and alive. None of the fae knew exactly what sort of magic had done it, had leeched life itself from the earth. Callan's already watchful gaze on her had turned more intense, and for the first time since they left and had joined Lia's armies, he refused to leave her side.

"If they have someone with magic that can do this, I can only imagine they're capable of matching yours, maybe even nullifying it," he explained, grim-faced and sober. The shared grins and light-hearted talks of their home were done, stolen from them just as the life had been stolen from the land they'd now make camp on.

The humans had protested, fearing the land was cursed, but some of the elder fae, with gifts that made them able to detect such things, had declared it safe. Now, Eve had a show to put on that would hopefully rally the frightened soldiers before the final push into Coruscis to meet Gorias–wherever they were. Lia joined them just before sunset when Eve would attempt to revitalize the once plentiful grassland.

"You can do this?" she asked, her tone hopeful, despite the shadows that dimmed her summer sky eyes.

"I think I can," Eve replied, frowning. "Are you alright? The elders say the land isn't cursed if that's what's worrying you. It's perfectly safe here."

Lia shook her head, eyes closing briefly. "It's fine," she replied, though her expression remained haunted.

Unconvinced, Eve simply frowned. Something was going on with Lia, but right now, with thousands of people watching and waiting, she simply didn't have time to figure out what it was. With a steadying breath, she crouched, placing her hands in the dry earth, and closed her eyes.

Feeling and focus.

Exhaling slowly, she filled her thoughts with, well, life. The cry of a newborn baby, the first shoots of spring plants, a bountiful harvest at the end of summer, and a warm hearth to keep the winter air at bay. Each of those things meant life, in some way or another.

Moments passed by, and with each heartbeat she poured more of herself into it, stretching that invisible limb that her gift had become into the earth beneath their feet, stretching and spreading like the roots of a great oak. Everywhere it touched, life returned. She could feel the roots of the grasses expanding as the plants straightened, as their life was restored. Not far away, a copse of apple trees groaned as leaves sprouted, their limbs becoming laden with bright red fruit once more.

Her breath became shaky, she was pouring so much of herself into it now, and there was little left for her to give–but the job was not yet done.

Just a little bit more, she thought. *And then I can rest.*

A strong, familiar hand clasped her arm, pulling hers from the soil. Its twin lightly cupped her cheek. "You've done enough, it's time to sleep," Callan whispered against her hair as he lifted her to his chest, cradling her like a child. "Rest now, dove."

With her head against his chest, she did just that, falling into a fitful sleep against him, with the steady beat of his heart her lullaby.

She was home, in the deep forests of Darkegrove.

Though she didn't recognize the place specifically, there was no mistaking the enormous trees that towered over her, grown so thick that the sunlight above barely penetrated the forest floor where she sat. A cool breeze drifted from the north, likely chilled by the snow that capped the Sgiath, the ancient mountain range creating the northern-most border of the kingdom.

She knew she was dreaming, as there, just across the small stream that bubbled at her feet, sat a dragon. An actual dragon. Sleek and white, with silver scales here and there that seemed to sparkle, even in the minimal light that found its way this far beneath the canopy. It was massive, with sharp black eyes watching her intently.

Rising from the log she sat on, Eve tentatively took a single step forward. With only a low growl for warning, the dragon shifted in a shocking flash of light. Instinctively she threw her arm over her eyes, waiting until the last of the light faded.

"What a brave little thing you are," a feminine voice purred.

Lowering her arm, Eve was shocked to find a woman standing nearly within arm's reach of her now, barefoot in the stream. Draped in a gauzy white material split into two panels that barely covered her breasts and the space between her thighs, she was curvy, tan, and utterly devastating in her beauty. Night dark hair fell in gentle waves to her hips, swept back behind her shoulders. The eyes had remained the same, utterly black with no iris.

"Who are you?" Eve demanded, that very bravery steeling her spine. The woman's beauty and aura of power that seemed to ripple off of her in waves left little doubt in Eve's mind she had to be a goddess. This was a dream, she reasoned, so perhaps this was the goddess of dreams.

The woman began to walk then, a slow circle around Eve, a predator examining her prey. "I have many names," she replied in a lover's tone. She paused before Eve, trailing a sharp nail over Keithia's mark on her clavicle.

Eve swatted her hand away, earning a throaty laugh from the mysterious woman. "And they are?"

The woman grinned in response. "The Destroyer, Darkness, End of All Things, The Unending One," she paused, leaning closer to whisper. "Kore, The Void." Leaning back, she tilted her head, dark lashes lowering as she took in Eve's appearance.

"What do you want?" Eve demanded, courage beginning to falter. So this is who they feared, the one who led Gorias against them in some war with the gods. The one who would end the world, if the three queens of Aestera failed to stop her.

"What a delightful prize you are," Kore remarked with amusement. "And so impertinent. Perhaps when I've finished devouring your world, little queen, I'll keep you for a pet. I do so enjoy breaking the spirited ones." She tilted her head, dark gaze raking over Eve's body, biting her lower lip gently. "And you are so much prettier than your predecessor."

"I think not," Eve replied. This was a dream, it was *her* dream, and that meant she was in control. With a lift of her fingers, vines sprouted from the ground, aiming to wrap around Kore's throat, silencing her threats.

Kore snapped her fingers as the vines encircled her tan throat, and the vines disintegrated into ash. "Oh, there will be no more of that, little queen."

Panic blossomed as sharp talon-like nails aimed for Eve's throat.

Eve had no idea if Kore could kill her here, in this dreamscape, but she certainly wasn't going to stand around and wait to find out. Spinning on her heel, Eve took off through the dense forest, Kore's lilting laugh chasing her on the breeze.

"Wake up, wake up, wake up," she huffed as she ran. A bright white light flashed through the trees. Kore had shifted, and now a dragon, a gods damned dragon, was chasing her. "Oh shit."

"Little queen," Kore called, in a voice so ancient and terrible it chilled her to her very bones. "Why do you run when you know I'll find you? Such a waste of energy, and so very pointless."

"Eve!" Callan's shout echoed through the forest, distant and hollow. Her head jerked toward the direction of his voice, making her miss the raised root ahead of her. She sailed through the air for a heartbeat before crashing against the loamy earth. Wet leaves clung to her hands and knees as she shoved herself to standing once more and ran again.

"Wake up, dove, wake up!"

"Please," she sobbed. "Please let me wake up."

Her heart pounded, her lungs burned. Still, she ran, pushing herself harder as the sound of trees cracking and falling echoed behind her. Kore was so close now she could feel the thundering of her wings reverberating through the ground.

But that was her mistake, Eve realized, choosing that form for the chase with such a dense forest for Eve to hide in. She wouldn't be able to see Eve clearly, and if she wanted to actually land, she would have to shift or wait for another clearing.

Like the one I'm hurtling toward now, Eve realized, heart thundering.

Ahead, the trees grew more sparse, spaced apart to allow for...wait, a Black Pool? Like the one she'd nearly been drowned in. *The one that was a portal.*

With a cry of frustration and fear, Eve pushed harder, ignoring the screaming in her legs, the way her body begged for a rest. Ignoring even the utter horror that coursed through her as she leapt for the dark, endless waters of the Pool, and found herself sinking into its depths.

CHAPTER 48

LIA

"How could you?" Lia demanded, her voice little more than a harsh whisper in the darkness of her tent.

Bella, seated beside her on the bed, sighed. She'd asked this very same question several times already since Bella's unexpected attempt at teaching her to use her powers, and still, she remained in disbelief. "I had to push you past your self-doubt. Besides, I am the daughter of a goddess. It wouldn't have killed me."

Lia flopped back against the pillows with a grumble. "I didn't know that."

"I know," Bella admitted. "I am sorry I frightened you."

"Are you?" Lia asked, turning to look at Bella in the moonlight. Now that they'd traveled farther south, nighttime fires were hardly necessary, a blessing in Lia's mind. The opening at the top of her tent could be left wide, and with no billowing smoke to block any of the light, it felt almost as if they were outdoors entirely.

"Of course," Bella replied, wounded. "I know my methods were not okay but...I wanted to show you how capable you are, how powerful," she sighed. "You are amazing, my love, and you can do anything you want, but you have to believe in yourself. You needed the push."

Lia shook her head, gaze turning to the bright moon beyond their tent. "Don't ever do anything like that again, please," she whispered.

"Never," Bella promised, curling up against Lia's side, her arm draped over the queen's abdomen. "I will never do that to you again"

Lia closed her eyes, inhaling the scent of moonflowers that always seemed to cling to Bella. "I–"

Her words were cut off as Eve's fae friend, Leysa, she recalled, burst into the tent. Her dark face was grim as she spoke. "You need to come immediately, something has happened to Eve."

Moments later, hastily dressed in a simple tunic and leggings, Lia, with Bella at her side, followed the shifter to Eve's tent. Little explanation was offered along the way, only that after Eve's work with the vegetation, she had fallen into a deep sleep–and now something was terribly wrong. They arrived to find Callan sitting beside their bed, clasping Eve's hand. She was still asleep, red hair damp with sweat, pale face scrunched as if in pain.

"What's going on?" Lia asked as she took a seat on the foot of the bed. Placing a hand on Eve, she frowned. She was so cold, Lia could feel it even through the leggings that covered Eve's legs. Despite the warm air, sweat beaded her brow.

"She fell into a deep sleep after using her gift," the dark fae male behind Callan explained. Valerian, she remembered. "At first everything seemed fine, but then she started crying out and thrashing."

"We can't wake her," Callan added, his voice strained, hoarse. As if he'd been crying, or screaming.

Bella, hovering near Lia's side, leaned forward to look at Eve more closely. "Do you have anyone gifted by the dreamer with you?" she asked Callan.

"No," he replied, shaking his head. "My sister paced to Falias to see if she can track one down to bring here but–"

"The gift is rare," Bella finished, nodding. "I could ask my mother, but I doubt she would offer any real assistance here, and she isn't answering my prayers anyway."

"What about Keithia?" Lia asked, recalling the goddess of life and earth. "She would have a vested interest in keeping Eve alive, right?"

"She isn't answering either," Callan replied tightly. "None of them are." Leaning closer, he pressed his lips to her forehead. "What is happening to you, dove? Come back to me."

Valerian cleared his throat as he placed a hand on Callan's shoulder. "We hoped you might be able to help."

Lia blinked, surprised. "How? She isn't injured from what I can see..."

Bella exhaled slowly, and when Lia turned to look at her, the familiar silver eyes had gone cloudy. "A light in the dark, to bring the wayward home. Thunder crashes against silence, and the way forward is opened."

"Oh shit," Valerian mumbled.

Lia took Bella's hand in hers, meeting those silver eyes as they returned to normal once more. "Bella?" she prompted gently, giving the seer's hand a gentle squeeze.

"I'm okay," Bella replied, nodding her head. "That was strange."

"How so?" Leysa asked.

"I never have visions when I'm awake. It always happens when I'm dreaming." Her gaze turned to Eve. "I guess my mother deemed this one too important to wait."

"Your light," Valerian said, drawing Lia's attention. "A light in the dark, to bring the wayward home."

Callan's attention shot to Lia as if seeing her for the first time. "You have to try."

The intensity of his gaze and voice, along with the shadows that seemed to darken the room, chilled her. "Of course," she replied without hesitation. "I will try."

She had no idea what she was doing as she lay her hands on Eve's chest. If healing was a nearly impossible task, how would she even begin to project her light into someone else's dream? Despite the fear and doubt, she knew she had little choice. Her friend was in danger.

Lia began by willing herself to picture a beacon of light, a way for Eve to see the way out of her mind. Pushing with her power, she felt it grow, moving like wings to surround Eve in an embrace. And then...nothing.

Light surrounded Eve, but there was no change, no reaction. "I don't know what to do," Lia began, frowning.

"Because you need one who can tap into dreams," Lucia said from the doorway. "One blessed by the dreamer themself."

"We have none here with that gift," Callan growled in frustration.

"Oh, but you do, my child." Lucia smiled patiently. "You've never asked what *my* gift is."

Silence fell over the tent as each of the fae simply stared at the ancient queen.

"You?" Callan asked, incredulously. "My mother never said, *you* never said."

Lucia shrugged. "Most assume I bear Helie's gift, as my mother did before me. But I gained the favor of my father's patron, Endri, the god of dreams and inspiration."

Without waiting for further questions, she crossed to Lia. "Give me your hand, light-blessed, and pour your light into me. You will be the beacon. Callan, my dear, call out to her. She'll need to hear your voice to know it's safe."

Lia did as she was told, taking one of Lucia's hands into her own. Eyes closed, she pictured the beacon, a round ball of glowing golden light. She saw it floating in the dark, hovering, before willing it to find Eve, to guide her friend home.

"Come back to me, dove," Callan urged, his voice low and pleading. "Please come back to me."

CHAPTER 49

EVE

She was sinking into the darkness again. Water surrounded her, and she was going to die.

No strong hands were shoving her beneath the surface this time, and no hate-filled hearts were determined to see her die rather than accept a woman's right to rule. But there were also no benevolent goddesses here to tug her the rest of the way through the portal, to offer words of wisdom before returning her home.

Eve had just made one monumental mistake.

She had followed Callan's voice, but what if she was wrong about its origin? What if it had been simply a figment of this dreamworld or worse, what if Kore had been tricking her somehow?

Panic seized her heart, and she kicked hard, racing back toward where she thought the surface was. She couldn't be sure now, there was no light here to guide her, no telltale shimmer of sunlight on the rippling water to show her which way was up and which was down. In her desperate bid to escape, she had simply thrown herself into death's waiting arms.

But this was a dream, surely she would simply wake up?

The little voice inside herself whispered no, urging her to fight, to find a way out.

So she kicked harder and harder, until finally, a glowing light appeared. She paused only momentarily as a golden orb appeared overhead.

Was this a trick? Eve wondered, hesitating as her lungs began to burn. She didn't dare test her theory that you couldn't die in dreams. Tentatively she swam toward the light, if for no other reason than the lack of options left to her.

"Come back to me, dove. Please come back to me."

That was Callan's voice, and the light, it felt warm, like sunshine. It didn't matter if it was a trick, she was running out of time.

With every bit of her waning strength, she kicked, harder and faster than she thought possible, reaching a hand for the light until it led her to the surface–and as she broke through, she gasped, opening her eyes to see Callan, Lucia, and Lia standing over her.

"She's here," she coughed, grasping Callan's arm tightly, before breaking down entirely.

Callan's arms wound around her, holding her close as sobs wracked her body, the warmth of his body easing the remaining terror and cold of the nightmare.

Here was her anchor, her home, her love. The one place she knew she would be safe, no matter what came next. From the gentle trembling of his shoulders, she could tell that he too wept, from relief, she knew without having to ask.

"You're safe," he whispered quietly, voice ragged. "You're safe."

AN HOUR LATER, BATHED AND DRESSED, AND FINALLY WARM again, Eve recounted the story of her nightmare to the others. Brida, Cathal, and Mara had joined them in time to hear the story, and now each of her friends, and allies, sat in silence as they considered what she'd told them.

"She's a dragon," Leysa stated flatly. Staring at the ground.

"Only in dreams," Lucia replied. "It is only a ruse to frighten you, I'm sure. None of the legends say she can change forms."

Eve shuddered at the memory. "Well, it worked." Callan's arm around her tightened slightly, and she leaned against his shoulder. His touch anchored her, soothing the worst of the fear that lingered.

She was more angry than afraid, ready to go to Naia, find this last artifact, and then face Kore.

She wanted it over.

"So how did she get into Eve's dream?" Mara asked, frowning.

"Well," Lucia sighed, leaning back in her chair as the others each stared, waiting. "The gods can do it, so I am not entirely surprised that she managed to. I think that you'll find that those blessed by the gods will have some natural immunity to such invasions though." She paused, looking at Eve for a long moment. "Your use of power weakened you, and also told her exactly where to find you."

Turning her gaze to Lia, she added, "Be on your guard, light-blessed. You painted a target on yourself when you took out her army. I am rather shocked she chose to go after the life-blessed one first."

Why hadn't Keithia warned me? Or Macaria? Eve wondered. If the gods were helping them, then why not warn them of this danger? Unless they hadn't known somehow or, more likely, were keeping more secrets.

"What can we do to stop her from doing it again?" Lia asked, looking at her seer.

"I've taken the liberty of handling that," Lucia answered. "You'll find that simple herbs can offer at least a measure of protection in dreams, and I will be calling upon Endri for help. Assuming they listen, we should be secure from now on."

Eve straightened, nodding. "Well, let's hope the gods don't fail us now."

"Good luck with that," Cathal mused darkly, taking Mara's hand in his.

"We're getting closer," Callan said, ignoring his brother's remark. "Every step we take toward defeating her, the harder she'll fight back. We need to be ready for anything."

Murmurs of agreement sounded around the tent, and with only a few quiet goodbyes, the party dispersed. Only Brida lingered, hesitantly.

"I wanted to ask you something," she said, glancing between Eve and Callan.

"What is it?" Eve asked, sensing the tension beneath her cousin's words.

"Do you trust her? The fae queen?"

Callan sighed, his eyes meeting Eve's. "She will help the fae, but...be on your guard. She won't do anything to harm the humans directly, but I doubt she'll do much to help you if you need it either."

Eve's hands curled into fists at her side. "She'd let them die?"

Callan nodded once. "Maybe."

Brida's expression turned as hard as stone. "Thank you for the warning."

"You have us, and Avellon," Callan added. "We will always come to your aid if you need it."

Offering them a tight smile, Brida nodded once. "Thank you."

As she departed, Eve loosed a breath. "We need to make sure they're closer to us than Finias when the next battle comes."

"Agreed," he replied. "But let's worry about that later. Tonight, you need actual rest, and tomorrow, I need to call on my mother. She owes us an explanation."

CHAPTER 50

LIA

"Eyla is here," Bella announced breathlessly, as she rushed into the tent.

It was fully dark now, and well beyond the timeframe they'd been given by the men Lia had sent for Bella's daughter. Though she hadn't complained, Lia knew the seer had been worried for her daughter. As the hours passed, Bella waited outside, keeping herself busy by helping wherever she could with menial tasks around the camp, despite Lia's objections, and requests for Bella to rest.

Now that they'd finally arrived, relief and joy played across Bella's features as she grabbed Lia's hand, leading her out to meet her daughter. "She's going to be delighted to meet a real queen," Bella said over her shoulder as they made their way to the carriage rolling into the center of the encampment.

"I'm delighted to meet her as well," Lia replied, squeezing Bella's hand gently.

As they approached, the carriage door swung open, and one of the guards tasked with retrieving the girl held his hand out to help Eyla down. Completely disregarding his hand, she leapt from the carriage and ran straight into Bella's waiting arms with a squeal.

"How was the journey?" Bella asked, smoothing her daughter's braided raven hair as she looked her over.

"Long," Eyla sighed dramatically. "And bumpy!"

Bella laughed. "Eyla, I would like for you to meet someone very important. This is Aurelia, Queen of Avellon," she said, stepping to the side to allow Eyla to see Lia fully for the first time. "Aurelia, this is my daughter, Eyla Avoden."

"The queen?" Eyla whispered, her almond-shaped eyes widening. In contrast to Bella's silver, Eyla's eyes were a warm mahogany, the only stark difference between mother and daughter who so closely resembled one another.

"You may call me Lia, as all of my friends do—I think you and I are going to be great friends," Lia said with a smile. "I'm so happy to meet you, Eyla."

"Really?" Eyla asked, looking to her mother for confirmation.

"Really," Bella confirmed with a grin. For the first time, Lia saw real joy on Bella's face, and it warmed her heart. It was like seeing her whole for the first time, now that she had her child close and safe.

"Shall we go get you settled?" Lia asked, looking from Eyla to Bella and back. "And maybe you can tell me about your friend," she added, gesturing to the rather ragged-looking doll the child clutched close to her chest.

"Her name is Lilah," Eyla said, before turning to look around the camp with wide eyes. "There are a lot of people here."

"Yes," Bella replied. "There are. They are here doing a very important job, preparing to stand up against someone very bad and keeping all of us safe."

Eyla nodded. "Good job everyone," she said in the most grownup-sounding voice a child her age could muster.

"Let's get you settled," Bella laughed, as Lia led the way.

Lia watched as Bella's gown slipped to the floor, the whisper of the fabric against her skin the only sound. Slowly, she slid on a tunic and leggings to sleep in before hopping onto the bed beside Lia.

"I'm glad that Eve is okay now," Bella said eyes drifting closed as Lia rolled to face her.

"Me too," she replied. "Bella?"

"Mm?"

Lia hesitated. She'd intended to ask Bella to teach her more about her magic, how to control it better, but after saving Eve, things had almost settled back to normal between them and the idea of ruining that by bringing up Bella's last training exercise gave her pause. She hated the idea of fighting with Bella again, and even though her feelings were still hurt, she knew she had every right to be angry about what Bella did, rehashing it made her feel a little queasy.

So instead, she asked about the other thing on her mind. "What do you think the rest of your prophecy meant?"

"The rest of it?" Bella asked, opening her eyes slightly to look at Lia.

"A light in the dark, to bring the wayward home. Thunder crashes against silence, and the way forward is opened. The first is in danger, the second will be the beacon, and the third will find her way," Lia repeated. "The light in the dark, the beacon, those are me saving Eve, the first who was in danger, right? But what does that mean, thunder crashing against silence?" She frowned. "If the third is Naia, why does she need to find her way? She's in Thalassa and apparently ignoring us."

"I don't know, honestly," Bella said. "I never understand them entirely until the pieces all come together. You're right about the parts regarding you and Eve. I think that was my mother's way of telling us we were on the right path. As far as thunder, silence, and finding her way...I have no idea. I guess we'll have to wait and see."

Lia sat up in the bed, cradling her head in her hands. She hated waiting, not knowing what would happen next, but something else was plaguing her mind, had her intuition screaming at her. "Something is wrong," she whispered. "I can feel it but I can't explain what, or why."

Bella rose beside her, placing a comforting hand on her shoulder. "The whole world is wrong right now, it makes sense you'd feel that way. But if you feel like your intuition is speaking to you, listen. You'll figure it out in time."

"I hope so," Lia replied softly, gaze turning to where Eyla slept in a small cot, across from them.

I just hope it isn't too late for us all by then.

CHAPTER 51

EVE

Callan's pleas for an audience with Macaria went unanswered, as did Eve's to Keithia. Lucia sent her own messenger, informing them of her lack of success as well. None of the gods, it seemed, would deign to aid their chosen.

"Why aren't they answering?" Eve muttered, leaning back in her chair. It was past midnight, and she was exhausted. They would be leaving again at dawn and would be crossing the border into Coruscis shortly after that.

Long stretches of sand awaited them, with little shelter and water available. Callan had assured her it would be alright, that both fae armies had water-blessed among them who could call forth enough to keep the horses and soldiers hydrated for a while.

"I'm not sure," he admitted, as he moved around the tent, dousing lanterns before taking her hand in his. At her raised brow, he added, "You need to sleep. Come to bed."

"I don't take orders from men," she reminded him, lips twitching into a grin. It wasn't entirely true, not where Callan was concerned at least, especially when a bed was involved.

His answering grin told her he had the same thought. "They'll answer us, or they won't," he began, returning to the topic at hand. "We can't wait to see what they'll do, so we keep moving forward."

Nodding her agreement, both to his statement and the idea of sleep, she rose from the chair and let him lead her to the bed. Once beneath the blankets, with Callan's arms around her waist, his warm body pressed firmly against her back, she sighed. "The scouts haven't found anything yet. What if we're too late?"

Callan hummed thoughtfully, a low sound that reverberated through her. "I don't think so. If Kore had the cauldron, we'd know. I don't think she'd bother tormenting you in your dreams."

Eve considered his words, closing her eyes tightly against the memory of her nightmare. "I still don't understand how she trapped me in there," she whispered into the darkness.

"That's a question for Lucia, or Endri, I suppose."

"If they answer."

"If they answer," he agreed. His thumb slid over the back of her hand slowly, rough skin sliding against hers soothingly. "You need to rest. I'll be here, and Lucia's herbs will help keep us safe."

She wasn't so sure she trusted that, but sleep beckoned her like a lover. It had been a long, trying day and tomorrow would likely be worse. Northern Corsucis was brutal and unforgiving. They would need to push hard to reach the more hospitable southern reaches, where civilization could be found.

A messenger would be departing ahead of the main body, one last attempt to contact Naia before Eve would insist on Callan pacing her there. Something was wrong, she could feel it in her very bones. Instinct screamed that she needed to go now, but she couldn't appear in the palace at this hour, and the last thing she wanted was to offend Naia when so much depended on her believing their unbelievable story.

When sleep finally pulled her under, Eve dreamt only of lightning strikes, and complete, unending silence.

CHAPTER 52

LIA

They had been riding for hours, and the sun above was finally beginning to feel hot rather than just mildly warm. Some of the soldiers complained, cursing the lack of shade, but to Lia, it was bliss. Winter in the deserts of Coruscis felt almost like late spring in Avellon. As she rode at a gentle canter, she tilted her head skyward, relishing the warmth on her face.

"You look like a goddess when you do that," Bella said.

Lia laughed lightly, turning her gaze to Bella. "I certainly don't feel like one. I'm sweaty, and I smell like horse," she replied.

"I think you smell like sunshine," Bella grinned. "Sunshine and apples."

"Sunshine and apples?" Lia smiled back, confused.

"Well, more like apple blossoms I guess, but also a little like the fruit. Mostly like sunshine though; pure, beautiful sunshine."

Lia's heart gave a squeeze at Bella's gaze, the light that shone within her silver eyes as she spoke, as much as the words themselves. "And what does sunshine smell like?"

Bella tilted her head, considering. "Impossible to explain," she sighed. "But warm and beautiful. Perfectly fitting for you."

Lia laughed fully then, and something within her gave a little tug in

Bella's direction—and not for the first time. She'd been feeling this little tug in Bella's direction since the day she'd died, and come back as fae. But with everything else she'd been feeling and experiencing, she'd so far managed to bury it, to pretend it wasn't there like she so often did with things she didn't want to admit to herself.

She knew she was beginning to love Bella, but this thing Lia felt pulling her toward the seer, even when she wasn't around, felt like more than that somehow, and Lia wasn't entirely sure she was ready for more.

Her gaze drifted to Eyla, sleeping soundly in the saddle in front of Bella, her head resting comfortably against Bella's arm wrapped gently around the girl. There was also the child to consider. She was committing not just to the woman she loved, but also a child. Could she do that?

Were the promises they'd whispered to one another just mistakes borne of fear and passion? Something inside her screamed, raging against the very idea. No, she loved this impossible, infuriating, confusing woman, despite everything telling her it was a mistake. Despite her rather questionable teaching methods, despite all the secrets she'd kept, Lia loved Bella.

The thing inside her sang with joy, seeming to shout *yes, this is right*.

What that tug was, what it meant, she didn't know. Perhaps becoming fae had heightened her emotions alongside her senses. That was a question she would rather ask Eve than Bella. She didn't dare broach the subject, not when those words hadn't yet been spoken between them. Whatever her own feelings were, she had no idea what Bella might be thinking or feeling. Bella wanted a relationship, but that didn't necessarily mean love, certainly not so soon.

"What are you thinking about?" Bella's voice startled her, drawing her from her thoughts.

"Naia," she lied, with a slight twinge of guilt. "I think Eve is going to try to go see her in person if we don't hear back by the time we make camp."

"Is that wise?" Bella frowned. "There's no telling what's going on in Thalassa or what sort of reception fae might receive there."

Lia sighed, shaking her head. "I don't know, but I do know that Eve's mind isn't changed easily."

Bella fell silent once more, her gaze turning to the bright sun above. "We'll need to rest soon," she said, eyes moving to the column of soldiers ahead. They had taken to riding closer to the center now, for fear of Eyla's safety.

"Mhm. Lucia has people prepared to conjure water for the horses," Lia said, patting her own Zephyr's neck gently. The journey had been hard on them, especially with the change in climates, but they were coping well, thanks in part to magical help from the fae.

Without warning and with only a few wispy clouds above them, thunder cracked, startling horses and riders alike as a bright streak of lightning flashed across the sky.

"What in the name of the gods was that?" Lia breathed, as Zephyr settled.

Bella had gone still in her saddle, holding the awake and wide-eyed Eyla tightly. "We need to stop and make camp." Her gaze shot to Lia. "I have a feeling you were right about something being wrong."

Chapter 53

Eve

The storm disappeared as suddenly as it had appeared. Not a single drop of rain fell, despite the thunder and lightning that raged overhead for more than an hour. Camp had been made swiftly, and every eye seemed locked on the sky. Just enough water had been conjured to refresh the nervous horses, and what was left when they were finished was quickly dispersed, fear of lightning strikes on everyone's minds.

"Word from Thalassa, Majesty," the messenger said, placing the sealed letter in Eve's waiting hand before departing.

With shaking hands, Eve tore the letter open. Shock rang through her at the words and who had delivered them. Sinking onto the bed, she let the letter fall to the floor.

"What's wrong?" Callan asked, grabbing the discarded letter.

"Naia has been taken," she said numbly. The world spun around her. How stupid they'd been, how naive. Rather than letters they should have sent armies, or at least a few skilled guards. But they hadn't and now the worst had happened.

If Kore had her hands on Naia then all was certainly lost.

"Who is Maren?" Callan asked, placing the letter on the table gently, eyes on Eve.

Eve closed her eyes. There had been no mention of the cauldron, or who had taken Naia. Perhaps Kore hadn't yet found the cauldron. Maybe Naia's disappearance was somehow unrelated. As if fate would be that kind to them.

"Her sister," she explained. "And emissary. She has assumed responsibility as their mother has taken to bed, too heartsick to handle it."

"Will Maren help us?" he asked, voice distant, considering.

Eve laughed, the sound hollow even to her own ears. "She says yes. They've seen no signs of Gorias near Thalassa, and she is sending scouts to the surrounding areas to be sure. Naia must have received my earlier letters because Maren says she only just found them."

"When did she go missing?"

"A few days ago, after the battle in Avellon, why?"

"Then there is still hope. If Kore found the cauldron, and had its bearer, she would almost certainly be coming for the two of you and your artifacts next. But she hasn't done that. Which means either she has only Naia, or neither of them."

She mulled his words over. He was right. With possession of two artifacts and presumably two bearers, not to mention the army of Gorias, there would be no reason for Kore to wait. She must still be searching for something, or someone.

"We'll need to get to Thalassa soon," Eve said slowly, recalling the distance. "Another two days, maybe three at most."

Callan nodded. "Assuming we don't meet Gorias along the way, I think it can be done in two."

Eve leaned back on the bed still dressed in her riding clothes, dusty and smelling of horse and sweat. "When all of this is over, we're going to stay in bed for a week."

Callan grinned at that. "I think that is a fabulous plan. But before sleep, I suggest a bath, dove," he added. "I don't mind the smell, but I think you'll hate having sand in your hair while you try to sleep."

Despite her complete agreement, Eve tossed a pillow at him. "Ass," she swore, halfheartedly.

"I love it when you call me names."

~

Thanks to the magic of a delightful fae blessed with the gift of water, Eve enjoyed a hot bath that not only saved her from sleeping in sand, but soothed her aching muscles. Days of riding had taken their toll, and though she would never have complained, relief from the pain had been sorely needed.

Finally in clean clothes and in their bed, Eve groaned as Callan worked out a particularly painful knot in her shoulder. "Have you seen the way Lia looks at Bella?" she asked suddenly.

Callan paused, smiling bemusedly. "I haven't really paid attention, to be honest."

"Do you think they may be mates? Bella isn't fae but..."

He shrugged in response, his glorious hands resuming their work and earning another groan of pleasure from her. "I've never met another demigod, so I can't be sure, but I don't see why not. Humans are different. Such short lifespans would make it difficult, if not impossible, to find a true mate. With our long lives, we have time."

Eve smiled. "How long?"

Callan paused. "Very long," he replied. "Why?"

"I want to see dragons," she explained, ignoring the bite of fear when Kore's dragon form flashed in her mind. "Are they awful? Dangerous? Or can you actually ride them?"

Callan sighed. The bed creaked as he moved to sit beside her on the bed. "Well, like us, it depends on the dragon. I've been wondering what it would be like to be inside you while flying through the air on the back of a dragon."

Eve shivered, her blood heating at the idea. Dampness pooled between her legs as the image flashed in her mind. Callan sitting, with her on top of him, riding him as the dragon soared higher.

"I think you like that idea," he mused.

The familiar feeling of shadowy tendrils tracing their way up her bare thigh. She said a silent prayer of thanks that she'd chosen to wear only a long tunic, foregoing the leggings thanks to the warm night. Her core tightened as the shadows crept closer to the apex of her thighs.

Rolling onto her back, she grinned at him. "I thought you wanted me to rest," she whispered. Sleep was certainly not what she wanted right now, and the sentiment was mirrored in his own darkened gaze as he grinned in response.

"And you will, later," he said.

Shadows gripped her wrists, pinning them above her head as he undid the buttons of her tunic with excruciating care and an utterly unhurried pace. Her heart pounded in her chest, a sound he could hear thanks to their bond. The shadows between her legs stilled, just shy of reaching her clit.

Desperation for contact had her squeezing her thighs close, the friction sending a small wave of pleasure through her. "Callan," she pleaded.

His answering laugh rumbled through her as he moved, sitting on her thighs as he bent down to claim her mouth with his own. Like the movement of his hands, now tugging the tunic open to bare her breasts, the kiss was slow, precise.

Sliding a single finger down one breast, he stopped at the peak, pinching her nipple lightly between two fingers, before replacing them with his mouth, tongue flicking against it. A small groan passed her lips, and he rocked back, a pleased grin playing across the face she loved so much.

Sliding off of her, he wrapped her legs around his waist, positioning himself between her thighs. Finally, the shadow between them began to move again, teasing her clit with small, slow circles. It was the best kind of torture. Her blood was pure heat coursing through her veins as the pressure began to build, a dam ready to burst with her release. Another shadow joined the first, this one sliding inside her, moving in and out in time with the first that now began to vibrate as it circled. Her climax came hard and fast. Her back arched off the bed, and she cried his name so loud that she was certain the entire camp had to have heard.

"Quiet now, dove, your pleasure is mine and I don't share," he whispered, rising to remove his own clothes. "Next time, bite those pretty lips to keep quiet, or I'll do it for you."

Her eyes widened as he settled between her legs once more, his proud length on full display as he leaned forward, claiming her mouth in a more intense, bruising kiss.

"We'll see," she replied, in mock defiance, as he sat back. She tugged against the invisible bonds, desperate to touch him, to feel him in her hands.

He chuckled, the sound dark and full of wicked promise, and then entered her in one swift motion, drawing a strangled cry of surprise and pleasure from her. Remembering his words, she bit down on her lower lip, keeping quiet as he began to move. Pulling one leg over his shoulder, he pushed deeper, determined it seemed, to draw out those cries of pleasure. To test how quiet she could be. Angling her hips, he hit the spot inside of her that sent a shudder through her, pure pleasure so intense that the second time she came, she cried out once more, unable to hold it back.

As promised, he leaned forward, biting her lower lip gently, just once, before flicking his tongue over it. "A promise is a promise," he breathed, before joining her as she tumbled over the edge.

CHAPTER 54

LIA

Bella had been right, as had Lia's intuition that something was amiss. Her thoughts turned to the news Eve had shared earlier in the evening: Naia Colvari was missing. Though the cauldron remained hidden or lost, it was still grave news, and the remaining two queens would need to be on their guard until they could discover where Naia had been taken.

The sword took its usual place on the table nearby, and as Lia lay in bed, listening to the quiet sounds of Bella and Eyla sleeping, she stared at it. Eyla had fallen asleep quickly after dinner and snored quietly in the cot they'd added to Lia's tent. Bella wanted to remain close to Lia, and where Bella went so did her daughter.

Even in the dark, the sword seemed to almost glow with its light, faint and barely perceptible, but it was there. How long had her ancestors been carrying this sword, wielding it in battle, and passing it down through the generations, with no knowledge of its true power and origin?

The Sword of Light. They'd known what it was called at least, and knowing the goddess who had bestowed her gift on Lia, she had no doubt the name was fitting.

Would it blind her enemies as she had? Or would it heal the

wounded? A small part of her longed to find out–the part of her that had been born the day she died. While the other part of her, the one that clung so tightly to who she had been before this war had started, hated the very idea. Retribution and hope. Equal parts in one woman. Two sides of the coin that made up Lia Vallyse now.

Bella shifted suddenly, a small noise of annoyance or upset signaling whatever she dreamt of was unpleasant. Lia studied her face, illuminated by the moonlight. She could be having another vision, or perhaps just a nightmare thanks to everything they had been through and everything that was yet to come. Bella had predicted the fall of their kingdoms, and so far, they had managed to save Avellon. But Coruscis remained in danger.

Bella's eyes flew open, and she turned to Lia with alarm etched into her features. "She's searching. She scours the desert, furious that she cannot find what was lost. She's coming. She's coming," Bella whispered. "We need to get up. Something is already happening."

Without questioning, Lia rose from the bed and quickly pulled on a pair of leggings with the long tunic she'd intended to sleep in. If she'd learned anything by now, it was to listen when Bella issued a warning. Fear flooded her. They weren't ready to face Kore head-on, were they? They had two of the artifacts, but maybe Kore did as well. And Naia. How could she keep everyone she loved from harm, with so many unknowns?

Bella followed, dressing in silence, casting glances at her daughter every so often.

"Stay with her," Bella commanded, grabbing her own sword from where it lay. "I will go and see, but I don't want to wake her or leave her alone. You'll be safer here with the guards outside."

She frowned, ready to argue. If something was amiss, she needed to see for herself. Lia knew Bella wanted to protect not only Eyla but her as well, but there was a time for hiding and a time for meeting danger. "I should go, we can have a guard stay with her–"

"I don't trust anyone but you," Bella interrupted shaking her head. "You know how to fight, and you have your magic...and I don't want you out in the open until we know what's going on. If there's to be a battle, I will send someone else to guard her so that you can lead your people."

Lia sighed, but nodded. "Alright."

"Thank you," Bella whispered, pressing a swift kiss to Lia's lips before departing.

Finding herself alone with only a sleeping child for company, the little voice within Lia screamed that she had just made a horrible mistake.

CHAPTER 55

EVE

E ve fell swiftly into a deep sleep with Callan's arms wrapped around her like armor, protecting her from whatever may come. She couldn't be sure what woke her sometime later. Perhaps it was the silence, now that the wind had settled to a dead calm, or maybe it was her gift, the very earth warning her of the danger, but Eve sat straight up in bed, dragging Callan from sleep alongside with her.

"Something is wrong," she whispered in the dark. No alarm had been raised, and from the quiet sounds of conversation she could only barely make out, the guards were still on duty outside.

Rather than question her or reassure her that it was nothing, Callan stilled beside her. "What do you feel?"

Rising from the bed, she dragged a nearby robe around her shoulders and stepped out into the night, startling the guard nearest the tent flap. She hadn't answered Callan's question, but he followed silently in her wake anyway, letting her lead.

"Majesty?" the guard asked, blinking in the dim torchlight.

"Has there been any report of anything amiss?" she questioned, though her gaze fixated on the path that led beyond the camp and deep into the desert.

"No, Majesty, all is well, I assure–"

His words were cut off by a woman's shout, soon echoed by others.

"The watch has spotted someone," Callan murmured, taking Eve by the hand and heading toward the commotion.

"There," the guardswoman who had raised the alarm shouted, as they neared. "I saw someone approaching."

"Just one person?" Callan asked, confused.

"A woman," she confirmed.

Sure enough, treading through the sand toward them was a feminine form, instantly recognizable to Eve the moment she lifted her head to look at the gathered fae.

Emilia's lovely pale face was illuminated by the light of the moon, and though she looked exactly as she had the day she'd tried to murder Eve, something about her was *wrong*.

Stopping several feet away, well out of the reach of the guards and soldiers who had now formed a protective ring around Eve and Callan, Emilia smiled.

"Is this truly the welcome you offer your dearest friend after such a long time apart?" she purred, in the same feline tone she'd always used. "Surely you've forgiven me by now." Emilia's head tilted slightly, the move unnaturally jerky. "I've forgiven you for leaving me to die, and for choosing to be his whore rather than the queen we needed you to be."

Callan growled, shadows gathering around him as Emilia's gaze darted to him briefly before returning to Eve. She lifted a hand to her mouth, wiping at something dark that had begun to trickle from the corner of it.

"How are you here?" Eve asked, voice firm despite the fear and anger that had her hands trembling.

"Oh I am to be a message," Emilia sighed. "I had hoped I would have more time to play, to repay your mercy," she said, practically spitting the word at Eve. "But it appears my time is running out." She examined the liquid coating her fingers a moment, pouting. "Shame."

"Say what you came to say, voidspawn," Callan commanded, tightening his grip on Eve's hand. Whether to steady her or himself, she wasn't sure.

Emilia rolled her eyes and pinned Callan with a bored stare. "Boring."

Turning to Eve she continued, "You are to give up this foolish cause, you have no hope of victory. The Unending One bids me to tell you that if you bow before her, she will let you live." Emilia's face split into a vicious grin. "As pets. For her to use however she sees fit—both of you."

"Fuck that," Eve growled, reaching out with her magic, calling upon the earth beneath them to aid her. A chasm opened beneath Emilia's feet, swallowing her as she screamed, the sound somehow wrong, filled with many voices instead of just one. Within seconds, the earth enveloped her entirely, and whatever wore the skin of her oldest friend vanished beneath the sand and stone entirely.

The guards gaped at her. She could feel each and every stare as if they'd reached out and touched her with their hands, but she ignored them as she turned to Callan.

"That was strange. She's already made this threat once, why do it again?"

"Maybe just to rattle you further?" he guessed, frowning.

"I don't think so. I feel like there's something we're missing. I need to see Lia."

"Alright," he agreed. "But take the guards with you. I know you're capable of defending yourself," he added, seeing the argument building in her eyes. "But it would make me feel better."

"Fine," she conceded, "but it won't be necessary."

"I know," he smiled, pressing a kiss to her lips. "My Queen is utterly terrifying."

CHAPTER 56

LIA

Every minute ticked by with impossible slowness. She'd asked the guards outside if there had been any word at least five times since Bella had left, and each time they'd said no, assuring her they would alert her immediately should anything change. Through it all, Eyla slept soundly, blissfully unaware that something might be wrong.

Perhaps Bella was mistaken? Her visions didn't often specify timing, so it was possible that whatever she was afraid of simply hadn't happened yet.

She was nearly ready to go to the guards once more, this time to demand someone get her an explanation when a shift in the air behind her had her tensing. The hairs along the back of her neck stood up, alerting her to a presence that hadn't been there seconds before.

"Do not cry out," a male voice said, barely above a whisper. Too quiet to be heard outside. "Or I will slit the girl's throat."

She didn't dare test the veracity of the threat, keeping silent as a grave as she turned slowly to meet the intruder. Dressed in pale grey, his form was undeniably masculine, and impossibly dark eyes stared at her coldly. Aside from that, there was little she could tell about him, thanks to the mask that covered the entirety of the lower half of his face and the hood that covered his hair. He had to be fae, that much she knew without seeing his ears. Nobody else could have made it inside without being detected. Truthfully, even a fae shouldn't have been able to, thanks to the wards the fae had promised to put up.

In one hand, he held the Sword of Light, with the other, he gripped her arm so tightly she knew it would bruise, yanking her closer. "This will not be pleasant," he said flatly.

"No–" she began, only for the words to die on her tongue as darkness and wind enveloped them. A strangled cry of surprise spilled from her lips despite her best efforts to remain calm, and before it was over, she found herself in what appeared to be remarkably well-preserved remains of a fae structure, illuminated only by a pair of roaring braziers.

Tiny bits of stone bit into her knees and palms as she fell forward, suddenly shoved free of his grip. *I have to get back, I have to get away,* she thought, delving deep into herself to call upon her magic as Bella had shown her, using her fear and determination as an anchor.

There was nothing there. Only emptiness greeted her as she called out for her magic, as if it had never existed to begin with. Had Helie stripped her of her gift?

"I think you'll find that won't work around me," he said coldly.

"Who are you?" she demanded, rising to her feet to face him.

Tugging the mask free, he revealed his face–rugged with tan skin defined by a nasty scar that ran the length of the right side of his face. "Call me Jabez, since you and I will be spending some time getting acquainted." His gaze swept over her and she stiffened. There was no lust in his eyes, to her relief, only cold hard calculation.

"My goddess wants the secrets pulled from you; peeled from your very skin if necessary."

Lia watched silently as he walked slowly to a table she hadn't noticed before, and paled at what she saw there. Gleaming silver instruments, from wicked sharp blades to what appeared to be clamps, lay strewn haphazardly across the surface. Directly behind him, her roaming gaze snagged on another table, this one bare save for leather straps hanging from the sides. Her heartbeat was a dull roar in her ears. If she didn't get away now, awful things were going to happen here.

"I will never tell you whatever it is you want to know," she said defiantly, hoping her words would remain true. This must have been what Bella was so afraid of, what her instincts had been warning her against. If only she had gone along with her.

No, she realized, shaking her head against the thought. *There is no telling what would have happened to Eyla if I hadn't been there. At least she is safe.*

He merely sighed, shaking his head. "I wouldn't be so sure of that," he replied, tracing a finger along one of the instruments idly. "Shall we get started then, little queen?"

~

Blood dripped on the stone floor.

Thanks to the fae senses she now possessed, she could hear every drop Jabez wrung from her. Her new senses had also made every bruising touch more painful and every swipe of his blade more excruciating than the last.

Time had ceased to have meaning, and in what she'd learned was a temple to the fae god Vidar, the god of silence and restraint, devoid of any windows to indicate the time of day, she had no way of knowing how long she'd been his captive.

Rolling her head to the side, she surveyed Jabez's back as he examined his instruments, no doubt deciding what to use next.

"Why haven't you asked me any questions?" she asked, her voice hoarse, throat burning. She had screamed, raged at the gods for abandoning her, begging for mercy.

At first, she had been ashamed that he could elicit the reaction from her. She had wanted to be stronger, to show no fear.

Now, she simply wanted it to be over.

"I was just getting to that," he replied idly, as if they were discussing the weather.

Lia sighed, turning to gaze at the stone ceiling again. There was a mosaic above her head, images of what looked like a man, but she couldn't quite make out his features. From time, she assumed, or perhaps the artist had simply left his features deliberately vague. The images of the gods back home had always been without features, as they were always depicted with their backs to the viewer, a reminder of the fact they had abandoned their children, her father and Alfie believed. She had never put much thought into it herself, but she was certainly feeling their absence now.

Returning to her side, Jabez now held a small silver cup in his hand. Gripping her head, he lifted it from the table as far as the leather bonds across her chest and shoulders would allow, pressing the cool lip of the cup to her dry, cracked, lips.

"Poison?" she spat, attempting to turn her head away.

His grip tightened on her hair, not allowing for even the smallest movement. "Water," he replied with an impatient sigh.

She eyed him warily but parted her lips, allowing the liquid into her mouth. It certainly tasted like nothing but tepid water, still a balm to her aching throat despite the warm temperature.

All too soon, the cup was taken away, her head released to fall back against the hard table with a thunk. She barely even registered the faint pain, thanks to her other injuries. Looking down, she grimaced at the sight.

Her shirt had been ripped open, and cuts of varying size and depth marred her tanned skin. Likewise, her leggings had been cut from her, and her legs bore vicious bruises from the beating she'd received with a metal bar, alongside more gashes and cuts. One blow had been hard enough to shatter one ankle.

"Where is the Queen of Coruscis?" He asked, leaning against the table, carefree and unbothered by the sight of the woman he'd so cruelly tortured.

Lia couldn't help the bitter laugh that erupted from her. "Are you serious?" she asked incredulously. "Your people have her."

Jabez frowned, dark brows coming together tightly. "Hmm," he hummed thoughtfully as he straightened. "You wouldn't lie to me, would you, little queen?" he inquired, reaching back to grab the metal bar again.

Lia's heart sank to her gut. Fear reared its ugly head once more. She couldn't bear another beating with that thing. Closing her eyes tightly against the tears that welled, she shook her head frantically. "No, no, I'm not lying," the words as much a plea as they were an answer.

Cool metal trailed along her thigh slowly, and she jerked against the bonds, crying out from the pain the movement caused. "I'm not lying!" she shouted. "We got word she was missing and assumed you had her."

She had made a vow to herself, and to him, that she would tell him nothing. But where was the harm in admitting this? It told him nothing, and she truly had no idea where to even begin looking for Naia, so it wasn't as if she could tell him anyway. Shame coated her throat. The excuse felt hollow. She was saving herself more pain, and at what cost?

His warm breath met her ear as he leaned close, whispering, "I believe you." She kept her eyes squeezed tight, not wanting to watch the next blow as it fell.

But the blow never came. Instead, the bonds across her chest and thighs fell away, the sudden absence of their constant pressure making her gasp. Pain wracked her body as he lifted her from the table, cradling her like a bride.

"You'll rest while I await orders," he said, walking her to the corner, where a cot waited. Gingerly laying her on the hard bed, he straightened, examining her ruined ankle. "I don't think you'll be going anywhere on that, but just in case you're stupid enough to try, know that your magic will not work here and that I will be close by."

Rolling to her side, she cried out as her ankle screamed thanks to the movement. He was right, there was no way she could stand, much less try to run.

All she could do was pray to whatever gods may be listening.

CHAPTER 57

EVE

Bella met Eve, and the personal guard Callan had insisted on, halfway to Lia's tent. "What happened?" the seer demanded.

"Kore sent a message in the form of my oldest friend," Eve replied tightly.

Bella's brow shot up. "Please explain."

So Eve launched into the tale of what had occurred with Emilia back at Darkegrove, explaining her death and then reanimation, with no small degree of guilt. By the time they reached Lia's tent, Bella's eyes were dark, her expression somber.

"That's awful, I'm sorry." She paused, just outside of the tent. "Lia and I both had a feeling something was wrong, but I had no idea..."

Eve dismissed the rest of her statement with a shake of her head. "You had no way of knowing. But I need to speak to Lia. Something else is wrong, I think maybe it's Naia."

Bella nodded her agreement and they stepped inside, offering a brief nod to the human guards outside the queen's tent. "I think you're right, Lia has been saying–"

The seer froze, staring into the darkened tent, inhaling sharply.

"What's wrong?" Eve asked, looking past her. "Where is Lia?"

Bella's gaze shot to the small girl still asleep in her cot. "She should be here," Bella whispered tightly. "I left her with Eyla, to keep them both safe."

"Guards!" Eve called out, wincing as the girl stirred.

The pair of guards entered immediately, confusion on their faces.

"Where is your queen?" Eve demanded, rounding to face them.

"We thought she was still in here," one of the men replied, face paling. "Nobody has been in or out since she last asked for an update, at least an hour ago."

"She's been taken," Bella breathed, hand flying to cover her mouth. "Alert your soldiers, have everyone begin searching for her immediately."

"What's going on?" The sleepy voice of Bella's daughter drew their attention, though her question went unanswered. Even her mother, moving to give her daughter a comforting hug didn't dare reply.

Eve nodded her agreement with Bella's order, fear seizing her heart. "Send word to King Callan, Lady Brida, and Queen Lucia immediately. We will all search for her. She must be found right away," she ordered her own fae guard, who departed instantly.

Bella gasped, leaping from her daughter's cot and striding to a table in the corner. Eve followed her gaze, in time to hear Bella let out an impressive string of curses. "They've taken her, and the sword," Bella said, turning to face Eve, expression dark.

"Gods help us," Eve murmured, dread settling in her gut. "I need to get back and secure the crown."

A flash of light outside the tent drew her attention, and moments later, Leysa appeared. "Callan sent me to help," she said.

Nodding her thanks, Eve said, "Can you ask the shifters to take to the sky? Perhaps they can see something we can't from the ground."

"Of course," Leysa replied. "Some of them already have, scouting to see if there are any more surprises out in the sand."

Bella brushed past Eve, determination evident in her stride.

"Where are you going?" Eve asked.

"To get more help," Bella replied, casting a glance over her shoulder. "I'm going to talk to the gods."

CHAPTER 58

LIA

"It seems you'll be with me for a while longer, little queen," Jabez said suddenly, drawing Lia from the edge of sleep as he returned. He went to grab her from the cot, but Lia struck, landing a sound blow against his face.

The look of surprise on his face had satisfaction blooming in her chest, but it was short-lived as he simply sighed, pulling her over his shoulder. Pain wracked her as the fractured ankle bumped against his body, drawing a despondent sob from her.

"That was a waste of energy." With more care than he had used to pick her up, Jabez laid her on the torture table once more. Pausing, he looked her over. "I hope you know I don't enjoy this."

She snorted in response, swiping at the tears that streamed down her face. Pain, frustration, and desperation were a storm inside her. "I'm sure," she bit back. "Only men who get off on causing pain do things like this."

Jabez sighed, shaking his head as if she were a petulant child. "That is where you are wrong, little queen," he replied, pinning her arms. The now familiar pressure of the straps tightening against her chest had panic soaring, and she struggled against the bonds, to no avail. "I feel nothing when I look at you, or when I hurt you," he replied. "I see a job I have been tasked with, nothing more."

Lia simply stared back. Somehow the knowledge that he felt nothing at all made it worse. If he lacked feeling entirely, then there could be no hope of mercy. "How is that possible?" she asked, if only to keep him talking a little longer, anything to buy time before he started to hurt her again.

"I once served the god Vidar," he replied, pointing upward to the mosaic above them. "Silence and restraint. The most devout of us took our vows quite literally. We embodied silence, going years without speaking and even silencing our very minds. We did not dream, did not allow ourselves to feel. We *were* silence."

Leather pressed firmly against her thighs, pinning them to the table as he yanked the strap tight. A rather pointless step, considering she couldn't run. "But you don't serve him now," she said, glancing upward.

"No," he replied simply, "I do not. He abandoned his children." For the first time, she saw the faintest hint of emotion flash in his dark eyes. "Now, I serve the only goddess who remained, one who cares for her devout servants as a mother to forgotten children."

"Kore," she seethed, shaking her head. The one who wanted to end the world, to destroy everything, and for what?

His gaze snapped to hers, warning clear in his eyes. "Speak her name with respect, little queen, or you will not like the consequences."

Lia's blood turned cold. As bad as things had been so far, the look in his eyes told her they could get far, far worse. "So," she asked, still desperately clinging to her small reprieve, this short conversation that kept his next ministrations at bay, "why is she doing this?"

Jabez rocked back on his heels, considering her a moment. "You want a tale, little queen?" he asked, watching dispassionately as she nodded, before turning to his instruments. "Then I will tell you–while I work."

Lia's heart sank. The time she'd bought herself was at an end. She didn't bother to stop the sob that wracked her as Jabez returned to her side, a small pair of pliers in hand. "There was once a king of Gorias, known as Arawn the Glorious..."

~

Lia was back on the cot again, and this time it didn't take long for her to fall asleep, or perhaps more accurately, pass out from the pain. She knew she was dreaming when she found herself whole, without pain, and sitting in the middle of the very same field she'd spoken to Helie in once before.

But there was no goddess to greet her this time, no gift waiting to be bestowed. Only the seemingly endless sea of grass and wildflowers as far as the eye could see. A warm breeze stirred, and as the sun warmed her upturned face, she hoped this was her afterlife.

Maybe I died.

It was a morbid thought, one that sent a fresh wave of guilt through her. She knew those she loved would be heartbroken, that she still had her duty to fulfill to save the world, but escape at this point seemed hopeless. Unless they found her, and soon.

"Wake up," a feminine voice she didn't quite recognize called. "Wake up, it's time to go."

Turning in place, she searched for the source, finding nobody around.

"Wake up. Now." The voice was more urgent but still distant.

A jolt of fresh pain sent a shockwave through her, and as she cried out, the warmth and peace of her dream were ripped away. She was once again on the cot, staring at the floor ahead of her...and a woman's bare feet.

Her gaze drifted upward slowly. Had Kore finally come? Did she want to relish the kill herself or did she simply intend to see to Lia's torture on her own?

"Finally," the woman muttered.

To Lia's shock, she met the gaze of the goddess Araceli, Bella's mother. "*You* came?" she asked, sounding as dumbfounded as she felt.

Of all the gods who might've answered her prayers, Araceli was easily the one she least expected.

"Yes, and we must go before I'm discovered," she replied impatiently, reaching for Lia's arm and holding it tight. Her attention flitted to Lia's ankle, silver eyes darkening. "This will hurt, I'm sorry. I do not possess the power to heal I'm afraid."

Lia opened her mouth to reply but closed it quickly as the torture chamber disappeared in the blink of an eye. The scream that came from her as she was yanked into darkness left her throat burning. Pain was no longer simply something she felt, she *was* pain incarnate. Every fiber of her being burned, and as she began to fall unconscious once more, she could have sworn she heard Bella crying her name.

Chapter 59

Eve

Eve brought the damp cloth to Lia's brow once more, wiping away the blood caked to her forehead. Her once golden blonde hair was the color of rust, her tanned skin a full shade paler than it had been. Her injuries...those had nearly made Eve vomit upon seeing them.

Bella sat beside Eve, still clasping Lia's hand tightly as the healer worked to stabilize Lia's broken bones. "My mother says she will do what she can," Bella began, casting a small glance at the healer, a fae woman from Finias. "Helie may not come though, because of how close they believe Kore to be."

Eve snapped, "They're afraid."

Bella sighed, nodding her head in confirmation. "Yes, and while I understand why, I will never forgive them for not risking it for her."

"And where the fuck were *you* when she was taken?" Aelius snarled. He'd demanded the same answer a handful of times since Lia had been returned to them, but no matter how many times Bella explained her reasoning, he remained unsatisfied.

The seer shot to her feet, carefully laying Lia's hand on the bed. "I'll be back," she said before storming out of the tent.

Soaking the rag into the now dirty water basin, Eve cast a sidelong glance at Aelius. "You know it wasn't her fault," she said. "They would have taken her anyway, either by killing Bella or waiting until Lia was alone."

Aelius scoffed, barely sparing the tall, dark soldier who stepped inside a glance. "Bastien," he said by way of greeting. "Any news?"

"Actually yes, for you," he said, his eyes settling on Eve.

Her brow rose slightly. "For me?"

"Yes, the pretty fae girl, with dark hair and grey eyes," he began, clearing his throat. "Ah, she asked me to come for you, said you'll want to talk to her."

Frowning, Eve dropped the rag back into the basin and rose to her feet. "Did she say why?"

"No, Majesty," Bastien replied, offering a slight bow.

Eve hesitated. If Cora wanted to speak to her, she had no doubt it was important, but she also hated the idea of leaving Lia's side.

Reading her expression, Aelius, said, "I'll be with her, and I'll play nice when the seer returns."

"And I'll make sure he does," Bastien added, taking a seat beside Aelius.

Satisfied, Eve cast a final glance at her injured friend and sent yet another silent prayer to Keithia. She could grow herbs for the human healers and had been able to provide some aid in that way, but healing was not her gift.

No fae had yet come forward from Lucia's army to offer aid. Leysa and Valerian had gone to their own camp to find someone blessed with Helie's gift, but apparently, it was uncommon in the northern kingdoms, for some reason.

Not every fae bore a gift from the gods, and in fact, it was rarer than Eve had expected, given that so many of her friends were blessed. Hope remained, however, that someone would be found with the capability to at least ease the worst of Lia's injuries.

To her surprise, it was Valerian who waited for her outside. "I've come to pace you to Cora," he explained. "It's urgent." His normally cheerful demeanor was cast in shadow, something clearly bothering him.

"What's happened?" she asked, heart sinking.

"Not here," he replied quietly enough that only those with heightened hearing would be able to overhear.

Despite the worry that flooded her, Eve nodded her understanding, taking his outstretched hand. They whirled into darkness, and in the span of a heartbeat found themselves in Eve and Callan's tent, where her mate, Cora, Cathal, and Mara all waited.

"What's going on?" she asked, stomach dropping as she took in their dour expressions.

"We've been betrayed," Cathal said, striding from one side of the tent to the other, looking positively murderous.

"That's a bit of an overstatement," Cora sighed from her seat by the table.

Beside Cora, Mara shook her head. "Hardly," she replied, gaze lingering on her mate.

"Someone just tell me what's going on," Eve said, glancing around the room.

"Lucia's daughter, Zia, dropped the wards around Avellon's camp," Callan said finally.

A pebble dropping to the floor would have sounded like a boulder in the silence that fell over the room as she processed what Callan was saying.

Valerian paced away again, leaving Eve to stare in shock at where he had been standing a second before. "He's gone to bring someone else to this meeting," Callan explained. "Leysa is organizing with some of our people who are taking over Avellon's wards and protection."

"We're stretched thin with guarding Brida's people too," Eve said quietly, her gaze shifting to Cora. "Why did she do this?"

"We don't know," Cora answered. "But I suspect it was likely just because she hates humans."

"What?" Eve blurted. *That would have been nice to know long before now*, she thought, her attention darting to Callan. "Why didn't you tell me that?"

Callan sighed, casting a long-suffering glance at his sister. "It isn't entirely true, that's why. She doesn't hate them, she simply-"

"Views them as beneath us," Cathal finished. From his tone, Eve suspected it was a shared sentiment.

"And nobody suspected she would do this? Are we sure she isn't working with Kore?"

Mara laughed, actually laughed, at that, her manicured nails tapping against the wine glass Eve hadn't noticed before. "No, but we'll find out soon enough."

Eve's head was spinning. All of this had unraveled while she cared for Lia? How much had been known, or suspected, and kept from her?

Callan, reading the accusation in her gaze as she looked at him, shook his head. "We really did not know, dove, not until you were gone to care for Aurelia."

Eve nodded, closing her eyes briefly. She believed him. The rest of them, she wasn't so sure, but Callan wouldn't lie to her. "Okay, so who did Valerian go after?"

"Lucia's eldest daughter," Callan answered.

"This is going to be quite entertaining," Cathal said, face splitting into a devious grin.

Eve turned as the air behind her was disturbed, announcing Valerian's return. Instantly, he appeared, with a tall, thin woman on his arm. With dark skin and jet black braids that fell to her hips, adorned with gold hoops, she bore a remarkable resemblance to the goddess Helie, save for her eyes that were a dark brown, rather than the goddess's gold.

"This is Princess Alyona, of Finias," Valerian said, releasing the princess's arm, and stepping away.

"So you've heard what my sister has done to the humans," Alyona said without preamble, expression grave. "Now let's discuss how we're going to fix it."

CHAPTER 60

LIA

A scream erupted from her lips as Lia awoke with a start. Fear, more than pain, coursed through her as she thrashed. Her gaze darted around her, taking in her surroundings. It was dark, barely lit by a small lantern on a table.

Panic gripped her heart, but eased as she realized there were no gleaming instruments there to tear her skin or break her bones scattered across the tabletop–and that it was moonlight above, from the peak of her tent.

Her tent, where she was safe because the goddess Araceli had rescued her.

"You're okay, you're safe," the masculine voice said beside her, gently placing a hand on her shoulder.

She screamed again, trying to scoot away on the bed, before recognition set in. It was Aelius who had spoken, Aelius who was touching her arm, not Jabez. Aelius who would never harm her.

"I'm sorry," he said again, pulling his hand away as realization darkened his blue eyes.

Closing her own, Lia shook her head tightly. "It's okay, I just...I didn't know where I was for a moment."

She sat up, straightening, and every move hurt, though considerably less than before. She still couldn't move her leg correctly, and the ankle Jabez had shattered, she saw, was still a deep shade of purple and nearly twice the size of the other.

"There were no healers?" she asked, frowning. "Helie didn't..." Letting the words fall away, she sighed. Of course Helie hadn't come. She hadn't come when she was being tortured, only the goddess Lia had assumed hated her came when she pled for rescue. Why would it be different now?

"You've been seen by healers. They've treated you with herbs and poultices," Aelius explained, scowling. "But so far the fae either haven't found someone with healing magic, or they haven't sent them."

"Queen Evelyn is trying," said another, and Lia turned to find Bastien seated behind her. "I'm sorry, I didn't mean to startle you," he said, offering a small smile.

"It's fine," she said, forcing a smile in response. Their presence was a balm to her wounded heart. Her twin and the man she'd known her entire life, essentially another brother to her, had stayed, she knew without asking, to watch over her. But still, she hurt. A cloudy sky, where the sun wasn't quite ready to shine again. "Where is Bella?"

Bella's absence was a shock and for a moment, hurt almost as much as a knife to the gut.

"She was here all night," Aelius replied. "She took her daughter to another tent so that she didn't see you like this, and she leaves occasionally to go and check on her."

Bastien glanced toward the tent flap, adding, "She should be back soon."

Lia relaxed then, some of the tension easing from her shoulders. "Okay," she replied, more to herself than the others.

"We're going to keep looking," Aelius said, leaning closer as he examined the bruises and cuts along her legs, visible thanks to the short nightgown she wore. "For a fae with healing magic."

Someone had changed her clothes, she realized, and cleaned the blood from her skin. A healer, she assumed, making a mental note to thank them later.

"I can do it myself," she said, straightening.

"You're too weak–" Aelius protested.

The tent flap opened, sending a jolt of pain through her as she startled.

"You're awake," Bella said breathlessly, eyes wide with relief. "And too weak for what?" she added, looking at Aelius.

"She wants to try to heal herself," Bastien explained, sighing.

Bella paused, her gaze meeting Lia's. For the span of five heartbeats, they simply stared at one another. She couldn't read the emotion she saw swimming in Bella's eyes, but what she felt in her own heart was tremendous relief and love. That tug she'd been ignoring was unbearably taut, ready to rip the heart from her chest if needed, anything to be closer to Bella.

"Then she should do it," Bella replied, closing the distance between them. Brushing past Aelius, she climbed onto the bed with Lia, slowly, to avoid jostling her leg too much, and enveloped her in a careful hug. Rocking back so that she was perched precariously on her knees at the edge of the bed, she looked Lia over. "She can do anything."

Aelius cleared his throat, rising from his chair and moving to stand by Bastien. "I really don't think-," he began tightly.

Lia cast a warning glance at her brother, but Bella slid into his chair easily, unbothered by her brother's tone. "You can do this," Bella said, offering a smile that made Lia's heart ache.

Nodding, Lia shifted into a comfortable position and closed her eyes. She pictured her favorite meadow, where sunflowers grew so tall she could barely reach their bright blooms. Where the warm spring breezes would make waves in the tall grasses and as children, she, Bastien, and Aelius would pretend to be a ship's crew, sailing away to a distant and magical land.

She heard her mother's laugh and felt the familiar squeeze of Aelius' hand in hers, the little patterns their own special language developed as children. Warmth flowed through her—the warmth of a springtime sun kissing her cheeks, chasing away anything that made her sad or hurt.

A sharp gasp sounded from behind her, and she didn't know if it was Aelius or Bastien who had leaned forward first, lightly touching her shoulder, but soon a second hand joined the first– and then a small, female hand was slipping into hers.

The sensation spread from her chest, down her abdomen, her legs, and to her ruined ankle. Warmth like she had never known caressed the most broken pieces of her body, sliding against her skin as comforting as a mother's touch.

Her eyes remained closed as she focused on the feeling of three of the people she loved most in the world supporting her, pouring their love into her as she healed herself. When the warmth finally began to recede, she opened them, a small gasp escaping her as she beheld what she'd managed to do.

The ankle that had been so badly ravaged was normal again, no sign of bruise or misshapen bone to be seen. Her legs, from what she could see, were healed, though pale pink scars remained from her time being held by Jabez.

Relief and exhaustion swept over her. Healing herself had taken so much out of her, so much energy, but she had done it. She had managed to harness her power and use it as her own, without guidance or help from a goddess.

"It didn't take away all the scars," Aelius said, surprise etched into his tone.

Bastien hummed thoughtfully but said nothing, and Bella, she was only staring at Lia, understanding swimming in her silver eyes.

"I need to sleep," she said, before anyone could start asking questions or fussing over her.

"Of course," Bastien replied, releasing her shoulder. She knew without looking that he had taken Aelius by the arm. He would likely have to force her brother out.

"The guards can remain close," she said, turning to look at her brother, who was in fact ready to protest. "But I want to be alone, just for a while. Please." She looked to Bella then, hoping the seer would understand her need for privacy, despite how much she'd missed them, how desperately the other part of her wanted to keep them close.

With lingering looks, each of them shuffled out, Aelius and Bastien pausing to give her a peck on the brow each, and Bella, a more lingering kiss pressed to her lips.

Once alone, she pulled the nightgown higher, revealing the scars that she'd chosen to leave behind. Her ankle had to be healed so that she could stand and fight. When the next battle came, she would be standing alongside her own people, sword raised, ready to face whatever Kore and Gorias had to throw at them.

The scars would remain so that she never forgot what they'd done to her, the parts of her that they'd tried to break–the parts she could only admit to herself they *had* broken.

But her people would not see that, would not see the weak, hopeless woman she'd become on Jabez's table. They would see only their queen. Strong, fearless, and filled with hope and light.

With that thought to comfort her, Lia settled into the bed and drifted into sleep.

DRESSED IN STUNNING GOLD SILK THAT HUGGED HER slender form perfectly, Helie offered Lia a warm smile. "Hello, Aurelia."

Barely resisting the urge to stomp her foot like a child, Lia gaped at the goddess. "Where the fuck have you been?"

The curse felt strange on her tongue, as did the disrespect. She never cursed at people in authority, ever. But there was rage blooming in her chest now, and for the moment at least, she didn't care if she angered the goddess.

To her shock, Helie just sighed. "It is regrettable that I was not able to come to your aid."

"Regrettable?" Lia repeated, jaw still hanging open. "How is it that the one who hates me so much could come but you couldn't?"

The corner of Helie's mouth twitched slightly, her expression giving nothing away. "You mistake fear for her child for hatred, my dear," she replied lightly. "She should not have come to your aid either. It was incredibly reckless of her and put us all at risk."

Snapping her mouth closed, Lia tucked that information away for later. "Why are you here now?"

Helie took a small step forward, and though fear had her wanting to step back, Lia held her ground. "I've come to check on you," the goddess sighed. "In the only way I can." She glanced around at the open meadow they'd once again met in. "But I seem to recall being told that wards were being put up to protect your dreams from intruders. Strange that they–"

In an instant, the bright sunny sky of Lia's dreamworld vanished. Darkness replaced the light, nothing but barren soil replacing the tall grasses that had danced in the wind moments before. Helie's golden eyes widened with what Lia could only assume was terror. "Wake up!" she commanded before disappearing as well.

Wake up, wake up, wake up, she repeated, fear coursing through her veins. Something was coming, she could feel it in her very bones, and she knew without a doubt she did not want to be here when it arrived.

Something wet was touching her hand. Something wet...and warm. Looking down, she saw nothing, but as the sensation grew more defined, she gasped, eyes flying open as she woke.

The strange, wet feeling on her hand remained, even as the rest of the dream turned nightmare faded. A sort of lapping sound had her head turning to the right, only to find a bear–an actual bear–licking her hand gently.

The shriek that erupted from Lia was neither queenlike nor strong, earning what she could've sworn was an exasperated sigh from the bear, who sat back on its haunches and stared at her expectantly—waiting for what, she didn't know.

Did bears live in the desert? she wondered. She thought back to her lessons as a child and couldn't recall a single mention of bears in Coruscis. *So maybe this one traveled south especially to make me its lunch,* she thought with a bit of hysterical laughter.

"Okay," Lia breathed shakily, scooting back, gaze darting to the tent flap as Aelius burst inside.

"I told you she'd panic," he sighed, shaking his head at Bastien, who followed immediately behind him. The bear turned to look at them, giving a light shake of its furry head.

Lia blinked. Their reactions confused her. Why weren't they afraid or doing anything to get the bear–*the very large bear*–out of her tent?

"He's a shifter," Aelius explained, resting a hand on the bear's head. The bear quickly shook her twin's hand free, huffing once.

A shifter, she exhaled slowly. Right. She'd forgotten about the fae shifters with Eve's army. "Eve sent the bear?" she asked, gaze darting to the bear in question.

"His name is Amias," Bastien supplied helpfully, reaching up to pet the bear, who to Lia's surprise, leaned into his touch. "And he volunteered to come help watch over you. Queen Evelyn asked for volunteers from their army to help with our security since–"

"We should wait," Aelius interjected. "Eve asked to explain the situation herself, and she's on her way now."

Lia frowned, bear momentarily forgotten. "What situation?"

Bastien and Aelius exchanged a glance. "The one," Bastien replied, "about a princess of Finias betraying us, and leaving you unguarded."

CHAPTER 61

EVE

"So it's true then," Lia asked from her bed, dutifully ignoring Amias, who lay beside it, still in his bear form.

I probably should've sent a note, Eve thought, lifting a hand to hide the silent laugh she had at the memory of her friend's fear-fueled rant about waking up to find a bear in her tent.

"Yes," she replied. "Lucia's youngest daughter, Zia, pulled her protection from your army and then fled. There was some...animosity toward humans we weren't entirely aware of. But we're working to determine if there is more to it or not."

"How?" Lia asked, gaze drifting to Amias again as he stretched and yawned.

"Lucia's eldest daughter, Alyona," Eve explained. "She is going to see that her sister is found and questioned."

Lia blinked at Eve. "Oh. Can we trust her?"

And that was the question on everyone's minds. A lot was riding on the word of the fae princess, but they had little choice in the matter. The people of Finias would hardly accept Eve or Callan intervening in their political affairs, and they certainly could not afford Finias abandoning them entirely, or worse, an outright fight with them.

"We don't have much of a choice," Eve replied honestly. "We've taken over placing wards around your camp, and some of the shifters have volunteered to help," she explained, gesturing to Amias. "We have to leave the rest to Alyona. She claims to not share her sister's opinions of humans, and she seems genuinely angry with Zia."

Lia fell silent, a thoughtful look playing across her features. As she straightened her legs out in front of her, Eve's attention snagged on the scars still marking her tan skin. Her heart gave a squeeze, sympathy for her friend's suffering washing over her. Tears threatened, but she knew that Lia wouldn't welcome them, and the last thing she wanted was to cause Lia more pain.

"You kept them," she observed quietly, a statement as much as a question. If Lia's gift was nearly as strong as she suspected it was, the scars should have been easy enough for her to heal away.

Lia didn't answer immediately. Her summer sky blue eyes turned to her ankle, the one that had been mangled when she'd been brought in, now healed perfectly. "I did," she replied, tone wary.

Eve looked away as the image of Lia, broken and bleeding, flashed in her mind, sending a chill down her spine. Lia had been so near death. Even now, as healed as she was physically, a light had gone out in what had once been one of the brightest souls Eve had ever known. She could only hope the brilliant, hopeful spirit that made Lia so special would return, one day. The scars on her body she could have healed, but the ones Eve knew her soul bore, those would take time.

"Why?" she asked, meeting Lia's gaze. It was a struggle to keep the pity off of her face

Lia sighed, eyes closing briefly. "To remind me that if this didn't break me, nothing will."

"You are the strongest person I know," Eve began slowly. "But it's okay to feel it, to cry, to fall apart," she finished, casting a glance to the tent flap. Aelius and the others waited outside, refusing to go very far from Lia. Bella, especially, had been reluctant to leave the two queens, and shifter, alone long enough for them to talk. "If you don't want them to see, I understand, but nobody will judge you or think less of you if you need to fall apart. Keeping it in is only going to make it harder. Trust me, I know."

"I can't," Lia replied, shaking her head. "If I start, I don't think I'll ever stop." Waving her hand once, Lia took a deep breath. "Tell me about Alyona."

She wouldn't press Lia any further about it. Eve could understand better than most the need to stay strong, to wait for the right moment to let it all out, to fall apart. She'd allowed herself only a moment when her mother had been taken from her, only a moment when she thought the same of Callan.

Lia would find her own way to get through this, and her friends would be there for every step, whatever she needed. Now, it seemed, she needed to think about anything but what she'd been through.

"She's...fierce, but quiet," Eve began, recalling the brief conversation she'd had with the princess. Even from the short interaction they'd had, she could tell Alyona was whip-smart and fiercely loyal to her people. "She loves her sister, but disagrees with her actions, and she's concerned there's something else at play that even she doesn't know about. She is very much her mother's daughter, and I think she will be a fierce ally."

"Do you think Zia is allied with Gorias?" Lia paled.

"Truthfully, I don't know," Eve shook her head. "Alyona doesn't believe so, but we can't be certain until we question her."

Amias grumbled, but whatever his opinion was it was lost on Eve. Too bad speaking to animals wasn't one of her gifts. If it was important though, Amias would have shifted and said whatever it was aloud.

"I don't like it," Lia said, scooting to the edge of the bed. Eve started to rise, to help Lia stand, but stopped as Lia waved a hand. "I'm not getting up, I'm just getting comfortable. Besides, there's a bear in my way."

Eve couldn't help but laugh at the wariness in Lia's tone and the way she eyed Amias as if he were a dangerous predator. Which he admittedly was, but not when it came to Eve or Lia.

"He can take another form if it would make you more comfortable," Eve offered, earning a long-suffering sigh from Amias. "But this is the form he prefers."

"It's fine, I'll get used to it," Lia replied with a smile that didn't reach her eyes. "Will you let me know if you learn anything new?"

The question was a clear dismissal, and Eve rose to return to her own camp, and Callan. "Of course," she replied, watching Lia carefully. "Do you want me to send the others in?"

Lia shook her head, still eyeing Amias. "I need a minute. He'll stay, right?"

"As long as you want him to," Eve promised. "If you need anything, he'll make sure I'm alerted right away."

As she left Lia alone, eyes shadowed and body scarred, she silently vowed if she ever found the male who'd taken Lia, she would shove vines so far down his throat they'd come out of his ass.

CHAPTER 62

LIA

"So," Lia began, scooting closer to the side of the bed and gingerly stretching her legs over the edge. She tensed as her bare feet grazed the small space between the bear shifter and her bed. She hadn't tried to stand since she'd been rescued thanks to her ankle, but it was healed now, and standing should be easy, only fear had kept her from trying. "You're a fae who turns into a bear."

Amias grumbled in response, rolling his ursine body to a sitting position. Strength rippled and radiated from beneath the thick almost-black fur as he stretched. Curious brown eyes watched her carefully as she tested the ankle, pressing her foot harder onto the ground.

No pain. The relief was so intense it nearly brought tears to her eyes. She hadn't completely doubted her healing ability, but to actually see proof of it was emotional in a way she hadn't expected. She'd managed to heal herself, using magic she still didn't entirely understand, and mended bone and flesh.

"And, when you're a bear, you still think like a fae? You don't follow base animal instinct alone?" she asked, slowly pushing herself to stand. Her legs were every bit as wobbly as her voice, though she suspected that was from nerves rather than any real weakness. She felt strong, physically at least. Her fae strength had been returned to her as soon as she'd finished healing her injuries; as if her body needed the reminder that she was safe, alive, and still fae.

Perhaps with enough time, Lia thought, she could turn that healing light inward and heal the scars she still bore on her soul.

Her new guardian rumbled in response, dipping his head and pressing his nose gently to her arm. The offer was clear. He would help her stand if she needed it.

"I'm okay," she breathed, reaching up to run her hand through his fur. Soft and warm beneath her touch, it soothed her nerves. "Thank you, for volunteering to help me. It was very kind of you."

Amias chuffed in response, and if bears could blush, he almost certainly would have been. The thought drew a light laugh from her. "I need to pee," she said casting a glance toward the curtained-off area that would allow her the privacy she needed. "You might want to go outside." The comment had the bear rolling his eyes.

"Right, okay then," she sighed, before heading to see to her needs.

Amias had moved to the center of the room by the time she finished and watched her closely as she sat on the edge of the bed once more. He held up a paw as if asking her to wait, but before she could ask why, a bright light flashed, instantly revealing an olive-skinned fae male in place of the bear. A little shorter than herself and lean but well toned, as revealed by the tight black leathers he wore.

"I thought formal introductions might make this a little less awkward," he said by way of greeting. "Hello, Queen Aurelia, my name is Amias Mordin, and it is a pleasure to finally speak to you."

Lia gaped. It was one thing to know the bear who had been by her side, who had just listened to her pee, she cringed, was a fae, but to actually see it was another thing entirely.

"Hello," she said awkwardly. "I suppose you can call me Lia now that we've shared that intimate moment." The joke was lame, but to his credit, he laughed.

"Well, if it makes you feel better, people pee in front of me all the time when I'm in bear form. Usually it's out of unbridled terror because they mistake me for a real bear about to eat them, but still," he replied, shrugging.

Lia laughed in response, the first real laugh since she'd returned. It made her heart feel a tiny bit lighter, and for the first time in a while, she felt a little like her old self again.

"Well, I guess I shouldn't be so embarrassed then." She paused as Amias took a seat in one of the chairs across from her, letting him get settled before she launched into the questions burning at the back of her mind. "What do you make of this thing with Princess Zia?"

Amias tilted his head, considering. "Well, I think that Queen Evelyn is right," he said thoughtfully. "I wasn't there for the meeting, but I've heard enough of Princess Alyona to make me think she can be trusted. Most importantly, I agree that we have no other choice but to see how this plays out."

Lia nodded. She thought the same herself, truthfully, and hadn't expected a different answer. "Tell me about yourself," she said next. "We're going to be spending a lot of time together."

"What do you want to know?"

"Do you have family back in Falias?" she asked, wondering what it was that drove him to join the fight.

Amias' oval face split into a broad smile. "I have a husband and two children. My husband wanted to join me, but the kids needed one of us to stay home. They're young," he explained. "Too young to be left alone. Twin girls, Terra and Sidra. They're two years old."

"That's very brave of you," she said, offering a smile in return. "I'm sure you miss them, and they must miss you as well."

"I do," he agreed. "But I know that I'm doing the right thing. I'm helping to give them a future."

Her heart ached for him. The choice to leave his family behind to fight against such a grave threat must have been incredibly difficult. But she was also impressed by his courage, his will to do what he could to protect the world, and his family, from those who would destroy it. How many men and women in her own army did the same?

They were the reason she must remain strong, must continue to stand and fight, even when all seemed lost.

"Thank you for telling me about them," she said, offering a smile.

"Of course–" His words fell silent as he looked toward the tent flap. Whatever he heard or sensed was beyond even her own enhanced hearing.

She threw her arm over her eyes as white flashed in the tent with Amias' shift into his bear form. Only then did the sound of grass crunching outside reach her ears, announcing someone's arrival, and Amias quickly took up a position between Lia and the tent flap. Lia gripped the sheets tightly as he lowered his head slightly, paws pressing into the floor of the tent firmly, prepared to defend her if needed.

"It's okay," Bella called just before stepping inside. "It's just me."

Instantly, Amias relaxed. The easing tension in his form signaled her own, and she released her tight grip on the sheets. A sigh of relief sounded through her as Bella entered, the sight of her love chasing away the rest of her fear entirely.

"What happened?" Bella asked, eyes widening.

Following her gaze, Lia looked down at the sheets she'd been holding so tightly, only to find the pale blue had turned black, as if burned.

"I don't know," Lia replied honestly, her voice wavering. "I guess I must have accidentally used my powers."

Amias pressed his wet snout against her knee gently, his body plopping onto the floor with a thunk.

"You'll learn to control it better," Bella assured her, "with time and practice." She hesitated, shifting from one foot to the other as she dragged a hand through her long raven hair.

"What is it?" There was something Bella wasn't saying, as clear on her face as if she'd spoken the words aloud.

"Eve wants to pace to Thalassa to find out what's going on with Naia Colvari, and she wants you to go with her."

Lia blinked. Of everything she'd expected Bella to say, that was probably somewhere near the bottom of her proverbial list. "Oh," she began, eyeing Bella's lovely face for a moment, eyes narrowing. "You're concerned I'm not strong enough."

She crossed to Lia then, falling to her knees in front of her. "No, sunshine, that isn't it at all." Bella's touch was a brand on her skin, her fingers pressing gently against the inside of her knees. "I know that you are strong, and you can do anything. It's just...I worry. I don't like the idea of us being apart again."

Lia sighed. Of course. Bella could never leave Eyla alone, not even here surrounded by guards, not after what had happened in this very tent while her daughter slept. Fear for her daughter would keep her here, while at the same time, she would be afraid for Lia every moment they were separated.

"I'll be fine," Lia soothed, placing her palm against Bella's cheek. "Eve and I will be together, along with whomever she has pacing her. Everything will be fine."

Bella nodded, though she still looked unconvinced. "Callan," she supplied. "With help from another fae, I'm not sure who."

"See?" Lia said, forcing a smile she didn't feel. "I'll be perfectly fine with them. Nothing bad will happen."

CHAPTER 63

EVE

"Hold tightly onto Tori," Eve instructed a slightly terrified-looking Lia. "She will get you there safely, I promise. It'll be disorienting, but close your eyes, that helps."

Lia nodded tightly, doing exactly as Eve instructed as she stepped into the tall, blonde, fae female's opened arms. Tori, one of Cora's most trusted friends. had volunteered, desperate she'd said, to get away from Cora's moping. What that moping was about, Eve wasn't entirely sure, but she made a note to find out when they returned.

"Hold on tight, dove," Callan purred into her ear. Heat coiled low in her belly, and she gave him a playful slap on the arm.

"Tease," she muttered, laying her head against his chest. As darkness and wind swept around them, his answering laugh warmed her.

SHE HADN'T SEEN THE HALLS OF EVERTIDE SINCE SHE WAS A small child. The sight of the domed room with soaring ceilings decorated with frescoes depicting images of the sea in various states, peaceful with rolling waves, storms lashing a lost ship, and the horizon at sunrise and at dusk, had her inhaling sharply. The room was stunning, the shades used by the artist a perfect complement to the warm sandstone that made up the entirety of the building. She wondered if the gazing pool that sparkled like gemstones in the bright overhead sunlight still graced the inner courtyards reserved for visiting dignitaries. The one she and Naia had once turned into a swimming pool, much to their parents' dismay.

"Something's wrong," Lia cautioned from just behind them, returning Eve's thoughts to the present.

Eve nodded her agreement, warning bells sounding in her mind. Word had been sent ahead to Naia's younger sister Maren, the princess turned regent, to prepare her for their sudden, and likely alarming, arrival. Eve had expected waiting guards, perhaps even some advisors or trusted courtiers, but what greeted them was utter silence.

She opened her mouth to call out, only to be stopped by the sound of bare feet against the polished floor. Someone was approaching swiftly. Her grip on Callan's arm tightened briefly, releasing as their greeter arrived.

Stepping out of an archway that led off of the main room, Maren herself appeared. Clad in a thin, gauzy gown of pale pink, with her wavy dark brown hair hanging freely to her hips, she looked less a princess and more a wandering waif.

"Of course something is wrong. My sister has been taken, and according to you, our world is threatened," she replied, tone sharp. "But now you're here to ask questions and to seek our help. So explain."

Eve cast a sideways glance at Callan before returning her attention to Maren.

"There is an ancient goddess set on destroying the world, for reasons we don't entirely understand, and apparently, the three of us human queens," she said, words spilling out faster than she'd intended. "Well, two of us formerly human, now fae, are destined to save everyone."

Maren's gaze slid to Lia as she stepped up beside Eve. "We want to help find your sister," Lia cut in smoothly, "because it's the right thing to do, but also because the very world depends on it."

Maren eyed the group for a moment, silent and unreadable. Eve's heart thundered in her chest. If Maren turned them away now, or if she didn't believe, all could be lost. They had come so very far, had been through so much...

She took Lia's hand in hers, giving a squeeze gently. They were in this together. No matter what happened next, they would stand united, and when Naia was found, she would stand alongside them as well. Whatever Kore and Gorias threw at them next, they would fight it with their heads held high.

"Follow me," Maren said finally, turning on her heel to lead them back the way she'd entered. "You're wearing slippers with your gowns?" she asked, gaze flicking to Eve and Lia in turn.

Eve nodded. She'd dressed in a flowing emerald gown made of layers of thin fabric that fell loosely around her, leaving most of her thighs bare, revealing the twin blades strapped to either thigh in sleek black holsters. Atop her carefully smoothed curls, the Crown of Darkegrove.

Lia had chosen white for the occasion, twin panels held in place at her shoulders and waist with gold ornaments, and a silken underskirt that covered her legs entirely. At her waist was the Sword of Light, fastened to a gilded and jeweled scabbard that perfectly complemented her own crown of golden spires.

A different sort of armor, for a different sort of battle.

The decision to keep the artifacts close to them had been an easy one, following the attack on Lia. If they held them, it was reasoned, then Kore wouldn't be able to take them—at least not without facing the two queens who now knew they could wield them.

Not that either of them knew *how* just yet.

"Yes," Eve replied for both of them. Dainty slippers had been chosen for practicality as much as fashion. Heels would have been difficult should a fight occur, and boots would have painted an odd picture when they needed to appear as normal as possible.

"Then you may follow me through the center of the hall," Maren said, casting a glance toward Callan and Tori as they stepped into the long, sunny hallway. "There is a delicate mosaic here; most shoes are not permitted. Slippers are fine."

True to what Maren had described, the center length of the hallway was made entirely of tile in varying shades of blue. It was reminiscent of a summer sky meeting the sea, but with no specific rhyme nor reason for the placement of the tiles that Eve could discern.

Waving a hand at the sides of the room, she indicated smooth paths with no tilework, just wide enough for them to walk single file. "You may walk there."

"This is stunning," Eve said as Maren led them further into the castle. "I don't recall seeing this when I visited as a girl."

Maren laughed lightly, the sound airy and carefree as a songbird. "You wouldn't have," she explained. "Children are not permitted in this wing. You'll see why in a moment."

Brilliant sunlight shone in through the massive windows that lined the hallway, nearly as tall as the walls themselves, thrown open to welcome both the bright natural light and salty air that drifted in from the sea beyond. Though the sea was not yet visible from where they stood, with only tall palms and rolling sand dunes visible from one side and a small but lovely courtyard on the other, there was no doubt they were close to the ocean.

Soon, they arrived in a round room, with winding stairs that led both upstairs and down, and a closed door to the left. No windows graced this room, but from below Eve could make out what sounded like the crashing of waves. With a glance over her shoulder, Maren led them down the spiral stairs and into the most lovely room Eve had ever laid eyes on.

The entirety of the room was made of windows. Each of them opened outward, welcoming the sun and sea breeze that drifted in merrily from the ocean, not more than a minute's walk from where they stood. Potted trees and exotic flowers she'd never seen before filled the area, and in the center, a large, pale wooden table, covered in maps. Chairs were placed around the room, grouped in sets ranging from two to six, and a fountain bubbled in one corner, covered in green and blue tiles in a pretty pattern that resembled waves.

"This was Naia's office," Maren explained, gesturing to a desk in one corner that Eve had overlooked, thanks to the plants that had nearly hidden it from view.

Tori whooshed out a breath and shook her head. "I would never get anything done here," she mused.

Eve nodded her agreement, as Lia hummed thoughtfully.

Maren smiled and led them to a set of six chairs with a perfect view of the ocean. "So you're going to look for her."

"Yes," Eve replied, as they all sat. "We would have come sooner, had we known she was missing."

Lia unfastened the sword at her hip laid it across her lap carefully, earning a quiet stare from Maren, who ignored the slight admonishment in Eve's tone.

"You didn't disarm us," Callan remarked, tilting his head slightly, "and I've seen no guards since we arrived."

Maren turned to him with an appraising look. "Because I know her brother well," she explained, turning her attention to Lia. "Quite well," she continued, a faint blush creeping into her bronze cheeks. "I trust him. He said you were coming to help and that I could trust you. So I do."

She could feel Lia stiffen beside her, but Eve didn't dare look over to see Lia's reaction to the emotion that showed so clearly on Maren's face.

"I'm glad that Aelius was able to make this meeting so smooth," Eve interjected before Lia could ask questions. "Tell us what happened to Naia."

"Mm," Maren replied, gaze shifting to the sea beyond the open windows. "We received word of your coronation, Eve, and then of your troubles in Darkegrove. Naia waited to see if Darkegrove would call for aid." Sighing, she looked down at her hands, clasped in her lap. "Then we received word of your father's illness," she said, looking back at Lia. "Aelius left, to help tend to your father–"

"Forgive me, Princess, but time is short," Callan cut in.

Maren's gaze slid to Callan, cat-like brown eyes narrowing. "About a week before I wrote back to you, my sister vanished from this room," she said tightly. "We don't know how."

Eve's gaze darted to the open windows, noting the lack of walls or other visible security between the castle and the sea. "Evertide is hardly a fortress..."

Maren sighed wearily. "What you do not see are the walls that enclose this stretch of beach, making it private for the use of our castle and its inhabitants only. Or," she added, leaning closer, "the four armed guards who were with her at the time. They were found dead, strange arrows lodged in their throats. Their bodies were left on the ground just outside of the windows here." She flung a hand toward the windows that led to the beach. "These were our most seasoned soldiers, each of them deadly and well prepared to defend her. After the attack on Dark-egrove, we took no chances with her safety."

"Strange how?" Lia inquired.

"Made of ash," Maren replied. "We've no ash trees at all in Coruscis. They're rare even in the north, as I understand it. So why make arrows from trees that are so difficult to find?"

Eve inhaled sharply. There was no doubt then. What small bit of hope remaining that Naia's disappearance was unrelated was dashed entirely.

"Four wouldn't have been enough," Callan said plainly, casting a glance at Eve. "Gorias took her, I do not doubt that, but the question is, how did they lose her?"

CHAPTER 64

LIA

Ice flowed in Lia's veins. Gorias had successfully taken two of them now.

Was Naia now suffering, as Lia had, at the hands of a torturer without the ability to feel any remorse for his actions?

Jabez's face flashed in her mind, and she tensed. Her pulse was racing, and her breath began to come in quick bursts. Closing her eyes, she willed herself to calm, to breathe normally. Jabez could not get her now, not here, not again. One hand gripped the pommel of the sword tightly, though when it had found its way there, she couldn't say.

The sensation of someone's hand taking hers had her eyes flying open. Eve was there, giving her hand a gentle squeeze. "You're safe," she said quietly. "And you are not alone."

Maren watched intently but said nothing about Lia's reaction. Instead she asked, "So it's true, what I've heard. You're both fae now?" Her attention shifted to Eve, who now stared at the princess. "You said so yourself when you arrived, 'formerly human'."

"Yes," Lia said, finding her voice at last as she looked at the woman her brother had apparently been involved with. She wanted to know more when there was time. Were they in love? she wondered. "We both died and then were reborn as fae. A gift from the gods."

Maren blinked, the only outward sign of her surprise. "Yes, your letter mentioned the gods," she said to Eve. "Will they intervene to save Naia?"

No. She wanted to scream. *No, they'll leave her to suffer and wish for death.*

Pressing her mouth closed so tightly her jaw ached, she gave Eve's hand a squeeze. This was not a question she could, or should, answer. Not when they had done so little to help her when she needed them most.

"We hope so," Eve replied, her thumb sliding over the back of Lia's hand comfortingly. *I'm here*, the gesture seemed to say.

"If the worst should happen," Lia began, inhaling and exhaling slowly to steady her frayed nerves, "I think whatever god has chosen her will intervene as ours did."

Looking at Eve, she smiled grimly. "There is something we need, in the meantime."

Maren frowned as Lia faced her once more. "What do you need?"

"There is an artifact, one that must not fall into the enemy's hands. A cauldron, hidden somewhere here in Evertide."

Maren began to shake her head, confusion sweeping over her face.

"It would be an heirloom," Callan added. "Something passed down through the generations with likely no solid explanation as to why, or one that doesn't seem to make sense."

Leaning back, Maren laughed once. "Actually, there is something like that, but I'd forgotten about it entirely."

"Where is it?" both queens demanded at once.

Blinking, Maren rose from her seat. "Right over here actually," she replied, making her way to Naia's desk. As she returned, Lia could only gape. In her hands was a small iron pot with three legs, and inside...a small plant.

Eve made a small noise of shock, and Callan flat-out guffawed. Maren frowned, examining the artifact-turned-flower-pot in her hands as she sat again. "Well, we knew it was old, and my grandmother told us it must remain in the family, but we didn't know why."

"That um..." Lia said, closing her eyes as she held in the laugh that threatened to escape her. "That's a gods-created artifact, one of the greatest weapons on Aestera?" she asked, looking at Callan for confirmation.

"I assume so," he shrugged, still shaking his head in disbelief. "But I've never seen it myself, and without getting verification from the gods themselves we can't be certain."

"How would you do that?" Maren asked.

Lia studied her, the princess turned regent. The woman who had acted as emissary for much of her mother's rule and all of her sister's. Behind her kitten-soft appearance, there was a sharp mind, she knew, but also a kind heart. She'd spoken to Maren a handful of times when she'd ventured to Avellon on official visits. Their shared acquaintances had sung her praises, and none had ever had an unkind word to say about her.

Aelius, strangely, had not spoken of her once, though they clearly knew one another. Why hadn't he told Lia about their relationship? Had he been worried over the political ramifications of the match? Or had he simply not thought it important enough to share? It would be a good match, she thought, considering what she knew of Maren.

Maybe he didn't tell you because he didn't want to remind you how alone you were back then. With a sigh, Lia dragged her attention back to the topic at hand.

"We can each call upon our patron god," Callan explained. "Eve can call to the goddess of life and earth; Aurelia, the goddess of healing and light–"

Lia rolled her eyes slightly. "If they deign to answer," she cut in. "We would like to take it with us," she said suddenly, earning sharp looks from the other three fae. They had agreed to ease into this, but this discussion about the gods was beginning to make her stomach hurt.

Maren stilled, her fingers tightening on the cauldron. "Why?"

"We need it to fight this evil, and it's not safe here any longer," Lia replied. "If they got in to take Naia, then they'll certainly get in again to try to take that."

Maren's shoulders fell as she looked down again. It was cold, explaining it that way and in such a harsh tone, and very unlike her. "I'm sorry," Lia added. "I haven't been feeling myself lately. I did not intend to be so rude," she explained, tone softening. "Forgive me."

Maren nodded, looking at Lia once more. Behind her brown eyes, her sharp mind was clearly at work. "Take it," she said. "Find my sister, and make them pay." Turning to Callan as she held out the pot, she added, "I am sorry but your armies cannot enter Thalassa. If you need to move closer, you may camp near Serona. It's a short ride, and I can ensure that supplies reach you if you need them. Let me know if there is anything more you need."

Callan inclined his head in thanks, taking the pot from her with care. "Thank you," he said, as everyone rose to their feet.

"Please," Maren added, looking at Lia, "tell Aelius I would like to see him when he's able. There is something we need to discuss."

As the others began to ready themselves to pace back, Lia paused. "Are you in love with my brother?" she asked suddenly, surprising even herself.

"Yes," Maren replied matter of factly, straightening and meeting Lia's gaze levelly. "I am. Very much."

"Then I will be sure he returns to you, as soon as possible," Lia replied with a smile.

CHAPTER 65

EVE

The cauldron was placed within Eve's encampment, safely ensconced with the crown. When Valerian had laid eyes on it, he'd cackled until he cried. Even now, hours after returning, Eve still caught him staring at it, shoulders shaking with barely contained laughter.

"Should we just leave the plant?" Leysa asked, giving Valerian a light smack on the shoulder. "Pull it together, babe."

Callan rolled his eyes at Valerian. "Gods above, Val, it's not *that* funny."

"I think we should," Eve replied, ignoring them. "It could be a useful disguise? If we're even right about it being the cauldron."

Rising from her seat, Eve moved to the cauldron. Her fingers slid over the broad, smooth leaves of the plant inside idly. They'd called upon the gods repeatedly, and as before, their prayers had gone unanswered.

"I wish one of them would answer us," she sighed, turning to face the group. "So we can find out for–"

"How did you summon me?" Keithia demanded, appearing suddenly in the middle of the group. Her eyes were wide, bewilderment and a small amount of rage etched into her features.

"I have no idea," Eve replied, gaping. "We called you but–"

"You found it," Keithia interrupted, crossing the tent to stare at the cauldron. "You used its powers to summon me." She frowned turning to Eve. "But you were not gifted this power, you shouldn't have been able to..." With an incredulous laugh, Keitha trailed off, gesturing to the plant that resided in the cauldron. "Do you know what this does?"

Each of the fae shook their heads silently.

"This cauldron was blessed by storm and sea, and desire and pleasure. The cauldron of the sea grants your desire, what you need most at the moment. This plant somehow channeled a bit of its power, Evelyn, allowing you to use it thanks to my gift to you."

Valerian burst into laughter again, drawing the attention of everyone else. "You have to admit," he said, "this whole thing is ridiculous."

Eve couldn't help the grin that tugged at her lips. Turning to Keithia, she asked, "So this is *the* cauldron then?"

The goddess sighed irritably. "Yes." Her gaze darkened as she added, "Do not summon us again. The Void can detect our presence, and it puts all of us in danger. We will come to you when it is safe to do so and only then. Be safe, children."

Before anyone could reply, she was gone as suddenly as she'd appeared.

"So, magic plant lady, can you summon us some proper beds, or maybe a juicy steak?" Valerian teased, earning a sigh from Eve and a laugh from the others.

"We should be very careful," Callan said, changing the subject again. "And we need to find Naia as quickly as possible."

Eve nodded. "Agreed, but where do we start?"

THE FIRST STEP, THEY'D DECIDED, WAS TO MOVE THEIR CAMP closer to Thalassa, just outside of Serona as Maren had offered. True to her word, supplies had been delivered within hours of their arrival, though how Maren had managed to arrange it on such short notice, Eve had no idea. Even the local tavern had been generous enough to provide ale for the soldiers.

They were all in desperate need of a break, and for once, with no obvious threat looming on the horizon, they were able to take one as they worked to find where Naia had been taken. A task that they were quickly realizing was near impossible.

"They could have paced her anywhere," Eve sighed, poring over reports from the scouts and shifters that had taken to exploring the surrounding areas. "Why would they even stay in Coruscis?"

"Because of that," Callan replied, gesturing to the cauldron where it sat on the nightstand by their bed. "They won't go far until they've gotten their hands on it."

Leysa arrived as Eve contemplated another update from a scout, essentially reporting that they'd found no sign of Gorian soldiers or the missing queen.

"Some of the shifters have spotted scouts wearing Gorian colors, searching ruins a few hours south of here," she said, plopping into a chair. Eve waited for her to pour herself a glass of the chilled wine Maren had sent over earlier in the day before she continued. "An old temple, not sure who it's for though." She drank deeply, sighing as the glass left her lips.

"But what are they looking for?" Eve asked, frowning. Surely if Lucia knew that the cauldron had been entrusted to Thalassa, so did Gorias.

"One of the shifters was able to get close enough to pick up a few words," Leysa said, leaning forward. "They're not looking for the artifact. They're looking for Naia—and whomever she left with."

Eve blinked in surprise. "What?"

With Leysa's answering grin, realization smacked her in the face. "She's with someone else," she whispered, disbelief settling over her. "But who?"

Leysa shrugged. "I have no idea, but it's strange right?"

"Very," Callan replied. "It was almost certainly Gorias that took her, from the arrows they'd used. But I have no idea what could have happened after."

"Maybe she escaped," Eve mused aloud.

"Perhaps with the intervention of a god or another fae," he said thoughtfully.

"Majesties, you're needed right away," the guard called from outside. "It's urgent."

Rushing out of the tent with Leysa in their wake, Eve and Callan headed straight for the crowd that gathered several feet away.

"What's going on?" Eve demanded as the crowd parted to reveal soldiers wearing the colors of Finias.

"Word from our High Queen," one of the men said, casting a wary glance around them.

"Lucia?" Eve asked, heart speeding up. They had been sent no news of Alyona's quiet rebellion and had only dared to hope she would be successful.

"No," he replied firmly. "Princess Alyona of Finias bids you well and would like to reaffirm the alliance between the armies of Finias, and those of Darkegrove, Falias, and Avellon, from now until the end of all things. Zia, formerly Princess of Finias, has not yet been found, but High Queen Lucia wishes to ensure the safety of her allies. Those sent in search of the traitor are rejoining our forces and will be here by morning, led by Princess Alyona as our High Queen wishes to handle the search for her daughter personally."

The search for Zia had so far yielded little information, but what they had been able to learn from her guards was troubling. Unlike Naia, the fae princess hadn't been taken. Instead, she'd walked into the desert under the guise of checking the wards, refusing to allow her guards to accompany her. They'd been suspicious enough to alert her mother, but by the time Lucia arrived, Zia was gone. Inside her tent was a note with only two words. *I'm sorry.*

Their own people were stretched even thinner, now that they were sending the shifters out in search of Naia only Amias had been able to remain with Lia. The rest of the protection they'd offered had been taken up by some of the other fae from Falias, but she'd feared it wasn't enough. Now, with help from Finias once more, the protective wards and spells could be reinforced more often and with less strain on the fae performing the magic.

"Please assure your high queen of our continued support and

thanks for her aid," Eve replied, dismissing the guards who bowed and departed for their own camp.

"Alyona did it," Callan said, taking Eve's hand in his.

"She did," Eve replied, relieved. "Now we just have to find Naia, and end this."

CHAPTER 66

LIA

"So," Lia began, eyeing her brother as he settled into the chair across from her own. "How long have you been sleeping with her?"

Bastien cackled beside Aelius, and Bella, at Lia's side, pointedly looked elsewhere.

Aelius merely grinned. "I'm sorry, dear sister, you'll have to be more specific, there are so many *hers*."

Lia narrowed her eyes, seeing right through the facade. The teasing smirk he bore didn't reach his eyes, ever so slightly narrowed, and his hands, hidden beneath folded arms, had tensed into fists. It was likely that nobody else had noticed the telltale signs of Aelius' lying, but she knew him better than anyone and would always know when he wasn't being truthful. The only reason she hadn't noticed before was that she hadn't been paying attention, and she damn well was now.

"Oh, I think you know exactly who I mean," she countered. "Maren Colvari sends her regards, and asks that you to come see her as soon as possible."

All humor drained from his face entirely as he straightened. "Is she okay? Was something wrong when you visited?" he asked, voice tense.

"No," she assured him, surprised by the reaction. *He's serious about her*. A shock for her twin, who took a different woman to bed nearly every week, sometimes more often. He had, to her knowledge, never been serious about any relationship before. "She's fine, I think she just wants to speak to you. She didn't say why."

Aelius sighed, leaning back in his chair.

"So it's serious?" Bastien asked, brow raised. He hadn't known either, she noted.

Aelius grunted, grabbing a glass of wine from the table and drinking deeply.

"Do you even know who that belonged to?" Bastien asked, grimacing.

Aelius ignored him, settling his gaze on Lia entirely. "It's serious," he began, wiping his palms against his thighs. "We met when she first visited during her mother's reign several years ago, but we didn't start seeing each other until I went to Thalassa a few months before Father..."

Lia nodded, recalling his departure clearly. He'd gone at their father's behest for some diplomatic reason or another, the details of which she couldn't remember. It had annoyed her because she hadn't been allowed to join him, as her father had begun readying her for the throne in earnest and wanted her close.

"You love her," Lia supplied, smiling softly at her brother. It warmed her heart to see him care, really care, for another person outside of their family and Bastien. It would do him some good to settle down.

"I do. But it's complicated," he admitted, "and private."

Lia held her hands up in surrender. "I will press no further than, dear brother."

Bastien and Aelius snorted at once. Lia shushed them, gesturing to the cot where Eyla slept near her own. With Amias as added protection and with Alyona now seeing to the wards that her sister had abandoned, Bella had felt it safe to return her daughter to the tent they now shared.

"I will make sure she's on her best behavior," Bella offered, earning an appreciative glance from Aelius.

"You can try," Lia replied in a sing-song voice, her heart light and unburdened.

A low chuff sounded from the tent entrance, announcing Amias' return. Aelius and Bastien both tensed as he entered, watching warily as the bear shifter ambled inside.

"Never going to get used to that," Aelius said, shaking his head.

Amias dutifully ignored him, pressing his nose to Lia's arm gently in greeting before plopping down beside Lia's bed in his usual place.

"Well, you should," Lia replied, offering the bear a smile. "He's going to be around until this is finished. He's actually quite good company, once you get to know him."

A sound as close to a laugh as a bear could manage sounded from Amias.

"I'll take your word for it, and bid you goodnight, sister," Aelius said, rising from his chair.

Bastien followed suit. "We're going to join the search for Naia tomorrow," he explained. "It'll be an early start."

Later, when they were alone, this little family she'd somehow found herself creating and their unexpected guardian, Lia lay on her back, relishing the peace and quiet. Bella had fallen into a deep sleep nearly as soon as her head had met the pillow. She couldn't be sure if Amias was asleep or just lying quietly, but it made no difference.

Silently, she sent a prayer of thanks to the bright moon above. Thanks for her rescue, and thanks for the woman who lay in bed beside her, snoring softly. She owed a great deal to the goddess who was responsible for both, and as she drifted off into a blissfully dreamless sleep, she could have sworn the moon shone a bit brighter.

CHAPTER 67

EVE

The midday desert sun was nearly blinding. This far inland, with the sea an hour's ride from Serona, there was little relief from the breeze. Even in winter, Coruscis was hot, dry, and as far as Eve was concerned, miserable.

Callan had taken her out into the dunes, far enough away from their camp that they could practice undisturbed. Bella, Eve had been told, would be doing the same with Lia, later in the day. They would practice separately for now, because they did not yet know what would happen when they tried to wield their artifacts, and they couldn't risk accidentally injuring each other, or worse.

"I'm not sure what to do," Eve said, placing the crown atop her braided hair. "It doesn't feel the same as my magic. I can feel it there now though, the power. Like it's humming when I touch the crown. I've never felt that before."

"Maybe it's because we have all three of them together," he suggested. "I will write to Lucia when we get back, perhaps she'll know. Reach out for the power you feel, call upon it as you use your gifts, and see what happens," Callan coached, taking a place far behind Eve.

Nodding, she looked to the dune ahead of her. With the gift

bestowed on her by Keithia, she called upon the stone buried far beneath the sands, willing it to rise from where it rested.

The ground shuddered and groaned as a boulder rose, breaching the surface of the earth before halting suddenly as Eve released her pull on it.

She held her breath, fear and anticipation coursing through her veins in equal measure. "Okay," she breathed, "I'm doing it." She brushed against the power residing in the gemstone hidden in her family's crown, gently, coaxingly. A test to see what it would do.

Nothing happened.

She could feel Callan at her back, his presence anchoring her as she pushed harder, willing the ancient stone to do something...anything.

Still no response, until—

You beckon me, Bearer? Ancient and wary, a quiet voice whispered in her mind. She had awakened something, but what...she did not yet know.

"Who are you?" she asked aloud. Callan stepped around her, worried gaze meeting her own. "It speaks to me," she explained, eyes wide.

"Be careful, dove," he warned, frowning.

I am the Stone of Rule, it said, finally answering her question. *You have no need to fear me, High Queen. I obey no command but your own and exist only to serve you.*

"Serve me how?" Her gaze remained locked on Callan's, heart pounding.

Do you not know? As long as I rest upon your brow, your reign as High Queen is blessed, and the goddess-given gift you bear will not fail you.

"It can't be silenced, even by the Samach?" she asked, incredulous.

Callan's eyes widened in silent question.

Not even by the god Vidar himself as long as you command it, but only if I am with you.

Eve sighed. "Thank you," she said, frowning. "Who is Vidar?"

Silence, Bearer. He is silence.

"Will you just be listening until I call on you then?"

I will only awaken when I am needed, the Stone replied. *Until then, I slumber.*

"Then do that, now," she replied. "I will call upon you when I'm ready."

As you command, Bearer.

True to its word, the stone fell silent, the power she'd felt awaken subsiding until it was once again barely perceptible. Waiting.

"What happened?" Callan asked. "What did it say?"

"I can defeat the Samach," she said, hope blossoming inside her. "It's going to help us win."

CHAPTER 68

LIA

"It talked to you," Lia repeated, dumbfounded.

"Sort of," Eve replied, waving a hand. "I could hear it in my head. I'm wondering if the Sword will do the same for you."

Lia's gaze shifted to the sword in question, lying on the table nearby. "Aelius never spoke of hearing voices," she said. "He used it for years."

"I know," Eve explained. "That's because he isn't the bearer."

Right, of course. She sighed. "I can try. I was going to take it out to the dunes and practice in a few minutes anyway, with Bella, Amias, and Tori."

Eve nodded. "Good, try reaching out to it with your magic when you do," she said, offering a smile. "Maybe it can tell you exactly what it does, like the Stone did for me."

A part of her dreaded hearing a strange, incorporeal voice in her head, but the idea of getting more information about what this magical artifact did intrigued her.

"Oh," she said, stopping Eve just short of leaving, "has there been any word on Zia or Naia?"

Dark red waves bobbed slowly around Eve's face. "No," she sighed, shaking her head, "not yet. Callan is meeting with Alyona now though, I'll let you know if there's anything new."

Smiling her thanks, Lia waited until Eve had departed before running a finger along the hilt of the Sword of Light. "Well, I guess we'll see what you can do," she murmured, casting a glance toward Amias, who watched her carefully in his bear form. "Let's go."

The wind was picking up, Lia noted, glancing skyward at the bright sun overhead. It was a cloudless day, with endless blue skies and warm sunshine above. Sand began to spin and dance along the dunes, carried by the wind. They wouldn't be able to remain out of the camp for long, she'd been warned. Sandstorms were known to pop up out of nowhere, and it would be too dangerous to remain outside the tent if one did.

Amias had the form of a desert cat, impossibly large, nearing the size of his bear form, with sleek fur nearly identical in color to the dunes. Standing close by her side, he scanned the surrounding area constantly, ready to defend her should a threat arise, and Tori hovered a few feet away, frowning at the sun above as if it had personally offended her somehow.

"Okay, so we'll stay behind you," Bella said, taking a position directly behind Lia. "Hold the sword in front of you and just...will it to obey you. I think."

"Shouldn't you know how this works?" Tori asked. "Your mother is a goddess."

Bella laughed. "Well, even if my mother knew, and I'm not convinced she does, she would never tell me. Despite being the goddess of prophecy, she almost never shares what she's seen, because they can change– and maybe a little because she likes keeping secrets."

Tori snorted in response, but fell quiet as Lia pulled the Sword from its scabbard, and held it out straight in front of her. The metal hilt felt warm in her hands, maybe a little warmer than it should have but perhaps that was just her imagination.

"Okay, now talk to me," she whispered, knowing but not caring that the fae at least could hear her. Eve had told her to reach out with her magic, she remembered, so she did.

Closing her eyes, she pictured the sun above and willed a bit of its warmth to flow from her hands to the Sword.

Ah, a small, sweet voice called in answer. *Finally.*

You're the Sword of Light, she thought back.

Yes, Bearer, what is your command?

Lia's heart raced, her palms growing damp around. The voice in her head was eerie and unnerving. Somehow ancient, and childlike all at once; it sent a chill down her spine.

Tell me what you do, how you can help me win this war.

A sigh, and then, *When you hold me in your hand, I will be your mightiest weapon, against even your greatest foes. None can silence your magic, and my light will blind any who stand in your way.*

Even the Samach?

Even the Samach, Bearer. None shall be mightier than the Bearer and her treasure.

You can't act without my command, correct? Eve had said as much, but it didn't hurt to be certain.

Only the bearers may command each of us. We answer only your call.

Thank you, Lia replied, sighing with relief.

I will slumber until I am required, Bearer.

The feeling of power receded until it was nothing more than a whisper against her palm. Turning to the others, she smiled. "I have what I need."

Tori's brow furrowed. "But nothing happened, you just stood there."

Bella shook her head, eyeing Lia carefully. "I think plenty happened."

Lia's answering smile was one of hope, of certainty for the first time in a while now. "Let's get back to camp."

Chapter 69

Eve

"They've found her," Callan announced, stepping into the tent where Eve sat reading. Things had been quiet, eerily so, as they waited for a sighting of Gorias or of the two women they searched for.

Her book closed with a snap before being tossed onto the bed, the steamy romance utterly forgotten now. "Naia?" she asked hopefully.

Shaking his head, Callan gave her an apologetic frown. "I'm sorry, dove, no word on Naia. But we did find Zia. Hopefully, she can give us some answers."

"Where is she?"

Callan stepped closer, taking Eve's hand in his. "They're holding her in Lucia's camp. It'll be faster to just pace there."

"Okay," she replied, stepping into his arms.

They arrived in a large tent, nearly the size of their own, crowded with the royals of Finias and their guards. Seated in the middle of the space was a petite teenage girl with short, curly dark brown hair and wide, clear blue eyes. She remained unbound, but with the number of guards and other fae, binding her was hardly necessary.

Lucia, standing at her daughter's side, stared at the girl, lips pressed tightly together.

"Tell them," Alyona said, from her other side, earning a sigh from the woman who stood behind her. Lucia's other daughter, Eve guessed. Her hair was so short-cropped she was nearly bald, the style a perfect compliment to her sharp features, but it was her eyes that gave her identity away. They were identical to Lucia's, down to the striking colors—one light blue, the other honey gold.

Lifting her gaze, Zia met Eve's stare evenly. "The earth-blessed one," she said, her voice as delicate and clear as a bell. "Figures. Where is the other?" she asked, looking to Alyona now.

"On her way," the crown princess replied.

"Then I'll wait, so I don't have to repeat this again." Straightening, Zia stared past Eve at some random point on the side of the tent. Tension radiated off of her as she sat in silence, until finally Lia and Tori appeared just behind Alyona.

"Finally," the captive princess muttered, glancing at Lia. "The light-blessed."

"Now tell them," Alyona ordered again, impatience seeping into her tone.

Zia glared at her sister but did as she was told. "I was approached in my dreams," she began, gaze drifting around the room. "Unlike my mother and sisters, I was granted no blessing by a god. Unusual for royalty," she sneered at Lucia, "and embarrassing for my mother."

Lucia winced, turning away from her daughter.

"So the Divine Void approached me. She told me of her plans for this world, to make it anew, granting us all equality. To remove the gods who show such favoritism and who abandoned us when we needed them." Her gaze danced between Eve and Lia. "You will not win. The gods do nothing but lie to you."

"Did you join her?" Eve asked, frowning.

Zia sniffed. "I couldn't find them. I'm sure she's looking for me, as one of her favored."

Alyona rolled her eyes. "Or, you did what she needed you to do, allowing her crony to kidnap the Queen of Avellon and torture her," she snapped, leaning closer to her sister. "This monster used you. You are a fool for believing her poisonous lies."

"That's enough," Lucia said quietly. "We have what we need."

Turning to Eve she added, "Zia has no idea where they are. She was told they would find her, but when she wandered into the desert as she'd been commanded, they never came."

Eve nodded. It seemed there was little information to be gained from the girl. "What are you going to do with her?" she asked, frowning. Surely she couldn't remain here, where she could easily cause more trouble, especially if Kore decided to try again.

"She's being sent home, with Nisa," Lucia replied, gesturing to her middle daughter, who inclined her head in greeting. "She will ensure that Zia causes no more trouble, and wards will be placed by others to prevent her dreaming, since she cannot be trusted to do it herself."

It was clear that Zia's actions pained Lucia greatly, and she could only imagine the difficulty it caused her to send her youngest child away, to know that she had tried to help bring about the end of the world. Sending her home was hardly a permanent solution, but it would have to do for now.

"Queen Evelyn," Lucia added, "I received Callan's letter. I am afraid I know nothing about–" she paused, casting a glance at Zia, who rolled her eyes. "The matter he asked me about. I wish I could be of more assistance."

"Thank you anyway," Eve replied, turning to Lia who had watched in silence. "We should speak in the morning," she said. "I want to hear about your...practice run."

Lia nodded, offering a warm smile. "I have a lot to tell you."

Watery sunlight streamed in from the opening overhead as the three queens and one queen-to-be gathered in Eve's tent in the early morning hours the next day. It was well past time for Brida to be brought into these discussions, she'd decided, since she would soon be leading Darkegrove in earnest.

"Wow," Brida breathed, after Eve relayed the story of the artifacts, the three queens turned bearers, and the fact that they were apparently reincarnated.

"I want to ask you more about that," Lia said, looking at Lucia. "Can you tell us anything about who we used to be?"

Eve had wondered the same, had begun to question how much of her soul was truly hers and how much belonged to this ancient fae who had borne the Stone before.

Lucia offered Lia an apologetic smile. "I'm afraid I know little of the story, but what I do know is that each of the four were women, and they fought in the great battle to stop Arawn and Kore, as I explained before."

It wasn't much. In fact, the only new information was that the four bearers had been women before. "I wish we knew more," Eve sighed. "Perhaps the gods could tell us?"

"I'm sure they could," Lucia replied.

"But will they?" Lia countered.

Brida shifted in her seat. "If they were women before and women now, does it stand to reason that the bearer with Gorias is a woman? That could help us narrow down who we're looking for."

"Not necessarily," Lucia said. "It could simply be chance that our three bearers are women once more. I think the easiest way to locate the spear's bearer will be to look for who Kore keeps the closest. Obviously not an easy task."

An utterly impossible one, Eve thought bitterly. She doubted they would get that close until it was time to kill her. "Can we stop her with only three of the artifacts?"

"Another question for the gods, I'm afraid," Lucia replied.

"Tell me about mates," Lia blurted. She had been sitting quietly, a contemplative expression on her face, thinking, Eve had assumed, about the task at hand.

Lucia's brow rose slowly, her lips twitching at the corner. She hadn't smiled since she'd arrived, no doubt due to her daughter's betrayal and now absence. "What do you want to know?"

Lia's cheeks flushed. "How do you know if you've found yours?"

"I think our dear Eve can answer that," Lucia replied. Eve suspected Lucia could've answered it as well, but she simply shrugged and explained what she knew.

"It's...it's impossible to stay away from them. You feel constantly pulled toward them, like a string connects your heart to theirs," she replied, recalling what it had been like after she'd turned fae. "It's not something you feel when you're human, but for a fae it's impossible to ignore."

Brida watched with interest, remaining silent as Eve explained.

Lia's lips pressed together for a moment. "Does it make you love them?"

"No," Eve shook her head. "It doesn't force love, it just...brings you together."

"It's not necessarily about love," Lucia interjected. "You can find your mate in someone who makes you feel complete, as a friend or a lover," she replied, expression turning wistful. "You may find that you come to love that person in time, or you may not."

Lia nodded, expression turning lighter. "Thank you." Her attention shifted to Eve then. "It spoke to me, the Sword."

Eve straightened. "Like the Stone," she grinned. "What did it say?"

Lucia held up a hand. "They speak?"

"Only to us, in our minds," Eve said, glancing at the box that held her crown, lying on the bed nearby.

"That's so strange," Brida muttered.

"It was," Lia agreed. "It explained how it works, and it said my powers can't be silenced when I'm holding it." Lia's hand drifted to the Sword, lying across her lap.

Lucia smiled, really smiled. "Remarkable," she breathed. "Now we just need to find our wayward queen."

"And hope that she gains her powers in time," Eve added. Her thoughts turned to the deaths that she and Lia had experienced in order to gain their own. She shuddered at the thought. "The other fae kingdom should return when she does. Murias, right?"

"Indeed," Lucia replied, "and they will be a formidable ally. Their armies were the strongest of us. Their king and queen are both excellent strategists."

"Then I hope it happens soon," Eve said.

"Gods bless her," Lia murmured.

"Literally I hope," Brida added with a nervous laugh.

Chapter 70

Lia

Lia returned to her own tent shortly after the meeting with Eve and the others, head spinning with all she'd learned. She'd suspected that Bella was her mate, ever since the tug in her chest had started pulling her closer and closer to the demigoddess, but as she often did with things that made her uncomfortable, Lia had ignored it. Now, the pull was so overwhelming that it could no longer be ignored.

She went over what she wanted to say in her mind once again.

I love you, and I think you might be my mate.

She just had to say the words. Get them out and see what happens.

Bella and Eyla were seated on the floor, looking through a children's book, when she stepped inside. Lifting her head, Bella offered Lia a smile that had her mind emptying with a whoosh.

Any doubt that had remained vanished in the span of a heartbeat.

Here was her mate, her heart, her love. Forever, they'd promised, and forever it would be.

"Oh good," Bella said, rising to her feet. "I was hoping you'd be back soon, I want to show you something."

"What?" Lia asked lamely.

"Eyla darling, take Amias and go find your tutor," she said.

Eyla scrambled to her feet, waving at the bear shifter seated in the corner, as watchful as ever. "Hi Lia," she said with a grin, before running out, Amias in her wake.

"You wanted to show me something?" Lia asked, smiling after Eyla.

"I found this amazing place close by," she replied, taking Lia's hands in hers. "I already spoke to the guards. "Tori will come with us, as well as a few others. It's close by, so it should be fine. The scouts have already checked it out too, and it's clear." She grinned, making Lia's heart skitter. "You're going to love it."

Bella led Lia through the camp by the hand, guards trailing a discreet distance behind. Stepping out into the open expanse of the desert, with no tents, carts, or soldiers to block their view, Bella pointed into the distance. Squinting, Lia could just make out the shape of trees, a small copse of them.

Lia turned to Bella with a confused smile. "I see the trees, is that where we're going?"

Bella grinned in response, urging Lia forward with a tug of her hand. "Yes," she replied as they set out. As they walked, Bella gave Lia's hand a squeeze. "You took me to that lake, the first time, remember?"

Lia nodded, cheeks heating. How could she have forgotten? Her thoughts drifted to the two of them standing in the rain, drenched and making promises to one another, to her tasting and touching Bella for the first time. It had been one of the most important nights of her life.

"Of course," Lia replied, "I wanted to take you swimming, but then the storm came–"

"Exactly," Bella interjected as they reached the oasis. "And now, I've found a way to make up for it."

"There's nothing to make up for, that night was incredible," Lia countered, capturing Bella's lips in a swift kiss.

Laughing, Bella shook her head as they broke apart. She dropped Lia's hand and set off into a run. "Come and catch me, Queen of Avellon," she taunted.

For a moment Lia could only stand and blink at Bella as she ran across the sand. Dark hair flying wildly behind her with her arms flung wide, she reminded Lia of some fantastical bird, or perhaps, more accurately, a dragon, passionate and fiercely protective of those she called her own.

Embracing the moment, Lia let out a resounding *whoop* and followed Bella straight to the oasis. She found her prize, standing with her back to the cool, clear waters, waiting with a bright grin.

"I win–" Bella began, tilting her head slightly.

Without thinking, Lia ran straight for Bella, catching her in her arms and leaping into the pool behind her. Bella's squeal of surprise was cut short as they broke the surface of the calm water. Lia pushed off the sandy bottom to rise to the surface, finding Bella already there, treading water and staring at her incredulously.

"I win," Lia quipped, splashing Bella playfully.

Bella's silver eyes narrowed. "Oh, we'll see about that," she replied. "I'm going to–"

Her words were cut short as Lia pulled her close, pressing their lips together. The kiss was deep, devouring, and full of need. When they pulled apart, Bella sighed, shaking her head slightly.

"I could drown happily now," Lia teased.

"Only in me," Bella replied.

"Gladly." The cool water was a balm to her skin that suddenly seemed aflame. To look at Bella set her afire, as if pure sunlight flowed in her veins.

Glancing down, Lia laughed. She hadn't given them time to remove their clothes. The light gowns they'd taken to wearing to withstand the warmth of the desert sun were likely ruined now, as well as the sandals they wore.

"I've ruined our clothes," Lia observed.

"That's okay, at least we got our swim," Bella replied.

Later, wrapped in the towels a guard had gone back to retrieve for them, they sat on the shore, watching the calm waters in silence.

"I need to say something," Lia began slowly, not daring to meet Bella's gaze. "But I'm worried you might not want to hear it."

"Nothing you could say would scare me away," she affirmed.

Taking a steeling breath, Lia closed her eyes. "I think you might be my mate."

There was silence, heavy, dreadful silence as Lia waited for Bella to respond. Finally, she opened her eyes and turned to Bella to find her grinning.

"Is that all?" she said, shaking her head slightly. "I've known that since the moment we first kissed. I just...I thought it would frighten you so I was waiting for you to figure it out on your own."

Lia gaped for a moment as she allowed the thought to process. This beautiful, sometimes infuriating woman was her mate. The one soul perfectly matched to her own, the one whom she would spend the rest of her incredibly long life with. "I am so lucky," she said, pressing her lips to Bella's.

"Forever," she whispered.

"Forever," Bella agreed.

Chapter 71

Eve

Night in Coruscis was stunning. Nearly as beautiful, Eve was forced to admit, as those in the north. With no trees or mountains to block the view, the night sky above was a blanket of shimmering stars. More expansive and endless than Eve could have imagined.

"I will miss this," Callan mused from beside her.

Desperate for some fresh air and a break from being trapped in a tent with nothing to do but wait, they'd taken a short walk to the top of a dune not far from their tent. Still within the bounds of the Falias encampment, as everyone had been given strict orders to remain close after nightfall.

With each passing day, the fear of an attack by Gorias grew. Word had been sent to Avellon and Darkegrove, searching for any sign that Gorias had returned northward for some reason, but so far, no sign of them had been spotted.

It was as if the entire army had simply vanished.

"I will too," she replied. "When we finally get to return home."

Callan cupped her cheeks gently, their gazes meeting. "We will end this," he said quietly. "And when we do, I will make sure the very mountains sing your name. As you deserve."

Closing the distance between them, Eve pressed her lips to his, her palm resting against his chest. His steady heartbeat beneath her touch was her anchor when things began to feel out of control, when she felt lost in the proverbial woods. He was her home, and he would always be her biggest supporter.

"Thank you," she replied, grinning. "I think just one mountain will do."

A low growl from nearby had them both turning in time to see a white wolf stalking straight for them. Callan frowned. "What's wrong?"

With a bright flash, Cora shifted into her fae form, familiar pale pink gown and all. Her dark hair was braided back, revealing her lovely face, currently the picture of sheer anger.

"Why did you ask him to come? Why?" she demanded, flinging her arms wide in frustration. "You know it isn't safe here! And you," she all but shouted, pointing a finger at Callan. "You couldn't even tell me? I know you hate him but this is cruel."

Callan rose to his feet, offering a hand to Eve as she did the same. He frowned at his sister in confusion and impatience. "I have no idea what you're talking about, Cora. Stop yelling at me."

Cora's gaze shot to Eve. "Was it you then?"

Eve blinked, shaking her head. "I don't know what you mean, Cora. Who is here?"

Cora's face crumpled, and tears began to fall. "So you didn't ask him to come?" She sighed, wiping the tears away and composing herself. "Mason is here. I don't know why. I just got word. He's with Lady Brida's people right now."

Surprise raced through Eve like wildfire. "I need to find out why he's here, right away." She turned to Callan. "Pace me there?"

"Oh, you're not going without me," Cora interrupted.

Callan sighed. "Fine, we'll take horses," he suggested. "Cora can run."

With a glance, the two women agreed silently and set off to find out why Mason Sinclair had arrived in Coruscis.

∾

"Eldred is–" Mason was saying to Brida and Leith, only to stop short as Cora stepped inside.

"You're really here," she blurted.

Eve's brow rose high, her gaze turning to Brida, who simply shrugged.

"I was going to tell you," Mason began, glancing around uncomfortably. "Maybe we should talk somewhere privately."

Cora's cheeks turned pink, and she looked back to where Eve and Callan waited.

Eve offered a smile. "I'm sure that we could step outside," she began, glancing at her human cousins.

Brida looked inclined to say no, likely from the curiosity Eve could see swimming in her blue eyes, but Leith took her by the arm and gently led her outside.

"Just let us know when you're finished," Eve said gently to the pair, knowing she and Callan would know exactly what was being said, and when they were finished. Cora likely knew that too, she knew, but they would at least attempt not to listen in out of respect for the apparent couple.

"How long has that been going on?" Callan asked once they were outside.

Eve laughed, shaking her head. "I think since the moment we arrived in Falias, my love. You've never noticed the way he looks at her?"

Callan grumbled. "I've been too busy worrying about what he's saying to you to notice how he looks at my sister," he paused, expression darkening. "I don't like it."

"No," Eve said gently, placing a hand on his arm. "Let her be happy. She'll hate you if you make this harder for her."

He sighed, his gaze cutting to Brida and Leith, who had wisely remained silent. "Fine."

"What was he saying about Eldred?" Eve asked, turning her attention to the human leaders.

Brida shook her head slowly. "Eldred is working with the Council of Nine and overseeing matters in Darkegrove. He's presented your terms; making me the queen in exchange for you to step down and relinquish your claim on the throne of Darkegrove."

"And?" Worry coursed through her. If they refused to recognize Brida's claim, if they pushed back she would have to–

"They said yes," Brida beamed. "They've agreed, and the council is drawing up the necessary declarations."

Eve sighed with relief, turning to Callan with a sad smile. Letting go of the throne was hard. It had been her dream to see change brought to Darkegrove, to see women counted as equals for the first time in five hundred years.

A ruling queen was only the first step, a monumental one, but still only the first. It had cost her so much, her mother's life and nearly her own, as well as those who had died defending her or trying to stop her. Now, after all of that sacrifice and death, she was walking away from the throne she'd fought so hard to win.

"You're not giving up on them," Callan said, reading her expression. "You've achieved what you wanted. Darkegrove will have its queen, and you will still be there to support her."

Her heart swelled even as tears stung her eyes. "Thank you," she whispered, linking her hand with his.

"We're finished," Mason declared, from just inside.

"Finally," Leith mumbled, wrapping his jacket tighter around his shoulders.

Mason ignored him as they all stepped back in. "Did Lady Brida tell you?" he asked Eve.

"She did, thank you for everything you've done to help," she said, offering her critic-turned-ally a smile. They had come a long way as well, from the council room of Darkegrove where he'd all but called her a whore, to now, where he bowed in deference.

"Of course," he replied, casting a glance at Cora, who watched carefully. "We, ah..." he began, turning a nervous eye on Callan. "We're together."

Callan stared at Mason in silence, expression flat and unreadable. To his credit, Mason stood fast, waiting until Callan spoke finally, never faltering beneath his glare.

"Don't hurt her."

There was an undeniable threat beneath those words, and Mason's brow rose slightly. "Never," he promised.

Cora rolled her eyes and stepped in, taking Mason by the arm. "We should get back to our camp, I'm sure our people are wondering after their fearless leaders," she teased.

As they departed, after a quick rush of goodbyes between them all, Eve climbed atop the horse she'd share with Callan for the return ride. "Be kind to him, Callan. He loves her."

"Not as much as I love you," he teased, nipping her earlobe gently.

She laughed as a shiver of desire ran up her spine. "You can't know that for sure."

"But I do, dove. There is no love in this world greater than ours," he whispered, his warm breath dancing along her bare neck. "There is no heart that beats for another more intently than mine for you. I will forever stand in awe of everything that you are."

CHAPTER 72

LIA

The banging woke her, dragging her from a deep and dreamless sleep. Thanks to the new wards that Alyona had seen to, it had been easy to fall into bed, Bella's arms around her, and allow herself to drift into sleep with the quiet sounds of Eyla snoring softly and Amias grumbling as he found a comfortable place between their beds.

Why are the soldiers practicing at this hour? She wondered, her gaze drifting to the greyish sky, visible through the peak in the tent. Dawn hadn't yet arrived, she realized with annoyance and lifted her head to listen.

Amias was on all fours, staring at the tent entrance with an intensity that sent a chill down her spine.

"Are they erecting something new?" she asked, wondering if perhaps the thumping she heard was the construction of a new tent or something. Amias' low grumble in response was answer enough. She shook Bella awake, swiftly rising from the bed and dressing.

"Mm, what?" Bella asked sleepily.

"Something's wrong," Lia whispered. "Get up, moonlight. We have to get dressed."

Without questioning, Bella rose immediately and began to dress in her own tunic and leggings, as Lia had. Within moments they were both dressed and armed, Lia with the Sword of Light, and Bella with her own sword at her hip.

Amias' head swung toward them moments before Aelius and Tori stepped inside. The thumping sound continued, growing in intensity and volume steadily. Realization had her stomach dropping. Not *thumping*, but *war drums*. Gorias was here.

Reading her expression, Aelius inclined his head. "Tori is here to pace Eyla to Thalassa. Maren will keep her safe."

Bella started for her daughter, waking the sleeping child as gently as she could and helping her dress. "You're sure?" she asked Lia's twin, gaze hard even as her eyes swam with fear.

"I'm sure," he agreed, tone softer than any he'd used with her before. "The shifter scouts have already checked. Gorias approaches from the west. Thalassa will be safe as long as we stand."

And if we fall, well, nowhere in Aestera would be safe for long, Lia finished for him silently.

Lia could only watch, heart aching, as Bella cupped Eyla's cheeks gently. "My brave girl," she whispered, her cheerful voice in stark contrast to her shaking hands. "Remember Tori?" Eyla nodded, blinking sleepily at her mother. "Well," Bella continued, "she's going to take you to meet another new friend. Her name is Princess Maren and she's very nice. Mama will catch up with you later, I promise."

"It's okay, mama," Eyla whispered, wrapping her arms around Bella's neck. "I know you will."

A strangled sob came from Bella as she wrapped her arms tightly around her daughter, walking her over to Tori. "Don't you leave her there if you feel even for a second that it's not safe."

Tori nodded, lips pressed together firmly. "I will make sure she's safe, you have my word."

Eyla was passed from Bella to Tori quickly. "I love you, sweet girl," Bella said just before the pair vanished.

Straightening, Bella turned to Lia. "Let's go send them to the void."

～

"We don't have Naia yet," Lia said quietly as she came to stand beside Eve. Aside from the few gently rolling dunes, this part of Coruscis was little more than a flat expanse of sand until it met the sea. With her earth-blessed gift, Eve had managed to build a dune for them to stand on, high enough to see over the line of soldiers from a safe distance.

"I know," Eve sighed, taking Lia's hand in hers as they surveyed the armies spread in front of them. "They'll keep looking, and we'll hold our ground for as long as we can."

The combined armies of Avellon, Darkegrove, Falias, and Finias stretched far and wide. Thousands of men and women pledged to defend their world from the monster threatening it. Far ahead, just close enough to be seen now, the front lines of Gorias began to appear on the horizon. The battle wouldn't begin for a while yet, Aelius had explained while he and Bastien had escorted her here, to the place where she and Eve would try to wield their gifts to defend their armies. For now, it would be posturing, waiting until someone decided to throw the first figurative stone.

Like last time, Bella insisted on being with the soldiers, fighting shoulder-to-shoulder with the others. She had no offensive magical gifts of her own, but she was wicked fast with a blade and tough. Their brief goodbye flashed in Lia's memory.

"I love you, sunlight. Stay safe, do what you can to help but don't you dare burn yourself out. I know that you're strong, but remember you have limits–and if things start looking bad, go get Eyla and run. Run as far and as fast as you can."

"I'm not running," Lia had balked. "I'll stand with my people until my last breath."

Bella shook her head. "Please. Promise me. I need to know that you're safe, and I need to know that Eyla is safe. I can only trust you with that."

"But your mother–" Lia began to argue.

"If we fall, and Kore gets the artifacts, she'll kill the gods first. All of them."

Lia fell silent then. Bella was right. It had been made clear to them that the gods were the target of Kore's rage, though they still did not know why. "I promise," she said reluctantly.

Bella's hands gripped the sides of Lia's face tightly, pulling her close and capturing her lips in a desperate kiss. "Stay alive for me," she whispered.

"And you stay alive for me, moonlight," Lia ordered, wrapping her arms around her mate. "We'll see each other when it's over."

"Are you okay?" Eve asked quietly, drawing her from the memory.

"As much as possible," Lia replied, offering a small smile. "Have you sent a prayer to Keithia?"

Eve glanced sideways at Lia. "Have you sent one to Helie?"

Lia laughed. "No, but we should. Maybe they'll listen this time."

"We can hope."

Hope is all we have, she thought, not bothering to say it aloud.

She had carried so much hope with her, all of her life.

Hope in the good of others.

Hope for the future she could see Eve making for Darkegrove.

Hope that when her father passed, Lia would make a good ruler.

But now, clad in her gleaming gold armor, and staring out at the army that nearly dwarfed their own, hope was but a tiny kernel held tightly in a too-tight grasp.

CHAPTER 73

EVE

"Any minute now," Callan said as he came to stand beside her. Dawn was finally breaking and the sun already beginning to warm the desert.

"You have to go." It wasn't a command or a question, just a simple statement of fact. He wouldn't be able to remain here with her and Lia, no matter how much either of them wanted him to. He needed to be with Valerian, who she could already see making his way to the front of the lines, issuing commands to the fae soldiers as he did.

"I do," he admitted, as they turned to face one another. "Remember, dove, focus and feeling." His hands slid down her arms, heat trailing in their wake as they moved down the skin left bare by the short-sleeved tunic she wore. Leather armor had been placed over it, similar in shape to a corset, with straps over her shoulders. It would help to keep her safe should a sword try to pierce her abdomen, but if everything went to plan, nobody would get that close.

"I've got her," Cathal said, drawing Eve's surprised attention. Like last time, she'd known that Mara would remain close, but to see Cathal here was not expected.

"You're not going down there?" she asked, turning to Callan for confirmation.

"No," Cathal replied as Callan shook his head. "I'm staying close to help keep the three of you safe so you can do your thing."

Mara stepped up beside him then, dressed in armor that mirrored Cathal's, sleek and black, made of supple leather. Her long dark hair had been braided the same way Eve's had, in a crown around her head. "My magic doesn't work long distance," she said. "His does. He'll be more of an asset than I was before."

"And I don't want a repeat of last time," Callan added. "Someone got close to you and that can't happen again."

"I think it's starting," Lia said quietly, pointing to where Gorias approached. Sure enough, the incessant drumming had finally stopped, and the previously still line of soldiers had begun to move forward.

Callan's hands gripped her face gently as he turned her to look at him. "No greater love," he whispered, pressing his lips to hers in a brief but intense kiss.

"None," she agreed, placing a hand on his armored chest. With one last swift kiss, he was gone, paced to the front lines to issue commands.

"That was–" Cathal began as he and Mara stepped up to her right.

"Don't," Eve said sharply. She couldn't deal with whatever snarky thing he was about to say right now.

"I was going to say," he replied, exasperated, "that was impressive, him leaving his mate here. I know how difficult that had to be for him." He glanced at Mara, whose soft gaze met his own. A silent conversation, no longer than a few heartbeats passed between the mates.

Eve said nothing in response as she tore her gaze away from the intimate moment to scan the line of soldiers ahead, trying to get a glimpse of her friends.

"Where is Leysa?" Lia asked, scanning the crowd herself.

"With a few other shifters, still looking for Naia."

A low chuffing sound announced a new arrival, and to Eve's surprise, Amias ambled up to Lia's side. Her brow rose in silent question at the shifter in his bear form. His gaze swung toward Lia and back to Eve, steely resolve in his wide brown eyes. Point taken. He was going to keep protecting her.

"Get ready then," Eve said to all of them at once as shouts broke out from below. Rallying cries from commanders, echoed by the men and women who followed them.

Reaching for the magic deep within, she stretched out with that invisible limb as the first wave of Gorian soldiers came within range. A wall of stone erupted from the ground, then rammed back down as hard and as fast as it had broken out, dragging screaming soldiers into the chasm she'd created. Several others, unable to stop in time or pushed over by those behind them, tumbled in after.

So few, she thought. *That took out so few of them.*

From atop her magic-made dune, she watched as the Gorian forces came to a halt. Her own fae archers fired then, an impressive volley raining down on the enemy across the divide. But Gorias had magic on its side, and swiftly, shields went up. Made up of wind, ice, or even, to her surprise, pure shadow.

"They've blessed them as well?" Lia breathed beside her, echoing the surprise that rocketed through Eve.

"Of course," Cathal replied with a snort. "You may be the chosen ones, but there are generations of magic flowing through fae veins–on both sides." Lifting his hand, Cathal sent a wave of power toward the chasm Eve had created, and fire sprung to life inside, making the barrier between the armies that much more treacherous.

"Nicely done, my love," Mara purred.

For several moments, magic blasted back and forth between the two sides, doing little damage to either thanks to the wards both had erected. The crown atop her head hummed with magic, ready to be wielded as she saw fit.

Not yet, Eve thought. *We wait until we have to.*

"It won't hold them long," Cathal said. No sooner had the words left his mouth than two figures broke forward from the Gorian ranks, arms thrown open. The sky above cracked wide, and rain fell out of clouds that had not been there moments before, dousing Cathal's flames after a few moments. The ash arrows fired by the foe on their side quickly swept away by gusts of wind, no doubt conjured by others behind the storm-callers.

Eve sighed in frustration as the fighting once more came to a brief halt. Cries of surprise echoed through their ranks as something began to move from within the Gorian army, something huge.

"What is that?" Eve demanded, rising on her toes to see.

"They didn't," Cathal said, awestruck.

"They did," Mara confirmed.

"What did they do?" Lia demanded, straining to see. Amias grumbled in warning.

"I didn't know they still existed," Cathal said, as much to himself as the others.

Frustration flooded Eve. "What still existed?" she questioned, turning sharply to Cathal.

Mara's eyes were wide as she shook her head, taking Cathal's hand in hers.

"Fachan," Cathal replied, pointing.

A massive creature ambled from somewhere behind the Gorian ranks, though how he hadn't been spotted before was an absolute mystery. Easily three times as tall as the average man, with a singular eye that dominated his pallid grey, hairless head. He was monstrous, a being of myth and legend. As were the fae, she supposed, but this...this was the thing of nightmares.

Behind him, grasped by one of his enormous three-fingered hands, he dragged a large wooden ramp. Where he had retrieved such a thing in the middle of the desert, she had no idea.

"How did he–" she began as the fachan flipped the ramp over, creating a path for Gorias to cross her trench. Wide enough for them to cross five wide. It would be a risk though, to cross over the trench leaving them exposed to the soldiers waiting on the other side. More than a risk, she corrected, an absolute slaughter.

It made no sense, she frowned, inhaling sharply as another ramp appeared in the fachan's other hand. "How?" she demanded, without looking at Cathal.

"They can conjure," he sighed. "Only a few times though. They have limited magic, but they're damn hard to kill." She could hear the smirk in his tone as he added, "Though they do hate fire."

"Take it down," Eve commanded.

"With pleasure," he replied, stretching a hand toward the beast.

Flames sprung to life around its feet, causing it to panic. Swatting at its own legs with the ramp in an effort to put out the flames, it only succeeded in spreading them further, and now the ramp was on fire.

Cathal's laugh of victory was cut short as suddenly, his flames vanished, and the previously terrified monster dropped his second, charred and damaged ramp across the gorge she'd created.

The Samach had finally come out to play.

CHAPTER 74

LIA

"Where are they?" Cathal murmured, tugging his sword free from the scabbard at his back.

Lia's gaze swept over the line, blinking in surprise as the fachan vanished, but her shock at the display of magic from the creature was doused as her gaze fell on an unremarkable group amongst the Gorian ranks. Something within her chilled.

"There," she and Eve said simultaneously.

"Well, that's creepy," Cathal muttered, cutting a sideways glance at the two queens. Beside him, Mara already had a pair of deadly sharp daggers in her hands and a watchful gaze on the fight unfolding in front of them. "You two are the only ones who can stop them," he began, as shards of ice began to rain down from the clear blue sky, impaling several of their own soldiers. Shields flew up, made of wood and steel not magic, thanks to the intervention of the Samach.

"They can be that selective?" Eve asked, tension creeping into her tone.

"Apparently," Cathal remarked. "We'll be here to help if any break through, but gods help us if they do. You have to take out the Samach if we have any hope."

Lia's gaze met Eve's and they nodded, linking hands as they both reached for their artifacts.

I need you, she whispered in her mind, calling on the ancient Sword as she pulled it free.

What is your command, Bearer? The eerie double voice cooed in reply.

The Samach, there, she replied, fixing her gaze on the group of four that had chilled her to her very bones. *Blind them.*

As you wish, Bearer.

Bright light, unyielding in its intensity, flared in front of the four who commanded silence. Shrieks erupted as they clutched their faces. Within moments of her attack, Eve acted. Vines sprang forth from the ground, pulling and strangling the four fae until the screaming stopped.

Shadows erupted from the front lines in front of Lia. Callan.

Eve grinned, a hand flying to her heart as his shadows raced across the divide, flinging several of the Gorian soldiers into the chasm that once again erupted in flames as Cathal's magic returned to him. Soldiers from Finias soon joined the magical assault, just as the first Gorian soldiers began to brave the wooden planks. Wind and water, and even, to Lia's surprise, what looked to be bits of gleaming metal surged forward, taking down Gorian after Gorian.

The planks groaned beneath the armored soldiers but held fast. Shields of wind stopped the arrows and magic that threatened to pummel them. Below, Bastien's voice rang high above the sounds of battle, screaming orders as they crossed, sword meeting sword for the first time.

Her head whipped to the side at the sound of Aelius calling out in warning. They'd finally begun to go around the chasm, she realized, attacking the human army at the left flank. With barely a thought, Lia sent a wave of light, blinding the first of the Gorians to attack and buying Aelius precious moments.

"No," Eve breathed, as more and more began to cross, somehow pushing their own forces further away from the chasm. It shouldn't have been possible, given the bottleneck the small crossing created, and yet—

"Windcallers," Cathal explained. "They're using wind to push us back."

"Not for long," Eve replied tightly. Lia watched as, just across the chasm, a group of fae were pulled beneath the sand by grasping vines. Within moments their own forces rallied, retaking their position with ease.

Where is Bella, she wondered, scanning the chaos below. It took only moments for her to spot her mate, fighting shoulder to shoulder with fae from Finias. Their line was holding fast, she saw with relief, easily pushing back the wave of Gorians who had made it across.

"Lia," Eve warned, gesturing to where Bastien had been before. She couldn't see him now, couldn't see any of the men he'd been surrounded by. Only Gorian soldiers stood there now, but where– a scream tore through her throat as she saw it. Bastien fighting on the charred ramp, with three others at his side. *They're trying to stop them from crossing,* she realized just as the first loud crack sounded.

No. The word echoed through her. Bastien stilled, shouting something she couldn't hear, and his men began to retreat. Either unaware or unconcerned about the danger, the Gorian soldiers pressed on. Bastien remained, walking backward as he met blow for blow, defending the retreating backs of his soldiers.

"Bastien, run!" she screamed as loud as she could, eyes burning. She knew she was crying, sobbing, in front of the others now, but she didn't care. "RUN!"

Eve's own strangled cry sounded as she ran in the opposite direction. Lia didn't bother to look, not when Bastien, the friend she called brother, was in danger.

The second crack sounded, and the ramp began to buckle. He was close now, so close. If he would just turn and run he could–

The ramp gave way without warning, and all who were standing on it vanished into the flaming chasm beneath. Grief and terror wracked her very soul as she continued to stare at the place where the ramp had been just moments before. Her throat burned as she screamed his name. She could bring him back, maybe with the sword she could–

No, Bearer. Not even with me can you revive the dead.

What's the point of you then? she demanded bitterly.

To save the rest of you, the Sword replied simply.

Dragging her gaze away, Lia looked to the rest of the battle. Gorias had finally swept in around the right flank. Eve's temporary reprieve was all but useless as Gorian soldiers began to pace across, now that more of their own army was distracted at the flanks.

"Aelius," she whispered, turning her attention to where he was rallying their forces. To her relief, there he was, leading a charge that was actually managing to push back the Gorian forces.

Eve returned to her side, pale and shaken. "They almost killed Cora," she choked. "She was in her wolf form, and they had her surrounded, three of them with spears. But some of the others got to her in time."

Cathal's attention snapped to Eve. "Tell me she's alive."

"She is," Eve confirmed. "She's being taken to the healers. I saw some shifters carrying her away."

Cathal simply nodded, turning his attention back to the Gorian soldiers he was currently immolating.

"Why haven't they attacked us?" Lia blurted suddenly.

All four sets of eyes on the dune turned to her suddenly.

"Now that is the question," Cathal replied.

"Maybe because they know they have the artifacts," Mara suggested.

"I think that would make them more likely to," Eve countered.

Dread settled over Lia and she turned to Eve. "Unless," she began, reading the same realization in Eve's eyes, "they're waiting for *her* to arrive."

"Shit," Eve whispered.

"Be ready," Lia said, earning a grumble from Amias, who pressed his hefty body against her side protectively. "She'll be coming."

CHAPTER 75

EVE

The battle raged on for what felt like hours. Brida's line had nearly buckled twice but had been reinforced by soldiers from Finias. Now, they were all exhausted and had managed to do little more than hold their own. While Gorias wasn't advancing, neither were they.

A horn sounded from the east, making Eve's heart stop as they turned. Had Kore arrived like she and Lia had been expecting?

But rather than the muted grey mountains of Gorias, the riders who approached bore the standard of Coruscis, white waves cresting on a sea of turquoise. Maren had finally sent aid. Their commander, an older woman with salt-and-pepper, short-cropped hair and sharp, dark eyes stopped before them.

"We're sorry it took so long," she said briefly, before leading her soldiers into the fray.

They must have been given their orders already, as they simply dispersed into the field, filling in the gaps where they were most needed, and for the first time, they began to actually push Gorias back. It had taken the combined armies of five kingdoms, but they finally matched their enemy in strength and numbers.

She scanned the field for Callan and the others. Cora had been taken to the healers after taking an ash arrow to her shoulder. Still in wolf form, she'd been carried off, gravely injured but still alive, she'd been assured.

Valerian is okay, she sighed with relief as she watched him take down two Gorian soldiers with one broad sweep of his sword. From what she could see, he didn't seem injured. A silent prayer of thanks went up to the gods.

Her focus shifted to Callan, fighting down there somewhere. It took only a moment to find him, her gaze landing on the explosion of shadows far to the right. He was surrounded by at least five enemy soldiers, and holding his own though he was slowing.

One man went down, clutching the sides of his head as Callan spared him barely a glance. Two others dropped their swords as tendrils of shadow wound around their necks, snapping them. The third, at Callan's right side, lifted his blade attempting to take advantage of his distraction, only to be gored by a boar shifter who charged in at the last moment. Callan felled the fourth with a swipe of his twin blades.

And the fifth– *"Oh gods,"* she breathed. He was making right for Callan's back, and her mate didn't seem to see him. With a shriek of rage, she flung her power out toward the would-be assassin. Spearing directly up from the ground beneath the man, a thick vine impaled him. Callan spun in time to see the man go limp on top of the impossibly sharp vine. His gaze shot to Eve, and he grinned, actually grinned. She shook her head, turning her attention back to the fight happening closest to them.

It took exactly three heartbeats for her to realize what was happening–for Lia to come to her side, linking their hands as both of their gazes shot to the west where a dense shadow had begun to take form.

"What is it?" Cathal asked.

The air seemed heavier now, weighted in a way that went beyond the seriousness of battle. Slowly, the fighting began to subside as the impenetrable darkness began to sweep across the desert, moving toward them at an alarming rate.

"Fuck," Callan said from behind her suddenly.

"Is that what I think it is?" Cathal asked warily, tugging Mara closer to his side.

A low rumble emanated from Amias' throat at Lia's side.

Eve gave Lia's hand a squeeze, never once taking her eyes off of the horizon.

"She approaches, Bearer. Can you feel it?"

"I know, I feel it," she replied aloud.

"Feel what?" Mara asked quietly.

"The Void...the nothingness," Lia said, horror-struck.

"Kore is here." Eve's heart beat a steady staccato as fear coursed through her veins.

The end was here, and they were still without Naia. There was no winning this fight. With bone-deep certainty, she knew that without all four artifacts on their side, they had no real chance of winning. Naia could have given them a better chance, but they didn't even have that.

"We're going to die," Cathal remarked almost blandly. "Shall we run for it, my love?"

Mara sighed. "No, darling," she replied. "We will fight."

"As you wish," he replied, resigned.

Callan stepped to Eve's side then, taking her free hand in his. There would be no long, heartfelt goodbyes. Not this time.

Her heart ached as Lia stepped forward, still holding Eve's hand in her own, and scanned the crowd below. She knew without asking which two she searched for, and for Lia's sake, she hoped they would arrive before the darkness.

CHAPTER 76

LIA

Aelius remained where he was, with the men and women under his command. Even as he whipped around, meeting Lia's gaze, she knew he wouldn't leave them. Placing a hand to his heart, he offered her a smile. Not a word needed to pass between them for her to understand. He was saying goodbye, and that he loved her. Willing warmth into her veins, Lia sent a small burst of healing light for him, and hoped he would understand.

The darkness loomed ever nearer as she searched for the other half of her heart with eyes that burned. Her heart gave a lurch as she saw Bella, rushing straight toward them. Her familiar silver eyes were bright and wide as she arrived, out of breath, with blood caking her dark hair and face.

"You're hurt?" Lia asked, raising her free hand to heal her mate.

"No," Bella said breathlessly, "I'm fine, save your strength."

Amias moved to the side to allow Bella to take a position beside Lia, and the seven of them watched quietly as Kore made her approach.

"She's dragging it out," Cathal remarked drily.

"She means to frighten us," Eve replied, sharing the same thought Lia had.

"Well, it's working," Mara whispered.

Lia straightened. If their enemy wanted to wield darkness to terrify them, to pacify them, then she would use her light to do the opposite. "Trust me," she said to nobody in particular as she raised her free hand and pushed as far as she could with her magic. No heat, no healing, no blinding, just light, pure as a summer day.

The moment it met the two, the darkness abated. For a moment, everything seemed to pause. Every breath seemed to still as every human and fae below waited, watched to see what would happen next.

Kore's darkness seemed to pause, as if she too was considering Lia's actions.

But then without warning, just as hope began to bloom anew from the tiny kernel that remained in Lia's soul, Kore pushed back.

The darkness she commanded pressed back against Lia's light with such violence that the sky itself seemed to shudder. Eve squeezed Lia's hand gently, and she felt the firmness of the earth beneath her feet as Eve poured her own magic into her, grounding her.

Life and Light pushing against the Void, against the darkness that threatened them all.

Sweat beaded on Lia's brow with the strain of holding Kore at bay, at maintaining the power it took to keep her darkness from overtaking them. Even with the extra push from Eve's gifts, it was too much, the strain too great.

"I can't–"

Just when she thought her magic would falter, when that last ember of hope began to gutter in her chest, a small hand slid into her own. Power like she'd never felt before crackled in her veins. With another push, the light she'd called to challenge the Void pulsed, flaring brightly as lightning skittered across the sky.

A wail of frustration echoed across the sands, and some small forgotten piece of her soul screamed in terror, shrinking back from the sound. To her shock, the Void surrendered, pulling back across the sky so quickly it would have been missed had Lia blinked.

A gasp sounded from Eve, and she knew, as she turned her head, exactly who she would see standing beside her.

"Where is my cauldron?" Naia Colvari asked, as Lia's eyes met hers.

BEFORE YOU GO...

ENJOY A SNEAK PEEK OF THE FINALE TO THE *CRESCENT QUEENS* TRILOGY...

They gathered in the secret place, the last one hidden from *her* view. Not even the prayers of their human children could reach them there. Fear was thick and heavy as iron as it weighed down upon each of the gathered gods. All of them were there, he noted, scanning the crowded vestibule. The upper level was just as full, he could tell, from the many faces he saw looking down from the balcony above.

"Lir."

He turned to face Araceli. The goddess of the night sky and prophecy, as mad as she was lovely, was one of the few who had gotten involved in the war that threatened them all, thanks to her daughter's entanglement with Aurelia Vallyse.

"You've made some of us very nervous," he said, the corner of his lips tugging upwards. He had a part to play, she'd declared, thanks to the artifact he'd helped create so very long ago.

Lir hadn't yet decided if he would accept the fate Macaria had laid at his feet, despite the push from Keithia and Helie. That determined duo had been on his ass from the beginning to offer the cauldron bearer his boon.

Perhaps, if she proved herself up to the task, he would.

"Time is running out," Araceli stated, her gaze distant and her voice soft. *Prophets*, he thought with mild disdain, as she continued, "The girl with the heart of thunder must be claimed. All will be lost...all will be lost..."

Lir raised a brow and turned his gaze back to the gathered gods. All eyes were on the center of the room, where the god of sight had opened a viewing pool.

Images of the war played across the still water. Sword clashed against sword as the battle raged before shifting to the hilltop where Helie's chosen had been forever changed and drew her first breath as a newly created fae.

Light, pure and deadly, erupted from the sword bearer minutes later, decimating the Void's army.

To his surprise, Lir felt the first stirring of hope in their success. Perhaps these mortal women would rise to the challenge after all. Mind made up, he turned, and left their sacred space for the first time in centuries.

It was time for him to meet his own chosen in person and determine for himself if she had what it took to save them all.

The Crescent Queens Series

Book One

Queen of Earth and Stone

Book Two

Queen of Light and Solace

Book Three

Three queens will rise. Three queens will save the world....but at what cost?

The final battle begins in book three of the Crescent Queens Series, coming soon.

Acknowledgments

Where to begin?

A huge thank you to B.T.B for my incredible map once again. You brought the world of Aestera to life in a beautiful way.

For my editor Kathy, thank you so much for polishing all of the rough edges, and for your overall kindness. I can't tell you how much I appreciate you.

To the Platonic Square, you guys are the very best cheerleaders, sounding boards, and so much more. Love you all....*platonically*.

And last, but certainly not least, to my husband Eric. I would never be here without you. Thank you and I love you.

About the Author

Tricia Meyers is an avid reader and writer of fantasy romance, a collector of too many pens, a part-time coffee enthusiast, and full-time mom. Writing has been her passion since childhood and has always been an outlet for her creatively.

Queen of Earth and Stone is her debut novel, and passion project that rekindled her dream of being a full-time author.

Find out more on www.authortriciameyers.com.

facebook.com/tricia.d.meyers

instagram.com/tricia.m.books

tiktok.com/@tricia.m.books

goodreads.com/authortriciameyers